William Torrens McCullagh Torrens

Memoirs of the Right Honourable William, Second Viscount

Melbourne

Vol. 1

William Torrens McCullagh Torrens

Memoirs of the Right Honourable William, Second Viscount Melbourne
Vol. 1

ISBN/EAN: 9783337186081

Printed in Europe, USA, Canada, Australia, Japan

Cover: Foto ©Raphael Reischuk / pixelio.de

More available books at **www.hansebooks.com**

MEMOIRS

OF

THE RIGHT HONOURABLE WILLIAM

SECOND

VISCOUNT MELBOURNE.

BY

W. M. TORRENS, M.P.

IN TWO VOLUMES.

VOL. I.

WITH A PORTRAIT.

London :

MACMILLAN AND CO.

1878.

PREFACE.

Some historic tribute, it will be owned, is due to the memory of a man who by the space of forty years took part in pro· moting every legislative change which subsequent experience has approved, and who in three successive reigns filled some of the most responsible offices of state. And if the recollections of his public life be found entwined with those of unbroken friendship and domestic tenderness, while not a boastful phrase, ungenerous act, or word of flattery addressed to monarch or to multitude needs extenuation or apology, they can but furnish one more proof that he who makes least claim to lofty motives is oftentimes most worthy of respect and love.

I could have wished that some one more competent had undertaken the task of chronicling the best doings and sayings of Lord Melbourne. But time wears on, personal recollections fade, and contemporaries one by one drop into the grave. In a little while longer I felt that it probably would be too late, and that regrets would then be vain. My own acquaintance with public affairs began while he was minister, and the impression he made on me, of genial temper, broad-heartedness, civil courage, practical wisdom, and fine humour, has not been effaced by any combination of high qualities in the statesmen I have subsequently known. He was not an orator, a jurist, or a financier; no statute bears distinctively his name, and no volume is inscribed with it. He did not even take the trouble of writing letters for effect; and his correspondence, like his conversation, was never in full dress. But a colleague who knew him well said to me when speaking of him,—"He was a great gentleman;" high-minded without assumption, munificent without letting it be known, careful of the interests of the Crown without compromising his self-respect, faithful to party without harbouring ill-will to opponents, outspoken almost to a fault, yet never taking advantage of confidence or wilfully inflicting a wound; sensitive as a woman to misrepresentation, yet of all men the most placable and ready to forgive a wrong: a man sorely tried in the relations of private life, yet never suffering his griefs to mar the happiness of those around him by a murmur at the pain he was doomed to endure. No wonder he had fewer enemies and more warmly attached friends than many men of his time. Such geniality, however delightful and endearing, would not, indeed, of itself perhaps justify a claim to historical remembrance. But circumstances in some degree exceptional enabled him to earn a reputation for administrative skill which has not frequently been surpassed. Unlike his predecessors in office, power came to him late in life, and when habits of luxurious leisure unfitted him, as was feared, for the performance of its onerous duties. The elasticity of his nature, and a noble ambition to vindicate the early expectations formed regarding him, enabled him to win credit and confidence as Secretary for Ireland and afterwards as Minister for the Home Department, in very difficult times. The verdict of colleagues, whose collective weal and individual ease are necessarily at stake, is often more severe than that of the public at large. Melbourne was, in fact, popular with both; and when at last he was placed at the head of affairs, he evinced a maturity of judgment and finely-tempered tenacity of purpose which, in seasons of perplexity, rendered him indispensable to his party, and secured him a longer tenure of office than has been enjoyed by any Premier of our time.

From the varied correspondence to which I have had access I have endeavoured to draw the chief materials for these Memoirs. My acknowledgments are especially due to the Duke of Wellington, Lady Monteagle, and the Marquis of Lansdowne for the papers respectively placed by them at my disposal. But to a great extent I have preferred to weld together traditional and documentary materials, rather than to reproduce at length letters which in part have lost their specific interest, and in part could hardly have been written with any idea of eventual publication. Two or three subjects of a personal nature I have abstained altogether from noticing, not because their fair discussion would, in my opinion, tend to depreciate the value set upon the character of the minister or the man, but because I reject as wholly untenable the claim of idle curiosity into the affairs of the dead, merely on the pretence that the living were illustrious. Whatever seemed to me fitted to explain or illustrate the acts or motives of the statesman I have given unreservedly : about things in no way calculated to serve that purpose I am willing to bear the burthen of having exercised a disinterested discretion.

CONTENTS.

CHAPTER XI.

PROGRESS AND REACTION.

CHAPTER XII.

CANNING'S ADMINISTRATION.

CHAPTER XIII.

DUBLIN CASTLE.

CHAPTER XIV.

THE IRISH CHANCELLORSHIP.

CHAPTER XV.

THE WELLINGTON ADMINISTRATION.

CHAPTER XVI.

IN THE LORDS.

CHAPTER XVII.

HOME SECRETARY.

CHAPTER XVIII.

THE REFORM BILL.

CHAPTER XIX.

PARLIAMENT REFORMED.

CHAPTER XX.

EXECUTIVE AND LEGISLATIVE DUTIES.

MEMOIRS

OF

VISCOUNT MELBOURNE.

CHAPTER I.

ANTECEDENTS.

Manor of Melbourne—Secretary of State to Charles I.—Puritans and Cavaliers — Vice-Chamberlain to Queen Anne—The old Pleader of Lincoln's Inn—Sir Matthew Lamb—First Lord Melbourne— Brocket Hall.

IN one of the pleasant valleys of south Derbyshire, not far from Ashby-de-la-Zouch, stands the ancient church and modern town of Melbourne. The manor was in Norman times part of the demesne of the Crown. Granted successively to more than one favourite of the hour, and resumed on some real or imaginary pretext of forfeiture; it was given by Edward III. to his brother, and it long remained among the great possessions of the house of Lancaster. In Tudor days a castle on the north bank of the stream, "metely kept in repair,"* was held for the king: the neighbouring hamlet thriving apace, by dint of certain handicrafts, into a busy market town. The severed fiefs of York and Lancaster, once more re-united in the heritage of royalty, were by degrees distributed again in recompense for service done; and Melbourne Manor was in 1604 conferred by James I. on Charles, Earl of Nottingham, from whom soon afterwards it passed to the family of Huntingdon, and subsequently to that of Hastings. A survey at the close of Elizabeth's reign noted " a faire ancient castle, which Her

* Leland, 1550.

Majesty keepeth in her own hands;"[*] and, from a drawing attached to the survey, there is an engraving in the 'Monumenta Vetusta'[†] from which the outworks seem to have been of considerable extent. Camden somewhat later speaks of the structure as going to decay, and by the end of the century it had nearly disappeared.

By a curious whim of mediæval patronage, an interest in the weal of Melbourne had likewise been given to one of the spiritual peers. King John conferred the church and parsonage-manor on Walter Malclerc, Bishop of Carlisle, and suffered him to annex both permanently to that see. In 1229 he obtained a grant of a fair on the Nativity of the Virgin to be holden within the precincts of the episcopal manor during five days. His successors found Melbourne a pleasant resting-place on their way to the North, and sometimes went no farther. On the plea of Border troubles, Bishop Kirkby tarried longer than usual, and finally made up his mind to hold his ordination there. As the realm became more tranquil and journeying grew less hazardous, the diocesan fixed his country seat in Cumberland, and without the transitory title of "palace," the not undesirable mansion was let on lease to Sir John Coke, in possession of whose descendants Melbourne Hall has ever since remained.

The worthy man was the second son of Richard Coke of Trusley, who had been bred to the law, but quitted that profession on his marriage with the heiress of Thomas Sacheverell in the neighbouring county of Nottingham. His eldest son Francis, who married the daughter of Lord Holles, inherited the maternal lands of Kirkby, attained the dignity of knighthood and sat in one of the brief parliaments during Elizabeth's reign. A younger brother, George, took orders, and late in life became Bishop of Hereford; while his sister's husband, Valentine Carey, was raised to the see of Exeter. John, being of a studious turn and diligent in all his ways, rose late in life to an eminent position. Sent early to Cambridge, he became a fellow of Trinity in 1584, and subsequently

---

[*] Lyson.　　　[†] Published by the Society of Antiquaries.

Professor of Rhetoric. Until his prime was passed he tarried at the University, then travelled abroad, and was nearly fifty years of age when he resolved to settle down in Derbyshire and lead the life of his progenitors, in hospitality and charity, hunting and falconry, of which last he seems to have been very fond.

His academic friends had not forgotten him, and to the first parliament of Charles I. he was sent as member for the University. There he made divers speeches of the practical and prudent sort; the times being still but half awake, and the light that was in him, though steady and useful, shining only through narrow horn-lantern pane. Fuller* quaintly praises him for being governed by good maxims:

That no man should let what is ungrateful or dangerous appear under his hand, to give envy a steady aim at his place or person, nor mingle intimate with great men made desperate by debts or court injuries whose fall have been ruinous to their wisest followers; nor pry any further into secrecy then rather to secure than shew himself in no point to a friend which might empower him to become an enemy.

Through the influence of his kinsman, Lord Brooke, he was made Secretary of the Navy, a post of very subordinate importance in those days, but in which he was so commended as to obtain a more profitable place as Master of Bequests. In the third parliament of the reign he was again returned for Cambridge, and, upon the death of Sir Albertus Morton, was made Secretary of State. While things went well he was a good official, faithful and frugal, deprecating change and war, and the dissipation of his master's substance in vain shows. But when the clouds began to lower, and religious feuds to warp the minds of men, he was hardly equal to the tasks which unforeseen devolved upon him. The protracted effort to impose the Liturgy on Scotland by haughty edicts, polemical diplomacy, and at length by force of arms, failed,

* 'Fuller and Lloyd Worthies.'

as the Scots averred, because they were stout of heart, and, as the king's advisers told him, because his officers had no stomach for the war beyond the Tweed. But Charles felt he had incurred a heavy loss of credit both abroad and at home. His melancholy looks were a mute reproach to all in his employment. Secretary Coke was stricken in years, the best of whose ability was spent, and whom none of the powerful or ambitious courtiers regarded.

He was a man of gravity—says Clarendon—who never had quickness from his cradle; who loved the Church well enough as it was twenty years before; and understood nothing that had been done in Scotland, and thought nothing that could be done there was worth such a journey as the king had put himself to. Every man shifting the fault from himself, and finding some friend to excuse him, it fell to Secretary Coke's turn (for whom nobody cared) to be made the sacrifice; and upon the pretence that he had omitted the writing which he ought to have done, and inserted some, which he ought not to have done, he was put out of his office by the dark contrivance of the Marquis of Hamilton, and the open and visible power of the Queen.

The historian adds that Strafford, seeing its injustice, strove to prevent his removal, and succeeded in having it suspended for a time, but her Majesty and the courtiers were too strong for him, and the upright man was dismissed to make room for the elder Vane.

Announcing the event to his eldest son he wrote:—

You have heard me declare my desire, and endeavour to obtain in this evening of my age some time of repose at home, wherein nothing did retard my resolution more than the persuasion of my friends, that I must not abandon the public whilst my being upon the stage might either advance for good, or at least give interruption to the prevailing of evil, wherein though I know not how little I could prevail in either, yet my tenderness was such that I durst not break out till God should make my way. And now since the world is satisfied that it is not my own act, I both contentedly and cheerfully submit myself to God's will, and the King's. What sense good men have of it you shall hear of much by others. For me, assure yourself I shall come home unto you with as much quiet, and with as calm a mind, and with as little repining and complaining or spleen against any one, as any ever went from court to a country life after so long and so many employments.

Laying aside all that might remind him of the days he had passed at Court, he proposed to live with his son at Melbourne, and calculated closely what establishment would suffice for both: " a bailiff, a clerk, a butler, a cook, a falconer, a groom, a footman, and a young fellow to bake and brew and keep the tercels."

Sir John the younger sat in the Long Parliament, following the counsels of Pym and Manchester, but much disquieted by the subversive notions that eventually prevailed. He was named one of Strafford's judges, and assisted throughout the trial, but at the end did not vote, accounting for his absence to his father by some misapprehension as to the hour fixed for the decision. On the outbreak of the civil war the old man was driven, by fear of the quartering in his house of some of the new levies, to seek shelter with Danvers, his son-in-law, at Southlam in Leicestershire, having written in vain to Essex for protection from the troops under his command. He assured the general " that his heart was faithful, and his prayers assiduous for the prosperity of the Parliament wherein consisteth the welfare of the Church and State."* But like many of the gentry and professional classes, the family was viewed with distrust by strong partisans on both sides, as waverers and undecided ; because, like Falkland, they wanted peace, and the triumph neither of the Puritans nor of the Crown.

* September 20th, 1642.

Sir John writes to his father in the second year of the civil war :

I pray God to continue you in good health and preserve you in safety through the troubles of the times. I hope my letter came safe to hand through the unsafety of the way.

In another, the 16th of January :

He is exceedingly grieved that his father through the misery of the times should be enforced to remove from his house at Melbourne at this season of the year.

His letters are without signature, and bear the marks of hard usage on the road. From Leicestershire the octogenarian with difficulty made his way to the neighbourhood of Tottenham, where the brother of his second wife, Alderman Lee, resided, and where in September 1644 he closed his eyes.

Among the townsfolk at Melbourne, the greater part were for the King, and they set about repairing some of the outworks of the castle, said to have covered two-and-twenty acres in Plantagenet times ; but long since fallen into decay. Sir John Gell ordered a detachment from Derby to occupy the town, and levelled the remains of the crumbling fortress to the ground. The commanding officer, Major Swallow, found the manor excellent quarters, and established himself there for some time. Baxter, the well-known preacher, mentions that while on a visit to his friend at Sir John Coke's house, he was taken ill, and by the doctors sentenced to die, whereupon, thinking he had done with this troubled world, he began the work upon ' Everlasting Rest,' which he survived to publish, and by which his name is still widely kept in remembrance. Yet Sir John the younger was named with Lords Pembroke, Derby and Montague, Sir Walter Earle and others of the Commons, as commissioners to receive the captive King from the Scottish army ; and by them he was conducted to Holdenby in Northamptonshire.

Charles distinguished General Brown, Sir J. Holland, and Sir J. Coke from the rest for the consideration shown him in the performance of their unwelcome office; telling them at the same time, "it was one which unbecame gentlemen of a free mind." Like others of the moderate party, Coke hoped until the last that the great struggle might end in general amnesty and accommodation of differences. But when he saw the monarchy overthrown, he went into voluntary exile, and died at Paris in the following year.

His brother George was among the bishops who protested against the enactments made during their enforced absence. The revenues of his see were in consequence estreated, his palace occupied by Colonel Birch, and his private estate appropriated by that worthy until the Restoration, which the deprived prelate did not live to see. His nephew Colonel Coke, who inherited the family estate, was more fortunate. A pleasant gentleman, and well-favoured, he won the hand of the heiress of the Leventhorpes in Hertfordshire, and being popular with his neighbours, he was returned for Derby to the complaisant House of Commons of 1685. His father had been expelled the Long Parliament for his steadfastness in the royal cause, and he had been bred in like principles; but when James II. spurned the remonstrance of the Commons, and instead of militia, told them he meant to employ a standing army, the House was daunted and dumb. At last Colonel Coke rose and said, " I hope we are all Englishmen, and not to be frightened by a few hard words:" but they sent him to the Tower for his temerity. In 1688 he raised a troop of horse with Lord Devonshire, and obtained the rank of colonel. And while travelling abroad died in 1692 at Geneva.

Thomas Coke inherited from his father, soon after the Revolution, the family estate. Without the ability requisite for great affairs, his winning manners and good looks early made him popular in his county, for which he was returned, soon after he came of age, with Lord Hartington : he subsequently sat with Mr. Curzon in three successive parliaments of Anne. Though his name is not mentioned in debate, and neither Steele or Prior thought him worthy of an epigram, he seems to have been considered an influential man.   Lord Chesterfield, who had been brought up with the Prince of Orange, and, after his coming into England, had no little weight with government, gave the rising Commoner his daughter in marriage. The Earl complains to her of the conduct of her brother Woottan, and says he would go out of the world with satisfaction if he had a son like her husband. Even after her death in 1703, Chesterfield continued to be solicitous for his advancement. He is spoken of, indeed, as one of those who stood well with the politicians of both parties, for in 1706 he was made by Godolphin a Privy Councillor and Vice-Chamberlain to the Queen, an office he continued to hold under Harley and St. John. In 1709 he married the beautiful Mary Hale, one of the maids of honour whom Swift mentions as "the toast" of the day. When Mr. Coke "did him the honour to ask him to dinner" she happened to be from home, being engaged to her friend Lady Sunderland, whose mother—the difficult Duchess—described her as "a very pretty young woman, and of very good family." She was the daughter of Richard Hale of Codicote, in Herts, whose grandfather sat for the county in the parliament of the Restoration; and whose brother Sir Bernard Hale, an advocate of note, was made Chief Baron of the Irish Exchequer in 1722. He subsequently became a puisne Baron at Westminster, and died in 1729 at his house in Red Lion Square.

In times when faction rent society in twain, and change of administration not unfrequently involved impeachment of chiefs and the sweeping dismissal of subordinates, it needed more than ordinary repute and tact to keep a position envied or influential. In what the skill of Coke consisted, or where his influence lay, it is not very easy to determine.

He seems to have been a genial, tolerant, and generous man, who had many friends and few enemies. With Gay.

and Bolingbroke he lived on terms of intimacy, while Pope, who spared nobody, quizzed his fine person and showy office under the epithet of "Sir Plume." In the 'Rape of the Lock' the deputy lord of the ceremonies is sent by the angry fair one to demand the surrender of the ravished tress :

> Sir Plume, of amber snuff-box justly vain,
> And the nice conduct of a clouded cane,
> With earnest eyes, and round unthinking face,
> He first the snuff-box opened, then the case.

A maiden sister resided at Melbourne, took care of his children there when young, and kept together his interest in the county by judicious management, whereof her loving letters advertised him circumstantially from time to time. All her skill and assiduity, however, in the practice of good neighbourhood failed to baffle the ambition of Sir Godfrey Clarke, who in 1710 resolved to contest the county. If the Vice-Chamberlain would have come down in time, she was sure his presence would have saved the seat; but, too indolent or too secure, he came not till too late; and his adversary won. The chroniclers of the period are content with noting that he retained his place at Court in the succeeding reign under Townshend, Stanhope, and Walpole. He was appointed likewise to a Tellership of the Exchequer, a lucrative office which he held until his death in 1727, as well as his place in the household. Nor were these the whole of his acquisitions. In the will of the political pluralist is the recital of a grant in reversion by George I. of the Surveyor-Generalship of Customs, worth besides fees £500 a year, to him for his own life, that of his son, and that of his son-in-law John Fanshaw. This, with the family inheritance and the manor of Melton Mowbray, the marriage portion of his second wife, was entailed on their only surviving son, with remainder to their only daughter Charlotte, to whom, as well as to her half-sisters, suitable fortunes were already secured.

His eldest daughter by Lady Mary Stanhope espoused

Lord Southwell; his second had been early asked in marriage by Mr. Thornhill, but on a question regarding settlements the engagement was broken off. Some years later the proposal was renewed; and the lady, who blamed others for the previous misunderstanding, announced that this time she would not leave the business to Mr. Lamb. The legal adviser whose circumspection the lady contemned was a practitioner of long standing at Southwell in the adjoining county; who as little as herself then dreamed that in his posterity the lands and honours of the Cokes were destined to descend. He died in February 1735, dividing his property between his two sons Robert and Matthew.

Left parentless in childhood, the care of George Coke and his sister devolved upon the family of their mother, who continued to reside in Hertfordshire. Besides his landed inheritance, the accumulations of his minority lay at the disposal of the young squire. For a time he lived at Melbourne and afterwards in London, but his passion seems to have been for foreign travel, in which he spent several years. In 1740 the hand of Charlotte was given to Matthew Lamb, whose father has been already named, and whose uncle had bequeathed him a considerable fortune.

The name of Peniston Lamb is entered, the 7th of October, 1708, as that of a student in the books of Lincoln's Inn. The term of legal probation was then seven years, and it was not, therefore, until the opening of the following reign that he was admitted to practise at the bar. Early bent on mastering the occult science of real property law and the intricacies of equity drafting, he had long been qualified to earn a considerable income by what was called pleading under the bar, and to give advice which his clients found to be safe and wise. He lived unmarried all his days; while his younger brother took to wife a lady of whose charms and virtues little is known, but who bore several children, of whom a daughter and two sons were destined to migrate westward and to have their names identified with those of folk of quality. Peniston went on pleading and demurring, weaving settlements and ravelling threads of adverse wile from month to month and year to year, till, looking upon parchment, he had ceased to view and had half forgotten that there was any shire in the realm but that in which he laid the venue of his life. Still, as his balance rose at Child's, he dreamed occasionally pleasant dreams of estates there-after to be settled strictly in tail male on his own or his brother's progeny; and when his hair grew grey, he gave up dilatorily rather than deliberately the former alternative, and vouchsafed hints, every year more plain, that if his nephews showed capacity to raise their family in the world as much as he had done, he might——, but further this deponent sayed not. His brother at Southwell heard whispers of these things and pondered them in his heart. Robert, his eldest born, took to Latin and was fond of choral service. Here was fitness for the Church; he had the best of schooling, went to Cambridge, and in due time took holy orders. He too, like Uncle Peniston, seems to have been proof against the witchery of the sex, a point of resemblance which, however it may have touched the equity draftsman's heart, did not prevent him from providing by special cove-nants that if the said Reverend Robert should marry, the lands to be purchased by the executors should be settled strictly upon his issue, or in default thereof upon Matthew and his heirs male lawfully begotten. This condition proved to be the golden hinge on which eventually the gate of splendour opened to the family.

Peniston Lamb died in 1734, and was buried in the Chapel of Lincoln's Inn. His brother did not long survive him, leaving his acquisitions in Nottinghamshire to his children.

Robert rose by gradual steps of preferment until, 1744, he became Dean of Peterborough. He lived a devout and charitable life, ripening mutely for the bishopric to come. Matthew followed his uncle's calling, and mastered the difficulties of legal lore while he was still comparatively young. Through the introduction of his kinsman he became known as a useful energetic man, who had a taste for the improvement of land and an instinctive faculty for developing its resources.

For many years he is understood to have acted as confidential adviser to Lords Salisbury and Egmont in matters relating to their extensive estates; and being ever careful to turn opportunites to account, he profited largely by the knowledge thus gained of men and circumstances. His legal acumen and business capacity gave to his opinion no inconsiderable weight as adviser and referee; and it was probably on a well-founded estimate of his practical fitness for the post that he was selected to be standing counsel to the Board of Trade. To the competency bequeathed by his uncle he steadily added gains arising from his own exertions; and in 1741 he thought he could afford himself the luxury of a seat in Parliament, and agreed accordingly for one that stood waiting to be hired at Stockbridge. It was the way of the world at the time; for lawyers, soldiers, men of letters, and younger sons, the only way of getting without uproar or ruinous expense to Palace Yard. A son was born in January 1745, to whom the name of Peniston was given, and subsequently two daughters, Charlotte and Anne, of whom the latter died in childhood.

In 1746 Matthew Lamb purchased Brocket from the representatives of Sir Thomas Winnington. Several farms originally forming portions of the estate had been alienated from time to time by its prodigal owners. All of these were gradually bought back by the new possessor. But the old Hall was suffered to remain as it had been left by the family, long extinct, whose name it bore; and the indolent stream of the Lee widened and narrowed at will as it wended its way through the park, its rich banks overgrown with sedge and reeds, furnishing the best cover for snipe in all the country round.

Not long afterwards the unlooked-for tidings came that his brother-in-law had died suddenly at Geneva, leaving the whole of his goodly inheritance to his sister and her son.

Mr. Lamb, though he seldom spoke in Parliament, being indeed little of a party man, had sufficient influence to obtain in 1755 the honour of a baronetcy. Thenceforth he sat for Peterborough.

The cathedral city had neither mayor nor corporation. The suffrage was by scot and lot, Lord Fitzwilliam exercising the same degree of influence " as in the case of his burgage tenures at Malton, or his corporators at Higham Ferrers."* The steward or bailiff of the Chapter officiated as returning officer. At rare intervals, attempts were made by lavish outlay to beguile the electors into forgetting that they were merely nominal. In this way, Mr. St. John was returned in 1699; but the election was set aside the following year on petition. After that the placid course of nomination ran so smooth that for two or three decades no trace is to be found of any contention on the subject; " Scot and Lot " periodically did the drinking and the shouting : that was all.

Sir Matthew's residence in town had hitherto been in Red Lion Square, then inhabited by judges· and king's counsel. But opulence was already moving westward ; and accordingly in 1756 he bought a house in Sackville Street, Piccadilly, where he dwelt for the residue of his days. Beyond his advisorship to the Board of Trade, his baronetcy, and a secure seat in Parliament for life, his ambition did not soar. The cup of his content was full ; yet fortune would have it overflow. His brother became bishop of the diocese where he had so long been dean, and his daughter wedded Lord Belasyse, heir of the house of Fauconberg. If his son gave little promise of learning or of wit, and preferred Melbourne woods to Cambridge Halls, his father was consoled by his comely features, gentle manners, and docile disposition.

Sir Matthew died, after a short illness, in his sixty-fourth year, bequeathing Peniston realty and personalty estimated at nearly half a million sterling. To these were added, not long afterwards, the savings of the frugal bishop, who sur-

* Oldfield, ‘ Representative History,’ vol. iv. p. 287.

vived his brother only till the following year.   Lord Belasyse
was returned in the room of his father-in-law.

Young Sir Peniston and Lord Garlies were named to
George Selwyn, the proprietor of Luggershall, as eligible
candidates; and, though hardly acquainted with either, he
agreed to return them both for his borough as supporters of
Lord North's administration.*   An intimation was subsequently made to Selwyn, that if he wished, Wigton might
in lieu be placed at his service; but he thought he could
take care of himself, and he did so, without incurring the
obligation.

Sir Peniston continued to represent for many years the
hamlet in Wiltshire, which had returned two members from
the days of Edward I. The qualification in the lapse of
time had become so doubtful of definition as more than once
to puzzle committees.   There were, now and then, contests
for one or both the seats between candidates without scruple
as to expenditure.   But before the close of the century an
arrangement was come to between the two principal proprietors in the neighbourhood, which secured to their
respective nominees in several parliaments the unpurchased
privilege of legislators; and to the voteless village the
uncoveted blessings of electoral peace.†   The members who
ironically bore its name at St. Stephen's were never heard in
debate, and were not often told in division. In the meagre
records of the period it is difficult indeed to trace their
existence; and in private memorials no mention is made of
their attendance save on remarkable occasions.

Without any of the talents which those who went before
him had turned to account, the young baronet found himself
at three-and-twenty a person of no small consideration.
Women persuaded him that he was handsome; politicians
only wanted to know what were his views; in the county it
was hoped he would reside constantly, and complete the improvements at Brocket his father had begun. Society opened

---

* G. Selwyn to Lord Carlisle, Jan. 1768.
† Oldfield, vol. v. p. 213.

its arms to so eligible a recruit, and before six months he
was the suitor, slave, and betrothed of one of the fairest
women of her time. Elizabeth, only daughter of Sir Ralph
Milbanke, of Halnaby in Yorkshire, was then in her twentieth
year; and if the portraiture and gossip of the day are to be
believed, possessed already the fascinations which eventually
gave her an influence so considerable in the world. Her
first picture, painted by Sir Joshua in 1770, was more than
once engraved.* It has the fault so frequently complained
of in his delineation of court beauties, that of betraying too
much desire for effect. But with the freshness of youth
there is mingled the unmistakable look of that ambition with
which throughout life this singular woman was animated.
Early in May her son Peniston was born, and with the
felicitations on the glad event were mingled those upon her
husband being created Lord Melbourne of Kilmore in the
County of Cavan. An Irish peerage was one of the honours
George III. was most ready to confer; and, as it was not
incompatible with membership of the House of Commons, it
constituted an intervening grade of social rank, which, as
the experience of his father's reign had shown, led the holder
frequently to look for imperial ennoblement.

The world did its best to spoil the youthful favourite
of fortune. While the joy of motherhood was new, Lady
Melbourne was devoted to her first-born, and delighted with
his praise. Reynolds persuaded her to be painted in the
attitude of fondling her child; and in simple garb made
her the subject of the charming picture engraved by Watson,
well known under the name of 'Maternal Affection.'

Ere the winter season came again, she was ready to
take part once more in the gaieties of the town. With the
Duchess of Richmond and Mrs. Damer, one of the most
gifted and accomplished women of her time, and with ever-
multiplying troops of friends she was content to float on the
stream of fashionable life. Masquerades were then in vogue,
and women of quality did not hesitate to adopt attire, at

* The mezzotint by Finlayson was published the following year.

balls where dress in character was the rule, which would
not be thought of in our day. Her name is mentioned with
that of the Duchess of Ancaster and Lady Fordyce as
" among the pretty fellows appearing in dominoes as masculine as many of the maccaroni things we see everywhere." *

In the following spring she persuaded her husband to
purchase a mansion in Piccadilly next to Burlington House,
which had been built for Lord Holland from designs by
Chambers, the architect of Somerset House.

Upon the site three separate dwellings originally stood,
one of which did not content the ambition of Charles Spencer,
second Lord Sunderland, who bought up the other two, and
added a library for the notable collection of books and
manuscripts subsequently transferred to Blenheim. " It was
noticed," says Swift, " that he had much fallen from the
heights of those republican principles with which he began "
as member for Tiverton, when he would not let himself be
called my Lord, and hoped to see the day when there would
not be a peer in England. Here he lived with exceeding
pomp, quarrelling with his imperious mother-in-law, Duchess
Sarah, circumventing his colleagues, patronising Addison,
and elaborating schemes for limiting the peerage: and
here he prematurely ceased from troubling, after which
Sunderland House became the possession of another, and
not less remarkable Secretary of State.

The family of Fox, like that of Coke, owed its uprise to
the favour of the Stuarts. Old Sir Stephen stood upon the
scaffold at Whitehall; and steadily refused to conform to
the will of Cromwell. Under the Restoration he was re-
compensed for loss and exile by more than one lucrative
post; and when at his instance Chelsea Hospital was
founded, he backed his advice with a donation of thirteen
thousand pounds. His eldest son held office under Walpole,
and became Lord Ilchester. The younger Henry squandered
his inheritance at play; then took to politics with a view
of retrieving his position; soon made his mark as a debater

* Reynolds' Diary.

of pith and versatility; was made Surveyor of Works by
Walpole, and Lord of the Treasury by Carteret. Then he
asked Lady Caroline Lennox in marriage; and when repelled
by her sire, stole her by the help of the Duke of Marlborough, who gave her away. Holland House, at Kensington, deserted and in disrepair, but encompassed with recollections, would under his renovating hand make such a
residence for his lady wife as no ancient noble could command in the vicinage of town. A lease for years was first
secured and then the fee. In 1755 Fox became Secretary
of State, but valuing opulence above all distinction, he let
himself down into the sinecure clerkship of the Pells in
Ireland, worth £2000 a year for life, and the Paymaster-
Generalship in England, whose percentages on all moneys
paid out of the Treasury, and all subsidies to foreign states,
together with the use of floating balances left in his hands,
enabled him in a few years to heap up wealth untold.* To
keep his places, and to advance withal his connections and
adherents, he voted sometimes with Newcastle, sometimes
with Bute, but always with the king. Offers of the first
place were more than once made to him, but in vain; he kept
fast hold of what was best worth holding; and not without
great difficulty and undying grudge towards former friends,
he was at last induced to relax his clutch upon being made
a peer. Tired of an ungrateful world, he resolved to trouble
himself no more with its affairs, and his precocious son
Charles James having already coaxed him to defray large
gambling debts, he was ready to dispose of his house in
town which he no longer wanted. Throughout his official
career he had been the contemporary and intimate of
Sir Matthew Lamb, who purchased Brocket in the same
year that he began restoring the "brave old house at
Kensington." †

* "In time of war the office yielded thirty, forty, and even fifty
thousand pounds in one year to its fortunate possessor."—Earl Russell,
'Life and Times of C. J. Fox,' vol. i. p. 2.

† H. Walpole, May 5th, 1747.

After he had betaken himself thither he sometimes let the house in Piccadilly, and when his sons Stephen and Charles first came into Parliament they took up their residence there. But at length he disposed of it for a considerable sum in 1770 to the son of his old friend, from whom it thenceforth bore the name of Melbourne House. The courtyard in front was at that time inclosed by gates, and the space now covered by the chambers of the Albany was a garden having an entrance opposite Savile Row. In its adornment large sums were lavished by Lady Melbourne with no ordinary taste and skill. Cipriani, who enjoyed a high reputation in his special walk of art, and whose substantial forms of nymph and cherub his countryman Bartolozzi had made familiar to the public eye, undertook to paint the ceiling of the ball-room. Wheatley, as eminent for his versatility in landscape, embellished several of the other apartments, while to Rebecca, fast rising into note under royal favour as a humorist in fresco, the remaining decorations were assigned. And then began that round of hospitalities of which for many years there seemed to be no end. Lord Melbourne boasted that on his marriage he had given the whole of his wife's fortune back to her in diamonds. He was very proud of her attractions, and cared not what expenditure contributed to enhance the *éclat* of her position. Sir Joshua became a greater favourite than ever, and, with other men of genius, was made welcome always to festive gatherings where the crowd went and came, and often to the friendlier receptions of the few. He painted in 1776 a third portrait of Lady Melbourne, holding her son by the hand, which was engraved in mezzotinto by Finlayson. Though less attitudinised, it is upon the whole less pleasing than those already mentioned. Lord Melbourne belonged to the Dilettanti and other clubs which consisted mainly of artists and men of letters. He was fond of the drama, and liberally befriended not a few of those who made it their profession. In politics he took no deep or earnest interest, attending irregularly at Westminster, and voting with his malcontent friends at Brooke's two or three times in the session. He had had in fact no training to business of any kind, and easily fell into habits of indolent dissipation, which he never probably made any serious effort to break through. At Almack's he played faro with Lord Stavordale, who once at a sitting lost £11,000, and on winning it back in a single hand at hazard swore at his ill luck, for "if he had been playing deep he might have won millions."* His cousin, Charles Fox, shone equally there and in the House of Commons.

The new nobility thought it became them to be more lavish than the old. Without being singular, Lord Melbourne indulged in all the pleasures of a pleasure-seeking time. During half the year he had more enjoyment in shooting-parties at Melbourne, or drawing the fox-covers of Hertfordshire, than in late hours in town. He was, upon the whole, a good-for-little apathetic, kindly man, who never had a quarrel in his life, and who probably never lay awake an hour fretting about anything. By George Selwyn he continued to be returned for Luggershall, with any one else who was acceptable to Lord North ; and having no trouble about his own seat, he was readily persuaded to help those who had difficulty in gaining or keeping theirs. At the election for Herts of 1774 he proposed Mr. Plumer, in a short and sensible speech said to be the best made on the occasion. His friend and neighbour Sir John Seabright performed the same service for Mr. Halsey, while Mr. Ratcliffe proposed Lord Grimstone: the Cowper and Dacre interest being on the one side and all the influence of Hatfield on the other. The day's amusement was said to have cost £4000, and the two first-named candidates were returned. Calvert and Seabright came in for the borough, and thus a very useful contingent in support of Government was secured.

Meanwhile the additional buildings and external improvements at Brocket were completed, and its fair mistress longed to render it all beautiful within. Mortimer designed,

* II. Walpole to II. Mann, February 2nd, 1770.

and with the assistance of Wheatley painted, the allegoric groups which decorate the ceiling of the centre drawing-room; and by degrees, to use the expression of her illustrious adviser in artistic matters, " the walls being hung with pictures, came to be hung with thoughts."

Throughout the American war Lord Melbourne when he voted had supported ministers, and at its disastrous close did not desert them. Increased taxation and accumulating debt weighed heavily upon commerce, whose wings were continually clipped at sea by the privateers. Petitions for retrenchment and peace poured in from many counties and large towns. Burke persuaded the chiefs of opposition to espouse the principles of economic reform, and though Shelburne was defeated in his proposal in the Lords, Dunning (his nominee for Calne) carried by eighteen, after hot debate, his memorable resolution, that by means of sinecures and pensions " the influence of the Crown had increased and ought to be diminished." In the minority we find the noble member for Luggershall. Burke's Retrenchment Bill to carry into effect the resolution was resisted at every stage. The king, incensed beyond measure at the arguments used on the occasion, which he said were personally aimed against himself, bade Lord North be of good heart, keep up the conflict, and things would mend. He did so for another year, Lord Melbourne and the members for Herts, both county and town, lending him their aid in the struggle to defer the threatened change.

In the new parliament chosen during the autumn the number of ministerial supporters was not much increased; and it was more than ever necessary to insure the fidelity of those who had been faithful found. Decorations and promotions were liberally bestowed. Several creations and steps in the peerage had been promised ; and in November Horace Walpole, dining at the Lucans, heard, probably from Lord Clermont—a man equally well-informed of moves at Court and of odds at Newmarket—that Lord Melbourne was about to be made a Viscount, and in time would read *En voilà pour aujourd'hui.* In the same breath he adds, Lord Clermont told them that Scipio had first introduced toothpicks from Spain, a fact he did not know before, or that his lordship knew Scipio to be anybody but a racehorse. The Gazette before Christmas ratified the rumour.

CHAPTER II.

EARLY SURROUNDINGS.

Birth and childhood—Prince of Wales's household—Guests and
intimates—Class-fellows at Eton—Mrs. Damer—Lord Egremont—
Exchange of mansions—Prize Declamation at Cambridge—A
winter at Glasgow.

ON the 15th of March, 1779, Lady Melbourne's second son
was born, and at St. James's font received the name of
William. Peniston was then nine years old. Gentle, intelligent, and engaging, he began to concentrate all his
father's hopes and wishes, and daily to become more and
more a source of joy and pride. The Viscount never tired
of being told that his boy was like him; and in no companionship did he find pleasure so unmixed. His heir must
of course be sent to Eton, and in due time Cambridge, and
have masters if he would learn classics and accomplishments. But his own recollections of the interval between
childhood and manhood were nearly bare of all that related
to learning of any description, except that its acquisition
was irksome and a bore. If his son cared as little for
books as he had done, he could as well afford it, and would
probably be as happy. Peniston grew apace; held himself
well, had a high-bred look and air, was loved by everybody,
and by every dog about the place; would ride his pony
at anything, and no doubt in time would be a capital shot.
How he loved the boy, and how the young affectionate
nature, cheerful and pliant and easily pleased, coiled round
each fibre of paternal being, none saw or cared but she of

whom it came. Soon she felt however, that if the little stranger was to be prized and loved, all must come from her. And when he began to look around him and laugh up into her eyes and play at her feet, woman of the world as she was, her heart softened, all her best impulses were moved; and she vowed within herself devotion to the bringing-up and future destiny of her second son. Nor was it long before tiny sparks were visible of a nature very different from that which Peniston in infancy had shown. Let alone, he would amuse himself readily. Eat when not hungry no power could make him; but when he began he did uncommonly well. Not fretful, peevish or cross, he was nevertheless healthily troublesome. He liked mischief, would have his way, and was often wholly unmanageable. Three years later * Frederick was born. As children they grew up together, for the most part at Brocket, and were much attached; their features bearing marked resemblance, and many of their mental qualities being equally akin.

George III. had for some time been anxiously engaged with frugal plans of a provisional establishment for his eldest son. Economy in the prince's expenditure might be combined, he thought, with a continuance of parental control over his ways of life. The heir apparent might very well continue to live at St. James's or at Windsor, being allowed as much for robes and privy purse as he himself had had; and he would give him sixteen horses instead of four. But he might do with an equerry and two or three footmen less, not having a house to keep of his own.

The great difficulty I find—wrote the king—in having persons whose private conduct I think may with safety be placed about a young person, is not surprising, as I thank Heaven my morals and course of life have but little resembled those too prevalent in the present age; and certainly of all objects in this life the one I have most at heart, is to form my children that they may be useful examples and worthy of imitation. I should therefore be

* April 17th, 1782.

scrupulous as to the private lives of those I place about my son, though in other cases I never wish to be informed, unless of those great enormities, that must make every man of principle shun the company of such persons, but in the case of my children, my happiness as well as the good of the public is materially concerned in this investigation.[*]

What Lord North would have recommended, had his advice been really desired, it is useless to surmise ; he probably thought that while the prince was denied an establishment of his own, he might as well be surrounded by those whose tastes were congenial and whose position in life rendered it easy for them to contribute to pleasures which else he might seek in worse company. Many noble mansions were ready to welcome him, and Melbourne House was gayest of the gay. Its *poco curante* owner was proud to receive him ; Lady Melbourne was charmed with his visits ; and he soon learned to make himself at home. Sheridan and Fitzpatrick, Selwyn and Hare, contributed each in his special way to the mirth of the table, and whatever was fascinating and fair in the Whig saloons of the day was certain to be found in the company of the new viscountess. There also frequently came Francis, Duke of Bedford, and Charles Fox, then in the ripening promise of popularity and power, though damaged in character by the recklessness of his private life, and, in spite of all his father's liberality towards him, without a guinea.

As the time approached when the Prince of Wales would come of age, it became necessary to provide for him a separate establishment ; and Lord Rockingham is understood to have advised that such an allowance should be asked from Parliament as would enable him to maintain with befitting splendour his position as the first subject of the Crown. George II. had enjoyed £100,000 a year when the public revenues were far less, and when money went much farther in the purchase of every necessary and luxury of life. His son

* Letter to Lord North.

Frederick, though an object of parental dislike, received an equal allowance, and George III. himself had had the same ; but the minister vainly urged that these precedents should be followed. The king was dissatisfied with the conduct of the prince, and distrustful of the companions of his choice. Of late he had been much in the society of Charles Fox, who, far from deprecating the suspicion with which he thought himself unjustly regarded, went out of his way to declare that the grant of £50,000 a year moved by the Chancellor of the Exchequer was inadequate, that the hope of economy on which it was founded would not be realised, and that sooner or later Parliament would be called on to relieve embarrassment which its improvident parsimony was about to render unavoidable.

Had it remained with him, he certainly would have advised an establishment more adequate and suitable ; but the person most proper to decide on the business was of a very different opinion, and therefore it was his duty to submit.

The imprudence and unseemliness of such language from a Secretary of State did not prevent its being cheered warmly by those who began to call themselves the prince's friends. The Commons would readily have voted one hundred thousand a year had they been suffered to do so. The king, however, adhered to his resolve, and beside the separate revenue of the Duchy of Cornwall, could only be induced to add the colonelcy of the 10th Dragoons, the only military appointment the prince ever obtained and which he continued to hold until he ascended the throne. For his residence his father gave him the well known house, originally built by Henry Boyle, Lord Carleton, on a piece of ground leased to him in 1709 by Queen Anne for thirty-one years at £35 a year. It was described as part and parcel of the royal garden near St. James's Palace. His nephew, Lord Burlington, subsequently inhabited the mansion and gave it to his mother, from whom it was bought in 1732 by Frederick, Prince of Wales, being, as was said, delightfully situated for

a place of courtly pleasure; but the building itself was
tame and poor, hardly any place being capable of greater
improvements, and hardly any standing in more need of
them.*

There the widowed princess resided till her death.   The
gardens reached to those of Marlborough House, and constituted its chief attraction; for near the approach stood a number of dwellings not of the most sightly aspect.   Holland
designed a colonnade to serve as a screen, and erected the
portico which in later years was transferred to the façade
of the National Gallery.   When finished, Horace Walpole
pronounced the new palace in Pall Mall the most perfect
in Europe; the three chief apartments and the music-room
looking on the secluded grounds, and the vestibule, hall, and
staircase superb.   " But where the money was to come from,
he conceived not; all the tin mines in Cornwall would not
pay a quarter."† This consideration gave his Royal Highness
small concern.   The Chancellor of the Exchequer had had
full warning of what was likely to happen; and happen it
should.   To celebrate his birthday the prince was resolved
upon a feast; and Carlton House being still in the hands of
the workmen, the dinner was given to a numerous company
at the White Hart, Windsor, whereat, as Lord Melbourne
loved long afterwards to tell, a turtle was served weighing
four hundredweight—a present from the East India Board.

Appointments in the household of the prince were
coveted by all who had interest at Court or with Opposition;
and many were the jealousies and disappointments which
they caused.   Lord Lewisham was made Warden of the
Stannaries and Lord Melbourne was named Gentleman of the
Bedchamber, with Lord Spencer Hamilton, son of the sixth
duke of his name.   The place of the latter was subsequently
filled by Lord Charles Somerset, and some years later by
Lord Clermont.

At the ball given on taking possession of his new home

* 'Critical Review of Public Buildings,' p. 75, 1734.
† Letter to Lady Ossory, September 17th.

the heir apparent received the gratulations of all that was best born and most beautiful in the land, as sung in after-years by the granddaughter of his wittiest and merriest confidant—

> They crowd around me like young girls peeping,
> And seem to question me which is most fair!

On none were admiring eyes more fixed than on Lady Melbourne, then perhaps at the zenith of her popularity and attraction.

Maria Cosway, wife of the well-known miniature painter, had exhibited not long before at the Academy two or three historical pictures giving evidence of much originality and feeling. Her acquaintance was sought by many persons of distinction, and it became the fashion to bid high for the possession of her works. The Duchess of Devonshire visited her studio; and at the request of the prince she painted some remarkable portraits. One of them was that of Lady Melbourne, which remained at Carlton House until removed to the Corridor at Windsor.

At the general election of 1784 no contest provoked so much passion or proved so memorable as that of Westminster.* At the end of the tenth day's poll, Fox had three hundred and eighteen votes less than Sir Cecil Wray. The exultation of his opponents knew no bounds, but their rejoicings were premature. Surprise, disappointment, and rage bewildered the adherents of the Whig chief, and his cause would have been irretrievably lost but for allies who had never taken part in such a fray before. Georgiana, Duchess of Devonshire, then without compeer as queen of fashion, openly undertook with the aid of her sister Lady Duncannon and Mrs. Crewe to canvass for the leader of Opposition; Lady Melbourne, Mrs. Damer and others took a part less prominent, but not less enthusiastic. On the twentieth day the majority was reduced to eighty-four; the struggle became keener than ever; and the profusion of blandishments and inducements

* March 1784.

were on both sides unparalleled; for, the example once set of female interference, the Countess of Salisbury and other Tory ladies sought to exert a counter-ruling influence over the electors. On the thirtieth day Lord Hood was still head of the poll, while Fox was but one hundred and sixty-six above his other competitor. And when on the fortieth day his victory was announced, it was by a majority of no more than two hundred and thirty-six, out of thirteen thousand votes. The protracted suspense, and the violence of the passions which had been excited during the conflict, together with the bitterness of disappointment, caused, ere its termination, by the tidings of multiplied defeat in other cities and towns, all served to intensify rather than abate the delirium of triumph. The carriages of the Duchess of Portland and the Duchess of Devonshire, each drawn by six horses, took part in the procession from the hustings to Piccadilly, where, in front of Devonshire House, the orator was received by his " Grand Electress " and presented by the Prince of Wales with a wreath of laurel.

Meanwhile in the clear air of Hertfordshire the younger children of the household throve apace; and at each recurring holiday-time delighted more and more the ever onward and upward spirit of their mother. Peniston was too old for companionship with the youngsters, but their joyous freaks amused him, and he entered often into their childish play. Their mother was delighted, and she persuaded Reynolds, though overladen with engagements more than he could execute, to undertake a group illustrating in their varied ages the fraternal love of her children. By some it has been said that the idea originated with himself, as in the well-known painting which keeps in memory, at Holland House, the youthful gallantry of Charles Fox towards his cousin, Lady Sarah Lennox, beneath the window whence her mother is observing them. We only know that the veteran President of the Academy entered genially into the realisation of the design, and made two or three studies of the pranksome younger boys and of their more staid and thoughtful elder. Peniston is portrayed as encouraging Frederick and William to romp about him, while there is in his features the mingled look of amusement at their gambols and of dreams less childish passing through his mind. The 'Affectionate Brothers' was one of the last pictures finished by Sir Joshua, and in conception, grace, and vividness of expression, it is eminently worthy of his fame. It was first engraved in mezzotinto by Bartolozzi; and subsequently in a smaller size by S. M. Reynolds. The youngest is in the dress and attitude of a spoilt child still an inmate of the nursery; while the vivacity and force of the picture are concentrated in the unruly youngster; who, according to Sir Joshua, gave him more trouble than he liked, and whom he used to bribe into brief intervals of quiet by promises of another ride on his foot. And he looks it still—a hearty, gladsome, wayward little fellow, with a soft roguish eye and gesture full of provocation.

A few months afterwards, George, not yet three years old, was painted by Maria Cosway, in the allegoric style she affected, as the 'Infant Bacchus.' The picture was said to be particularly happy, and was probably as like as the delineation of chubby and rosy features is by those who love them, usually said to be.

Emily, the only daughter who survived the period of infancy, was not born until 1787. In expression and in spirit she bore a striking resemblance to her mother, and as she grew up attracted and attained the attachment of all around her. In after-life William and his sister found innumerable points of sympathy, and her influence with him was great.

Of those who were intimate during his boyhood at Melbourne House, he remembered none in after-life with greater pleasure than the widowed daughter of General Conway. While yet a girl, her desire to excel in art had received a singular impulse from some passing words of David Hume. In a morning walk she saw him give a shilling to an Italian boy who offered him some small casts from the antique for sale, asking thoughtlessly what he saw worth encouraging in such a calling. The philosopher gently rebuked her, saying that, valueless as these cheap copies seemed to be, they were the produce of genius and skill beyond any she possessed; and that no modern attainments enabled one now to produce anything comparable to them. Piqued by his reproof, she resolved to try what she could do in modelling, and after some little time presented him with a head, in wax, of merits so promising that he made amends by cordial praise and incentives to pursue her studies in that direction. Her marriage with the eldest son of Lord Dorchester, though it brought her early into society, did not change her predilections in art. John Damer was a gambler, whose premature death left her without children, to follow the bent of her own tastes and inclinations. Her father's greatest friend was Horace Walpole, who took an interest in all she did, and by his advice she studied the elementary principles of anatomy from Cruikshank, and details of drawing and form from Cerrachi and Bacon. With Mrs. Crew she sojourned long in Italy, chiefly for the enjoyment and instruction its churches, palaces, and museums afford those who love art with devotion. Returning to England, she resumed with persevering zeal her amateur vocation. Her busts of Lady Elizabeth Foster, Lady Melbourne, and her mother, Lady Aylesbury, still attest the unaffected freedom and the uneffeminate delicacy of her style.

It was a caprice of the time to paint or mould likenesses in allegoric character, and young Peniston Lamb was represented by her in marble with the classic insignia of Mercury. The heads in relief of Thame and Isis on the keystone of Henley Bridge were the work of her chisel; and she took especial pleasure in transferring to marble the forms of her dumb favourites, though in this species of delineation she never perhaps attained the life-like touch of Lady Dacre. For a present on his birthday she brought Horace Walpole an osprey, whose plumage she had elaborated with peculiar care; and in acknowledgment he engraved its pedestal with the graceful flattery,

Non me Praxiteles fecit, at Anna Damer.

Her house was the centre of attraction for artists and men of letters, to not a few of whom she rejoiced in rendering timely and essential service. Angelica Kauffmann painted the best portrait of Mrs. Damer which remains; and through her the latter became acquainted with Maria Cosway, whose craving for admission within the exclusive fences of society she helped oftentimes to gratify. Mrs. Damer was one of Lady Melbourne's earliest, truest, and most intimate friends. When Brocket was adorning she was ever ready with suggestion or caution; always with a reason, and that a good one, for any deviation from customary style or breach of conventional rules of embellishment, she sympathised with her friend's love of magnificence, but her finer taste preferred harmony to glitter, and subdued colouring to fantastic show.

Both were fond of theatricals, and in the impersonation of character on the private stage had few equals. Fox, Fitzpatrick, and Sheridan, with all the young men of talent or of *ton* that were led by their example, were ready to aid by pen or voice or sympathetic presence whatever cast their fair friends chose. For the veteran critic of Strawberry Hill, the child of his greatest friend had the greatest charm, and he was seldom better content than when complaining that he was put to his wits' end at Twickenham to find at short notice a dinner good enough for her and Lady Melbourne.

Another intimate of both ladies, who equally delighted in all that was best in art, and whose great possessions enabled him to become one of its most generous and judicious promoters, was young Lord Egremont.*

George O'Brien Wyndham, while yet a boy, inherited great possessions. His grandfather had been the confidant

* Born December 18th, 1751.

and compeer of Bolingbroke, his father the colleague of
Grenville and Bute. Reynolds has preserved the expression of his features, which were singularly fine ; and
Fox is known to have said of him at eight-and-twenty,
that though he had no experience in business, and had
never been in office, he would rather take his judgment on
the India Bill than that of most other men he knew.
Petworth, rebuilt in the preceding reign by the Duke of
Somerset, had been filled by him with treasures of painting
and carving such as no other country house in England
could boast ; and the delight of its new possessor was still
further to enrich its halls and chambers with whatever
seemed to him most noble in design and beautiful in execution of the sculpture and painting of his day. He loved
the companionship of men of wit and art, and took less
pleasure in playing the patron than the host. Gainsborough
and Flaxman were his guests for days and weeks together.
With the entertainment of a palace they found a school
where they might study, by what light and at what hours
they would, the masterpieces of Holbein, Van Eyck and
Anthony Moore, Titian, Correggio, Hobbema, and Claude.

In early life Lord Egremont professed to be no more
than a man of pleasure, given to hospitality, fond of the
turf, content to be a cause of war among strategic mothers.
Rather shy and taciturn, many outshone him in the ball-
room, none in the morning ride or garden walk. There
was in his voice and manner, say his contemporaries, that
fascination for women, and even for men, which neither knew
how to resist. At Melbourne House he was a constant
guest, and through a long course of years his friendship and
sympathy were never wanting. Old Horace snarls at him in
his characteristic way as " a worthless young fellow ; " * his
offence being that, having proposed to Walpole's niece, Lady
Maria Waldegrave, he had seemed to grow cold, whereupon
the lady's relatives in a pet threatened to break off the match,
which, when he took them at their word, they much repented.

* Letter, July 24th, 1780.

He long remained unmarried, but his tastes were eminently social, and one of his greatest pleasures was to invite not only his friends, but their children to his princely house in Sussex, and to witness the varied enjoyment of pastimes provided for all ages. Some of the brightest scenes of William Lamb's childhood were in Petworth Park, where he and his brothers used to gambol all day long. Arthur Young had been a frequent visitor, and under his advice the old deerpark was disafforested, and Petworth, like Holkam and Woburn, lent its name to a school of improved agriculture. Except at Wentworth, there was not to be found in England stabling so extensive or a stud so numerous or high-bred; and its owner liked to be reminded that few great races had been run in his time in which some measure of success was not ascribable to him.

In 1790 William Lamb was entered at Eton. Among his class-fellows were Charles Sumner, destined to become Archbishop of Canterbury; Charles Ellis, afterwards Lord Stuart de Rothesay; and Sir Charles Stewart, the last two distinguished in diplomacy; Tullibardine, afterwards Duke of Atholl; F. Male, who enjoyed a high repute as a physician at Birmingham; and one who, in his way, attained more notoriety than any of the rest, George commonly known during the Regency as Beau Brummel. In the class above him were Henry Hallam the historian; and Assheton Smith, well known for his scientific inventions, still more for his long-asserted leadership in the hunting-field. In the class below him was Henry Fane, of whom he then knew little, but whose name, after the lapse of half a century, was destined to be associated sadly with the least fortunate and defensible proceedings in his public life.

A singular incident in family history occurred about this time. One day the Duke of York, a frequent guest at Piccadilly, complained to Lady Melbourne that he was tired of his residence at Whitehall; and that he longed for the possession of a house like hers, which he particularly admired. With her usual naivete, she replied that she in her turn desired the opportunity of looking on the park every morning when she rose, and that, were it possible, she would willingly exchange the chimes at night of St. James's for those of the Abbey. His Royal Highness vowed that anything was possible to her; and recurring to the subject frequently, the Viscount, who at first treated the affair as a joke, and then as one of his wife's unaccountable whims, was persuaded to consider seriously the feasibility of making the exchange. The pleasure of the king was the first thing to be ascertained; for the Duke was affectionate towards his father, and a special favourite with him.

The mansion, which occupies the space between the Horse Guards and the Treasury, and which was originally built by Payne for Sir Matthew Fetherstonhaugh, had been vacated for the use of the Duke in 1784 by Sir Jeffery Amherst, and was thenceforth held on lease from the Crown. The entrance stood some distance back from the street, and, to please its new occupant, a circular hall and portico were added by Holland soon after he had executed the colonnade in front of Carlton House for the Prince of Wales. Lord North, cheerful as ever, though grown quite blind, heard of the changes that were making, and said when they were described to him that "things were coming to a strange pass when the Duke of York was sent to the Round House, and the Heir Apparent to the Pillory."

Before Christmas it was agreed that the proposed exchange should be carried into effect; and in the course of the ensuing autumn the transfer actually took place. His Royal Highness assigned by deed the capital messuage and premises situate at or near Whitehall, and the furniture therein, together with the Old Lottery Office, and other the premises which his Royal Highness then held or had made application to the Treasury to hold by lease from the Crown for the term of fifty years, to Viscount Melbourne, who on his part transferred and made over all that and those the messuages and tenements situate and lying between Burlington Garden and Sackville Street and between Savile

Row and Piccadilly, &c. Thenceforth the titles of the two mansions were simultaneously transposed. The dwelling in Piccadilly was called York House, and subsequently the Albany; that in Whitehall took the name of its new proprietor, by which it was known during the rest of his life.

The seventeenth Parliament of Great Britain met on the 25th of November, 1790, to which were returned for Newport in the Isle of Wight Viscount Palmerston and Viscount Melbourne, whose sons, then pursuing their studies at Eton and Harrow, were destined to be associated in after-life so intimately. The Rev. Sir H. Worsley was then patron of the borough. Lord Melbourne vacated his seat in 1793, when, his son having come of age, he wished him to take his place, and Peniston was returned accordingly. The Viscount himself did not re-enter the House of Commons.

With the sons of other Whigs of quality William was sent to Cambridge; he was entered on the 7th of July, 1796, as a fellow-commoner of Trinity, and he went into residence in the October following. It was not with him, however, during the next three years the ordinary course of pleasure and nothing more. Though he would not learn by rote, to read long and hard he was not ashamed. Already it would seem as though he had beaconings of ambition. Not a bad classic when he quitted Eton, he acquired during his stay at Trinity a fairly extended acquaintance with the ancient poets and historians whose works were then among the books of the undergraduate course. But his studies were seldom bounded by the limits defined in lecture notice; for he was not reading for class, but to satisfy his own curiosity and love of information. From mathematics he turned away with distaste and aversion somewhat similar perhaps to that which Macaulay has confessed. In preference he gave himself to ethical speculation, in which throughout his life he never ceased to take peculiar interest. The law being assigned him for a profession, and political life pointed to by his mother as within his reach not remotely beyond probation at the bar, he wished to be allowed to keep his terms in London simultaneously with those at Cambridge. No reasonable wish (seldom, probably, an unreasonable one) was refused by Lady Melbourne; and accordingly, on the 21st of July, 1797, the registry of Lincoln's Inn records that William Lamb was entered a student of law by the Right Hon. Henry Addington, Speaker of the House of Commons, one of the benchers of the Society.

At the close of Michaelmas Term 1798 he delivered an oration in the chapel of Trinity which won the declamation prize. It was the first composition of any length or importance he had attempted, and it was subsequently printed for private circulation. The theme was "The progressive improvements of mankind." By his hearers it was received with no slight marks of favour, and by friends and kinsfolk made the occasion of kindly criticism and undiscerning praise. Like so many youthful essays, it would doubtless have passed quickly into forgetfulness, had not a passage caught the fancy of Mr. Fox, who, to the surprise and delight of its author, quoted it in his speech on the character of Francis, Duke of Bedford, when moving a new writ for Tavistock.

After exhausting the rich vocabulary of encomium, the statesman said he would conclude with applying to the present occasion a beautiful passage from the speech of a very young orator. It might, he thought, perhaps savour too much of the sanguine views of youth to stand the test of a rigid philosophical inquiry, but it was at least cheering and consolatory; and that in this instance it might be exemplified, he was confident was the sincere wish of every man who heard him.

Crime, says he, is a curse only to the period in which it is successful; but virtue, whether fortunate or otherwise, blesses not only its own age, but remotest posterity; and is as beneficial by its example as by its immediate effects. *

* 'Speeches of C. J. Fox,' vol. vi. p. 472, March 16th, 1802.

The following is perhaps the most felicitous example of the style and drift of the essay :—

Before this discovery (art of printing) the improvement of man could not be termed progressive; it was confined in its operation, and liable to long and frequent interruptions. He emerged, indeed, from the woods and caverns; he assembled societies; he founded cities; he instituted laws and cultivated learning. The arts reaped their noblest triumphs. The canvas glowed with animation, the marble swelled beneath the chisel into life. Philosophy in her colonnades and gardens dictated her solemn truths; Eloquence poured her loudest; and Poetry breathed her most enchanting strains. The great and unwieldy empire of Rome, under which, notwithstanding the corruption of manners and the depravation of taste, the productions of genius were still admired and preserved, now tottered to its fall. The barbarous hordes descended from the North. Literature, having no reliance except upon perishable transcripts of her works, was soon involved in the common ruin. The statues were broken, the pictures were defaced, the volumes committed to the flames, and the precious relics that escaped the savages are but the venerable vestiges of genius, and the splendid fragments of excellence. An age of sterility intervened. A period of thick darkness long brooded over the earth; and the mind of man slept, deprived of all its energies, and forgetful of everything that it had been accustomed to consider honourable and great. The mass of mankind can be amended only by experience, and experience can only be acquired by time. Every setting sun leaves behind it new instruction; every day spreads truths already ascertained, confirms those that have been hitherto doubtful, affords tests to detect fallacy, and establishes precedents to guide uncertainty. While generation is following generation; while the sceptre of power is passing from the grasp of one nation into that of another; while the dank dews of night are imperceptibly wearing away the monument and the column; while cities are going to decay, and stupendous piles of marble and brass moulder into dust; the mind of man grows vigorous from time, and is ever struggling on with increased energy in pursuit of that perfection, which to have sought after, though, perhaps, it can never be attained, exalts and glorifies human nature.

The tone of the essay, which the sentence quoted by his illustrious friend has preserved from oblivion, is throughout hopeful and genial, rather than argumentative or profound. We catch no shadow of the desponding temper which the susceptible author must have been familiar with, just then, in the political society of Melbourne House. The vexed spirit of Burke had indeed sunk to rest; but the schism his irresistible enthusiasm and eloquence on behalf of Catholicity and royalty as essential elements of Christian civilisation, opposed in his mind to every form of democracy and every phase of sceptic thought, was still unhealed. Lord Spencer, Mr. Windham, Sir Gilbert Eliott, and the Duke of Portland had joined Mr. Pitt's administration : while the adherents of Fox were so weakened and disheartened that they had not long before, in a fit of abortive rage, formally withdrawn from attendance in Parliament : and it was among the seceders that the young essayist had opened his political eyes. It is not therefore undeserving of note that in this first effort are traceable, though undogmatically writ, the lines of confident and even sanguine faith in moderate and steady progress, which in maturer years Lamb was found ready to defend against the opposite extremes of reaction and revolution.

At the end of Trinity Term 1799 he took his degree, and bade farewell to Cambridge with its genial associations of culture and speculation, to return no more.*

* He is entered in the registry of the University as having matriculated on the 29th of June, 1799, and having graduated on the 1st of July following. It is clear that his matriculation must have been accidentally omitted at the correct time, and that he matriculated just in time to enable him to take his degree.

It was not unusual at the period in question for young
men of promise to attend the open classes of philosophy
and jurisprudence in one of the Scotch Universities.   On
quitting Westminster, Lord Henry Petty spent two years at
Edinburgh before entering Trinity ; and between Harrow
and St. John's, the bright-eyed, laughing, but diligent
Henry Temple resided for some time in the house of Dugald
Stewart, notes of whose lectures he long preserved with care.
Glasgow indeed no longer numbered Adam Smith among
her illustrious teachers; but her reputation as a seat of
learning continued to stand high ; and by the wish of Lady
Melbourne inquiry was made if her son could be received as
a resident pupil by Professor Millar, of whose well-known
work ' An Historical View of the English Government,' Fox
once said, " It is dedicated to me, and written on the best
and surest principles."   Lord Lauderdale wrote—

There is a young man who wishes much to reside in your
house next winter.   He is a younger son of Lord Melbourne's.   He has the reputation and I believe really
possesses uncommon talents.   He means to go to the
English Bar with a view to follow the law as a profession.
He is the only person I have ever yet recommended to
you of whom I think I could with any safety say that
you will have real comfort and satisfaction in having
him as a pupil.   I wish you to write me a letter such as
I may show to them stating whether you can have room
for him the time he must be at Glasgow &c.   It is the
Duke of Bedford who has applied to me about it.*

The matter being arranged, William Lamb spent the winter
of 1799 and part of the succeeding one in Scotland, devot-
ing his attention specially to the Professor's lectures on
history and law and to those of Mylne on metaphysics.   In
the Collegiate Debating Club he took a constant and
brilliant part, being distinguished for aptitude of historic
illustration, and for caustic humour in reply.

* From Walthamstow, June 11th, 1799.

CHAPTER III.

A YOUNGER SON.

Firing at the king—Brocket races—A play of doubtful authorship—Beau Brummel—Call to the bar—Lady Caroline Ponsonby—Death of elder brother.

LADY MELBOURNE's aspirations for distinction and influence renewed their youth as she gazed upon her favourite son. Accustomed to flattery, and too quick-witted to be deceived thereby, she probably gave little heed to looks and words of admiration of which he was the object, from daughters who longed to dance with him, and fathers who liked being asked to dine; and doubtless she as little recked the smile-enamelled fear with which he was regarded as a fascinating younger son, by every shrewd mother of quality. What would he settle into? what would he do in life? would he go high? would he go far? Would her spirit, would her name live again in him, as the mirror told her that his features would? and she thought, with a sigh, he will be young when I am old. She studied his nature, antithetically mixed as it was, and full of qualities and dispositions the most opposite—not as an artist, to catch the fleeting expression, or, as an analyst, to note and weigh the elements continually apt to effervesce, but as a woman of the world, whose maternal love was purified from worldliness where he was concerned. All the experience she had gathered, and keen discernment she would fain impart redeemed from cynicism, and without losing hold on him. For his sake she wished

him to be invulnerable before he went into the fray ; and
yet she could not bring herself to forego the hope that his
reliance upon her would never grow less fond.

On the 15th of May, an attempt was made by a man
named Hatfield, who had formerly been in the Guards, to
assassinate the king as he entered his box at Drury Lane
Theatre. The news spread rapidly, and soon reached
Melbourne House, where the Prince of Wales was dining.
Lady Melbourne instantly ordered her carriage, and conjured
her royal guest to lose not a moment in repairing to the
theatre, where his Majesty was said to have resolved on
remaining with the queen as if nothing had happened. The
prince, who was on bad terms with his father, affected to
disbelieve the rumour, and made various excuses for not
going ; but the good sense of Lady Melbourne prevailed, and
by desire of the prince, William Lamb, who happened to be
at table, accompanied him. On arriving at the theatre he
found the Duke of York already there, and after tendering
their congratulations to his Majesty on his narrow escape
they withdrew to the apartment where the offender was in
custody, and remained during the preliminary examination
of witnesses who saw him present and fire the pistol. Hatfield recognised the Duke, under whom he had served, and
said that he was a good fellow. His lunacy, real or feigned,
was confidently asserted by the king, who showed no emotion,
and laughed at Queen Charlotte's supposing "that any one
but a madman would shoot him." Before midnight the
prince returned to Whitehall to thank his hostess for
persuading him to earn for once the praise of filial duty.
His young equerry on the occasion was wont to tell the
story with humour all his own, making the best of it for his
Royal Highness, and dwelling with affectionate emphasis on
the promptitude and tact shown by his mother. He was
thenceforth more frequently included in the invitations to
Carlton House, and became unluckily an early partaker in its
revelries.

Up to this time Hertfordshire contained no racecourse

except Barnet, which had never been a favourite with the gentlemen of the Turf, and which, owing partly to its proximity to town, grew every year less agreeable and worse regulated. The prince declared that it was a reproach to a county so accessible without being suburban that it did not supply an eligible place of meeting. In reply to his appeal Lord Melbourne was persuaded to devote a portion of his park particularly well suited to the purpose required; and in the autumn of 1799 a subscription list was opened for Cup and sweepstakes, headed by his Royal Highness, the Duke of Bedford, Lords Egremont, Clarendon and Burford, Sir G. Wombwell, Mr. Hale, Hon. G. Watson, &c.; Lord Melbourne and Mr. Hale of King's Walden agreeing to act as stewards. Hospitalities lavish and prolonged contributed to insure success. Next year the county members, Mr. Thomas Brand and Mr. Peniston Lamb, were stewards, and each following season brought new patrons—the Duke of St. Albans, Colonel Whalley, Lords Cowper and Ossulston, and Mr. Heathcote. When these assemblages began William Lamb was not at home, and at no period of his life did he take much interest in the events or controversies of the turf.

Mrs. Damer still continued to be one of Lady Melbourne's kindest, as she was one of her oldest, friends. On his death Lord Orford left Strawberry Hill to her, who had for him no greater charm than her rare talents for dramatic representation. Mrs. Damer's taste had not changed with advancing years, and it was by her that the pretty theatre was added to the house at Twickenham. One of the first performances upon its boards was a two-act comedy found among Walpole's papers, entitled 'Fashionable Friends.' The manuscript was not in his handwriting, and it bore no author's name. The piece, however, was well got up, and pronounced inimitable by the guests bidden to the scene. Charles Kemble was amongst them; and wanting just then something novel, he conceived the idea of obtaining leave from the executors to bring out the play as a posthumous work by the author of 'The Castle of Otranto.' It was accordingly produced in April 1802 at Drury Lane, Kemble himself and Mrs. Jordan sustaining the principal parts.

Its reception was unfavourable, and after a second representation it was withdrawn. Some of the criticisms on its tone and tendency seemed to have piqued the executors into its publication, as the best means of refuting the harsh insinuations of which it had been made the object. This was stated in the advertisement to the edition published by Ridgway, of which but few were sold ; and even the glimmer of its ephemeral existence is now difficult to catch among the relics of dramatic mortality, and its ashes need not have been disturbed, but for the recent ascription of the authorship to William Lamb.* Nothing in Walpole's diary or letters furnishes any warrant for the assertion ; nor is there in the memoirs of the time any proof, direct or circumstantial, on the point. If, as appears not improbable, the piece was an adaptation from the French, it may have been a youthful essay in composition given to the octogenarian critic by some too partial friend ; and never having been returned, it is just conceivable that Charles Kemble was misled as to its acting qualities by learning that it came from Lord Orford's library. But how it should have ever come to be associated with the name of his youthful acquaintance does not appear. There is nothing either very good or very bad, very dull or very adroit, in the construction of the play, which turns on ordinary incidents of life in the luxurious quarter of the capital; and it contains some smart and cynical turns of expression, but hardly one deserving of remembrance. Mrs. Jordan may have done her best to make the character she played attractive, and Chippendale and Fisher are not said to have been wanting in their way. But the only wonder is how it should have occurred to the manager of Drury Lane to take the trouble of trying, at some expense, whether it would do to attract or amuse an audience.

Brummel, who was born in 1778, was more than a year

* Alliboue, 'Dramatic Authors.

older in ways and ideas. Already fastidiousness in diet
and in dress possessed him. While his playmates roamed
or rollicked with laughing disregard of drenching or be-
miring, and happy forgetfulness of what figure they cut as
they got back to supper, the incipient dandy was ready to
elude on any convenient pretence the apprehended soaking,
not so much on account of discomfort as at the loss of
dignity. In every particular of person and apparel, he
would come into class finished *ad unguem ;* and the pocket-
money Tullibarden, Ellis or Lamb spent on sweets or sports
the premature cockscomb devoted to knickknacks of the
toilet. He was never known to hack his desk or cut his
name on the wall, while every other boy had ruined half-a-
dozen penknives in the process; and Assheton Smith was
wont to tell, long years after, how well he recollected that
Brummel never was flogged through the school, a circumstance which the veteran fox-hunter thought little to his
credit. But he was liked, in spite of his priggishness, by his
tutor and his dame, to whom he gave no trouble, and by
class-fellows, with whom he was always ready to share what
he had, making fun out of nothing to keep up the general
glee. In discharge of the duties of fag, especially "as
toaster of bread and cheese, nobody ever equalled him."
Lamb, like others, often quizzed him for his formality, but,
on the whole, remembered him as not a bad fellow. He
spent a year at Oriel, where he did nothing but break the
rules; and completed his education in the Prince's regiment
of Hussars. By the time William Lamb came back from
Glasgow, and began to saunter down the shady side of St.
James's Street, the "Beau," having come to maturity, was
on the sunny side, just bursting into blossom. He had sold
his captaincy, disentangling himself, as he said, of the in-
human trappings of war, abjured the levelling appellation
of " Mister," and had set about squandering his fortune in
the most exquisite manner. The *entrée* at Carlton House
was all very well in its way ; but he meant to hold his court
at White's, and to make himself king of fashion.

Between the Etonians there was little in common but
the zest for sarcasm and the love of raillery; this was
enough, however, to make five minutes of each other's
company constantly pleasant, and they met every day.
Brummel gave dinners of six or eight at his bijou mansion
in Chesterfield Street, where more than one royal highness
came; while Melbourne House was one of the few so
fortunate as to have a *chef* worthy of his approval. The
refinement and versatility of his impertinence, though it
seldom amounted to wit, amused his old class-fellow. Lamb
too had his foppery, though of a wholly different kind.
He could not help knowing that he was uncommonly good-
looking; but his vanity disdained ornaments or oddities
adopted by others to gain notice. An air of carelessness of
what he wore, and how he looked and what he said, was his
earliest affectation, and it stuck by him to the last; for
nobody ever happened to have coats that fitted better, books
more full of ideas or worthier of being remembered; and in
conversation, words more nicely chosen and heavily shotted
with meaning. But, from the outset, some vague and unaccountable wish to be thought indolent and idle appears to
have had a witchery for him, which in the midst of the
highest responsibilities he never entirely shook off. Dandyism he always looked upon as a species of acting, amusing
when consummate, and surprising in a person of talent and
skill, but simply ridiculous in itself, and despicable in a
man capable of better things. To vie with Brummel, or
Alvanley, or Mildmay, never occurred to him, but he enjoyed
their society, and in a certain sense admired and applauded
the way they played their parts. The Beau had a fancy for
enriching his album with contributions in verse by contemporaries of rank and distinction; and thus were preserved
some Anacreontics and other stanzas, serious or playful, from
the pens of Sheridan, Canning, Payne Knight, and Lady
Granville, which else might have dropped out of remembrance.

At all periods of his life Lamb loved classic verse;

Greek most in youth, English most in age. The melody of
tenderness and the majesty of thought could in turn melt
him to softness or stir him into passion. Rhythm had for
his ear a spell, which even in the turn of his merriest jest is
traceable; and many fragments of versification remain to
belie the foolish sneer that he was one who had not music
in his soul.

TRANSLATED FROM ANACREON.

Come painter, who with skilful hand
  Canst rival even nature's art;
Come, painter, draw as I command,
  The absent mistress of my heart.

Paint first each soft and jetty tress,
  With which her graceful head is crown'd;
If colours can so much express,
  Oh! paint them breathing odours round.

Above her cheek, full, lovely, fair,
  Where modest blushes reddening glow,
Beneath her mildly curling hair,
  Describe with skill her ivory brow.

Ah! how to imitate her face
  Thy chiefest science will be tried;
Between her brows the middle space
  Nor quite confound nor quite divide.

Here let the eyelid's lash be shown;
  Here let her semblance bear complete,
Dark arching eyebrows like her own,
  Which meeting, scarcely seem to meet.

But, painter, do not here forget
  To give her eye its native flame,
Azure, Minerva-like, and yet
  As melting as the Paphian dame.

Her nose and cheek then fashion well—
  That white as milk, and roseate this;
Her lips like soft Persuasion's swell,
  Pouting and challenging the kiss.

Beneath her chin where dimples play,
  About her neck of Parian stone,
Let all the loves and graces stray;
  That happy spot is all their own.

At the end of Michaelmas Term 1804 he was admitted to the bar, Charles Christopher Pepys being called on the same day. For an hour the currents of their destiny just touched, and then diverged as though they were never like to mingle. Except the uniform of learning which they then put on, they had as little in common as any two young men of the time. The one had fixed his thoughts on Equity, the ambitious dreams of the other led him to prefer Common Law. The one was by art a pleader, and by nature a plodder; unattractive in person, ineloquent in speech, unacquainted with the accomplishments or arts of society; but doggedly determined to know all that was to be known in his calling, and to allow nothing to divert him from its pursuit. The other, versatile and brilliant, of noble presence, and with a thorough air of fashion, was willing (or thought he was) to undergo the drudgery of sitting in court, and reading text-books, and copying forms, and trying to forget for so many hours a day all that made life enjoyable, for the chance of some day making a hit in a speech to a jury, and thereby getting into the golden groove of *nisi prius* gain; or, after a certain time, being held qualified for some easy post, which the blandishments and banquets of Melbourne House might secure for him. He had already chambers at No. 4 Pump Court, Temple, where his name is entered in the Law List "of the Northern Circuit, Special Pleader." As casual acquaintances, Pepys and Lamb met now and then, just often enough to be kept in mind of one another's existence, and to feel, if they felt at all, how little they had to say to each other. The equity draftsman had no taste for politics, rarely went to Levée, and never had time to read the *Morning Post ;* and his companion for the Call Day had probably never the curiosity, during the next thirty years, to look at the pages wherein the deeds and arguments of Mr. Pepys, and all that he said to Lord Eldon and Sir Lancelot Shadwell—are they not written in the books of Vesey junior? How, at the end of the long interval, they once more drifted notably into contact, and became firmly bound to each other by the ties of mutual confidence, the sequel will disclose.

Part of the family wealth had come from the elder Peniston of Lincoln's Inn, whose life had been devoted to equity pleading. But his grand-nephew can hardly have been swayed in choosing a profession by the repute of an old gentleman who was dead many years before he was born. His studies at Glasgow, and still more the ambition to excel in argumentative fence which his practice in what has been called the Wrangle School of the University had kindled, were more likely to predispose him at two-and-twenty to saunter five days in each term from St. James's to Temple Bar, and dine off pewter in Lincoln's Inn Hall with noisy and needy comrades of his own time of life. Then as now, there was at the bar a sprinkling of younger sons, in whom had been instilled the prudent notion that if they were not to drop behind the rank in which they had been bred, they must make their way in diplomacy, the Church, or the law. There had been already mitres in the family; and as episcopal preferments were then dispensed, holy orders might have seemed to one of epicurean temperament the shortest path to competence and luxury. It was the heyday of ecclesiastical jobbing; deaneries and golden stalls were the recognised perquisites which courtiers and politicians appropriated according to their need or greed. Bishoprics were the rarer prizes in the game; but a parliamentary family of distinction might secure, at least, a spiritual peerage on the Irish establishment. Many houses with vast estates in land were thus founded; and nobody in good society thought the method scandalous or even questionable. For William Lamb, with all his early love of ease and enjoyment, there seemed, however, no fascination in this sort of solemn farce for life; and Lord Egremont, though withheld by no scruple of conscience on the subject, told him it was a pity that one who had so much promise in him should be thrown away in squabbling about tithe of agistment or cribbing a fortune out of Church lands by running his life against leases. He

would have him put on wig and gown, rather than scarf and
stole; use his brain and tongue like Murray or Erskine;
go into Parliament and in due time all the rest would come.
His mother, when she had time to think, thought so too; she
was very proud of her son, and would have done anything
to kindle in him the fire of ambition. He did read some
law during his student days; more history perhaps than law.
How these years glided by he was never able distinctly to
recall; but amid the distractions and delights of Devonshire
House and Petworth, Whitehall and Kensington, there was
much to keep alive the hope and purpose of a career.
There were gathered all the wit and talent of the day; old
Sheridan and young Canning, fastidious Windham and sardonic Francis, Monk Lewis with his spectre tales, and
Gilbert Eliot with his reminiscences of Burke; Hookham
Frere and Lord Henry Petty, Whitbread and General Fitzpatrick, Charles Fox and Lord Grey. There was another
mansion out of town, where most of these celebrities were
welcome, and where he began to feel himself a favourite.
Frederick, third Earl of Besborough had a villa at Roehampton. By his first wife, Henrietta, sister of the Duchess
of Devonshire, he had four sons and an only daughter, Caroline, then in her nineteenth year. Brought up chiefly by
her grandmother, Lady Spencer, she possessed many attainments then unusual in one so young, and a peculiar charm
of manner that more than compensated for the want in some
degree of other attractions. In person she was slight and
graceful, but of somewhat less than the ordinary height; her
features, small and regular, were not set off by any beauty of
complexion; only her dark eyes, which contrasted strikingly
with her golden hair, vindicated her claim to be reckoned
among the distinguished and prepossessing.

Some years of her childhood were spent in Italy with
her mother, then an invalid. Subsequently she was sent to
Devonshire House, and for a while was brought up with her
youthful cousins. Her account of life in the nursery is
curious. The children saw little of their parents; were

served on silver in the morning, and allowed to carry their plates to the kitchen in quest of the dainties they longed for. Their state of ignorance was profound. They imagined all people were either nobles or paupers, and that for the rich there was no end of money.

We had no idea that bread or butter was made ; how it came we did not pause to think ; but had no doubt that fine horses must be fed on beef.   At ten years old I could not write.   My kind aunt Devonshire had taken me when my mother's ill health prevented my being at home.   My cousin Hartington loved me better than himself, and every-one paid me the compliments shown to children likely to die.   I wrote not, spelt not, but I made verses which they all thought beautiful.   For myself, I preferred washing a dog, or polishing a piece of Derbyshire spar, or breaking in a horse if they would let me.   At ten years old I was taken to my godmother, Lady Spencer's, where the house-keeper, in hoop and ruffles, reigned over seventy servants, and attended the ladies in the drawing-room.   All my child-hood I was a trouble, not a pleasure ; and my temper was so wayward that Lady Spencer got Dr. Warren to exa-mine me.   He said I was neither to learn anything or see any one for fear the violent passions and strong whims found in me should lead to madness ; of which, however, he said there were as yet no symptoms.   I differ ; my instinct was for music ; in it I delighted, I cried when it was pathetic, and did all that Dryden made Alexander do.   But of course I was not allowed to follow it up.   The severity of my governess and the over-indulgence of my parents spoiled my temper ; and the end was that until I was fifteen I learned nothing.*

As Lady Caroline grew up she evinced great facility in the acquisition of languages ; and, not content with French and Italian, voluntarily endured the drudgery of learning Greek and Latin, till at length she was able to enjoy not

* Letters to Lady Morgan, ' Memoirs,' vol. ii.

only a classic play at Harrow, where her brothers spent
their school days, but was not afraid to undertake herself
the recital of an ode of Sappho. Full of romance in all her
tastes, she loved painting; and devoted to water-colour
drawing long mornings throughout every period of her life.
She had besides that most rare of graphic gifts, the instinct
of caricature, which she indulged, not always circumspectly,
but never spitefully, in a letter to a friend, or on the fly-leaf
of a favourite volume, or wherever else opportunity served
and fantastic impulse prompted. She dressed as she painted
and played, picturesquely; prematurely indifferent to opinion;
and never exactly in accordance with the mode. Above all
she was, as Lamb too soon found out, like nobody else in
conversation. She had no patience, as she said, with the
preliminaries; and skipped all the prefatory matter conven-
tionally deemed indispensable, about coming and not coming,
health and the weather, which bored her to extinction. To
any one she liked she gave her hand at a second or third
interview, without the least unmaidenly air of freedom; and
with any one she did not fancy she would not shake hands
at all. Very early her pointed and often puzzling questions
attracted the notice, and fixed the gaze of accomplished
visitors at Roehampton and St. James's Place, where she delighted to be present at one of her aunt's receptions. She
is one of the few young persons of quality mentioned in
letters at the time as remarkable for talent or originality;
yet it could hardly be said that her sparkling talk, though it
held in solution an abundance of oddity, quaintness, and
humour, often crystallised into wit. William Lamb found
her irresistibly fascinating, and this perhaps would not have
mattered if she had not found him better worth talking to,
quicker to catch her meaning, and, in short, more delightful
than anybody she had ever seen. The family took no
special heed of the growing intimacy; with her connections
and accomplishments, a second son having naught but his
allowance and his profession was simply not worth thinking
about. Good looks and good society might get him a rich

wife, if he must marry early; but who cared? that was his
own affair.   Lady Caroline had the ideas of a duchess, and
without much fortune would of course make an excellent
match by-and-by.   For the present it was natural that the
young people should amuse themselves in each other's
society; they were very much in the same set, and the
time passed happily when they were together.   Did Lady
Melbourne observe nothing of this, or ruminate, when alone,
on possible contingiences?

Meanwhile Lamb lost no time in joining the bar at the
Lancashire Sessions.   At the instance of Scarlett, who was
much taken with him, a solicitor at Salford sent him a guinea
brief: long afterwards he used to say that the moment of
greatest pleasure he remembered in life was that in which
he saw his name inscribed above the unexpected retainer.
He had fortunately little to do in the case; but he got
through it without making any mistake; and thenceforth
felt that he was really a member of the profession—the
profession which, with its many faults and foibles, has after
all done more than any other class or calling to shape the
civil history of England, and to mould the curious fabric of
our social and political order.   The die was cast; he had
done his first stroke of work, and he felt seven years older
for it in willingness to work and in determination.   No
second brief was left at his lodgings; and during the
remainder of the sessions he occupied himself in watching
how others did the business, and trying to understand the
strange dialect of the provincial witnesses, and the equally
unintelligible gibberish of legal phraseology, used in a sort
of oral shorthand.   At mess he was voted a decided acquisition.   Natural, outspoken, well-informed, joyous, shrewd
and comical, he promised to be a positive blessing to
the sessional circuit, whose chief hardship did not consist
in having to put up with bad cooking or indifferent beds,
but in having to endure, through long successive evenings,
close confinement in dull country towns.   Would he really
come to sessions regularly?   Certainly he would; he had

quite made up his mind, and he would be there without fail next time. In this promise he was quite sincere, but fate did not mean it to be kept. He came no more.

Family residences acquire a social climate of their own, not to be resisted in its influence by a susceptible nature born and bred therein; and never to be wholly forgotten even by the exceptional one whose idiosyncrasy would fain break out of the atmosphere. The climate of the house in Whitehall was courtly. The windows of the living-rooms looked across the park towards St. James's, whence by reflection not a little of its claim to distinction was derived. The new wealth of the Lambs had supplied the beautiful and ambitious daughter of Sir Ralph Milbank with the means of spreading the gilded nets of fashion; and within her subtle toils a rare succession of the gaily plumaged and idly chattering birds were to be seen, caught for a little while and then let go. But Lady Melbourne was not a woman to be satisfied with a show of brilliant equipages, or the celebrity of sumptuous banquets over which the guests lingered until dawn. Her husband had been made an Irish Peer, and a Lord-in-waiting, if not to his Majesty, to his most gracious son, who should be king hereafter. Farther on, the baron's coronet had been exchanged for that of a viscount, why not a seat in the Lower House for one in the Upper, and an Irish be transfigured into a British Peer? All this she accomplished by the arts of courtiership, and by those of fascination over clever men and high-born dames, epicures of quality, poets of renown, statesmen of note, and Princes of the Blood. Tradition has not preserved any evidences of her possessing wit, but Sir Joshua and Maria Cosway give us a vivid notion of her beauty; and that she possessed the spirit and the grace, the tact of society, and the instinct of *savoir-faire*, cannot be doubted. What sacrifices her indolent and undemonstrative mate had silently to endure, by what regrets his hours of solitude were haunted, by what jealousies his dreams were troubled, who will ever know? The only child in whom he seemed to take affectionate interest was Peniston, born to him in 1770, and while he lived the chief object of his pride and care. He appears to have transmitted something of his own passive character to his heir, who in boyhood was obedient, gentle, and polite; in adolescence studious, decorous, and fond. Arrived at man's estate, he became at once a court card in his mother's hand. That he might have a seat in Parliament, his father in 1793, as we have seen, made way for him at Newport; and subsequently he was, by a skilful combination of influences, returned for Hertfordshire. This distinction he did not long enjoy. Attacked suddenly by illness for which the physicians were unable to account, his constitution, never robust, rapidly gave way; and on the 24th of January, 1805, he expired in his thirty-fifth year. By this so unexpected event William Lamb became heir to the titles and estates of the family, and thence must be dated the beginning of his long and distinguished career.

The death of Peniston stilled in Lord Melbourne's lonely bosom whatever fitful echoes may have been wakened there by the aspirations of his wife. William, in every respect unlike his elder brother, had always been her favourite son; and in his noble features, quick perception, fine person, and audacious humour, he was the very realisation of all her cherished hopes, the darling object of her solicitude and love. But all her powers of suasion failed to place him in the position Peniston had occupied. It is said that, failing to procure for him the allowance of £5000 a year his elder brother had enjoyed, she induced a friend to remonstrate with Lord Melbourne on the subject, and to enlist, if possible, his interest for him who had become his heir. All was in vain, William must do with £2000, which was quite enough for him; he owned that he was very good-looking, lively, and clever in a certain way, but he could never be to him the son whom he had lost. He did not object to paying the requisite smart-money in order that the family might still be represented in Parliament, and accordingly a seat was secured at Leominster for him, who now abandoned all

thoughts of following the profession of the law, and thenceforth devoted his attention to public affairs.

The days of mourning for her first-born were ended, and
Lady Melbourne did not affect to conceal the hope and joy
with which she looked confidently into the future of her
second son. The prospect opening to him was indeed
golden. At six-and-twenty, without drawback or encum-
brance, or anxiety of any kind to chill his satisfaction, he
was about to marry her whom he had freely chosen, and
who had shown her preference for him when he was still a
younger son. A seat in Parliament, without the trouble
of a contest, and all that was pleasant and luxurious in
town or country life was his, either in possession or in
anticipation. It added not a little to his own and his mother's
happiness, that about the same time his sister Emily, to
whom from childhood and throughout the long continuance
of their subsequent lives he was deeply attached, was betrothed to Earl Cowper, one of the richest proprietors in
Hertfordshire, and a man whom every one esteemed. The
bright days of spring were spent partly at Roehampton and
partly at Melbourne, of which he had always brief fits of
fondness. He said he had a bath of quiet there which he
could never get in London; and but rarely at Brocket:
it rested and refreshed his spirits more than any other
change he knew. Early in 1805 he became the accepted
suitor of Lady Caroline Ponsonby, to the great satisfaction
of his mother, who appreciated all the advantages of his
adoption into the highest Whig connection in England.
Lord Besborough's cousin had married Mr. (afterwards Earl)
Grey; and not less nearly, his family was related to many
others of distinction.

Most of Lamb's relatives and friends were members of
Brooks's Club, admission to which was regarded as the
initiatory rite of Whigism. One of his sponsors was Mr. Fox,
who was favourably impressed by his gay incisive talk, and
who augured well of his design to devote himself to public
life.

On the 3rd of June his marriage took place with Lady Caroline, and on the 21st day of July his sister was married to Earl Cowper. Although it was then usual for the season to end with the king's birthday on the 4th of June, people did not go out of town this year so early, and we find mention made of dinner parties which were numerously attended throughout July and August. The Prince of Wales returned from Brighton on the 14th, and dined at Melbourne House, Lord and Lady Holland, Monk Lewis, Lord and Lady Besborough, their daughter and her spouse, and Lord and Lady Cowper being of the party. From the private letters of Lord Minto about this date, it appears that he too had tarried in London all this time :

I accompanied Lord and Lady Holland to Lord Besborough's at Roehampton yesterday. We had the two Mr. Lambs there, the eldest of whom, having been the second brother, was intended for the law, and appeared to me a remarkably pleasant, clever, and well-informed young man ; he is now the eldest son ; the other, George, seems merely a good-natured lad. They are very unlike : the eldest puts me in mind of Windham ; the other has something of the Prince of Wales, only stunted in height, but very like in some points of manner. Lady Caroline Lamb, wife of Mr. William Lamb, and daughter of Lady Besborough, was also there.*

The following week Whitehall was deserted for Welwyn, and the newly married pair spent the rest of the year between Panshanger and Brocket.

* Letter from Lord Minto, August 24th, 1805.

CHAPTER IV.

IN THE COMMONS.

Contemporaries in Parliament—Huskisson—All the Talents—The Catholic Question — Maiden speech—Plunket—Fall of Grenville —Second vote of censure—Discouraged as a debater—Birth of only son—Copenhagen.

THE news of Austerlitz reached England early in December; and before Christmas the rumour spread that the health of Mr. Pitt was failing fast. Should he be unable to meet Parliament early in the year a change of executive hands would be inevitable; for no one among his followers had weight or influence enough to face the lowering storm. Tidings of Trafalgar came too late to revive the spirit of the sinking minister; and on his decease Lord Grenville and Mr. Fox were called upon to form an administration. For three-and-twenty years George III. had kept his word not to admit the leader of the Whigs again to office, or any who openly adhered to him. The Prince, on the other hand, continued to profess the utmost friendship for them, politically and personally. He still frequented Brooks's, and if its chiefs did not possess his exclusive confidence, the younger members of the party had no reason to complain that he forgot them in his revels. Lamb and his brothers were frequently commanded to Carlton House, and his Royal Highness was not unfrequently a guest at Whitehall.

How All the Talents came together, what they achieved, and in little more than twelve months how unexpectedly they fell, can be but briefly glanced at here. In the new administration were combined nearly all the persons whom Lamb was accustomed to regard as public guides or private friends.   Fox, Windham, and Sheridan, who divided his admiration in Parliament, had for colleagues Lords Erskine, Howick, and Henry Petty, towards all of whom he felt the strongest ties of friendship. His wife's relative was Chancellor of Ireland, the Duke of Bedford Viceroy, and Elliot of Wells, the confidant of Burke in his declining days, was a second time Secretary. For an effective performance the parts were badly cast.

With good but irresolute intentions, Elliot went back to Ireland lamed in reputation by having served in the same capacity under Lord Camden during the evil days of 1798— still too near to be forgotten, too dark to be forgiven. We know now that he deplored and deprecated many of the atrocities of that shameful time, but the people justly associated him with a system in which he had been something more than a passive accomplice. His look and figure were as unlucky as the associations revived by his name. Solemn in feature and spare in person, the thinnest and palest man in Parliament, they will be sure to call him, said Fitzpatrick, the "Castle Spectre," and exclaim whenever he moves, "See where it comes again!"* Plunket and Bush were indeed made law officers of the Crown, but Curran by some unexplained infatuation was passed over, though he was by far the most popular man of the day; and he avenged himself by incessant jokes at the expense of the new officials, in one of which he affected to have learned by accident that the Chief Secretary had left testamentary directions that if he died in Ireland, to elude detection in the grave, his body should be buried in the barrel of a duck-gun.

Lords Holland and Besborough urged on Mr. Fox the folly of leaving such a man as Curran to chafe at neglect and injustice; for he had risked and sacrificed for the principles which the party professed to hold dear infinitely more than

* Lord Holland's 'Memoirs of the Whig Party.'

most of those who were then enjoying office : and his courage in bearding the ruthless partiality of the judicial bench had endeared him to an outlawed people. The just and generous heart of Fox sympathised with the outspoken discontent of Curran, and he told the Duke of Bedford that the error must be repaired. His Grace availed himself of the first opportunity, and by midsummer Curran was appointed Master of the Rolls.*

On taking his seat in the Commons, Lamb found himself surrounded by not a few friends and relatives new like himself to the duties and responsibilities of Parliament. Lord Althorp, lately returned for Okehampton, was a Junior Lord of the Treasury ; but, fonder of hunting than politics, he was seldom to be seen in the House except on the eve of a party division. Lord Duncannon attended better, though hardly yet evincing the aptitude for public business that eventually distinguished him. On the other side, close to Mr. Canning, sat the member for Liskeard, who by marriage had lately become a near connection of his own.

William Huskisson, the son of a Staffordshire squire, Lamb's senior by several years, had entered political life as secretary to Lord Gower when Minister at Paris; and by his aptitude for official work he had won his way to advancement. Soon after, he was named by Dundas to superintend the working of the Alien Act; this duty he discharged so well that at twenty-six he became Under-Secretary for the Colonies, and in that department gained much of the knowledge of external trade which subsequently made him an authority without rival in debate. In 1799 he married the daughter of Admiral Milbanke, uncle of Lady Melbourne, an officer who had seen much service and had earned the commendations of Lord Spencer when he presided at the Admiralty. Mrs. Huskisson was a favourite at Melbourne House; her husband, an amiable but formal man, with a certain air of *mauvais honte*, was little qualified

* The appointment is dated 28th June, 1806 ; it was vacated by resignation on the 22nd of February, 1814.

to mingle in the frivolities and revels there. It was not until the previous year that he had succeeded in obtaining a seat in Parliament: his opponent at Liskeard being Thomas Sheridan, with whom he had an equal number of votes at the poll, but whom as competitor he got rid of on petition, to the no small regret of William Lamb, who thought the latter far the better fellow of the two. During the brief term of Mr. Pitt's second administration Huskisson was Secretary of the Treasury; and he now prepared to maintain his reputation as a rising financier by sifting the estimates and criticising the Budget of Lord Henry Petty, whose inexperience in details gave him no ordinary advantage. Lamb understood little of the questions that arose in debate between them; but his sympathies were all with the Chancellor of the Exchequer; and he had nothing in common, either of tastes, habits, or prejudices with the clever but ill-assured man of calculations. Huskisson was then just six-and-thirty, but in countenance and bearing he looked considerably older. From some constitutional want of bodily vigour, or a strange fatality which clung to him through life, too many of his days were spent in the endurance of pain. In childhood he had suffered much from a broken arm; a day or two before his marriage his horse fell with him, and though he would not confess it at the time he was hurt severely. Not long afterwards, when crossing the entrance to the Horse Guards, he was knocked down by the pole of a carriage; and in 1801, while staying at Blair Athol, he dislocated his ankle in attempting to follow the example of others who undertook to leap the Moat: and being unskilfully treated, he was never afterwards free from a slight degree of lameness. Untiring in the acquisition of knowledge, conscientious in the use he made of it, and perspicuous and fluent in discussion, a high value was set on his aid by the leaders of his party; but he was not endowed with qualities calculated to win any especial favour in society: and for a time he and Lamb saw little of each other.

The Whig leader in the Commons succeeded, when the new administration was formed, in dissuading the Catholic leaders from presenting their petition during the session. If they did so he would as usual support it with all his power; but he warned them that if beaten, the Government would be broken up, and another formed bent on their absolute exclusion. Instead of risking what might prove an abortive effort to grasp all that they desired, he promised that measures should be brought forward to secure the Catholics in substance what they had then only in words—a right to equal promotion in the army, and to hold municipal offices; a revision of the local magistracy, and a bill for the commutation of tithes: " The effect of these measures would be partly to make the Catholics generally more contented, partly to enable them to come with additional weight and strength when they again asserted their claims." * After the death of Fox the popular party in Ireland sought by various means to ascertain when the partial concessions which had been promised by him were likely to be forthcoming. The Lord Lieutenant was mute, the Secretary inarticulate, and the Chancellor, who made but an indifferent judge, was too lofty to be audible. The removal of corrupt and oppressive magistrates lay with him, and this part of the promise of Mr. Fox, which needed no new statute, was not performed owing, it was suspected, to Mr. Ponsonby's fear of endangering his family influence in certain constituencies. One attempt he did make to break down the fence of sectarian exclusion wherewith every seat even of local judgment was girt round. By the terms of Grattan's Relief Act, which Pitt's administration, at the outbreak of war with revolutionary France, allowed to pass in 1793, Roman Catholics were admitted to the elective franchise, and such subordinate offices as were not excepted therein. They might not aspire to any then existing rank or dignity of the law, but the newly created function of salaried Chairman of Quarter Sessions was plainly not within the mischief of

* Letter to Mr. Ryan, 1806.

these reservations. Mr. Bellew, a gentleman of character and standing at the bar, was named by the Chancellor to act as assessor to the magistrates of Galway, and recommended by him as well fitted to be their chairman. It was hoped that his being the son of a baronet of old descent would extenuate the sin of his professing the ancient creed; but the justices were highly offended, and to all expostulations proved inexorable. The heart of the Government failed, and Mr. Bellew was persuaded to relinquish this invidious post for a pension of £400 a year. Foxhunting intolerance was left to blunder on undisturbed for twenty years more, and the community at large paid the annual fine for Mr. Ponsonby's abortive attempt to steal a morsel of right in a courthouse.

Grattan vehemently urged in private the policy and humanity of reforming the unequal and ruinous tithe system, which he described as a perennial source of distrust, oppression, and crime. Plunket, who drank out of the same cup with him, earnestly pleaded for some such measure. The moderate party out of doors, through Lord Fingall, offered to exert all their influence to postpone the agitation of the general question, if this indispensable measure, and one admitting Catholic officers in the army to the higher grades of rank and command, were carried without delay. The democratic majority disparaged these instalments, and foretold, if they did not actually hope for, their defeat. They dreamed not of the powerful ally who was secretly preparing to aid them, and to sow tares while ministers slept, in the field of gradual reform. That ally was no other than the King.

The new member for Leominster heard these and other subjects connected with Ireland freely and frequently discussed at Holland House and Roehampton; and the impressions then left upon his mind remained indelible. He then first learned the difficult but important lesson which he was destined subsequently to apply, with a thoroughness none had ventured to do before him, to retrieve the imperial blunder

of provincial oppression, and to win back to healthful
content the temper of a community poisoned by wrong : and
that it were mere folly and impotence to affect the pedantic
observance of rules ordinarily recognised in the administration of a country long accustomed to the equal treatment of
every class and creed. He knew, as yet, little or nothing of
the island with the government of which he was subsequently to be occupied and identified more than any minister
of his time ; but even to his inexperience the question
irresistibly suggested itself—why not govern through the
men whom the majority trust and honour, instead of by those
who are generally hated or feared ? And he learned likewise the yet more important principle in the policy of
concession, that it is never worth while, where a great evil is
confessed and a great want admitted, to attempt remedies by
halves. The inducement held out by Fox to the Catholic
leaders, that the instalment he contemplated was one which
would enable them to exact the rest, was of all others,
calculated to alarm the fears of ascendency and inflame its
antagonism ; or if not, and if in full view of future demands
unsatisfying concessions should be granted, why not offer to
pay at once the debt of justice in full ? To fritter away the
credit of the giver and the gratitude of the receiver, was not
more objectionable than needlessly to keep up agitation after
the main point in dispute had been yielded. It will be found
that, when Lamb came himself to deal with measures involving the same choice of difficulties, he preferred the manlier and
simpler course, and found therein the satisfaction of success ;
until on the occasion of the very last legislative measure to
which he was a party by the surrender of his own judgment
as to the inexpediency of stopping short halfway, he was
finally overthrown.

Meanwhile the session was suffered to pass without a debate on the general question of religious disabilities ; and the
partial relaxations promised as payments on account were
deferred to a more convenient season.

The death of Fox irreparably shook the credit and influence of the ministry. The portfolio of foreign affairs was given to Lord Howick; and the leadership of the Commons was likewise intrusted to him. Thoroughly conversant with the ideas and intentions of his distinguished predecessor, and having the entire confidence of Lord Grenville, he continued to pursue a policy unchanged with respect to the conduct of the war. His coldness, and inapproachability by the rank and file, strikingly contrasted with the affable and communicative manner of him who was gone, and tended, no doubt, to lessen the authority which his acknowledged talents and integrity were calculated to give him. But he possessed qualities of guidance and control that won respect from those who neither loved his politics or his person. Speaker Abbot, when asked who of all the leaders he had known did best the business at the table, said,

Beyond all doubt Lord Howick: even Pitt, though he had a great majority, and could accomplish marvels when he chose to exert his power of speaking, was neither so clear or so decided in the conduct of details; and of course Addington was not to be compared with either. But when Howick stated what he meant to do regarding a particular measure or motion, I knew exactly what to expect, and that he would suffer no departure from his word.

But the place so long occupied by Fox in the bosom of his friends and followers, no one could supply. He was perhaps the only parliamentary chief whose ascendency had been originally gained, and when lost through political dissension had been regained by the force of personal attachment. Other party leaders have commanded larger majorities and carried more great measures, but none before or since was ever so beloved, nor was the loss of any ever so lamented. Lamb had in childhood sat at his feet, and in youth hung upon his genial talk, and learned when he came to man's estate to regard him with sentiments of party loyalty which he could never feel for any other man.   Upon the pedestal of Fox's bust he wrote the following lines :--

> Live, marble, live! for thine's a sacred trust,
>   The patriot's name that speaks a noble mind;
> Live, that our sons may stand before thy bust,
>   And hail the benefactor of mankind!
>
> This was the man, who, midst the tempest's rage,
>   A mark of safety to the nation stood;
> Warn'd with prophetic voice a servile age,
>   And strove to quench the ruthless thirst for blood.
>
> This was the man, whose ever deathless name
>   Recalls his generous life's illustrious scenes;
> To bless his fellow-creatures was his aim—
>   And universal liberty his means!

On the 19th of December, 1806, Lamb moved the address in reply to the speech from the throne.   The renewal of exertions to resist the continual aggression of France had been rendered indispensable by the rejection of all terms of accommodation; and though we had but two allies left in Europe, he hoped and believed that the spirit of the country would not repine at the burthens and sacrifices that would be necessary to maintain our attitude of national resistance. The internal condition of the realm was prosperous and tranquil; all classes were contented, and our commerce flourished.

Mr. Canning moved, as an amendment, an elaborate counter-address, effusive in profession of devotion to the sovereign, and boastful of the courage and loyalty of the people, and pledging Parliament to greater efforts by sea and land to make good successes recently gained "notwithstanding the apparent inactivity of ministers," and their tardy and recalcitrant negotiations abroad.   Howick denounced the amendment and speech as unwarranted by fact, and as more fitting a charge of impeachment.   Castlereagh defended Canning, but was glad the amendment was not to be pressed.   The Talents then sought to strengthen themselves in

debate, especially on the Catholic question.   Ponsonby and
Grattan urged the pre-eminent worth of the aid in this
respect which Plunket could afford.   He was personally
unknown among the Scotch and English Whigs; but his
forensic reputation stood already high, and his old leaders
in the Irish Parliament recalled with enthusiasm the courage
and vigour of his denunciations of the means employed to
carry the Union.   At the beginning of 1807, at the special
request of Grenville, he consented to come into Parliament
for the close borough of Midhurst.   He was not long in redeeming the promise of his friends ; and on an early occasion
made a speech which Whitbread declared would never be
forgotten.   No intelligible report remains, and he himself
did not think it worth preserving.   His unwillingness at
all times to take the trouble of reproducing from memory
what he had spoken was almost insuperable ; and the
minute preparation of sentences and phrases beforehand was
a labour he could seldom bring himself to undergo.   On the
logical ground-plan and the well-proportioned pillars of his
argument he grudged no thought or care ; for his mind became thoroughly charged with any great cause he espoused ;
and all its powers were given cheerfully and unstintedly
to the development in due order, in the marshalling in
fit procession, resources of reasoning, sarcasm, illustration,
and invective.   Rhetorical vanity he had none ; and though
in his rich wardrobe of words the variety seemed inexhaustible, scarcely anything that could be termed a decoration
was to be found.   This was his only speech of any importance
during the two months he sat for Midhurst ; for after the
dissolution in May he did not offer himself again.   He
remained out of Parliament for five ensuing years.   Lamb
was among the most attentive of his hearers on the occasion
referred to, and among the most anxious of those who longed
to hear him again ; for Plunket, if he failed to dazzle and
charm him like Canning, swayed his judgment in Irish
affairs even more.   He preferred his masculinity of thought
and style to the whimsicality and sometimes extravagance

of Grattan; Plunket, he said, came nearer to his ideal of Demosthenes.

When the purport of the Catholic Officers Bill was explained by Howick to the King he raised no objection; and notice thereupon was given for the introduction of the measure. It was received in Ireland with general indifference, provoking no anger, and eliciting no thanks.

In his confidential correspondence the Duke of Bedford furnished the Home Secretary, for the information of the Cabinet, with a careful account of the various meetings of Catholics in Dublin during the spring, and of several interviews given by him to Catholic peers, and by Mr. Elliot to deputations of landed proprietors and merchants, at which this proposal of limited concession, and the expediency of petitioning for general relief from disabilities, were discussed. Lords Fingall, Ffrench and Gormanston, Sir Edward Bellew, Mr. Keogh, and Mr. Burke, are with others mentioned as persons of influence and weight; but no allusion is made, by name or otherwise, to Mr. O'Connell. Up to this time, and for some years later, Mr. Keogh performed somewhat languidly and condescendingly the part of leader. As a man of property and intelligence, he was uniformly treated with respect; but in meetings said to have varied from fifty persons to two hundred, there was not much room for the exercise of stimulating rhetoric; and the drenching showers of caution which fell upon their deliberations whenever the wind blew from the east and the mail-bags were delivered from London were not propitious to ignition when any sparks did fall. In general the measure for equalising the condition of Catholic officers in the army was regarded with silent indifference. At a public meeting Lord Fingall moved to defer any general petition for relief, lest it should impede the measure and embarrass Government; neither reason was thought of sufficient weight, but the former was hardly thought worth noticing.* While ministers were

---

* Duke of Bedford to Lord Spencer, Feb. 17th, 1807.

F 2

confidentially assuring George III. " that they could not look without great uneasiness and apprehension at the state of Ireland, which they considered the only vulnerable part of the British Empire," * and warning him that the situation of that country appeared to them " to constitute the most formidable part of the existing difficulties " † of the realm, the surface of discontent remained unruffled by a passing gust of complaint. It was the sullen torpor of despondency, generated by the memory, still fresh, of the horrors and miseries of ineffectual resistance, and by a hardening unbelief in hopes and promises of redress. The Whigs had been twelve months in office, and nothing had been done even through the medium of legislation. To the bulk of the community the obstacles that hindered them were utterly unknown; and save to a very few persons who had opportunities of private communication with members of the Government, their silence seemed, and could not but seem, evidence of insincerity. Even Moore, the especial favourite of their *salons*, could not refrain from blended ridicule and reproach :—

> As bees on flowers alighting ceased to hum,
> So settling upon places Whigs grow dumb.

With their apology before us, from the pen of one of the most candid and consistent amongst them, we may judge the Grenville cabinet more leniently, though he himself admits their conduct on the whole was indefensible.

George III. believed that he might with impunity reject their half-hearted counsel, backed as it was by no popular demand; and before the bill came on for second reading he informed his ministers that it went beyond what he could conscientiously yield. He had misunderstood, he said, the scope of the measure, and required that it should be withdrawn. Lord Grenville, the Chancellor, the Duke of Portland, the Chief Justice, and Lord Spencer were for compliance, and sooner than break up the Government their colleagues acquiesced. The King, having thus humiliated them, demanded

* Cabinet Minute, March 15th, 1807.   † Ibid. March 18th, 1807.

a pledge that under no circumstances should he be disturbed by such a proposition again. This was too much, and they all forthwith resigned.

Lord Holland owned to Lamb, in whom he placed especial confidence, that he was adverse to their withdrawal of the bill; but being the youngest and most inexperienced member of the cabinet, he thought it hopeless to resist. He believed that if the Duke of Bedford and Lord Spencer, who were primarily responsible, as Viceroy and Home Secretary, for the pledges given by Fox, had tendered their resignation in the first instance, they might have caused a schism among their friends; but public opinion would have done them justice, and public faith would have revived. The concession offered was confessedly the minimum of redress, for sake of which they hoped that all the rest would be allowed to stand adjourned *sine die;* yet that minimum they consented to abandon in a vain attempt to appease the crazy prejudices of the sovereign. Their submission, contrary to their conviction of what was intrinsically right, and what they had declared requisite for the safety of the realm, could not have been justified had it stood alone.

The surrender of our opinions—wrote Lord Holland some years afterwards—was, as I then thought and still think, quite wrong. It might in many cases prove as injudicious in policy as it was indefensible in principle... The impatience of the King to get rid of us spared us the embarrassment, and gave to our blunder all the effect and advantage of an act of dexterity. He put himself completely in the wrong, and relieved us from a situation from which it had otherwise been difficult to extricate ourselves with honour.[*]

On the formation of Mr. Perceval's Cabinet of resistance to all concession, Mr. Brand moved, "That it is contrary to the first duties of the confidential servants of the Crown to restrain themselves by any pledge, expressed or implied,

[*] 'Memoirs of the Whig Party,' vol. ii. p. 202.

from offering to the King any advice which the course of
circumstances may render necessary for the welfare and
security of any part of his Majesty's extensive empire."

Lamb seconded the motion in a careful speech. It
reads like a fragment of one of the many constitutional
pamphlets which lie thick in Hansard, and which can only
be accounted for, in their mutilated state, by imperfect
reporting, or by the failure of their authors to catch or to
keep the ear of the House. The instinct of that assembly
has been ever quick to discern when a gentleman meditates
inflicting on it a dissertation upon the general aspects of a
subject about which he has probably nothing original to
say. It may be that all he has written down and got by
heart is good enough for himself, as an exercise of mind or
as evidence *quantum valeat* that he has something in him,
or, if by good luck it is given in the journals next day, as
redeeming a hustings pledge to make himself heard at
St. Stephen's. But prize essays of the sort are not thought
good for them by the bulk of the House of Commons. A
witty or bitter attack is worth hearing; a humorous or
even a ludicrous defence is worth staying for, but a set dis-
quisition, philosophic, pretentious, or vague, is upon the
whole better not heard, for it tends simply to generate a
low fever of impatience, a sense of headache, and eventually
an ungracious cry of "Divide." The more faultless the
exercise the worse for its author's chance of getting it
listened to, because the less chance of interjection or interruption breaking the reproachful silence which gravely
warns to desist those who are not wanted. What is surprising is that so many clever men at their wits' end for an
occasion to talk should fall into the error, and only discover
their mistake when, after certain preliminary platitudes, the
chill of a general thaw comes over them, and they perceive
friends and foes gently melting away through the side
doors; there is nothing for it then but to break off with a
well-turned declaration that everything has been said already that needs to be said, and that the case is incon-

testable. The scrap of the speech ascribed to Mr. Lamb in 1807 reads like a paragraph or two in a letter from "Verax" to the Editor of the *Times* when everybody is out of town. A quaint quotation from Lord Coke nods threateningly over the field of view. "The great Keeper of the Seal," it is said, "maintained that the councillors of the king ought to leave simulation and dissimulation at the porter's lodge when they came to council." This notion, when worked out and applied to the outgoing and the incoming ministry in phrases trenchant and terse, might have been made to tell on the sensibilities of those who had lost and those who had won; but the working-out and the application do not appear—possibly never were uttered, though we may take for granted that they were all to be found clearly written in the pigeon-hole of some escritoire at Melbourne House.

The constitution of this realm required that the king in exercising the functions of government should take the advice of the two great councils of the nation, the Houses of Lords and Commons. But the slow progress as well as publicity of their deliberations would in many instances destroy that secrecy and interfere with that promptitude and despatch so often necessary to the success of the measures of the government. It had been adopted as a principle coeval with the constitution that the right and duty of both Houses to advise the sovereign might be deputed to a selection from the members of both Houses, chosen by his Majesty as his privy councillors, by whose advice every act of the government was supposed to be guided; and thus, as far as was possible in a human institution, to give to the free government of England all the advantages of secrecy and despatch which belong to an arbitrary monarchy. But what surety did the country possess that this duty would be uniformly performed by men who could restrain themselves by a pledge to withhold their advice from his Majesty upon any occasion, however important or indispensable? What security had the country against such men giving their sovereign the worst advice; or how could the people be secure of their liberties under the government of men who, for the sake of possessing power, could violate their duty to their sovereign, break their oaths as privy councillors and sink their responsibility as ministers? If such a doctrine as that of the pledge required were to be allowed to pass or to be sanctioned, the constitution would be at an end. Ministers might be men of rank and talent, but by signing such a pledge they would resign their duty as honest councillors of the Crown; and if the House were to sit silent on such a question, it would abandon that constitution which was its pride, its duty, and its glory to maintain, to preserve, and to defend.

Plunket in a long and able speech contended that the motion meant no reflection on the King; but those who had recently advised him had done a double injury, first in inducing his Majesty to believe that he was acting contrary to the interests of his people, and next in persuading him to demand an unconstitutional pledge.

Grattan supported the resolutions as did Sir S. Romilly, Whitbread and Howick. But on a division it was defeated by 258 to 226, after two nights' debate. Mr. Brand was complimented on the moderation and discretion of the motion, but no notice appears to have been taken of Lamb.

His only son was born on the 11th of August, 1807, and was named by the Prince of Wales, as sponsor at his baptism, George Augustus Frederick. Of the many hopes encircling his infancy none were destined to be realised. Miss Berry notes in her diary, the following May, with what maternal pride Lady Caroline took her to a room at the top of the house at Whitehall to see her little boy asleep, who then promised well, only that he seemed too big for his age. Next day he was seized with fits, which it was thought would prove fatal. Life unhappily was preserved, but only to himself to prove a burthen, and to his father a grief incurable.

Early in the session of 1808, the conduct of ministers was impugned regarding the memorable seizure of the Danish fleet, without any previous declaration of war, in breach of the recognised comity of nations. If meditated treachery on the part of Denmark had been discovered it might and ought to be disclosed. Vague suspicion, it was contended, could not justify the sudden and arbitrary demand by our admiral, at the head of an outnumbering squadron, that the ships of an ally lying at anchor in their own waters should be surrendered as hostages for future observance of peace. Such a precedent would be fatal to all sense of international good faith or security; and Parliament had, therefore, a right to know what specific grounds there were for imputing to the Danes a perfidious purpose which could alone constitute our vindication. In both Houses the correspondence was called for between the Foreign Office, and the English Envoy at Copenhagen. The motion being made by the new leader of Opposition Mr. G. Ponsonby, Lamb could not but take a lively interest in a contention the subject and character of which quickened the pulse of every man of political feeling at the time; and one can imagine how ill his undisciplined expectations of dashing and damaging onslaught were realised by the speech of his relative in moving that the secret despatches should be laid upon the table. The ex-Chancellor was, after all, but the equity pleader still. He opened the case very much as he used to do in the Court of Chancery, with precision and method, with many innuendoes in ambush, and the heavy pomp of a funeral cavalcade. No better foil could have been furnished to the brilliancy of Canning, radiant with exultation at the success of his first exploit as Minister for Foreign Affairs. Secure of a majority, and confident in his power of arousing all the national pride and passion on his side, he revelled in the boast that he and his colleagues had not missed a great opportunity as their predecessors had done, and that he had built up the national power and influence, which had been dilapidated by them. They had designed a similar expedition with reference to Portugal, where they failed to carry it to completion. He could show, if he chose to violate confidence, ample justification for doubting the sincerity and distrusting the stability of the Court of Denmark in its promise to keep neutral; but whatever the verdict of the House might be, for himself he would ever glory in the expedition to Copenhagen, for it had saved the country. Windham, equally warm on the other side, declared that it was an abandonment of the established rules of international dealing, and the beginning of a war of plunder. The stain on the national honour could only be wiped out by the parliamentary condemnation implied in the proposed resolution. Palmerston argued that ministers were pledged to observe secrecy regarding the information on which they had acted; while Whitbread did not believe Government could produce letters such as they pretended to possess. Not that he accused them of actual forgery of the extracts they had read, but if the contexts were produced, these garbled extracts would tell a very different tale. Ministers had vaunted having outdone Napoleon with the vigour and rapidity of their measures. France had slain a giant; and they had imbued their hands in the blood of a dwarf. Lord Granville L. Gower, from personal knowledge, attested the reality of the cause for apprehension that Russia as well as the other Baltic States had been secretly won over by Napoleon to a maritime confederacy for the extermination of English commerce; and Castlereagh denied that in time of public danger ministers were free to produce all the information they relied on. Angry taunts and bitter scoffs were interchanged throughout the night, and it was near six in the morning ere it was announced by the tellers that Government had triumphed by 253 to 108 votes. On this occasion—and likewise when the subject was revived by Whitbread some days later, chiefly with a view of declaring on behalf of Lord Grey that his despatches to Mr. Garlicke in 1806 had been unfairly quoted—Lamb voted with his party. But his confidence in their power to achieve anything was daunted; and his

belief in his own capacity for debate waxed so cold that he
did not make any attempt to speak during the session. His
attendance, like that of Althorp, at this period was desultory
and broken by many intervals devoted to pleasure; but he
was generally ready to be in his place when the elders
whom he trusted thought it needful or important. Plunket
had disappeared from the scene, not to be lured back by the
blandishments of Lord Grenville, or the offer of reappointment as Attorney-General by Lord Redesdale. Ponsonby and
Grattan and Newport led his convictions in Irish affairs; we
find him voting with them in favour of increasing the grant
to Maynooth from £9250 to £13,000 a year, to prevent many
of the students for the Catholic priesthood being sent abroad
for their education. In general politics he appears to have
usually voted in consonance with the opinions of those with
whom he lived. Among them the policy of the new administration was held in as much aversion as its capabilities
were treated with disparagement. Canning while he retained office, and after him Lord Wellesley, were indeed
exceptions to their disdain; but Perceval and Castlereagh
were habitual themes of depreciation; and Lamb had
not the vanity, while yet inexperienced in public affairs, to
set up for himself as a discerner of spirits. In the daily
round of refined and luxurious existence, time glided by.
The lot had fallen to him in pleasant places. As yet there
was no shadow on his path; and if, contrary to the belief of
Holland House, the Tories should last for ever, he was ready
to say with Mr. Fox, "that in the company of witty men
and pretty women, with plenty of fresh air, old books, and
nothing to do, life was very endurable."

Meanwhile the family continued to enjoy the favour of
Carlton House, the heir to the throne being present at
assemblies given by Lady Caroline and attended by Sheridan
and other intimates of the circle, tarrying at supper not unfrequently till break of day.*

* Miss Berry's Journal, vol. ii. p. 346.

CHAPTER V.

VOTES IN OPPOSITION.

*Charges against the Duke of York—Abolition of sinecures—Reform
of the criminal law—Restrictions on the Regency—A Lord of the
Bedchamber—Support of the war—Death of Perceval.*

HAD any one told either Lady Spencer or Lady Melbourne,
on coming to town early in 1809, that before Easter her son
would be found censuring by his vote in Parliament the
most affable Prince of the blood, he would have been deemed
a trifler or insane.   If any one had told the youthful and
idle politicians themselves that such an unwelcome duty
lay before them he would assuredly have seemed to them
as one that mocked.   Had anybody ventured to repeat
the prophecy a month later, when sinister rumours had
got into circulation of disclosures about to be made of malpractices at the Horse Guards, Althorp in half an hour
would have forgotten it at the next meet of the Pytchley
Hounds, and Lamb would have answered with an indolent
stare or a lazy laugh.   Yet so it was to be.   A test of the
very different metal of which the two were made was about
to be applied, unexpectedly and painfully.   There is no
reason to suppose that at this early period the judgment
of either was materially influenced by that of the other;
but the coincidence of the views they formed and acted
upon under all the circumstances, may be regarded as the
first link in the long chain of sympathy that bound them
together in political life.   To the careless observer they had

little in common.   Their pursuits and tastes, their ways
of life and notions of enjoyment were in all respects the
most opposite.   It could hardly be said that the political
opinions of either were as yet mature, or that as party men
their joints were yet firmly knit.   But there was in both of
them, unprofessed in wordy platitude and hitherto never
put to the proof, a genuine love of justice for its own sake,
and a fearless independence of character which inevitably
begot mutual confidence and respect, and eventually led an
ever-widening circle to look to and to trust them.

Lord Althorp had been more than four years in Parliament. His distaste for general society, his unacquaintance
with literature and art, his inveterate bashfulness—which
imparted a sense of hesitation to his utterance of earnest
thoughts, provokingly unlike their clearness and solidity—
had precluded his attainment of political influence out of
doors, except in his own county, the representation of which
he held without a contest from 1806 until he became a
peer. For two years he had worked hard at Cambridge to
gratify his mother's wish that he should be in the first
class, and by dint of self-denial of all his favourite amuse-
ments he succeeded in gaining the first place, a very unusual thing for young patricians in that day, then precluded from even competing for the higher honours of the
University.   He thus acquired a knowledge of the elementary science of calculation, which fitted into the matter-
of-fact texture of his mind and grew with it to maturity.
He became a scientific agriculturist and a valuable assistant
in public inquiries where the collation of minute facts or
the elucidation of complicated figures was involved.   For
a good while he was too much absorbed in country pursuits
to attend regularly at Westminster ; but by degrees he
took more interest in national affairs, rather for the sake of
the practical improvements in legislation he deemed necessary, than from any strong interest in party warfare.   The
Whigs knew he would always vote straight for what was
most liberal ; and the reporters knew what he meant to say

although he did not always succeed in saying it. When beaten, which was frequently the case, he was never seen to frown, and with an opponent he was just as good-humoured next day as with a defeated friend. His parents were more fond than proud of him, for never had accomplished and ambitious parents a more unambitious or ungraceful son. But they loved his sterling worth, and had implicit confidence that whenever tried he would be found worthy of his name.

Early in the session Colonel Wardle, an almost unknown and wholly uninfluential member of the ministerial party, gave notice of motion for an inquiry into the misconduct of the Commander-in-Chief, to whom he openly imputed corrupt connivance in the sale by his mistress of commissions and promotions in the army. People asked in wonder if he were in earnest, or what his antecedents were. Mr. Elliot and Lord Castlereagh had unfavourable recollections of him in Ireland, where he commanded a Welsh regiment of Fencibles during the rebellion of 1798, by whom some of the atrocities were committed that excited the indignation of the gallant Abercromby and the grief of the humane Cornwallis. Otherwise his antecedents had been obscure. His seat had been won by the profession of extreme opinions, but having neither education, talent or fortune, he had no chance of making way with his own side, and was taunted with seeking notoriety by playing up to the cheers of the other. The Whig leaders had no fancy, however, for such a recruit. Ponsonby, Tierney, and Lord Henry Petty gave ministers to understand that they discredited his imputations and regretted their utterance as a public scandal. General Fitzpatrick and Mr. Windham, who enjoyed the personal friendship of his Royal Highness, were more open in their condemnation, and Lord Grey was known to have spoken of the affair as a mean and miserable species of persecution.* If Mr. Perceval had met the motion with a summary refusal it is possible that no more would have

* Le Marchant's ' Memoir of Viscount Althorp,' ch. vi.

been heard of the matter, for no man of mark on either side was disposed to have his name associated with accusations which, if not incredible, it was generally supposed would never be substantiated. But the Duke had given such personal assurances of their utter groundlessness that the minister was tempted to challenge the accuser to the proof; and for many days the House was occupied in the examination of witnesses at the bar, whose revelations filled Government with dismay and the public with rage and shame. Attempts were then made to break down the value of the evidence, much of which would not have been admitted by a court of law; Romilly and Whitbread felt called on to interpose for the protection of witnesses and the elucidation of the truth; and it became evident that a growing section of ministerialists were getting ashamed of the transaction. Excitement out of doors rapidly waxed warm. On the other hand, all the influence of the Court was brought to the aid of Government, and in a House where so many members had virtually no constituents it was only surprising that a minority of two hundred should have been found steadfastly resisting Mr. Perceval's resolution exonerating the Commander-in-Chief from complicity in corruption. But many grievous charges had not been confuted; Wilberforce and Sir Robert Peel,* J. W. Ward, N. Sneyd, and other ministerialists voted with Opposition, and one hundred and fifty members did not vote at all. Next day Perceval informed the House that the Duke had retired from the command of the army, which he had held for fourteen years. Althorp moved that in consequence of his Royal Highness having resigned it was not necessary to proceed further in the matter. This implied censure was rejected by two to one, Lamb, Milton, and Whitbread voting in the minority.

The younger Liberals would have carried their virtual triumph further. Lord Folkestone moved for a committee of general inquiry into the existence of any corrupt practices in the disposal of offices in any department of the State.

* The father of the Statesmen.

He was supported by Mr. Whitbread and Lord A. Hamilton, but opposed by Mr. Ponsonby, Mr. Tierney, and Lord Henry Petty on constitutional grounds, and by Canning and Perceval on the part of the Government. Only thirty voted for the motion, against one hundred and seventy-eight; but in the minority were Lord Althorp, Lord Forbes, Sir John St. Aubyn, Lyttelton, Pelham, Dudley North, Western, Coke, Ord, Lord Ossulston, and Lamb.*

In the autumn Lord H. Petty was called to the Upper House on the death of his brother; and the Opposition lost in him their most popular and trusted leader. In a private letter Lord Palmerston notices the event with characteristic clearness of appreciation :

Petty's elevation to the Upper House is a great circumstance for us, not so much from the harm which he would have done us by his individualat tacks, as from the unity and vigour the Opposition would have acquired by placing him ostensibly, at least, at their head ; a situation for which he was well qualified, but into which there is not another individual among them whom they can with equal advantage elect.†

Hansard contains no record of Lamb in 1808 or 1809; but in 1810 he supported Mr. Fuller's motion to abolish sinecure places. He charged Perceval, who preceded him in debate, with misrepresenting the aims and motives of his honourable friend, who really sought to purify and not to subvert parliamentary institutions.

His objection to these places was that they had a tendency to introduce into Parliament men who could not be expected to give an unbiassed suffrage in any discussion, and who would at all times be ready to sell their votes for their offices.

He objected to these offices as not only offering means of venal support to administration, but as also giving birth and strength to a factious opposition to Government—

* Letter from Lord Althorp to his father, April 19th, 1809.
† To Lord Malmesbury, November 24th, 1809.

when those who vote and are numbered in the day of battle think they have reason to complain, if they happen to be overlooked in the distribution of the spoil.*

Though supported by Creecy, Lord Archibald Hamilton, and Whitbread, on an understanding that the subject would be revived when the report was brought up of the Finance Committee the motion was withdrawn.

Romilly found in Lamb a willing convert to the doctrines of merciful wisdom he sought to apply in the reform of the criminal law. Every abatement in the sanguinary catalogue of penalties for offences against property proposed by that gentle and sagacious preacher in the wilderness, had his cordial support. In May 1810 Romilly snatched a second reading in a thin house for one of what Bentham called his Anti-hanging Bills; but on a subsequent stage the zealots for the scaffold rallied to the rescue ; and though Canning, Wilberforce, Brougham, Abercromby, Sir. W. Grant, Granville Sharp, Lamb, and other disciples who loved and trusted him were at their posts, orthodox cruelty succeeded in throwing out the measure by a majority of one.

He likewise supported a motion of his friend Mr. Brand for an inquiry into the state of the national representation, with a view to a juster distribution of electoral power. Ponsonby and Whitbread, Tierney and Newport led a respectable minority in its favour; but Canning and Windham persisted in regarding English reform as but an abridged edition of French revolution; and they were able to lend ministers a decisive majority.

In October Mr. Lamb, accompanied by Lady Caroline, met Lord Palmerston at the house of Mr. Conyers, where there was a shooting party, but the woods were so full of traps and spring guns that the owner "dared not set his foot in any of his plantations lest he should leave it behind him." He shot better than his friend, who tells, in his own characteristic way, how he brought down but one brace of

* Hansard, vol. xv. p. 383, February 12th.

pheasants owing to the high wind which blew; but Lamb
was luckier, and always found the wind lower when he fired,
which was a knack he had through life, which stood him in
good stead in politics as in sporting.*

Towards the end of the year the illness of the king
rendered it necessary that Parliament should make provision
for the exercise of the royal authority, and resolutions were
submitted to the House having for their object its limitation
with regard to making peers and conferring offices for life.
Opposition contended, as in 1787, that the Prince of Wales
should be unfettered during his regency in the use of the
prerogative. Prolonged debates arose on the mode in which
Parliament ought to perform its exceptional function. Perceval would have them declare the right and duty of the two
Houses to supply the defect in the personal exercise of the
sovereign authority. Sir F. Burdett and Lord W. Russell
were for acknowledging the Heir Apparent as invested *de
jure* with supreme executive power without any abstract
declaration by Parliament implying their right to give or to
withhold it. William Lamb replied with much animation
that such doctrine comported not with sound constitutional
principle or usage; and was highly complimented by Mr.
Stephen and others on the excellence of his argument.

But when it came to the adoption of the proposed
restrictions Government found it difficult to carry their
recommendations. Lamb was intrusted by his party with
the duty of moving an amendment on the principal
resolution for limiting the functions of the Prince Regent.
He began by expressing his inability to follow the right
honourable gentleman through the more minute parts of his
able speech, but felt it to be his duty to submit some observations upon the general principles involved in this great
question to the consideration of the House. The right
honourable gentleman had now opened the plan under which
he proposed to commit, during the incapacity of his Majesty,
to his Royal Highness the Prince of Wales the government

* Letter to his sister, October 29th, 1810.

of these realms ; and it was for Parliament to decide how far that plan was expedient, or whether it was such as could with propriety be adopted. With respect to those functions derived under the king, but in the exercise of which he had no immediate concern, such as the administration of justice in the courts of law, it was evident that the royal authority had suffered no diminution, and that the powers of the executive were in their full force and vigour ; but where the mind of his Majesty was to be applied, where the personal judgment of the sovereign had to be called into action, there the executive was incomplete, and those powers were dead and gone, and dormant to as great an extent as would result even from the demise of the king. The question now, therefore, before the Committee was, whether they would supply those powers in a complete and efficient manner, or in the mode proposed by the right honourable gentleman. With respect to the precedents of 1788, upon which so much had been said, and to which so much authority had been ascribed, he must say that, having never been carried into effect, it wanted the great sanction of all authority, it wanted the sanction which every precedent should have, that of experience. It was in reality no precedent, and he was convinced that, had it been carried into effect at that period, the consequences would have been found to be most injurious to the country. But should any gentlemen, from deference to the characters of the eminent men of the day, and more particularly to that of the distinguished. individual with whom it originated, be inclined to look to it with more respect, they would do well to consider the times that had passed over in the interval, and the different circumstances in which the country stood and stands respectively at the two different periods. It was not enough, in describing that difference, to say with the right honourable gentleman that we were then in a state of peace and now in a state of war (and here he must beg to remark that there was a reprehensible levity in the right honourable gentleman's manner upon this part of the subject, which he

G 2

thought but ill accorded with its nature and importance).
The country was then not only in a state of peace, but of
internal tranquillity and safety; now it was engaged in
foreign war, oppressed with internal dissatisfaction, surrounded with peril and with danger. Such was the situation
in which they were called upon to constitute a limited
regency; but let gentlemen put it to their own minds,
then, whether, under such circumstances, a proposition of
that kind could with propriety be acceded to; and with
respect to the precedent of 1788, so much but so un-
deservedly relied on, let them reflect, whether, if the limited
government then projected had been carried into effect, and
his Majesty had not happily recovered, that government
would have had force or energy enough to weather the storm
of the French Revolution. It was not necessary for him to
speak here of the measures adopted at that period, or the
alarm which was spread in consequence of that great event;
men's minds were sufficiently made up on those points.
There might have been, and he had no doubt there were,
many persons in that and in this country who believed that
the alarms which prevailed in this country during the
French Revolution had no solid foundation, and were excited
without justifiable cause; but there were also gentlemen
who believed that there were real grounds for those alarms;
and he would therefore put it to those gentlemen to say, if
they believed that during the period of those alarms we
should have been able to weather the storm with the arm of
the royal prerogative so palsied and weakened? With
respect to external danger at the present moment, he had
not words to express his sense of it, and as to domestic
danger, though he had not much fear in general of opinions
that could be met with other opinions, he was not without
his apprehensions. What were called Jacobinical principles
in the former instance—the refinements of philosophy and
the speculations of theorists which characterised that day,
carried a sort of corrective in their own wildness and extravagance; but the doctrines which were now afloat were

much more dangerous, because more specious and more seemingly constitutional. But, after all, why should Parliament entertain such suspicions of his Royal Highness as were evidently to be inferred from imposing such limitations? He did not mean to offer any personal eulogium upon that illustrious personage, agreeing as he did with the right honourable gentleman in the impropriety and irrelevancy of it upon the present occasion; but still he could not avoid saying that he considered such suspicions wholly unfounded and unnecessary. Why was that illustrious person to be deprived of the necessary power for effectually exercising the royal prerogative? The right honourable gentleman told them that he would vest him with all the powers of that prerogative, necessary to carry on external war, because the interests of the country demand that he should have the most ample powers in that respect; but that it was otherwise in the internal management of the nation. Why did the right honourable gentleman make this distinction? Was not this a most dangerous doctrine? Are we not taught to consider the power of his Majesty and that of the country as one and the same, and that the one assists and supports the other? Are not the powers of his Majesty in external war materially influenced by the internal management of the country? With respect to the power of creating peers, he differed very much from the right honourable gentleman. The right honourable gentleman had been careful to state the few creations which had taken place during his administration; and he had been no less studious to point out a period wherein he conceived the power of creating peers to have been abused. But he would contend that the instance brought forward was by no means an abuse of the royal prerogative; and that these creations were highly necessary and expedient. They were necessary to give to the House of Peers an accession of property and influence corresponding to the growing prosperity of the nation. As to the danger of bad advice being given to the Regent, he could see no reason for assuming that a regent would be influenced by bad advisers any more than a king; and to his mind it appeared most clear that any arguments which applied in support of the restrictions in the one case would equally apply to the other. As to the household establishment, which the right honourable gentleman was at first unwilling to enter upon this evening, he would say, that the officers of the household are officers appointed for the purpose of supporting the splendour and magnificence of the Crown. The House would do well to consider that in all the plans of reform which had yet been submitted to them, no reformer had ever attempted to encroach on the magnificence of the throne. This had always been considered as essential to the executive; and surely they could not think it proper, in the present case, to attempt to disjoin that splendour from the executive. To his Majesty that splendour was now useless; it could minister to him no enjoyment, it could afford him no gratification. Why, therefore, should there be two households? Surely, in the present state of the nation, when economy was so necessary, and considering how little prospect there was of his Majesty's recovery, it was everything but wise to saddle the nation with two establishments, one for his Majesty and the other for the Regent. What, however, was the object of the proposed limitation of the Regent's control over the royal household? The whole object was professed to be delicacy to his Majesty, that his Majesty may find on his recovery the same persons around him whom he saw previous to his calamity. If this was the object, he must say that the method proposed no such security; according to this resolution the queen might remove them if she pleased, and he did not know that, in this respect, a tribute of delicacy was more likely to be paid by her Majesty than by his Royal Highness. But the body to which he alluded, the lords of the bed-chamber, &c., was also a political body, and the question now was, not whether the influence of such a political body should remain, but whether it should be put into other hands than those of the Regent? Many books had been lately written on the subject of the influence of the Crown, and some by honourable and right honourable members of that House. In some of these it was contended, and with great show of reason, that the influence of the Crown has not been lately increased, and was barely sufficient for the due carrying on of the business of the nation. He would put it to those gentlemen who entertained these sentiments, how they could conscientiously vote on the present occasion that the powers of the executive ought to be limited. He would put it to those gentlemen who had the most recent experience of the difficulties thrown in the way of Government by the different parties in that House, and in the country, to say, if they found the management of the public affairs, with the unimpaired vigour of the Crown, so very easy a matter. But if the influence of parties prevailed at present, what would they be during a regency? A regency, as was well known, was the period when factions of all kinds were sure to prevail the most. Was it the duty of the Committee, then, to weaken the arm of the executive at a period when it ought to be the strongest? He would therefore put it to the Committee, if it was not their duty so to legislate on the present occasion as to prevent the danger to be apprehended from the collision of these factions and parties, and so as to prevent the undue diminution of the influence of the Crown. He therefore moved, as an amendment, to omit the last words of the resolution, "subject to such restrictions and limitations as were connected with the custody of his Majesty's person, and the arrangement of his household," inasmuch as these were to become the object of future discussion.

Canning followed on the same side, complimenting his young friend—as he was glad in public as in private to call him—on the moderation of tone and the fitness of topics he had relied on ; and the amendment was only defeated in a full house by twenty-four.*

---

* 'Parliamentary Debates,' December 31st, 1810, p. 493 : "State of the nation—Resolutions respecting Regency."

One of the first acts of the Regent was to reappoint his brother to the command of the army. The scandals which had compelled him to resign in the preceding year were dying out, but they were not yet dead. A good many who had yielded to the clamour of public indignation now half repented their votes, and sober reconsideration of all the facts and circumstances of the case led others to an honest change of opinion. Lord Grey from the first had vehemently denounced the accusation of the Duke of York, and he never ceased to load with obloquy its authors, whose motives he declared to be dastardly and mean.

Ponsonby, without quarrelling with the younger men of his party in the House of Commons who adhered to the austerer view, deprecated Lord Milton's resolution, "That it was highly improper and indecorous in the advisers of the Prince Regent to have recommended the reappointment of the Duke of York to the office of Commander-in-Chief." Perceval justified the reinstatement of the Prince upon the ground that no opinion had been expressed by Parliament touching his personal honour, or imputing to him conscious participation in corruption.

In reply to the taunts and reproaches of Whitbread, who inveighed against those who had aided in driving the Duke from his office yet now acquiesced in his restoration, Lamb declared that he himself had voted for further investigation, having been persuaded at the time that such was necessary; but even then, had the question been taken on the unsatisfactory evidence adduced, he would have said Not guilty. He certainly had wished for the Duke's removal as a matter of public policy, hardly dealt with as he conceived him to be, and undoubtedly made the victim of a public cry; but the justice of the case had, he thought, been satisfied, and the compulsory retirement of a son of the sovereign from a post he had previously held with credit, in consequence of the votes of Parliament, would serve as a sufficient warning in future against want of administrative vigilance which, though morally innocent, was politically reprehensible. Many were

constrained by the recollection of their previous votes to
absent themselves; but forty-nine proved inexorable, while
296 recorded their acquiescence in the replacement of the
Duke.

When the restrictions on the Regency expired, at the
beginning of 1812, the statesmen who for five-and-twenty
years had endured the enmity of the Court, not less for their
attachment to religious freedom than because they were the
Prince's friends, naturally expected to be called to power.
Lords Grenville and Grey were indeed invited to form an
administration, and about the disposal of political offices no
difficulty was made. But when they demanded the right to
nominate afresh to all the offices in the household, the
Regent peremptorily refused. An effort was then made to
bring about a coalition with some of the existing ministers
through the intervention of the Duke of York; his creden-
tials for the purpose being a letter in which occurred the
expression made memorable by Moore in the parody, which
is perhaps the happiest effort of his satiric muse :

> 'You know, my dear Fred, I have no predilections,'
> My heart is a sieve, in which hopes and affections
> Are danced up and down for a moment or two,
> And the finer they are the more sure to slip through.

The Whig nobles disdainfully rejected all idea of fusion
with Perceval and Hawkesbury, and the Prince, to their
amazement and chagrin, placed himself unreservedly in the
hands of a party whom he had always professed to regard
with aversion and distrust.

But if he changed his political advisers, the Regent was
rather less inclined to alienate old friends who had hitherto
constituted his household. He wished Lord Melbourne to
continue Lord-in-waiting; and though the office henceforth
entailed more duties of attendance at Court than suited his
advancing years, the wish was construed as a command.

Throughout the latter years of the war Lamb supported
Government generally in the increasing votes they asked for
the army and navy. His admiration of Earl Grey and his

intimacy with Lord Holland would have drawn him the other way, but his convictions were more nearly those of Grattan and Plunket. While Canning and Wellesley held the seals of the Foreign Office he went cordially with them in the general scope of their foreign policy ; and, believing that in the life-and-death struggle to which the country was committed it was too late to hesitate or yield, he resolved to refuse no reinforcement of munitions or men which were deemed necessary to sustain the army of Wellington in Spain. The opposition of Fox to the original declaration of war with France, and the traditions of his placability and personal good-will towards Napoleon, from which his nephew never swerved, were frequently the theme of frank and sometimes of vehement debate between them. And although during his last brief term of office the great leader of the Whigs had occupied the ground of resistance to Bonaparte's dictation maintained by his deceased rival, it was not unreasonably contended that, had he lived to witness the further progress of the seemingly abortive struggle, and the vast cumulation of national debt incurred each succeeding year on terms more onerous, and entailing enhanced burthens of taxation, Fox would have sided with the friends of peace and left the despotic powers of the Continent to fight it out among themselves,—Lamb thought differently. He undervalued, probably, the evils of heavy taxation and of usuriously contracted debt, but he was right enough in arguing that fiscal or financial objections were not the basis of Fox's general view of foreign policy. Such considerations would not have outweighed with him those involving the freedom of the sea and the independence of the realm, and if he believed these to be in jeopardy he would not have stopped to ask if the augmented liability was eventually to be feared. How little his mind was fitted to estimate accurately possible or probable consequences of war was illustrated by a curious incident of his earlier life. A year after the struggle with America had begun he bet Lord Bolingbroke a thousand guineas to one that the national debt would never reach £170,000,000, and took the one guinea down, registering the wager at Brooks's with the condition that he was not to be called on to pay it until he was in the Cabinet. Within six years he had kissed hands as Secretary of State, and in the interval the national debt had risen from £127,162,413 to £231,843,631.

Lamb early showed a leaning towards the liberal conservatism of Canning, who had intimate relations with another independent section of which Lord Wellesley was the head. The ranks of both were recruited from the Whigs who thought Lord Grey too exacting, and from the Tories who disliked Perceval as a bigot. The personal friendship of Lord G. Leveson and Lord Carlisle for Canning softened the aversion of many of the former. Plunket avowed his attachment to Lord Grenville, who more nearly impersonated his ideas than any one else during the latter years of the war; and Grattan, whose confidence he completely shared, gravitated towards the same point. It would be difficult to say in what these various sections differed from one another, all of them professing to regard the abolition of religious disabilities as the distinctive feature of sound policy. But the egotism of leadership and the prejudices engendered in bygone collisions kept their respective chiefs sometimes at arms' length, and sometimes wholly apart. While the Government was barren in legislation and dull in debate, their accomplished and eloquent opponents were constantly originating convergent movements against them, which, but for mutual distrust, would probably have proved successful. Lord Grenville had been Premier, and could contemplate no second position. Lord Grey was ready to take the Foreign Office under him, but his hatred of Canning was inappeasable and Whitbread was identified with him. At a muster of the Bedfordshire Militia, of which the latter was colonel, Lord John Russell, then a youthful subaltern, expressed in conversation his regret at the news from town that some efforts at a coalition among the different shades of opposition had failed. "What!" exclaimed Whitbread, "the union with Canning?—never!" So many were the chasms, even in social intercourse, between those who were looking daily for each other's aid, and conscious that without it they could effect nothing, that up to this time, and for many years after, Lord Lansdowne was personally unacquainted with Mr. Canning.

At Devonshire House there was perhaps less of political exclusiveness; and there Lord Boringdon first announced the project of moving an address to the Regent in favour of an administration that would conciliate the confidence of all creeds and classes. The 19th of March was fixed in the Lords for its discussion; and there was a fluttering of anxieties about the roost of power. At Melbourne House several intimates of Lady Caroline assembled on the evening of the discussion to learn the earliest tidings. The debate lasted long; and near midnight Miss Berry found " Lady Holland and fifteen other ladies at supper, waiting the arrival of their friends from the House of Lords. They came at last, crest-fallen Whigs and the party of Canning, all except their chief. Lord Wellesley had entirely failed them at the hour of need, not having chosen to open his mouth." * He voted, however, in the minority of seventy-two with Lords Grenville and Grey. For the previous question, moved as an amendment by Lord Grimston, Government had a majority of ninety-three. Perceval did not long survive his triumph. What all the rival strategies of Opposition could not accomplish was effected by the desperate hand of a lunatic, on the evening of the 11th of April, as the minister was entering the House. The populace who crowded Palace Yard evinced curiosity, but no symptom of compassion or concern; and the business of new cabinet making began once more. An idler of fashion with a seat in Parliament, a residence in the centre of the official firmament, and married to a woman of wit and ambition was likely to enjoy keenly the animated suspense that ensued, and to learn more of men and things in such a period of transition than constitutional theories could teach him. Whigs and Canningites concurred in supporting the motion

* Miss Berry's Journal, March 19th, 1812.

of Mr. Stuart-Wortley on the 21st of May for an address
to the Regent calling upon him to take steps for forming
an efficient administration. In the division we find the name
of Lamb with those of Huskisson, Sandon, and Binning;
Ponsonby, Milton, Whitbread, Althorp, and Tavistock.
Ministers only ventured to divide upon the previous question, and even then were beaten by 174 to 170; for the
consequent motion, half an hour later, that the address
should be presented by the Privy Councillors in Parliament,
the same individuals voted, but they were then outnumbered
by a majority of two. Further negotiations for a junction
of parties followed, but each and all proved fruitless, and at
length Lord Liverpool was named First Lord of the Treasury,
a position which he continued to hold for fifteen years. The
seals of the Foreign Department were confided to Lord
Castlereagh, and, although it was necessary in his case to
treat Catholic emancipation as an open question, the
cabinet was emphatically constituted on the principle of
resistance to all measures of civil and religious concession.
Lord Eldon was promoted to the woolsack, and Mr. Peel
was sent to Ireland, where the whole of the executive acted
under the guidance of the Attorney-General, Saurin, in
accordance with the principle of Orangeism. At the end of
the session it was announced that a dissolution had been
resolved on. Everywhere the standard of "No Popery"
was unfurled; and in the new House of Commons many of
the advocates of liberal progress were no longer found.
Among those who thus disappeared was William Lamb.

CHAPTER VI.

OUT OF PARLIAMENT.

Books and opinions—Melbourne House—Byron—Domestic jars—
' Glenarvon.'

SEVEN years' apprenticeship, spent for the most part in
desultory reading and irregular attendance at St. Stephen's
(not to be named as real or genuine work), had failed to
make him, or even to make him fancy himself a master of
parliamentary arts.   It sufficed, indeed, to teach him many
things important to be known; but for the present
savouring only of disappointment and disenchantment.   He
had learned by experience that he was no orator, and that
plausibility, good taste, coincidence of opinion with many
who listen, sound logic, and an occasional dash of sarcasm—
not too saucy from a young man on one of the back benches—
will not command a hearing, secure a report in the morning
papers, or evoke a careless "devilish good" from the chattering
critics at the clubs next day.   In spite of many advantages
of person, voice, address, leisure, acquaintance, connections,
and not a few sincere well-wishers, he had as yet accomplished nothing which scores of young men of his class
had not accomplished on their way to epicurean obscurity.
Such advantages probably went for less at a time when
Parliament contained a much greater proportion of men of
birth, fortune, and social accomplishment than it does now.
But, on the other hand, the judgment of the House was more
exacting and less tolerant of commonplace.   Men who had

bought their seats in the political theatre were ready to back their party chiefs by sitting up all night and walking home to breakfast in the dead of the morning now and then. But occasions of prolonged debate were rare, and afforded few opportunities for neophytes to gain a hearing. For the rest, the majority of the House wanted to be amused or to be excited, or to be moved in some manner, grave or gay. Sheridan made them laugh, Whitbread and Burdett made them angry, Canning and Windham filled them as connoisseurs with delight, Tierney and Perceval with pleasure analogous to that which some of them took in a well-sustained match in the ring or the cockpit. They instinctively refused to be drawn down to Westminster, or to be detained there from more agreeable occupations, to hear their junior colleagues spout their exercises in debating. Ill done or well done, what did it matter to the nation, or to them, or to anybody except the ambitious adventurers themselves? They represented nothing of popular interest or popular sentiment; nothing but their own money, or their fathers' manors, or their uncles' longing for a blue ribbon. If endowed with indomitable perseverance and clothed with a hide of insusceptibility, they learned by degrees to say all they had to say notwithstanding the buzz of inattention or the spectacle of empty benches; and in the course of years acquired a character for persistency in speech which answered pretty well as a substitute for oratoric fame. Sensitive and fastidious natures like J. W. Ward and William Lamb froze in this atmosphere of neglect, and all but abandoned in despair the hope of ever making their mark or realising their ambitious dreams. The oftener they tried, the more painfully oppressive self-consciousness became—that deadliest of foes to all true success. Neither had to encounter anything worth mentioning of hindrance or enmity; that would have been too great luck, for it would have drawn him out of himself, and infused something of reality into exertion. Both listened with discriminating curiosity and gratification to those who were masters of the arts of fence and exemplars in those of

declamation. Again and again the desire of emulating what
they saw and heard impelled them to new efforts. Of the
two, Ward succeeded better than his friend, who cheered and
encouraged him ungrudgingly ; but his letters tell how little
he was deceived by the partial praise of friendship into
imagining that he had become a power in the House; and
Lamb, less painstaking, though certainly less morbid in
temperament, seems to have yielded to the benumbing
influences of parliamentary failure and domestic chagrin :
and upon the dissolution of 1812 he did not seek re-election
to Parliament.

Many of the Opposition lost their seats who could ill be
spared, owing rather to the selfishness of borough-owners
than to the oscillation of popular opinion. Brougham felt
that—

> Romilly, Tierney, and Lamb being out of Parliament was a
> great imputation on some of their friends, who must not
> thereafter talk of the fickleness and wrong-headedness of
> the people.   These professors of party attachments had
> no sort of scruple to dissolve the regular Whig interest, or
> leave it with one single leader in the House of Commons,
> rather than forego the gratification of giving some cousin
> or toad-eater a power of franking letters !*

Somewhat later, himself excluded, Brougham changed
his mind, and did not regret Lamb and Horner being left
out, because the former had become as much a Canningite
as Ward ; and the latter was so ill that nothing but perfect
rest would keep him alive.† He thought Lord Thanet ought
to bring in Tierney for one of his safe seats, but the men
of mere talent and worth had but a frail hold on the political
affection of men who loved to do what they would with their
own.   Close boroughs were part of their investments when
they were not part of their inheritance, and were sold, let,
or given away like other descriptions of property.   Sooner

---

* To Earl Grey from Brougham Hall, September 10th, 1812.
† To Earl Grey from Croxteth Park, October 16th, 1812.

than abandon the career he loved, Tierney took to fighting contested elections at Colchester, on which his wife, who was wrapped up in his success, lavished from time to time the chief part of her fortune. Lamb took it easier, and made no immediate effort to get back to St. Stephen's; though George Lamb thought there was a prospect of a seat for William through the Duke of Devonshire.*

While the zest for pleasure was unchilled, and the power of fascination at its height, study and reflection asserted their claim to comparatively little of his time. The ambition to show in debate would every now and then prompt him to work up a subject, as people say; and, with access to the best sources of information about the Court and in society, with a good stock of constitutional reading in his retentive memory, the labour could not have been irksome, and success might have been great had he been less sensitive to criticism and more sanguine or enthusiastic in temperament. But, like so many of the finest minds, the flaw of doubt continually marred his would-be whole-heartedness in the advocacy of broad and generous principles. He hated the creeping palsy of misgiving, and tried hard to conquer and resist it. But it would not be beaten away; nor, even when most carefully prepared, and assured of fellowship in argument by the men he most respected, could he get rid of the self-consciousness, which is the great hindrance to effect either in public or private utterance. In the worth of right, in the wisdom of justice, in the safety of courage, in the duty of toleration, in the prudence of generosity, and above all, in the divine satisfaction of contributing to the happiness and contentment of others, he was the firmest of believers; and thus it came to pass that his name is found inscribed among the combatants who conquered in all the great struggles against prejudice, privilege, fanaticism, and oppression, from the death of Pitt until his own. But for twenty years it must be owned that as a subaltern he gained little distinction in the fight; and this not because he lacked the spirit of emulation, but because

* Letter of Brougham, from Greeta Bridge, October 24th.

he wanted intellectual earnestness. He had no exclusive
faith in religion, or politics, or love. He could argue
eloquently, lucidly, wittily for Anglicanism, as against the
Curia, the Kirk, or the Tabernacle; but nobody could convince
him that there was not a deal of good in all these, and that
kindly, honourable, and learned men might not honestly
consider their pretensions superior. He would banter alternately Tories and Radicals for opposite faults; and he was
ready to speak or vote, stand forward or stand by, as the
honour of his party required. But he could not forget his
inherent weaknesses, and often infirmities, or be mesmerised
into the delusion that patriotism and wisdom were of the
Whigs alone. And the bitter experience of his private life
had sown tares in the field of his affections, till at length he
had made up his mind there was nothing for it but to let
them grow together unto the harvest. When this sad process
of disenchantment, and goodnatured despair of constancy
began who knoweth? who, if he knew, would have the cruelty
to tell? The heart knoweth its own bitterness, and the
stranger ought not to intermeddle therewith. Were there
propriety, there would be no profit in laying bare griefs and
agonies of a sensitive and excitable spirit. For the most
part, he was able, and he chose, to gulp down the poison of
his happiness; and with such antidote or anodyne as he
could lay hands upon, to live on, without more than occasional
wincing, manfully on the whole, usefully and cheerily.
One of his specifics, and one of the best of them, was
reading; gradually the habit gained upon him until books
became the companions of half his life; he took the same
pleasure in them that he did in the society of wise and
witty people. He communed with philosophers, theolo-
gians, scholars, poets, jurists, novelists, satirists, all in
turn; and sometimes mutely, sometimes audibly, combated
their notions or damned their spite. The result of reading
so varied, preserved, as it was, in memory so retentive,
showed itself notably in conversation, where, by the suffrage
of all who knew him, he was truly delightful. The quaint-

ness and originality of his manner, fitful, abrupt, full of irony, and at times of tenderness almost feminine, gave to his talk a charm specific and peculiar, unlike that of other men with whom he lived. Inevitably it was a continued irritant to the pedantic and impatient, the frigid and fanatical. Now he was accused of levity; now of cynicism. One blockhead was convinced that he was a mere trifler who had no opinions, another was persuaded that he was a high-born sybarite who disguised hard and heartless views for the selfish sake of passing popularity. Both were utterly mistaken; from first to last it may be said of him with truth that he was a better man than he affected to be.

Old books and new by turns attracted him. He delighted in the theological writers of the sixteenth and seventeenth centuries, and spent no little time in the study of patristic divinity. His familiarity with the subjects they discussed would now and then show itself in a striking quotation, or the correction of an inaccurate one by some one in his presence. He kept up his classic recollections, chiefly through Horace and Juvenal, of whom he never tired, and many of whose most suggestive passages he turned into English verse. One charming paraphrase, rather than translation, was published with his name in one of the annuals of a later period.

> 'Tis late, and I must haste away,
>   My usual hour of rest is near ;
> And do you press me, youths, to stay—
>   To stay and revel longer here ?
>
> Then give me back the scorn of care
>   Which spirits light in health allow ;
> And give me back the dark brown hair
>   Which curled upon my even brow.
>
> And give me back the sportive jest
>   Which once could midnight hours beguile,
> The life that bounded in my breast,
>   And joyous youth's becoming smile !

And give me back the fervid soul
  Which love inflamed with strange delight,
When erst I sorrowed o'er the bowl
  At Chloë's coy and wanton flight.

'Tis late, and I must haste away,
  My usual hour of rest is near;
But give me *these* and I will stay—
  Will stay till morn and revel here!

With Mr. Allen, the librarian at Holland House, he had innumerable polemics. Allen possessed great learning and discrimination in judging of the authenticity of manuscripts and the comparative purity of editions. As brusque as Lamb himself, he was more intolerant of opinions he deemed indefensible by logic; and having reasoned himself early out of all belief, he spent the rest of his life in trying to lead others to the same conclusion, or to laugh them into scepticism. He had, besides, the habit of saying of every man of superior intellect he knew, that at heart he was an unbeliever, though for policy sake he might conform to established usages. He was, in fact, a genuine bigot in materialism, and put about the notion widely that his accomplished patron, and most of those who were his favoured guests, held similar opinions. But of Lamb this was certainly untrue. Perplexity between conflicting views regarding the great mystery of existence saddened many of his lonely hours. He envied those who had got through the stage of doubt, and had done with it. He longed for a solution of his own misgivings, and read and argued on in the sincere hope of finding it. Far from wishing to be convinced of the truth of the negative philosophy, his nature turned from it with a shudder. Milton was among his favourite companions, and he would recite whole passages with exquisite feeling and expression from his works.

Whatever may have been the effects of life passed in the whirl of distraction and indulgence which characterised the early days of the Regency, they were nowhere more traceable perhaps than upon the young and impressionable dwellers at Melbourne House. Lady Melbourne had ceased, indeed, to be more than casually amused by whims or novelties; and she moved on in her own diplomatic way, observant of all that was going on around her in looks and spirits, less brilliant than she once had been, though still not a bit like sixty-two: in artifices of dress and arts of manner more consummate than ever. Like Lady Holland at Kensington, and Lady Spencer at St. James's Place, her ascendancy in the household was supreme; yet there were some things her influence could not control, some energies she could not fire. William would do anything to please her when asked; but she knew it was no use always asking him to work as others worked for political advancement. Disenchantment seemed to have spread its insidious spell over him; and though weary enough of *ennui*, she could not bring him, and he could not bring himself, to set about any undertaking requiring effort or toil. His wife, unceasingly active, spent her existence with as little concentration of aim. Painting, music, reading, writing verses, patronising plays, taking part in private theatricals, dreaming romantically, and talking in a way to make people stare; riding on horseback, often coquetting, sometimes quarrelling (she hardly knew about what) with her husband, trying to please her father-in-law, who thought her a fidget; and trying to please her child, whose wistful gaze of incurious wonder made her for the moment staid and sad:—these and a world of intermingling trifles filled up her time. But her versatility found no resting-place, and the fatal habit of mentally looking into the glass grew upon her day by day. Her quick powers of appreciation were thrown away upon a glittering crowd of forms and faces, but few of which she paused to look at long enough to be able to caricature. None of the remarkable persons whom she met in society fixed her attention or riveted her fancy. It was not a profitable condition of mind, but it had been well for her and all who loved her, had her butterflyhood continued longer. Out of the unknown a new influence was about to break

forth on English society, and especially upon that portion of
it wherein she moved, compared with which all other talents,
genius, and originality seemed to her but as so many dull and
motionless lamps, while the lightning was flashing in at the
window.   An instinctive sense of misgiving impelled her at
first to turn away; but when this new element of dazzling
and resistless power came so gently as not even to cause a
start, and in its vivid and seemingly harmless beauty
lingered and played all the summer evening round her, her
imagination was led captive to its will.

Up to this time the name of Byron, save to a comparative few, may be said to have been unknown.   Lord Carlisle,
though one of his guardians, had seldom inquired after him
during his college days; and on his coming of age forgot to
ask him to dinner.   When he took the oaths and his seat at
Westminster he was not recognised by any one of his peers;
and on the Chancellor offering his hand in welcome, as a new
member of the House, he mistook the courtesy for the form
of party enlistment, and took it so ungraciously that Lord
Eldon turned away with a frown.   Morbidly sensitive to
neglect, and attributing it to a slight deformity of which
nobody but himself thought or cared, and fevered with an
insatiable thirst for distinction, he published in 1809 a
satire in which he attacked nearly every critic and poet of
the day, in order to be revenged for the ridicule cast by
Brougham on his 'Hours of Idleness' in the 'Edinburgh
Review.'   With his Cambridge class-fellow, Mr. Hobhouse,
he spent two years abroad, and returned full of aspirations
as a poet and a politician.   Through Samuel Rogers, his only
acquaintance of note, he was introduced to Lord Holland, who,
more suo, forgetting the petulance of his 'prentice rhymes,
aided him cheerfully with information and advice for his
maiden speech in the Lords.   It was an undoubted success,
and he was forthwith enrolled as a promising recruit in the
ranks of the Liberal Party.   But in the crowd of celebrities
and competitors for notice at Holland House, his vanity
might have eaten its heart out with scant pity or heed, had

he not been able to lay the world under tribute in a very
different sphere. His speech, he thought, would prove a good
advertisement for ' Childe Harold,' which appeared a few days
afterwards. Rogers and Moore had seen it in the proof, and
foretold the triumph which awaited him. The former told
Lady Caroline Lamb that she ought to know the new poet,
and lent her his copy to read before the work came out.
Soon afterwards Lady Westmoreland introduced him to her.
Her first impression was unfavourable, and she wrote in her
diary, "Mad, bad, and dangerous to know." But the *éclat*
of his poem made him in a few weeks the star without rival
of society. Wherever he went, and he soon went everywhere, to use his own expression " the women suffocated
him." His air of abstraction and look of melancholy,
and the rumours put about of his eccentric life, all contributed to fan the flame. Emulation for his favour became
fierce, and the wiles spread for his bewitchment were innumerable. Lady Caroline avers that she spread none.
She had called at Holland House after a morning ride
through wind and rain; he was unexpectedly announced,
and she owns that she ran away to readjust her toilet before
they met. His grave attention pleased her; the interview
ended in his asking leave to call, and the acquaintance thus
begun quickly ripened into friendship.

He lived much at Melbourne House, where he was
received on terms of the utmost familiarity. For the talents
of society, in which Lady Melbourne had probably no equal
in her day, his admiration was unbounded. The world she
knew by long and keen observation, and whose scenes she
had the rare faculty of picturing by a few graphic touches,
was all a new world to him. There was hardly a person of
note among courtiers, politicians, artists, or men of letters,
from the time of Garrick and Chatham, whom she had not
known; and there was not a prominent character living
whom she did not weigh in the balance of her own judgment, and whose idiosyncrasy she could not when she would
accurately tell. This, with casual acquaintances, was not

often. Experience had taught her the thanklessness of
those who delight in another's unguarded candour. She
used to say that few men were to be trusted with their
neighbours' secrets, and hardly any woman with her own.
But she found Byron better worth gossiping with than other
young men of his years. He asked her questions which it
really interested her to answer ; and, notwithstanding her
habitual wariness and reserve, a remarkable degree of
confidence sprang up between them.

With Lady Caroline it was hero-worship. The fascination
wrought upon her susceptible and credulous fancy by his
account of his youth and foreign adventures ; his dark hints
at the hidden griefs, the sorrows of his loneliness, the pain
of early disappointments, and his real or pretended indifference to passing success ; the ever changing beauty of his
features, and the glittering splendour of his verse ; and all
these laid with a look and tone of ineffable gallantry at her
feet by one whose nobility dated from the conquest, fairly
bewildered her. It is all very well for those who have never
been brought within the perilous circle of such a spell to
talk pharisaically of the ease with which it might have been
resisted. But to be just, one must estimate antecedents and
surroundings ; the enervating atmosphere of dissipation, and
the *furore* about a picturesque poet of high degree. If these
things are not taken into account, what really is left but the
mingled echo of two names of whose brief association and
subsequent severance the world has heard too much and
understands too little. It was impossible that such intimacy
should not be remarked, but this was exactly what his
vanity wanted. With all his profession of democratic
enthusiasm, he was habitually swayed by aristocratic
feeling ; with all his romance in rhyme about devotion to
nameless and secluded beauty, he was vain as any coxcomb
of being greeted by smiles of quality, and to be known as
the favourite of supreme fashion. In the best set Lady
Caroline was just then one of the fair and fickle rulers.
Melbourne House was the centre of gaiety and revel.

My cousin Hartington wanted to have waltzes and quadrilles ; and at Devonshire House it would not be allowed,* so we had them in the great drawing-room at Whitehall. All the *bon ton* assembled there continually. There was nothing so fashionable. But after a time Byron contrived to sweep them all away.

For his overweening egotism, gratified by special recognition in the glittering throng, chafed at devotion to the pastime in which he could not participate. He preferred sentimental talk with a clever and wayward woman, whose self-idolatry, already too mature, ripened into fruit as bitter as his own. One who knew her long, and well, and who was more than others lenient to her errors, has said of her that her conversation had all the charm of intellect, fancy, culture, and a low musical voice : it had but one fault, that it was all about herself. There was an affinity in this respect between them which in itself became gradually the cause of disappointment and vexation. Craving on the one side, encountered exaction on the other ; and as neither knew how to stifle ill-humour or chagrin, he would grow moody and she fretful when their rival egotisms jarred.

> For the sensitive plant which could yield small fruit
> Of the love that it felt from the leaf to the root
> Desired more than all, it loved more than ever,
> Where none wanted but it could belong to the giver.

She brought him fresh verses on which she had spent half the sleepless night in an agony of hope that his eye would kindle and his lips respond to emotions she had thus endeavoured to express. But though he failed not to praise the well-chosen epithet and flowing rhythm, he was far too full of his own greater thoughts to be able, had he tried, to affect enthusiasm at the tinkling of her lyric bells. In her mortification, she would inwardly upbraid him with being

* The Duke had married a second time Lady Elizabeth Foster, daughter of the Earl of Bristol and sister of the eccentric Bishop of Derry.

like the rest of his sex, too self-engrossed; and the time was
to come when she would tell him so in no measured terms.
But with 'Childe Harold' she could not thus make free.

At a reception one evening Lord Holland took an antique
censer from a cabinet to show it to some learned guest; as he
passed Byron and Lady Caroline he turned and said
gallantly to her, "You see I bear you incense." "Offer it to
Lord Byron," she replied, "he is accustomed to it." How
soon the poet began to tire of the confidential iteration of
morbid fancies, which were not redeemed by grandeur of
outline or depth of colouring that marked those drawn from
the dark chamber of his imagery,—who can tell? But
he loved being conspicuous in everything; and above the
admiration of women he coveted the envy of men; and
liked being spoken of as a favoured intimate at Melbourne
House.

Throughout the year 1813 Byron continued to visit constantly at Whitehall and Kensington. The 'Giaour' and
'Bride of Abydos' kept his name before the public, and in the
estimation of his female critics maintained his reputation.
Lord Holland was too good-natured, and too loyal in everything to the taste of his wife, to be niggardly in his praise.
Other men more fastidious and outspoken in their criticisms
tried to induce the poet to take more serious interest in
politics; but without effect; his letters and journals evince
hardly a trace of sympathy or regard for the great events
which were stirring the heart of Christendom; and it seems
to have been for him too great a sacrifice of pleasure to attend
frequently even as a listener any long debate in the House
of Lords. His second speech did not attract much notice;
and with all his pretentious vows of zeal for liberty, he
was a soldier that, without encouragement of fife and drum,
could not be got to march. His time was spent for the
most part in flattering pretty women, or being flattered by
them; and by his own account he was not sure with which
of them he was most in love. Lamb grew tired of his airs of
self-importance, and laughed at his wife's exaggerated

estimate of his perfections. If sometimes provoked at her misplaced friendship, he anticipated that it would soon wear out; and sighed only at the illusion he was unable to dispel. He knew better what Byron was than she could ever know, and felt secure that ere very long he would declare himself bored, and betake himself to other company. There was another circumstance which no doubt influenced him, but of which few were aware. Byron had in confidence told Lady Melbourne his intention and desire to form a matrimonial alliance, in order that he might settle down at Newstead and take the part that became him in public life. Would she advise him? Did she not know every one worth knowing in the sphere out of which he did not care to wed? Would she not save him from the daughters of Heth? To the mind of the old lady thus consulted, no connection seemed more suitable than one with her young relative, the daughter of Sir Noel Milbanke, who, beside many other attractions possessed a considerable fortune, and was heiress to the barony of Wentworth in her own right. Without professing to fall in love, the poet offered her his hand. It was refused, but with so much kindness, and even compliment, that he readily agreed that they should continue friends, and upon indifferent subjects correspond.

At Cheltenham, then in highest vogue, many of those with whom he was most intimate—the Hollands, Cowpers, Jerseys, Oxfords, and Melbournes—passed September pleasantly. Lady Melbourne had more leisure there; she listened to his wandering talk and gave him good advice. Whatever it was, he believed it sound and wise. On receipt of a letter from her not long afterwards he wrote,—

I have had a letter from Lady Melbourne, the best friend I ever had in my life, and the cleverest of women. I write with most pleasure to her, and her answers are so sensible, so *tactique.* I never met with half her talent. If she had been a few years younger, what a fool she would have made of me, had she thought it worth her while, and I should have lost a valuable and most agreeable *friend.**

The 'Corsair' was followed by 'Lara.' The hero of the latter, writes Ward, " is just the same sort of gloomy, haughty, mysterious villain, as Childe Harold, the Giaour, the Corsair and all the rest. There is a strange mixture of fertility and barrenness. One would think it was easier to invent a new character than to describe the old one over and over again."†

On the 20th of April, 1814, the King of France entered London accompanied by the Prince Regent, who went to meet him at Stanmore. The Duke of Montrose, Master of the Horse, and Viscount Melbourne, were in attendance. A vast concourse of all classes awaited their arrival in town, and the populace, they scarce knew why (except that they had a certain notion that the end of the weary war was near), vociferously bade the Bourbon godspeed on his way back to Paris. Later on, the allied sovereigns came to thank in person the royal representative of England's constancy and courage, which had stood fast for them and theirs when all else in Europe quailed. For weeks London was in carnival. Rejoicings and festivities never ceased ; and those who, through evil report and good report, had helped to sustain the policy thus crowned at last with triumph, could not but feel, as Lamb confessed he did, historic exultation. He was very proud of his country, and not a little proud of having never despaired of its success. When all their other visits were paid, the Czar and the King of Prussia went with the Regent to inspect the great naval arsenals, and were entertained by the officers of the fleet.

On leaving Portsmouth for Goodwood, early on the 25th of June, their Majesties were received at breakfast by the Duke of Richmond. In the afternoon they visited Lord Egremont at Petworth, where a brilliant company, including

---

* Byron's diary, November 13th and 17th, 1813.
† Letter to Bishop of Llandaff, July 7th, 1814.

Lord and Lady Melbourne and William Lamb, awaited them. Thence they proceeded to Dover and embarked next day.

By letters patent of the 11th of August, 1815, Lord Melbourne was created a peer of the United Kingdom, as Baron Melbourne of Melbourne in the county of Derby. He took the oaths and his seat on the 5th of February, 1816. Early in this year Lord Byron had married Miss Milbanke with the advice and approval of Lady Melbourne, and in spite of many petulant warnings of evil to come from Lady Caroline. Her cousin might be learned, and pious, and philosophical, but she was quite unsuited for a soul that was all sensibility and romance. It would never do; she was quite sure of that. A woman that went to church *punctually*, understood statistics, and had a bad figure; how could Conrad find any real community of sentiment with such a being? But the real grievance was that Byron could no longer be a lord-in-waiting to her majesty expectant of Whitehall. Ere long he heard of her complainings at his absence and alienation; and he had the effrontery to address to his peevish and hypochondriacal friend the lines beginning—

"And sayest thou, Cara," etc.,

in which, to excuse the discontinuance of his visits, he tells her that in fact he is thinking of nobody else, and apologises for conjugal perfidy by the assurance that "falsehood to all else is truth to thee." The only palliation that can be suggested for all the inconsistent, exaggerated, and indefensible freaks in rhyme of which poor Lady Caroline was the theme, is the poetic license Byron gave himself of treating esthetically the impulse of the hour without the least regard to what had gone before or was to follow after, and with entire indifference to the obligations of delicacy and of truth. The world has already heard too much of his ill-starred union, and how, during its brief continuance, he was willing to have it believed that he still valued the society of Lady Caroline more than that of his wife. During Lady Caroline's temporary stay in Ireland a correspondence was kept up between them in prose and verse.   At length, on learning that she was about returning to England, Byron resolved to put an end to all future communication ; and did so in a letter which bore on its seal the coronet and initials of Lady Oxford, whom he knew she disliked.   Before she recovered from the illness that ensued, he had quitted England, and they met no more.

The publication of the well-known verses in which he made his affected sorrow known to the world, piqued her into an outward show of indifference which she did not feel ; but her mortification was deep, and her temper, ill-fitted naturally to bear the strain, became ungovernable.   Many tales, for the most part exaggerated, were put about in idleness or malice.   That which gained widest currency related to a page whom she was said to have ill-treated in a fit of passion.   Her own version of the affair, written some time afterwards, is very different :—

The boy was a little *espiègle*, and would throw detonating balls into the fire.   Lord Melbourne always scolded me for this, and I the boy.   One day I was playing ball with him, he threw a squib into the fire.   I threw the ball at his head, it hit him on the temple, and he bled.   He cried out, "Oh ! my lady, you have killed me."   Out of my senses, I rushed into the hall and screamed, "Oh God, I have murdered the page !"   The servants and people in the street caught the sound, and it was soon spread about. William Lamb would live with me no longer.   His family insisted on our separation.   While instruments were drawing up, in one month I wrote and sent 'Glenarvon' to the press.   It was written at night, without the knowledge of any one but a governess, Miss Walsh.   I sent for a copyist, and when he came she pointed to me seated at a table and dressed in boy's clothes.   He would not believe that a schoolboy could write such a thing.   In a few days I received him dressed as usual. I told him the author, William Osmand, was dead.   When printed, I sent it to my husband, who was delighted with it, and we became united just as the world thought we were parted for ever.

The truth was, that, in the interval which had elapsed, Lamb relented. Many of her eccentricities and incoherences had come to his knowledge for the first time, when it was supposed he was about to put her away. Vexed and humiliated as he had long been by what he deemed her unpardonable wilfulness, he could not bring himself to make a public example of one whom he had loved so passionately when life was young, and whose girlish fears and warnings that she was incapable of self-control he had vowed to disregard. Had he not left her with too little guidance? Ought he to fling her in the face of the hissing world, and from such a height of luxury and indulgence, down such a steep of ignominy, humiliation, and reproach? He felt he could not do it, and readily clutched at the excuse her strange and foolish novel unexpectedly offered to reprieve the but half-accountable offender. Others might say or think what they would, but he read in his mother's face, that face of marvellous expression even in old age, that her subtler nature and more resolute will would approve rather than disapprove his resolution. She could not bid him sacrifice his life to a crazed and fitful humour; but, if he had the generosity and determination to endeavour to exorcise the evil spirit, she would think more highly of his understanding and his worth. His wife had not upbraided him with forsaking her, but bowed submissively to what she called her fate, and for once surprised those around her by her equanimity. Near relatives were apprised of what was in contemplation, and consented to arrangements being made with such consideration and privacy that the outer world might still remain ignorant in some degree of the change of relation intended. The deed was prepared for signature, and when all the parties necessary for its completion were in attendance, he went to speak a few last soothing words to her about their son, who was to remain with her at Brocket as

before.   Her brother and the man of law waited patiently
for awhile, and then impatiently for a good deal longer ;
and when at length the former went to the parties to the
meditated act of renunciation, he found her seated beside
him feeding him with tiny scraps of transparent bread and
butter.   And so the storm blew over for that time, and she
made all manner of promises to be tractable, and obedient,
and calm.   But the spoiled child of fortune and affection,
though for the hour sincere, was not to be so easily cured of
spoiling.   The evil spirit had departed for the moment, but,
unhappily it returned.

While the scandal of Lord Byron's separation from his wife
was still recent, the story of ' Glenarvon ' was announced,
which uncontradicted rumour ascribed to Lady Caroline
Lamb.   Curiosity was on tip-toe to peep through a window so
unexpectedly opened into the home of youth, beauty, and
fame prematurely and mysteriously abandoned.   The good
and the bad, the wise and the unwise, were equally eager to
read the book.   All were alike disappointed.   It was merely a
rhapsodical tale, published before any one was aware who
could have prevented its appearance, and which owed its brief
celebrity to the portrait it was supposed to contain of Byron
as he was in social life.   His friends not unreasonably protested against imputations unexpectedly cast upon him in his
absence and from such a quarter.   Save in passing sarcasm,
he does not seem to have taken any notice of the attack, and
the glaring points of difference between his known career
and that of the hero of the tale sufficiently negatived the
hypothesis that the picture had been literally meant for
him.   If likeness there were, it was a preposterous caricature.   In a fit of indignation, his friend and subsequent
biographer, Thomas Moore, wrote a review of the foolish book
which he was about to send to the ' Edinburgh,' when Horner
interposed, and without much difficulty convinced him of
the inexpediency of doing so.   In some journals it was
handled with severity not greater than it deserved ; consideration for the feelings of family and friends made others silent.

That its perusal could have had any other effect upon Lamb than that of exciting his pity is inconceivable, and to suppose, as its erratic authoress did, that it justified to him her extravagant demeanour where the poet was concerned, is simply impossible. Whatever was blameworthy in her predilection for Byron or her manner of evincing it, it was far eclipsed by the infatuation and incoherence of 'Calantha'; while the incidents of fashionable dissipation are thrown into the shade by a grotesque combination of foppery and Whiteboyism. It was not surprising that all who felt concerned for her reputation and welfare should have concurred to deprecate the notion of her again trying her hand in fiction. But 'Glenarvon,' in spite of its defects, had had a sort of success which makes a publisher ready to advise a second venture; and before long she was busily engaged in weaving the plot of another story, which made its appearance in due time.

Byron on quitting England addressed to her the well-known lines beginning with

Farewell, if ever fondest prayer

He felt or affected pique at her travesty of the supposed incidents of his life; which he laughed at as a rather insincere production when Madame de Staël asked him was the likeness correct. But he admitted the identity by volunteering the admission that part of a letter of his as given in the story was genuine.

Lady Caroline was at Brocket when she learned what he had said, and forthwith ordered a bonfire to be prepared, in which she had him burned in effigy; and then transmitted to him an account of his sentence and execution. None of her compositions attained high commendation from the critics of the day. 'Glenarvon,' 'Graham Hamilton,' and 'Ada Reis' were the only novels acknowledged as the productions of her pen, though others were ascribed to her authorship. In the Annuals are to be found not a few stanzas of merit.

Ever impressionable, her husband yielded to the literary influences around him ; and now and then wrote pungently or picturesquely as the whim inspired him ; or snatched a torch .from some of the revellers in rhyme as they passed by, and waved it gracefully aloft as if to show that he too could versify if he would.   Here is a fragment preserved by Jerdan, who coaxed him sometimes to write in the *Literary Gazette*, and says that he was certainly the pleasantest of pleasant men :—

> What ! is the ancient Shepherd dead ?
>   The Patriarch of the Mountains gone ?
> And is all his white hair withered,
>   That once like snow in the moonlight shone ?
>   And is yon old dame left alone
> To battle with the world ?   Alas !
> How different from the thing she was !
>
> He was no common kind, who held
>   An idle occupation here ;
> Nor in fantastic dreams beheld
>   Wild visions from another sphere ;
>   But his mind was firm and clear,
> And many useful things could tell,
> And, at times, on loftier story dwell.
>
> Every bird that wandereth forth,
>   And every grass and herb that sips
> Nourishment from the rainy North
>   He knew, aye, and the dark eclipse,
>   The moon, the sun, and why he dips
> His head beneath the burning seas,
> And nature's many mysteries.
>
> Oh, he was well beloved there !
>   The very breezes seem'd to play,
> In fondness, with his silver hair ;
>   But now he's vanished from the day,
>   And shook his eighty years away.
> Free as his mountain winds is he,
> Let loose to immortality.

Huskisson, Palmerston, and Brougham were among the Christmas party at Brocket, where the first-named talked without reserve to Lady Melbourne of public affairs, of his belief that Canning would soon join the Government, and of his hope that her son would ere long re-enter the House of Commons. Arrangements were already in progress for his doing so through the friendly intervention of the Damers. At Portarlington twelve obedient burgesses went through the ceremony as often as desired of sending a new member to St. Stephen's. On the last occasion the Earl in his *còngé d'élire* had nominated one Richard Shakespear, who was now about to accept the Stewardship of East Hendred in order to make room for William Lamb. Brougham wrote all he learned to Lord Grey. He had been for some time getting up his case about the continuance of the income tax, against which during the ensuing session he led the Opposition to unaccustomed victory.*

* See his letters to Earl Grey, January 9th, 11th, 22nd, 1816.

CHAPTER VII.

RE-ENTERS PARLIAMENT.

*Speech on reduction of offices—Returned for Peterborough—Speech
on the Address—Secret Committee—Death of Lady Melbourne—
George Lamb M.P. for Westminster—Memoirs of Sheridan*

To appease the angry cry of dissatisfaction at the maintenance in time of peace of military establishments un-
precedentedly large, for which no probable need could be
shown, Lord George Cavendish moved an address to the
Regent, praying that steps might be taken without delay to
reduce the number of troops, and to retrench the civil expenditure. Palmerston defended the army estimates for the
year as moderate; 28,000 men was a reasonable force for
home service; and considering that there were still old
reckonings on account of the lately concluded war, and
garrisons to be provided for our newly acquired colonies, he
thought the Government ought not to be blamed for adhering
to the amount of eight millions already voted. When 1817
came they could better judge whether the standing force
ought to be reduced. Althorp, A. Baring, Brougham,
Duncannon, Grattan, Mackintosh, Milton, G. Ponsonby,
Plunket, Romilly, Tavistock, and Lamb voted for the motion,
but were beaten by fifty-six.

A vacancy having occurred in the representation of
Wicklow, Mr. Ponsonby retired from Peterborough, and
was returned without opposition for the county. Lamb
desired to replace him in the seat his grandfather and

uncle so long had occupied, and early in April he was
returned for the cathedral town; Richard Sharp being his
successor at Portarlington.

On the 7th of May, Lord Althorp moved for a select
committee to inquire into the pay of public officers, with a
view to retrenchment. Two days after his notice had been
given, a Treasury Commission was appointed, within certain
limits to inquire into new offices and augmented salaries;
but though its members were respectable men, he thought
it was the duty of the House freely to investigate the
matter for itself. Lamb spoke with much effect, objecting
especially that our military establishments had not been
reduced to a peace footing.

He thought that, after all the explanations which had been
given, strong grounds for inquiry still remained, an
inquiry which, without any disrespect to the members of
the new commission, would be better executed by a committee of that House. The Right Hon. the Chancellor
of the Exchequer had founded his objections on the
lateness of the session, and the tardy progress of a committee. He did not think that technical arguments like
these were suited to a period of such severe and general
pressure, or that they were such as could weigh with a
House of Commons anxious to discharge its duties to the
country. The House was now called upon to consider
whether they would at length give to the people those
benefits which they were expected to confer. It was
said on the other side that confidence ought to be placed
in the pledges offered by the Prince Regent's ministers.;
but he believed the pledge to which the public looked,
and on which they founded all their hopes, was the solid
and substantial one given by that House, in its defeat of
the minister's project for renewing the property tax. If
the House did not redeem the pledge then given, they
had only excited idle expectations, and acquired a delusive
popularity. He could assure the noble Lord, that his

absence from a seat in that House, to which he had only
returned this session, had but served to confirm his conviction of the embarrassed situation of the country, and
of the extraordinary symptoms which had accompanied
the return of peace.   It was not, he admitted, surprising
that a war which had shaken every throne in Europe, and
driven every system of finance except our own through
the ordeal of bankruptcy, should in its conclusion be
attended with extraordinary effects.   Such multiplied
disasters could not pass over our heads like a summer
cloud, and leave no trace behind.   The country, however,
had done its part ; nothing was to be seen but a spirit of
cordial co-operation, and mutual desire to accommodate.
A noble Lord opposite had talked of attempts of pro-
pagating a base delusion.   He had seen with as much
regret as the noble Lord a few exaggerated statements in
different publications ; but in that House, and on the part
of his honourable friends, he denied that any practices
had been adopted or any topics adverted to which were
calculated to produce erroneous impressions.   In point of
fact he did not believe that any delusion existed in the
public mind in relation to this subject.   The public were
as little led astray into wild expectations, and had as
clear and distinct a view of what was practicable in retrenchment, as the noble Lord.   What was looked for was
example, and the effect of just principles adopted with
sincerity, and carried into operation with vigour.   Since
the period when he had first the honour of a seat in that
House, he had never seen in it so much apathy to considerations of economy—an apathy too well corresponding
with the disposition of the Government.   He begged,
however, to warn ministers, and to implore the House not
to entertain the belief that a similar apathy was to be
found in the present silence of the people.   It was an
unfortunate coincidence that this indifference hitherto
manifested, except on one memorable occasion, should
occur at a period when popular meetings were suspended,

and the expression of the public voice was consequently relaxed. Friendly as he was to such declarations of public feeling, he should be sorry to see the functions of the executive assumed on these occasions; and it would be most painful to him to find that a persuasion prevailed that, without the constant superintendence of the constituent body, there was no security for the public service. Should such an opinion however prevail, it would be owing solely to the conduct of ministers. In ordinary times, inquiries of this nature were better intrusted to the Government; but under extraordinary circumstances, and when retrenchment was to be carried far, and to be directed to great objects, he was satisfied that ministers had neither the courage nor the means of carrying it into effect by their own influence, and he submitted, therefore, the propriety of arming them with the authority of that House. He believed, indeed, that no inquiry or reform instituted under the sanction of the present ministers could be effectual, or give satisfaction to the public. It was true, perhaps, that no possible system of retrenchment or reform could satisfy all the hopes which sanguine spirits might conceive; but the mere mention of the word inspired nothing but distrust, when applied to the existing administration. He had had many opportunities of marking this impression on the public mind. It was chiefly founded on the attempt to impose unconstitutional taxes, and to procure the consent of Parliament to exorbitant estimates, both of which they had been compelled to relinquish. This feeling gave a new colour to the language universally employed, and created an opinion that it was necessary to watch every motion of the Government, and that the best and only security for their conduct was to withhold from them the public supplies. He begged them to reflect that they held in their hands, not only their own character and responsibility, but the character of the country and the safety of the constitution. Their measures most certainly, instead of exciting confidence or affection had hitherto produced nothing but alienation, jealousy, suspicion, and distrust.*

At the close of the session Canning became President of the Board of Controul, an office which he continued to hold for several ensuing years.

The harvest of 1816 was the worst since the beginning of the century, and at Christmas the price of wheat rose to 103 shillings a quarter. After the quotation of eighty shillings was passed, importation was free; but the unwise law which prohibited clearance for consumption under that price, had prevented any considerable stock from being accumulated in bond; and when relief was wanted to avert famine, the requisite supplies were not forthcoming. Bitter cries of reproach were heard in every manufacturing town, and merciless invectives directed against those in power, for having at the close of the war offered such a sacrifice of popular industry, health, and comfort, in the hour of victory.

Parliament met on the 28th of January, when Mr. Ponsonby moved an amendment to the Address declaring that the pressure of distress was graver than at the conclusion of any former war; but that to maintain the patience of the people it was incumbent on the House by a severe and vigilant exercise of its powers to prove to their fellow-subjects that the sacrifices it might be their painful duty to make were strictly limited to the real necessities of the state, and to express regret that the measures of the most rigid economy had not hitherto been pursued.

Lamb's speech in support of the amendment was as follows:—

He admitted that the noble Lord who had opened the debate, and the honourable gentleman who had seconded the Address, had in some points touched upon and explained with ability the state and prospects of the country; they had forcibly dwelt with exultation on the general state

* Hansard, May 7th, 1816, pp. 338–40: "On Lord Althorp's Motion for appointing a Committee respecting Public Offices."

and situation of the realm, and in one of the topics of their gratulation he most fully concurred; he need not say that he alluded to the prompt undertaking and effective execution of the armament against Algiers. The honourable gentleman who seconded the Address had, however, carried his feeling of eulogium into a sort of poetical enthusiasm on this event; he had described it as a proof to the nations of the earth that there was nothing selfish in the policy of Great Britain towards other powers; that her aid and co-operation were always in readiness to redress the injuries inflicted upon other states, and to relieve them in their hour of calamity. He was sorry to say that he could not concur in this unlimited panegyric, and before the honourable gentleman who had framed it could have wound his mind up to such a pitch of affectionate credulity, he should have turned his eyes to the systems which England had revived in Europe, to the dynasties she had restored and to the forms of government she had re-imposed. Had the honourable gentleman looked at the dynasties restored by British influence, he would have had his answer as to the liberal and enlightened policy of our ministers, in those of Spain and other nations, which they had reared from their ashes. Had the expedition to Algiers been undertaken on other grounds than those of national insult, he for one would not have concurred in its justification; great as was the principle connected with its object, he could never consent to Quixotic projects upon this general scale. England was, and he trusted ever would be, capable of maintaining her own dignity, and the Commons House of Parliament, her just avenger, would ever assert her title to that uncompromising claim. There was certainly no triumph more pregnant with satisfaction, or calculated to excite more heartfelt gratitude, than that to which allusion had been made. It was to be hoped that our great object was, on that occasion, most fully and permanently secured. The experience,

indeed, of past times forbade anything more decisive than
the indulgence of a hope on such an occasion. He was
satisfied that the conflict had been waged for a cause of
whose justice there could exist no doubt, and that it
had been conducted and terminated in the most efficient
manner. It was greatly the interest of England, and
indeed of the human race, that the atrocious slave traffic
should have been abolished. On no other part of the
speech could he bestow the same unqualified approbation.
One paragraph in the speech, which ascribed the present
state of distress to the sudden termination of the war,
was certainly founded upon a very unfair view of existing
circumstances; it was affixing to the end of the war that
consequence which ought to be attached to its continuance.
It was not its conclusion, but its long continuance which
had produced the effects which are now visible, and which
might have been obviated by the adoption of a different
course of policy. The war was the cause, and the distinct
cause, of the present prevailing distress; and if it should
appear in any future investigation, that an opportunity
had been culpably lost of terminating that war, and of
course with it a part of the public distress that was
incidental to its continuance, then the culpability would
attach to those who had ill discharged their duty, and
who became thereby responsible for the distresses, the
continuance of which they had caused. If, on the contrary,
no fair opportunity had been lost of terminating the war,
then the distresses which had arisen were unavoidable,
and must be met by patience and forbearance. Our
calamities had been produced by the war, though their
complete pressure was not felt till the arrival of peace;
they were thus connected with the peace in point of time,
but they could not be traced to the peace as their cause.
In this situation the great object for us to pursue was,
not to propagate a delusion with respect to the cause of
our distress, but to take every means of alleviating it, or
preventing its extension by supporting and maintaining

public credit. He stated this opinion, not from any fear that the recommendations of those who attempted to justify a breach of the national faith would be attended to, but from a firm conviction that breaking faith with the national creditor would bring no relief to the people, or .tend to remove, in any degree, the embarrassments of the country. On the contrary, he was convinced that such conduct on the part of the legislature would aggravate and extend them. If we were to trust to the dictates of experience we had it in support of this opinion. Some time ago the complaints against the landholder were as loud as they now were against the fundholder. These complaints were now heard no more, for there was no reason for them. Rents had been reduced, the landed interests were straitened in their incomes, but who had benefited by the change? The distresses of the manufacturing and labouring classes, instead of being alleviated, had been increased; they had been deprived of employment by the reduced circumstances of those who employed them, and found no advantage in the diminution of the income of those against whose wealth they clamoured. Any interference with the fundholder he was convinced would be productive of similar effects, instead of relieving our distress. Our situation should be supported with that firmness and patience that could alleviate every calamity, instead of leading us to attempt plans and expedients which might aggravate temporary sufferings into irretrievable ruin, by destroying entirely public confidence and national credit. But how were we to support public credit if we did not resort to such expedients? He would answer—by economy and retrenchment. Parliament, he hoped, was prepared for entering into economical reductions; ministers, he hoped, were prepared for the task; and the country, he hoped, was likewise prepared. He said, he hoped the country was prepared for it; for, although he meant no reflection against any particular individuals, he could not refrain from observing that those who now called for economy and retrenchment might be sorry that they were adopted. It should be recollected that retrenchment was not an unmixed good. A strict and rigorous attention to economy, and reduction of all our establishments to the lowest possible scale, must be productive of evils to certain individuals, and he was not disposed to underrate their sufferings; but the national good and the public security were paramount to all other considerations. The right honourable gentleman who had spoken last had contended that there was no necessity for the amendment, to obtain the object which his right honourable friend had in view, because the Address pledged the House to the same course of conduct as the amendment. This he would by no means admit. The Address merely pledged the House to take into consideration the state of the public income and expenditure; whereas the amendment went much further, and embraced an inquiry into the state of the nation in all its interests, financial, commercial, political, and colonial; examining all its concerns, its extensions of colonial territory, which was made the ground or the excuse of extending military and civil establishments—in short, the whole of our expenditure at home and abroad. Our commercial situation and system required revision, after such a violent change as it had lately undergone in the political circumstances of the world. The whole should be taken into consideration, with the view of ascertaining whether the regulations which had guided it in war should be continued or altered on the return of peace. There was one subject which pressed upon the attention of all, and which would be embraced in the inquiry that the amendment of his right honourable friend proposed—he meant the poor laws. The sums raised for the support of the poor, in the shape of rates, now amounted to a tax almost as great, and on certain classes of the community certainly more oppressive, than the property tax. It was impossible that eight millions a year could be collected or administered in

the manner, and for the purpose, in which this tax was
collected and administered, without the greatest oppression to the landed interest, and the ultimate diminution
of the industry and resources of the country. Not only
this, but many other subjects, demanded an inquiry which
might lead to amendments in our laws, institutions, and
establishments, mild and moderate in their operation, and
certain in their results upon the public prosperity and
happiness. Nor ought the House to be deterred from its
duty in adopting improvements and economical reforms,
by the rumours or the fears of any disturbances or
breaches of the peace which they either had heard or
with which they were threatened. His opinion on this
subject was always the same; it had always remained
unaltered, and he believed would do so. He allowed in
their fullest extent the rights of the people to petition for
any lawful object that they thought connected with their
interests, privileges, or well-being; he reverenced popular
meetings which were regularly and quietly conducted, he
reverenced the rights and the privileges which they
exercised, and he was disposed to attend to their represen-
tations, as much as any man; but when such assemblies
proceeded to violence, when they led to breaches of the
peace, he was for vigorous and immediate repression.
This conduct he would recommend, not only from motives
of public security, but from motives of tenderness and
mercy to the deluded persons themselves. He deprecated
all breaches of the peace, disturbance and riot, not only
for their immediate effects, but for their ultimate consequences. Tumult for liberty and right was not only
dangerous and destructive, but was a liar, and never kept
its promises. It led in the end, through scenes of anarchy
and blood, to a political tyranny, or military despotism;
the more fatal in its nature, and the more hopeless in its
consequences, from the circumstance that the people
were taught to seek refuge under its protection from
the more appalling evils of insecurity and confusion.

For these reasons he would give his cordial support to the amendment of his right honourable friend.*

While Charles Grant was speaking in answer to Lamb, a message of urgency from the Lords, demanding a conference forthwith in the Painted Chamber, was delivered by the clerks of their lordships' House, Black Rod and his Deputy being both accidentally absent. On his return from Westminster through St. James's Park, bullets had been fired and stones thrown at the carriage of the Regent, which broke the window, but inflicted no other injury. Lord James Murray, the lord-in-waiting, was examined at the bar as to the incident, and an address of congratulation having been voted on his Royal Highness's safety, the debate thus interrupted was adjourned till the following day.

Canning resumed the debate on the Address :—

An honourable gentleman, Mr. Lamb, who never spoke without making a deep impression by his eloquence and ability, truly observed, last night, that retrenchment is not an unmixed good. Such a process necessarily throws upon the world many meritorious and helpless individuals who are added to the numbers of the distressed and who augment the mass of discontent throughout the country. I state this not as an argument against reduction, but as an excuse for the frank avowal that in cutting deep it is impossible not to pain severely.

The amendment was lost by 264 to 112. The minority included Abercromby, Althorp, Brougham, Burdett, Ebrington, Mackintosh, Morpeth, Romilly, Tavistock, and Tierney.

Lord Cochrane presented a petition from Saddleworth, bitterly complaining of the neglect with which popular suffering was treated, declaring that no relief by way of charity would be of any use unless the grievances of the community were redressed by the concession of a thorough and compre-

---

* Hansard, January 28th, 1817 : " Address on Prince Regent's Speech, moved by Lord Valletort, seconded by Mr. Dawson."

hensive change, and averring that the existing House of
Commons did not represent the nation. A question was
raised as to whether such language ought to be tolerated by
Parliament, and the Chancellor of the Exchequer moved that
it be rejected. Lamb expressed his strong condemnation of
the revolutionary language held at public meetings during
the recess, and especially regarding universal suffrage and
annual parliaments :

But they ought to remember the emphatic language of their
Speaker, that their doors should be thrown wide open for
the statement of grievances; yet a line should be drawn :
those petitions which denied the authority of that House
and its power to make laws ought to be rejected, but the
present petitioners did not go to that extent; on the contrary, they fully admitted both those functions in their
prayer that the House would be pleased to pass a bill for
parliamentary reform. The petition from Bristol just
ordered to lie upon the table had prayed that the House
would receive and pass a bill for that purpose. The bill
was to be prepared out of doors, and they were to sit
there to receive and pass it. That was the popular doctrine now with the gentlemen who had taken the subject
of reform into their hands. They were to get the bill
ready and send it to the House of Commons, as a mere
formality, necessary to give it the effect of law. That
doctrine reminded him of what took place at the end of
the Civil War, when notions of a republic were generally
diffused. Serjeant Maynard and some of the old reformers
who still retained an attachment to constitutional forms
in the midst of all their republican zeal, proposed that a
king should be elected for the purpose of giving the royal
assent to bills; but that all other functions and authority
of royalty should be abolished. Upon the whole, he considered the petition as less objectionable than the former
one which had been received, and therefore he hoped it
would not be rejected.

Brougham and Canning took a similar view; and forty-eight members voted accordingly; but it was rejected by a large majority.

Before venturing to propose measures of repression, the executive resolved to take Parliament into its confidence, and to invite it to share its responsibility. A committee of secrecy was appointed to consider and report upon the information contained in certain sealed papers laid upon the table, which ministers believed would show an extent of seditious combination formidable to the safety of the realm. Opposition were invited to suggest names for the committee; and although, according to precedent, the ultimate actual choice was determined by ballot in the whole House, every one being free to modify the list as he pleased, the choice for the most part confirmed the list mutually agreed upon behind the chair. With Mr. Ponsonby were thus associated Lord Milton, Mr. Elliot, Sir Arthur Pigott, Mr. Lamb, Sir J. Nicholl, and Mr. Dundas. And when at the beginning of the following session the committee was reappointed for a like purpose, Lord G. Cavendish and Mr. Wynn replaced Mr. Elliot and Mr. Ponsonby. Evidence in support of the depositions and reports from the Home Office was brought before this parliamentary court of inquiry to aid its scrutiny and to shape its judgment. It is of the nature of such a tribunal that its consultations should frequently take the form of argument, and that its decisions should be come to not without controversy. Without such conflict of views it would indeed be of little use. But precedents forbid a disclosure of the divisions which take place on a proposed report or on any of its recommendations. It would, indeed, be incompatible with the idea of secrecy were lists of the majority and the minority upon important questions publicly recorded, when the grounds for such difference are withheld. The part taken subsequently in debate by members of the committee on the bills founded on the report, sheds, indeed, a partial light upon some of the questions which are supposed to have given rise to discussion with closed doors; but a speech in a popular assembly will always essentially differ from the condensed and contentious arguments suited to a committee-room. Service on committees of importance, where a man of intellect really devotes time and care to the investigation, and tries to carry others with him, or to resist their powers of suasion, is a special training of the best and highest kind; and few ordeals test more thoroughly the metal of which men are made.

For Lord Milton's amendment questioning the payment of war salaries to secretaries of the Admiralty during the expedition to Algiers, Lamb spoke briefly but much to the purpose. The vote, however, was carried by 169 to 114 in a strictly party division.

On the third reading of the Habeas Corpus Suspension Bill, Lamb, as a member of the Secret Committee, was ready to bear his share of any odium that might be excited by measures founded on their report; but he believed the bill to be required by the exceptional state of things that unhappily prevailed. A minority of 103, including Abercromby, Brougham, Burdett, Duncannon, Ebrington, Folkestone, Lambton, Mackintosh, Romilly, Tavistock, Tierney, Ponsonby, Althorp, and Cavendish, voted against the third reading.

Three days before the fatal illness of Mr. Ponsonby Lamb had differed from him in debate and division, and when he was gone he could not restrain his wish to pay a tribute of respect to the leader they had lost. He accordingly undertook the task of moving a new writ for Wicklow, prefacing the motion with a warm eulogy on the patience, temper, judgment, and urbanity of his deceased friend.

The plight of Opposition in 1817 was deplorable. Whigs and Radicals opposed one another, and no party chief succeeded to the authority of George Ponsonby, who for several years had filled the difficult post of leader. Tierney and Brougham were spoken of as qualified to replace him. In activity and versatility the latter was confessedly pre-eminent, but Tierney possessed temper, discretion, and standing in a far higher degree: and as he could be depended on to act loyally with the great Whig chiefs, they determined to have him for their representative in the Commons. In manner he was decidedly an improvement on his predecessor, whose bearing, haughty, cold, and repellent, aggravated the deficiencies of mind that came to him by nature. "He was the least eminent man," said Ward, "that ever filled such a station, and yet his loss was an event of considerable importance." But he was a man of independent means, of family connection, and of fidelity to his word. Tierney was in rather indifferent health, simply a soldier of political fortune, enterprising, clever, and a great swordsman in the wordy fray, but without a relative or follower in the ranks, and without decisive weight in counsel ; for by birth he was nobody, and when he had lavished his wife's fortune on contested elections he was poor.

Lady Caroline continued still to write, regardless of the dissuasions of her friends, and this year was published her third novel, 'Ada Reis,' by some deemed her best. It was violently opposed to many prejudices of society, and had little attraction for ordinary readers. She herself regarded it with no little pride, and playfully urged a friend with whom she interchanged literary confidence to uphold it :

All I have asked of Murray is a dull sale, or a still birth. This may seem strange, and I assure you it is contrary to my own feelings of ambition; but what can I do? I am ordered peremptorily by my own family not to write. All you say is true, and so true, that I ask you if one descended in a right line from Spenser, not to speak of the Duke of Marlborough, with all the Cavendish and Ponsonby blood to boot, which you know were always rebellious, should feel a little strongly upon any occasion, and burst forth, and yet be told to hold one's tongue and not write, what is to happen? You cannot do me a greater favour than to recommend and set abroad 'Ada Reis.' I will send you three copies, and with them the letters I have received from Gifford, Lady Dacre, and

several others whom you know. In the mean time I am
doing all I can for your future work upon Salvator Rosa.
I have received kind answers from the Duke of Devonshire, Lord Palmerston, and Lord Cowper, in which they'
say they will certainly obey your orders. You must
wait, but depend on the information. Will you, in return for the three Ada Reises, which I value at sixpence
apiece,—will you read the inclosed list, and serve me, if
you can, by trying to secure me a vote in Westminster
Hospital, in the case of a vacancy for a physician? it
may not happen this year, and it may in a month. I am
anxious to serve a physician whose name is Dr. Roe, and
as we both love Ireland, let me speak it to the honour of
that country, that he sprung from it. He has done
everything he could for my dear and only child. I therefore have done, and will do, everything for him. It is
Scotland, Ireland and England that are opposing each
other. You know you are all-powerful with the Opposition, and I hope for Ireland you will do your best. I will
do all I can for Salvator Rosa.*

Near the centre window of the drawing-room looking
into St. James's Park, the chair long retained its place
fastened to the floor, in which Byron sat for his picture to
Sanderson. Lady Morgan notes, in her diary, being received
in this room with the Countess D'Ameland, who seems to have
understood Lady Caroline's temper and manner, "more odd
and amusing than ever. There was no kindness she would
not take the trouble to devise for those who were in favour,
but it was hazardous not to accept the offer." Her song beginning "Waters of Elle," written in the autumn of 1818,
published with music, retained its popularity longer than
most West-end ballads. She delighted in the harp, on which
instrument she had attained considerable proficiency.

In consequence of a fall from her horse Lady Caroline
suffered, in December, from an attack of nervous fever,

* To Lady Morgan from Brocket Hall, undated, but obviously soon
after the publication of 'Ada Reis.'

2 K

which seemed at one time like to prove fatal. Her own
account of her recovery is too characteristic to be trans-
lated into other language than her own :

For one week I never swallowed anything. The moment of
danger is now passed, and I believe, in truth, I died; for
assuredly a new Lady Caroline has arisen from this death.
I seem to have buried my sins, griefs, melancholy, and
to have come out like a new-born babe, unable to walk,
think, speak ; but perfectly happy. So, finding myself
—after I had wished for death and died—alive again,
I made them carry me out into the air in a blanket,
and then, to the astonishment of every one, ordered my
horse next day, and sat upon it and would ride, and now
am well, only weak. I have positively refused to take
any draughts, pills, laudanum, wine, brandy, or other
stimulants. I live upon meal-porridge, soda water, milk,
arrowroot, and all the farinaceous grains. My mind
is calm—I am pleased to be alive—grateful for the
kindness shown me; and never mean to answer any
questions further back than the 15th of this month, that
being the day of this new Lady Caroline's birth: and I
hate the old one. She had her good qualities, but she
had grown into a sort of female Timon—not of Athens—
bitter, and always going over old, past scenes. She also
imagined that people hated her. Now the present Lady
Caroline is as gay as a lark, sees all as it should be, not
perhaps as it is ; and having received your very clever
letter, full of good sense, means to profit by it; but, at
present, like her predecessor, and like one of your country-
men, is going about wanting work. I have nothing necessarily to do. I know I might, and ought to do a great
many things, but then I am not compelled to do them.
As to writing, assuredly, enough has been written, besides
it is different writing when one's thoughts flow out before
one's pen, and writing with one's pen waiting for thoughts.*

* From Brocket, December 18th.

For some time Lady Melbourne had been in declining health, and in March she was made aware that her end was approaching. Firm and collected to the last, she spoke to her children frequently of their inevitable separation, and counselled each apart, in her own way, as to what she believed best for them in life. Even at the gate of death she would not quench the torch of that ambition which had lighted her devious and audacious path for well-nigh fifty years; but handed it to the son in whose destiny she believed, and bade him look high. Her parting words seem never to have lost the sharpness of their first impression. Her death took place on the 6th of April, 1818, at White-hall, whence, on the 14th, her remains were removed for interment in the family vault in Hatfield Church. The chief mourners were Earl Cowper, William, and George Lamb. Frederick was not in England.

The loss of his mother proved, in many ways, a serious one to Lamb. Though she never could accomplish all she wished in his favour, she was to the last watchful for his interest and versatile in expedients to promote it. More than all, she was for him the safest and best of confidantes. Up to this time no avowed estrangement had taken place between husband and wife; their pursuits were different, and their companions; her whims and oddities multiplied; and, as he could not cure, he resolved not to see them, or, when that could not be helped, not to remember them. He had reasoned himself into the conviction that the world knew very little about them, and that society held him in no way accountable for her unaccountabilities. No one but her immediate relations ever thought of talking to him on the subject. He continued, indeed, to be cherished and beloved by them all, for they knew how much he had to endure, and with what good-humoured fortitude he bore one of the greatest trials of a sensitive nature, that of being made ridiculous by her whom, of all others, he would have been proud and glad to see identified with himself in honour and esteem. What impatience and repining at the fate which

bound him for life to a woman he had once ardently loved,
and still was fervently attached to, when she was lovable,
feminine, and tranquil, but who, by her waywardness and
folly, every now and then outraged all his fastidious regard
for conventionalities, and humiliated him in the eyes of the
frivolous and tattling crowd. What struggles he had with
himself to choke down resentment, and to adjourn indefinitely the half-formed resolve to break with her once
and for all—we shall never know. From his mother he had
few secrets; none in domestic affairs. While she lived conjugal squabbles were more easily adjusted, or at least
smoothed over; for Lady Melbourne was in his opinion,
and not in his alone, a person of rare insight into character,
and she possessed a singular ascendency over the impulses
and tendencies of others. Affection for her daughter-in-law
she probably had none. Had she been ever so beautiful,
influential or wise, the old lady would have warred to the
death with a woman who had spoilt the happiness of her
idolised son, if warring would do him any good. But she
knew better. Long experience of the ways of the world
taught her to give him other counsel. She was ambitious
for him, and she knew that in the society in which they
moved there was every species of danger and detriment in
open separation. He was very handsome, very fascinating, and very susceptible. So long as the household was
preserved, there was little risk of his falling a prey to wiles
certain to beset him, if once the domestic bond were publicly
and irreparably broken. Notwithstanding all her sympathy
and aid, she knew that his pecuniary resources became every
year less adequate to meet his personal wants, and the obligations unreasonably thrown upon him : these requirements
would certainly be augmented heavily if he had to provide a
separate establishment suitable for her who bore his name.
He was in debt, but not yet to an extent that was formidable,
even though the possession of his inheritance might be long
deferred. But all this would speedily change for the worse
if Lady Caroline should cease to have her home at Melbourne

House, and designing persons once began to entangle him in the web of their enchantments. "Ah," he used to say long afterwards, "my mother was a most remarkable woman; not merely clever and engaging, but the most sagacious woman I ever knew. She kept me right as long as she lived." It is not difficult to imagine, though impossible to tell, in how many little ways, and by what subtle arts she contrived to quench sparks of contention, and to reconcile differences ere they gained head, to laugh ill-humour out of countenance, on either or both sides, ere it found angry words, and to create a diversion in favour of pleasure or peace when her intractable daughter-in-law seemed bent on mischief. The very presence of such a woman as Lady Melbourne, in her later years, was an insurance against dangerous incompatibilities taking fire. And when that presence ceased nothing could supply its place.

At the general election of 1818 the greatest triumph of the Whigs was the return for Westminster of Sir Samuel Romilly by a large majority over Sir Murray Maxwell, for whom Lord Castlereagh and all the supporters of the Government voted,—and by a still greater preponderance over Mr. Henry Hunt, then the idol of the populace. Upon Romilly's unexpected death soon afterwards, candidates of various shades of liberal opinion presented themselves. The Westminster Committee that had mainly contributed to bring in Burdett in 1807, of which Mr. Adams, a wealthy coachbuilder in Long Acre, Mr. Francis Place, clothier, of Charing Cross, and Mr. Brook, glass manufacturer, of the Strand, were the most influential members, undertook to find him a colleague after his own heart, and gave their support to Mr. J. C. Hobhouse, then best known as the devoted friend and confidant of Byron. An appeal to the electors, written by Place, staking the issue upon the principle of radical reform, appeared to Jeremy Bentham, who was consulted daily on the subject, to be just the right thing; and was considered by Tierney and Brougham and

Lord Robert Spencer as an insufferable affront to the Whig party. Hobhouse personally was known to all and liked by most of them; and he had the great merit of having a rich father who would spend any sum that might be necessary to carry Westminster. But that he should be returned in wanton defiance of the social and political influence that had theretofore been paramount, was unendurable; and, come what might, a Whig must stand.

Neither Tory or Radical at first appeared willing to take the field. At the instance of his brother William, who undertook the arduous work of organising a canvass of the most difficult, because the most spoiled, constituency in the kingdom, George Lamb agreed to become a candidate. A joint committee of Whigs and Radicals gave him their support. Representatives of the great family connection, all of whose mansions stood within the city, figured in the list as in the days of Charles Fox, and afterwards of Sheridan. Sir Francis, however, did not approve of the selection, and after some days promised his support to Hobhouse. He professed to be an advocate of household suffrage, triennial parliaments and ballot. But this did not content many who had supported Mr. Hunt, and they accordingly brought forward Major Cartwright, who outbid both his competitors by recommending that the suffrage should be universal, and that a new parliament should be chosen every year. This it was supposed would decide the fate of the election by splitting the Radical party. Yet many circumstances conduced to render the event till the last moment doubtful.

In his address George Lamb asked the suffrages of those who had lately returned Romilly, simply on the pledge of his adherence to the principles exemplified in the political career of that distinguished man, and these he promised to make the invariable guide of his public conduct.* Though little used to figure before a querulous and turbulent audience, he had acquired as an amateur actor some facility in elocution; and his pleasant features and good

* Address to Westminster, February 12th, 1819.

temper won him as much favour as could be expected from
the crowd. He parried questions meant to entangle him
in his talk, with adroitness so as not to give offence, and
steadily refused to be pushed beyond his promise to walk
according to the liberal light as it had shone forth calmly
in the votes and speeches of his illustrious predecessor. All
the arts of female suasion were pressed into requisition on
his behalf. The Duchess of Devonshire and Lady Melbourne
were no more; but their memory was recalled by Lady
Georgiana Morpeth and Lady Caroline Lamb, both of whom
succeeded in winning many doubtful suffrages. Among
these they hoped to reckon William Godwin, then at the
height of his literary fame, but whom neither of the fair
canvassers had ever seen. The philosopher was supposed to
be inaccessible to ordinary blandishments, and it was thought
advisable to approach him deferentially. On the 25th of
February he was rather surprised, but, as it would appear,
rather more pleased, at receiving the following note:

Lady Caroline Lamb presents her compliments to Mr. Godwin, and fears his politics will incline him to refuse her
request of his interest for Mr. George Lamb. She hopes,
however, it will not offend if she solicits it.

He replied without delay:

You have mistaken me. Mr. G. Lamb has my sincere good
wishes. My creed is a short one. I am in principle a
Republican, but in practice a Whig. But I am a philosopher,
that is a person desirous to become wise, and I aim at that
object by reading, by writing, and a little by conversation.
But I do not mix in the business of the world, and I am
now too old to alter my course, even at the flattering invitation of Lady Caroline Lamb.

Thus began an acquaintance which in due time ripened
into intimacy.

William Lamb, who never could be got to work energetically for himself at an election, threw all his energies into the struggle for his brother. His influence with moderate men among the ministerialists was personally considerable. Although no positive certainty could be had that at the last moment a government candidate would not appear upon the scene, it grew less probable every day. Two votes had been taken a few days previously in the House of Commons giving an addition of £10,000 a year each to the Prince Regent and the Duke of York. Tierney had led the opposition to both, and had been supported by Scarlett, Denman, Wilberforce, and Brougham. Ministers were too well satisfied with their majority of more than one hundred in the new parliament to embroil themselves in the Westminster election. Mr. M'Donald, who had recently made a very popular speech in the House of Commons, proposed the Whig candidate on the hustings.

Hobhouse was proposed by Sir F. Burdett and seconded by the Hon. Douglas Kinnaird. Major Cartwright was proposed by Mr. Nicholson and seconded by Mr. Bowie, who thought Hobhouse did not go far enough. Lamb was at first ill received, but quickly gained a hearing; rank and property sided with him against the democratic brewer. Out of 2763 votes polled for him, 1070 had been plumpers for Sir Murray Maxwell at the previous election some months before; and the fact was flung at him subsequently by way of proof that he was at heart a ministerialist. Hobhouse was distanced by hundreds and Cartwright by thousands.

Later on in this year Sheridan died, and William Lamb was among the well-born crowd who followed him to the grave. His admiration was unbounded for his genius. He had never, indeed, heard him at his best; and continually in his company during his latter years, he could not be unconscious of his foibles and his faults; the after-glow of his fame, and the fascination of his talk even in the clouded period of his decline, were for so lenient a judge and so generous a critic irresistible. Tom Sheridan was, besides, his personal friend; they were not far apart in age, and were

closely knit by sympathy in taste and turn of thought. Ere
many months had passed Lamb communicated to his friend
the notion of becoming his father's biographer; and as few
things are pleasanter, and none easier, than to build in the
air a monumental shrine to keep in remembrance the great
abilities and achievements of one we have known and loved,
he gave himself up for a season to the enjoyment, and
persuaded himself the while that at last he had hit upon
something in the shape of work, that would be not only
useful, but that would make him a name. He went in for
a preliminary course of reading in Old English comedy from
Beaumont to Congreve, and long afterwards he used to
excite the wonder of the superficial and the admiration of
the learned frequenters of Holland House by reciting whole
colloquies from Wycherley and long speeches from Massinger.
This was preparatory to writing the earlier portions of his
work, and delightful preparation it was. Then there was a
course of more laborious study in the orations, English,
Irish, French, Roman, Greek. Their differences of style and
comparative anatomy had for him a charm that they never
had before. It was very much owing to the working of his
thoughts at this period that his predilection for the condensed and laconic, over the diversified and diffuse, was
crystallised into principle and reduced into practice. He
liked the speeches in Livy, and still more those in Sallust
and Tacitus, better than those of Cicero himself, who he was
sure must have bored the Conscript Peers, thinking a great
deal more of their costly suppers than of the virtue of their
republican fathers: but in his opinion the model of statesmanlike eloquence was to be found in the orations in Thu-
cydides. Of the earlier Irish school he had little or no means
of judging. Fox and Windham were the *penates* of his
house, and the latter was with him a sort of idol. Canning
he could listen to for ever; but the man who he always
said was the most irresistible in argument he had ever heard
was Plunket. By the time he had come to settle conclusions
about all these, something of his youthful preference for

Sheridan was shaken; for he could not reconcile them with his unbridled freaks of fancy and tendency to over-decoration. This did not cool his biographic zeal, or abate his ambition to be the author of a book that every one would read. After many postponements and changes of design he at length began, and actually wrote the introductory portions of the Life of the orator as we have it now.

But the drudgery of seeking out, and testing and winnowing the materials for a consecutive narrative stretching back into the days of Garrick and Wilkes, was a dreadful reality for which his studies and philosophisings had not the least prepared him. Repartees were easily remembered, and the number of nights that 'The Rivals' and 'The Critic' ran was chronicled to his hand in the records of Covent Garden; but what put it into the dramatist's head to write as he did, how he managed to live while he was writing, and fighting to get it properly played; and then why he did not write on instead of turning aside into politics; and why when he had made the greatest speech of his day and generation, and was offered a thousand pounds next morning if he would give a correct report of it, he would not, could not, or at all events did not, though he had not at the time a thousand pence to spare—— all this thoroughly bewildered the intending biographer. He had got together all the best marbles and bronzes, sacrificial tools and incense-burners for his temple, but to go quarrying for the stones and digging out the rubbish for the foundation, or making the cement and trowelling it into the numberless interstices that must be filled up——Heigh-ho! perhaps somebody else would do it better: why not Thomas Moore, an enthusiast by nature, a skilled workman by trade? There was some hesitation and some demur: the poet instinctively knew that, professionally considered, it was not a job that would pay; people would expect too much, and if for himself he was to forage for materials, they would find that they had got too little for their money. Yet if he did not perform that more laborious part of the work, for which an author gets no thanks and few traces of which are ever discernible at all, how was it to be done? Moore was just then in the highest vogue, and the brilliant fragments of the great polisher and setter of intellectual diamonds were ten times more profitable, and a hundred times easier to supply, than circumspect and circumstantial biography of a man, half of whose associates and antagonists were still living. It was too late to detect many of the lies, and too soon to tell many of the truths about him. Moore was told by everybody he dined with that he was just the man to embalm Sheridan's memory in frankincense and myrrh. The Minstrel Boy liked the compliments better than the work, and took to it reluctantly. Lamb proffered him all the aid in his power, and sent him his notes and sketches, with the introductory chapters which only were written. Eventually they made their appearance, with little adaptation, at the beginning of Sheridan's Life, accompanied with due acknowledgments.

CHAPTER VIII.

KNIGHT OF THE SHIRE.

M.P. for Hertfordshire—Repressive legislation—Second contest for Westminster—Death of George III.—Proceedings against the Queen.

THROUGHOUT the manufacturing districts, open air meetings in favour of Radical Reform took place during the autumn. No breach of the peace occurred, and the local magistracy did not feel themselves called on to interfere until, upon the 16th of August, an assemblage estimated at seventy thousand persons, collected from various contiguous districts, met under the presidency of Mr. Hunt at Peterloo Fields near Manchester. The military formation of the converging columns as they marched to the rendezvous, and the exhibition of caps of liberty and flags with ominous inscriptions, above all the dreaded purpose of the demonstration, impelled the magistrates to order the yeomanry to disperse the multitude; and upon their getting helplessly entangled and wedged in by the people, a troop of hussars was called on to clear the ground. No resistance was offered, but in the confusion and terror which ensued many persons were severely injured, and six or seven killed. Ministers advised the Regent to thank the county justices for the promptitude of their loyalty and vigour in crushing sedition and preserving the peace; but on careful consideration, their legal advisers told them that the existing state of the law against popular manifestations was clouded with so much doubt that it was difficult to say what really constituted an abuse of the liberty of publication, of meeting, or of speech. Several measures of repression of the most stringent kind were thereupon prepared under the direction of Lords Sidmouth and Eldon; and Parliament was summoned to meet in November to confer upon them the validity of law. Before they were taken into consideration by the Commons, Lord Althorp moved for a select committee to inquire into the state of the country, with a view to ascertain the cause of the discontent and distress which had led to the recent manifestations of a desire for organic change. He was supported in debate by Douglas Kinnaird, Milton, Brougham, Duncannon, Tierney, and William Lamb, who said that:

On reviewing all the circumstances of the case, he found it absolutely impossible to doubt that inquiry into what had taken place at Manchester ought to be immediately instituted. This was necessary for the character of the magistrates themselves. To the argument which seemed to be principally relied on, that a parliamentary inquiry would prejudice proceedings about to take place in a court of justice, he would reply that, in a case of national importance, this was an inconvenience that must be submitted to. In the next place, he would remark, that he knew of no pending prosecution that would bring the whole case before any of the ordinary tribunals; and for himself he would say, that in his opinion nowhere could so impartial an investigation of the circumstances take place as in a committee of that House. If it were admitted that the magistrates had acted legally, still an important political question must arise on the discretion which they had exercised, and this made a parliamentary investigation desirable. He was apprehensive that coercive measures, in the present state of the country, would prove injudicious, and was afraid that more meetings like that at Manchester might be expected if something was not done to conciliate and tranquillise the public mind. A measure, he understood, was to be brought forward by an honourable friend of his, the object of which was to effect a reform in Parliament. He should be ready to support it if he thought its provisions were good. He had hitherto objected to the plans of the advocates for parliamentary reform, because he thought them not calculated to effect their object, and tending to degrade rather than to improve the representation of the people. He should certainly vote for the motion.*

It was rejected, however, by 323 to 150 ; a preponderance by which, with little variation of relative numbers, the whole of the six Acts were passed. Throughout the controversy the Grenvillites aided ministers, and on one critical occasion Plunket's voice rallied many waverers and, it was believed, saved them from defeat. Lord Grey brooked ill being thwarted by any who had ever acted with him. He spoke angrily of the veteran statesman with whom he had so long been associated, and he was said to have written in offensive terms to a friend in Ireland of the conduct of Plunket. But the intervention of Lord Lansdowne, who had better temper than either, reconciled the differences, ere they had become public, between Plunket and Grey.†

The new year opened in political and social gloom. Industry sought in vain an adequate price for its produce ; labour failed to win enough of bread, and enterprise looked round with languid gaze. Political repression was beginning to bear fruit in seditious plots. Early in the winter Lord Sidmouth had information of designs to overthrow the Government by means of a sudden outbreak in the capital, to be responded to by armed risings in the manufacturing towns. The agencies of espionage were forthwith redoubled. The Home Office tightened the cords of rigour,

---

* Hansard, vol. xli. pp. 554–55, November 30th, 1819.

† Plunket to Sir John Newport, January 9th, 1821. Lansdowne to Plunket, January 24th, 1821.

and loosened the purse-strings of reward for the betrayal of crime. But perjury grew faster than prevention; and dark promises of discovery ended for the most part in discovering nothing. Late on the 29th of January the tolling of the great bell of St. Paul's announced that George III. had passed away. For eight years the Regent had exercised all the powers of royalty, and henceforth he would enjoy the long-coveted name. At the Privy Council on the morrow he appeared to be unwell, and ere he could be proclaimed, his physicians confessed themselves uneasy at symptoms of acute inflammation. Both Houses of Parliament assembled, according to law, for the purpose of taking the necessary oaths; and adjourned until after the royal funeral. For several days George IV. was thought to be in imminent danger; as if death, having mocked him with the gift of a crown, was lurking near to make away with it again. He had not yet, however, wasted wholly the natural strength of his constitution, and the malady yielded by degrees. His first act on being reassured of life was to desire the Premier to prepare without delay a bill of divorce against the Queen, and his next to command the Archbishop of Canterbury to omit the prayer for her in the Liturgy. Doctor Howley meekly complied: Lord Liverpool refused to obey. The King was wroth, and peremptory in the reiteration of his commands. The Cabinet met, adjourned and met again; submitted reasons as to the impolicy and deprecations of the scandal necessarily attendant on such a precipitate act: and finding expostulation fruitless they resigned. No set of public men could be found to take their place on condition of giving the pledge they had refused, and his Majesty, sore against his will, consented to the question being left in abeyance so long as the Queen should remain abroad. Lord Liverpool engaged, on the other hand, to institute parliamentary inquiry into her conduct if she should return to England. In the midst of these discussions Lord Sidmouth received warning that an attempt was maturing by a few desperate men upon the

lives of ministers. The sanguinary deed was to be perpetrated on the 23rd of February at Lord Harrowby's
house, where the Cabinet were to dine. The dinner was
postponed; Thistlewood and his gang were surrounded
at their rendezvous in Cato Street, and eventually brought
to trial, found guilty, and executed. Parliament was kept
together long enough to vote the new civil list; but men's
thoughts were busy with preparations everywhere for the
general election.

It was during the session of 1819 that Canning, in a
bantering speech against parliamentary reform, was betrayed
into the use of personalities which regard for the dignity of
debate and for his own high reputation would have equally
forbidden. They escaped at the time with a protest from
Lambton, which had little effect; but, stirring the wrath of
the Rota Club, where advanced Liberals like Douglas Kennaird,
Sir Robert Wilson, Burdett, and Bickersteth periodically
dined, it provoked a reply in the shape of a pamphlet which
attracted no little attention. Canning, whose foibles it
rudely exposed, ascribed it to the pen of Sir Philip Francis:
it was really from that of Hobhouse. Success tempted him
to try his hand again in reply to Lord Erskine, whose views
did not differ materially from those of Canning. He assailed
in unmeasured terms the whole system of representation as
it then existed; and asked the question, " What prevents
the people from marching to the House, pulling the members
out by the ears, locking the door and flinging the key into
the Thames? Knightsbridge Barracks!" This was brought
to the notice of the House by Mr. Courtney,* and after brief
debate was voted a false, scandalous, and seditious libel.
The publisher having given up the author, he was sent to
Newgate by ninety-eight to sixty-five votes.

Next to being a victor the best thing was to be a victim.
The Rota drank his health up-standing with all the honours;
and the Radical Committee were more proud than ever of
their man. Hobhouse received no end of visitors, and lived

* Afterwards Earl of Devon.

as well as usual on what he called the wrong side of Temple Bar.

George Lamb had not been able during the session of 1819 to allay the discontent of the Radicals in Westminster. He had voted sometimes with the Government, sometimes with his colleagues, and sometimes not at all. His speech in support of Burdett's motion for parliamentary reform was stigmatised as half-hearted, because he thought, as many earnest Liberals of the period did, that any general measure of change was then unattainable, and because he offered to vote for the gradual transfer of seats from boroughs found to be corrupt to populous counties and towns. Sir Francis, amid professions of personal regard, rated him for his Whig caution, and complained that his backing was akin to that ridiculed by Falstaff.

If we were all sure of attaining the age of Methuselah, we might, by possibility at least, hope to see some good effected in this manner before we died ; but in our circumscribed sphere of existence to entertain such a hope from such a source would be as absurd as for any parliamentary reformer to vote for a candidate who entertained such puerile ideas on the subject.*

Nor was the knotted lash of Cobbett sparingly laid upon him. Stoutly advocating the claims of the rival whom it was resolved to bring forward again, he revelled, as was usual with him, in alternate scolding and banter.

If you, electors, belong to that indecisive, vacillating class of mere wishers, mere grumblers, hair-splitters, and oppositionists, who are satisfied with representatives, who sit out a debate in silent admiration of the wax candles and the Speaker's wig, and finish with voting in a hopeless minority, —then indeed I shall not attempt to influence your choice. Take, if you please, this Mr. Lamb, this yearling of the flock which Tierney folds ; make him your pet, your House

* Address to the electors of Westminster, February 25th, 1820.

Lamb: but for your cause, gentlemen, if by that word I understand your property, your liberty, and your national character, I fear that in the hands of Mr. Lamb your cause will be lost mutton.

Meanwhile, Hobhouse lay in Newgate, whither he had been sent on a Speaker's warrant for a libel on the House of Commons. Brougham and others would have dissuaded George Lamb from offering himself again for Westminster; and he was not disinclined to follow their advice. Sir Robert Wilson on his behalf communicated with the local leaders early in February, disclaiming any wish to cause useless division, and intimating that the Whigs would stand by and look on if they could be sure that the Radicals would not abuse the concession by crowing over them. Service, who was prominent amongst them, readily accepted the proposal for his own part, and assured him he might depend on Place behaving handsomely. Hobhouse, whom Lamb had visited in prison, hoped to avoid a contest, and plied his adherents with suggestions to that end; amongst the rest, that one thousand signatures should be promptly obtained for a banquet to be given him on the day he was liberated by the dissolution. This he thought would have a decisive effect on the minds of the rest, of the constituency. Government, full of internal distraction and despondency little understood out of doors, renounced all thoughts of contesting Westminster; and certain of their friends signified their intention to support any moderate Liberal who might stand. In a family conclave at Melbourne House it was unwisely resolved to try the issue of another contest; and the constituency, being then far smaller than it is now, the first foot-fall of canvassing was speedily overheard by the watchful ears of rivalry. Hobhouse, from his not unendurable dungeon in the City, wrote to his friend at Charing Cross :—

George Lamb positively starts; some Whigs have made efforts to prevent him, but he will try. I do not think that anything public should be done yet. The later the canvassing is delayed the better for us; it will be in our favour if we wait until all the great folks are out of town,* as they must be speedily in their various counties.

After another fortnight of preparation the addresses of the three candidates appeared; and as William Lamb's return for Hertfordshire was not to be opposed, he devoted himself for some weeks to the Westminster election.

On the 9th of March the contest began. G. Lamb was accompanied to the hustings by his brother, and was nominated by Mr. Wishart, and seconded by Mr. Evans, of Pall Mall, both supporters of Romilly and Burdett. He offered his hand to Hobhouse, who took it cordially, but he wholly failed to gain a hearing. The multitude were all for Hobhouse and Burdett, and rapturously cheered their liberated champion. Hobhouse complained that G. Lamb had upbraided him with the publication for which he had been incarcerated, and reproached him with having had in 1819 the support of those who voted against Sir S. Romilly and for Sir Murray Maxwell. He therefore called him the ministerial candidate. This justified him in opposing one who had shown no active sympathy with the cause of the people. He acknowledged that his rival had visited him in Newgate, then why should he reproach him with the sentiments for uttering which he had been sent thither? George Lamb justified himself by saying that sympathy for a friend whose political indiscretion had brought him into trouble was not inconsistent with reprobation of language all reasonable men condemned. He was not afraid to stand by an honourable man even when he thought him in the wrong; but he did not expect to find his having done so made the occasion of a taunt.

While the event was pending, Sir Francis was compelled to attend the assizes of Leicester, as defendant in the trial of an *ex officio* information filed by the Attorney-General against him for a seditious libel on the Government re-

* Letter from J. C. Hobhouse, February 11th, 1820.

garding the Manchester massacre. Sir W. D. Best tried
the case; and the jury, under his direction, found for the
Crown. The issue of the Westminster election five days
after was taken as the popular reversal of the verdict, and
Sir Francis was more the idol of the multitude than ever.
When the conviction at Leicester was known in town, a
placard appeared in these terms:—

Electors of Westminster, Burdett has been convicted.
Hasten to the poll, and show by your votes how you love
and venerate him.

The *Morning Post* observed that as probation in a jail
was evidently preferred to probation in parliament, and as
conviction of a crime was sufficient warranty for Westminster suffrages, to have two convicted libellers at once
was evidently a great "hit,"—and the chance of having one
out of prison at a time might add much to the perfection
of Radical representation.

The friends of Government stood aloof generally, only a
few, from personal regard, recording their votes. Burdett
was returned by 5327, Hobhouse by 4882, while Lamb
polled but 4436 votes. George Lamb, however, did not long
remain without a seat, being returned for Dungarvan, then
a close borough of the Duke of Devonshire's, in the room of
Captain (afterwards Sir Augustus) Clifford, who had been
appointed to a frigate under orders for the Mediterranean.
Whatever ill-humour the Westminster contest occasioned,
the rival candidates did not quarrel, and Hobhouse continued
to visit at Melbourne House as before.

Government were thought to have rather gained strength
by the new elections; and Castlereagh continued still to
lead the Commons; while Opposition lost soon afterwards
by the death of Grattan, one of its most venerated chiefs.
The first session of the new Parliament proved singularly
barren of good fruit. Sir J. Mackintosh, on whom Romilly's
legislative mantle had descended, succeeded in carrying two
bills abolishing capital punishment for a number of minor

offences,* notwithstanding the fears of Lord Eldon that small tradesmen would be ruined if shoplifters to the value of five shillings were not hanged. But the peers, by his advice, rejected the mitigation of punishment in the case of poachers, who blackened their faces at night; and Lamb found with regret that other humane clauses, in which he had supported his friend, must be abandoned.

Public attention unhappily reverted to the liturgical scandal caused by omitting the name of the Queen. Conjecture was busy as to the course she would pursue; and many who pitied the misfortunes of her early wedded life, and who would fain have saved her from exposure and ignominy, advised that she should be left the undisputed possession of her rank, and given an allowance sufficient to maintain it, with a view to her residing permanently abroad. But the reckless and lawless omission of her name in the service of the Church was an insult hard to bear; and the orders sent to ambassadors at foreign courts to disown her claim as Queen Consort, and to deprecate her recognition by the Governments to which they were accredited, filled the cup of provocation to the brim. The rights and privileges of a Queen Consort had long been established and defined; and that which had been hitherto observed as an assurance the most solemn of her dignity as Princess of Wales was the coupling her name in the Book of Common Prayer with that of her husband. While his father lived, this had been uniformly done.

Very properly, says Lord Campbell, it was directed that Caroline should no longer be prayed for as Princess of Wales, and very improperly that a new form of prayer for the Royal family should be used from which her name was entirely excluded.

It was worse than idle to argue that in the sovereign, as temporal head of the Church, is vested a discretion, for the

* 4th June, 1820.

use of which he cannot be called in question. Irresponsibility might with equal freedom, but with equal folly, be pleaded for his sending *congé d'élire* to a dean and chapter to nominate a dotard or blasphemer bishop of their diocese; or for any other act of arbitrary caprice tending to subvert the ecclesiastical system established by law. A constitutional monarch does not so trifle with his prerogatives. He knows that they are public trusts, not personal privileges; and that to be preserved, they must be exercised not only with decorum, but in the spirit of exalted equity. To bid the nation on its knees, brand with scorn an absent woman, unconvicted by law of any crime, and against whom no charge had ever been preferred in any public tribunal, was not only immoral, because ruthless and vindictive, but unconstitutional in the highest degree, as condemning the desolate and oppressed unheard. A secret commission to gather evidence of the Queen's alleged misconduct had in the preceding year been sent to Milan, and such of the Cabinet as had perused its report might feel persuaded of her guilt. Canning refused to break the seal of the copy sent to him, and returned it, saying—

He would not give any countenance to the notion that he acquiesced in a procedure he so thoroughly condemned. Let her be impeached of treason, if treason could be proved. Let her be put away publicly by the highest court of the realm, as one who had forfeited her right to share the throne. But until convicted and condemned, she was entitled, like every other subject of the realm, to be deemed innocent; and to prejudge her cause by royal authority was to insult a defenceless woman, to violate the first fundamental principles of law, and seriously to compromise the Crown.

Unhappily for George IV., Canning stood alone; and finding his position in the Cabinet untenable, he resigned the Board of Control. Beside the members of Opposition, many independent supporters, like Lord Wellesley and Mr. Ward, shared these views, and in a short time the current of public opinion set in strongly in the same direction. Before leaving Italy, Queen Caroline appointed Mr. Brougham and Mr. Denman her Attorney and Solicitor General; and made known through various channels her resolution to return to England. Thenceforth his Majesty would listen to no sound advice. In common with nearly all his friends, both Whig and Tory, Lamb deplored the infatuation of the King and the evils which it was too obvious would ensue from a public trial. Few were less disposed than he was to wound the pride of the new monarch, or to yield to what he felt to be popular illusions as to the character and conduct of his wife. Living in the circle where all she said and did from the time of her marriage was known, he paid little regard to the plausible extenuations of her reckless and unseemly behaviour. But he had no confidence that, once embarked in a judicial investigation so unusual, and for which Parliament was so ill qualified, justice would really be done. Bills of divorce were, after all, in his opinion, clumsy and coarse expedients for releasing injured parties from an intolerable bondage. They had grown into use in comparatively modern days; and the practice, even where the public in general hardly listened or looked on, and something of the proprieties of a high court of equity were observed, was not free from serious objection. Sometimes peers who had heard but half the case voted on the third reading of a divorce bill. Sometimes the decision was practically left to the Chancellor and the other law lords. But the Commons, obeying with singular forbearance a wise instinct of justice, had almost invariably abstained from discussing the merits of such bills. His mind revolted at the prospect of the opposite course being pursued, as it would be inevitably, were a measure introduced to dissolve the royal marriage. Even in the Upper House, it would be impossible, under the circumstances, to dissuade the great body of the peers from voting; and the scenes that were likely to occur in the Lower House filled his imagination with disgust and dismay.

He had many an anxious conference on the subject with Brougham, who was a constant visitor at the house of his younger brother. Lord Ellenborough had desired her Majesty's Attorney-General, on the first day of Easter Term, to take the precedence to which he was officially entitled in Court; and his friends were delighted for his sake at the professional prominence the otherwise valueless distinction gave him. But they were not without fears that his besetting love of notoriety might blind him to some of the worst consequences of the struggle that seemed impending. With his energy, versatility, and eloquence, to lead in a suit between King and Queen in the High Court of Parliament, with the nation for an audience, was a temptation hardly possible to resist; yet Lamb, who understood him well, and saw him daily, always acquitted him of blame in the transaction; and though part of his conduct remained unaccounted for, no one ever accused him of misusing his influence to draw the unhappy Princess needlessly or hastily into the struggle. She did not, indeed, disguise at first her misgivings of the thoroughness of his devotion to her cause. She considered him to incline, in point of fact, too much towards compromise; and she would have superseded him in favour of Sir James Scarlett, had he been willing to accept the charge.

Great efforts were made to dissuade her from returning to England; and at one time it was hoped that they might prove successful. On the indiscreet persons about her, who naturally wished to exchange the insignificance of a fourth-rate household at Rome, for the luxury and splendour of an English Court, was laid the blame of her ultimate decision. But her Majesty was not in reality swayed by them, or by any feeling or opinions save her own. Impulsive, vain, ill-educated, and unscrupulous—the best advisers would probably have failed to turn the most wilful of women from her purpose. She had cleverness enough to know that she could make herself intolerable, if not formidable, to the husband who had deserted, wronged, and insulted her. She sought reparation for private injuries, revenge for public affronts; and the opportunity had come. In her six years' exile she had outlived all remains of self-respect, and shrunk not therefore from discussions fraught with indelicacy and shame. Even before quitting England in 1814, she had ceased to be regarded with respect by those of her court whose consideration was best worth having; and all that had been told of her by general rumour since tended still further to lower her in estimation. On landing at Dover, early in June, she was saluted, it was said, through mistake, by the guard; and she was greeted with enthusiastic cheers by the crowds awaiting her from far and near. In a womanly and courageous appeal to the nation, without a word of reflection on her husband, she called for justice and demanded the recognition of her rights. Her progress was a series of triumphs, and the middle and working classes in London received her with rapturous welcome. The rage of George IV. could hardly be controlled. He went in state the same day to Westminster, and upon retiring sent a message to both Houses directing inquiries to be made forthwith touching the conduct of the Queen. The evidence had been long preparing, and, in a sealed bag, was laid on the table of the Upper House by Lord Liverpool, on that of the Lower House by Lord Castlereagh. The Lords adjourned in silence till the morrow. The anger of the Commons burst into a flame not to be extinguished for several months to come.

Who and what was her accuser? The question was paramount to all others in the popular mind, and troubled, above all others, the legal advisers of her adversary. The right of recrimination had always been admitted in proceedings for divorce; and to set up a new and exceptional practice at variance with established law, would, it was felt, destroy all semblance of consistent justice. Technically, the Chancellor satisfied himself that a distinction might be drawn sufficiently plain to warrant a refusal of proof that his Majesty's conduct disentitled him to relief from the nuptial tie. Ordinary bills for dissolution of marriage were always founded on the petition of the party complaining, who was treated throughout as a plaintiff in a suit. In that capacity he was liable to retaliation; and if his hands were not clean he was refused redress. But the King had not petitioned, could not therefore be called a plaintiff, and was not consequently liable to counter charges. Infidelity by a queen consort was by old statute-law high treason; but it could not be alleged that any corresponding crime could be committed against the state by a King; and therefore the analogy failed.* These specious distinctions might satisfy a majority of the Upper House; but who would guarantee that the fundamental principles of criminal equity would be put in abeyance, out of regard to distinctions so special and formal, by a majority of the House of Commons? Lord Essex used to tell how George III., about to mount his horse for a morning ride, noticed that the heir apparent, whom he desired to accompany him and who stood uncovered by his side, wore a wig, and he asked sharply why he did so; the Prince replied "that he found himself subject to take cold, and that he had been advised by his physician to take this precaution." His Majesty turned to the lord-in-waiting, and said, "A lie ever ready when it's wanted." And if once the controversy were opened, who would set limits to the suggestions and imputations likely to be made? The dissolute life led by George IV. subsequently to his marriage was simply notorious; he had never taken any pains to conceal his excesses of any kind; and there lay in ambush, hardly concealed, a charge against him which, if brought forward publicly in debate, could not there be set at rest, and which directly affected the validity of his title to the crown. He was said to have previously married Mrs. Fitzherbert, and she was still alive. Relying on his solemn word of honour, Charles Fox had undertaken to deny the fact; but finding that he had been duped, he addressed to the Prince reproaches without precedent or parallel in the history of scorn; and

* Private letter of Lord Eldon to his brother, September 1820.

when Lord Grey was asked to patch up matters by saying something in Parliament about misapprehension of meaning on the part of Fox, he peremptorily refused. The documents connected with the transaction remain to this day in a box which cannot be opened without the consent of parties never likely to agree in the breaking of the seals.

From the day that, to obtain a grant to pay debts, the denial referred to was given to Parliament, distrust of the royal veracity never could be stilled. It came at length to be regarded by courtiers and statesmen as a matter which it was idle to discuss; and anecdotes innumerable were told illustrating the universality of the impression. When Regent, he once called on Lady Spencer to ask her to do him a great service. He wished her to choose a person of attainments and accomplishments to be governess to the Princess Charlotte. Above all things, he desired that the lady should teach his daughter always to tell the truth. Lady Spencer betrayed by the expression of her features what was passing in her mind. On which his Royal Highness observed, " You know I don't speak the truth, and my brothers don't, and I find it a great defect, from which I would have my daughter free. We have been always brought up badly; the Queen having taught us to equivocate; and I want you to help me in the matter."

Negotiations for a compromise, conducted by the Duke of Wellington and Lord Castlereagh on one side, by Mr. Brougham and Mr. Denman on the other, led to nothing. Queen Caroline would have consented to live abroad if her regal station were recognised by the Austrian or Sardinian Government at the instance of our own, and if her name were restored in the Liturgy. The King refused; and the proceedings in both Houses were resumed. Mr. Wilberforce made a despairing attempt to induce the Queen to waive her pretensions, and confide implicitly in the honour and discretion of Parliament. An address to this effect was carried against the Opposition; Althorp, Brougham, Duncannon, J. Russell, Mackintosh, Whitbread, Scarlett, Graham, Tierney,

Denman, and W. Lamb voting in the minority.   George
Lamb did not vote.   As this was hardly a question on which
difference of opinion among persons on the same side might
not be reasonably entertained, it was regarded as decisive of
the course which each individual who voted had made up his
mind to take in the controversy.   On the 3rd of July a
select committee of the Lords reported that a *primâ facie*
case had been established against the Queen ; and on the
following day Lord Liverpool introduced a bill of pains and
penalties depriving her of the title, prerogative, rights, and
privileges of Queen Consort ; and declaring that her marriage should be dissolved.   Discussions on the mode of procedure, examination of witnesses, and arguments of counsel
occupied many weeks, to the great detriment of public morals,
and serious damage to the authority and reputation of
Government.   At length, on the 6th of November, after, a
debate of four days, the second reading was carried by 123 to
95 ; ministers and other holders of office at the will of the
prosecutor voting in the majority, and more than sixty of
their usual supporters declining to give it their support.

Public impatience overflowed at the announcement that,
after a decision which was virtually equivalent to defeat,
the bill was to be passed through a committee without a
day's delay.   The conscience of Lord Liverpool staggered
beneath its burthen ; and he suffered this further stage to
be completed before attempting to make a stand.   But in
the Cabinet, on the evening of the 9th, he proposed that
the bill should be withdrawn.   Lord Eldon stoutly resisted
its abandonment, and sharp words were exchanged between
the Chancellor and the Premier.   By way of compromise it
was resolved to feel again the temper of the House ; and to
move the third reading on the following day.   An exciting
debate was concluded by a speech of the Duke of Bedford,
who declared upon his honour that he believed the Queen
had falsely been accused.   The majority of one hundred and
twenty-three was found to have dwindled to one hundred
and eight, and the minority to have increased to ninety-

nine. It was clear that to send such a bill to the Commons, disowned by more than half the unsalaried peers who had voted, would be vain; and it was therefore withdrawn.

In the final division nearly all the friends and relatives of Lamb were told against the prosecution of the Queen. Devonshire and Bedford, Egremont and Spencer, Besborough and Fitzwilliam, Lansdowne and Grey, Holland and Cowper, contributed to secure the only result which in the existing state of national feeling was desirable or safe. In the great reputation won by Brougham during the protracted trial Lamb heartily rejoiced; for he admired intensely the self-reliant courage, untiring energy and inexhaustible versatility, of the man; nor could his keen perception of his volatility, or distrust of his overweening egotism, quench the sympathy he felt for one in whose company he took infinite pleasure, and even in controversy with whom he felt his own powers quickened into a higher life. It was at this period that the great intimacy began, which continued so many years uninterrupted, and the kindly memories of which no mere political breach could obliterate. Yet he was glad that the name he expected some day to inherit was not recorded among those who by their votes condemned the conduct of the King. At seventy-five, it could not be expected that Lord Melbourne should endure the excitement and exhaustion of sitting as a judge for thirty consecutive days on a state trial. With what feelings the old man learned the progress of the affair, it were worse than vain to surmise. Although he had retired from his place in the household, it was impossible for him to forget the confidence so long reposed in him. Beneath a tranquil bearing and impassive mien, one can well believe there ebbed and flowed memories of bygone days ill suited to the equanimity of mind becoming a juror in a suit brought by his sovereign. For once, infirmity and age were felt to be beneficent; for they exonerated him obviously, in the eyes of himself and of all others, from the duty of forming or pronouncing judgment. He had known

George IV. too early and too well, and yet he had received unnumbered marks of favour from him, the last being the coronet he wore. Upwards of one hundred and sixty peers shunned the scene of shame; assigning as varied pretexts as the unworthy guests in the Gospel who when bidden would not come. But with the venerable recluse at Brocket it was not necessary to make excuse; for enfeebled strength was too deeply written on his brow. And all who loved or cared for him rejoiced that he should be left undisturbed in his tranquillity.

Not so easy or so clear seemed to be the course which the subject of these memoirs had to pursue. Thinking as he did of the conduct of the unhappy Queen, and regarding as blind infatuation the fervour of popular passion on her behalf, he felt daily more and more the humiliation which Parliament and the country had been subjected to by her. He believed that indignation at the way in which she had been treated by her husband during fourteen years of provocation, was at the bottom of the hatred and fury manifested by all ranks in her defence. A man who could so illuse and insult his wife had no chance of a fair hearing from the people, whatever her frailties might be. The question was not, was she true, but, was he not false? Notwithstanding the imputations which every hour were publicly reiterated in the Government orders, she had the ineffable folly to bring in her carriage with her to the House of Lords the boy whom she said she had adopted, but about whom no satisfactory account could be given; and the mob shouted as she passed, "God bless your Majesty and your innocent child." Blatant absurdity was but the vulgar echo of more decorous and grave incoherency. It was, and could not but be, lamentable in the eyes of sensitive and honourable men. On the other hand, was it compatible with public courage or with public duty to stand aside on the plea of mere disgust? All the resources of espionage and menace, of vilipending and invective, of party organisation and Court influence, had been tried, and they had failed. The Bill of Pains and Penalties was abandoned in despair. A worthless, wayward, and as her own counsel believed, demented woman was become the darling of the populace, the balcony idol of a turbulent faction, and the heroine of millions of honest folk who knew but half the truth. Her partisans gave out that she intended to insist on being crowned in Westminster Abbey along with her loving lord. What she might attempt or do neither she or anybody else could tell. It was only clear that her name was a signal and her presence an incentive to mischief and confusion. With very few exceptions, women of rank and station could not be induced to visit her. She resented bitterly their abstention, and had even thoughts, it was said, of displacing Lord and Lady Hood, who had unflinchingly adhered to her throughout the trial, with a view to identify her cause more distinctively with the classes that had welcomed her. The prospect was dismal in the extreme, for all who wished a speedy end of disreputable controversy and the return of national attention to healthful and useful subjects of consideration.

Parliament adjourned for the Christmas recess, and ere it met again Lamb was one of many who had made up their minds that, under all the circumstances, the best policy lay in seeking to assuage every reasonable cause of irritation, and at the same time encouraging the Government to provide a liberal establishment for the Queen. Without ostensible grievance, it was hoped that the frenzy of the hour would cool, and that people would grow tired of her melodramatic cravings for applause. Appeals, public and private, were made to ministers to correct the initiatory error they had committed in the preceding year. On the 26th of January the member for Herts voted in a minority of 209 against 310 upon Lord Archibald Hamilton's motion for the restoration of the Queen's name to the Liturgy; on the 13th of February he was one of 178 who divided against 298 on the motion of Mr Smith of Norwich to the same effect; and on Lord Tavistock's subsequent resolution condemnatory of ministers for the course they had pursued, he voted with the same number against 324.

George IV. did not dissemble his anger at these re-iterated protests against his implacability. Folkestone and Althorp, Milton and Burdett did not surprise him ; but he was mortified at the votes of Cavendish, and vexed with those of Lamb. It was manifestly not the interest of the Whigs to rekindle his resentment. He made no secret of his discontent with Lord Liverpool, whose place he had more than once offered in vain to Castlereagh. They had begun to estimate the chances of a break-up in the administration, and to reconcile personal differences that might stand in their way if called upon to take the government ;* and politicians long excluded from power are seldom given to reprimanding the personal errors of the Court. Did their pertinacity in asserting their opinions in this affair of the Liturgy turn the scale of royal pique once more in favour of their rivals ? We know not, and probably will never know. It is only certain that ministers held on, in spite of their unpopularity, without any change, while the Queen lived ; that what was called a policy of conciliation was devised for Ireland, to be inaugurated by a royal visit, and carried into effect by Lord Wellesley's appointment as Viceroy, with Plunket for Attorney-General ; that Canning was at any price to be sent beyond sea ; and that Grey and his friends were to be shown his Majesty could do without them.

* Lansdowne to Plunket, January 24th, 1821.

CHAPTER IX.

*George IV. and the Whigs—Plunket's plea for religious liberty—
Lambton's motion for reform—Catholic Peers Bill—Death of
Castlereagh—Canning leader at last—Advice to Ward—Literary
friends.*

GRATTAN on his death-bed had bequeathed the charge of the
Catholic question to the most faithful and eloquent of his
disciples; and for its sake had bidden his son forgive, even
as he had forgiven, the greatest of his former foes.   Plunket
and Cartlereagh mourned alike his loss; and promised one
another to persist in the assertion of his principles of
religious liberty unto the end.   And to the end both kept
their word.

Early in the session Plunket, as Attorney-General for
Ireland, brought in the Relief Bill in a shape somewhat
different from that of former years, but in all essential
points the same; and on the second reading spoke as even
he had never spoken before.   Peel, who as leader of the
party of resistance had to reply, told Henry Bulwer many
years afterwards, that it was the finest speech he ever
heard.   Canning, over-sanguine, heard in it the trumpet
note of approaching triumph.   Mackintosh went home to
dream that he had heard Demosthenes.   Lamb's delight was
unspeakable.   Thenceforth Plunket's opinion had greater
weight with him on Irish affairs than that of any other man;
and to this must in some degree be ascribed the deflection of

M 2

his course from the straight and narrow way of Whiggery
for several ensuing years.

A motion of Mr. Lambton for reform was defeated by
a chance division of 55 to 43, there not being sufficient
speakers to carry the debate over the dinner hour.   On
the 9th of May a like accident was guarded against, and
the discussion was worthier of the cause.   Still there was no
general belief that organic change had approached the period
of ripening into legislative fruit.   On both sides there was
an evident disposition to generalise or speculate ; and when
Hobhouse had exhausted the stock arguments for household
suffrage, large constituencies, and short parliaments, no one
on the ministerial side took the trouble to reply, and the
debate would have died out had not the member for Herts
risen to express his dissent from certain of the doctrines of
his more advanced friend.   Like most of the Whigs who
leaned to Mr. Canning, he was disposed to deprecate making
reform a party question until religious liberty had been
achieved. He regarded, moreover, the extreme demands made
universally by popular assemblies at the time as wholly
impracticable, and calculated to harden the heart of resistance
against those measures of progress which began to look
attainable.   Ward's letters to Bishop Copleston at this
period described the uneasiness and despondency of the
moderate party in Parliament at the advocacy by men like
Lord Althorp, Mr. Lambton, Dr. Lushington, and Lord J.
Russell of comprehensive changes in the representation.
Mackintosh and Brougham would have been content to
leave many of the nomination boroughs untouched, and to
transfer seats to large towns from small places wherein from
time to time corruption might be proved on petition.   Had
the alternative of a new suffrage been left to the Liberal
opposition to decide, a great preponderance would have
ruled for twenty rather than ten pounds a year.   Lamb's
reply to Hobhouse touched skilfully the chords of this state
of feeling, and its success as a speech was long remembered.

It is easy, of course, to turn the telescope of experience
the wrong way, and call such improvements on the oligar-

chical system of representation then existing, diminutive
and dwarfish.   Why did not men who ten years later were
fain to force the passing of Schedule A. even at the risk of
convulsion, see beforehand what was coming, and boldly
anticipate the duty of wholesale redistribution ?   The answer
is plain and unanswerable.   The mob in Covent Garden
were ready for radical reform, but the mass of the community
were not ; and to force its adoption therefore by Parliament
would have been wrong had it been seriously contemplated.
The discussion of thorough-going theories with half-empty
benches at St. Stephen's was an easy way of acquiring
popularity ; and it helped, no doubt, gradually to educate
opinion.   But the minority, if taken at their word, must have
been driven to own that the changes they advocated could
in 1821 have only been imposed by the legislative will of
an insignificant minority, by dint of threats of physical force.
Looking back at things as they eventually fell out, who will
now hesitate to confess that it was better for the permanent
peace and welfare of the nation that opinion in favour of
electoral reform was allowed to ripen slowly and steadily,
instead of being prematurely snatched at and flung into the
wine-press of revolution ?

Lord Wellesley had demanded power to suspend the
Habeas Corpus Act, and the passing of the Insurrection
Bill.   Lord Folkestone opposed going into committee, as did
Spring Rice.   Lamb had such confidence in the Lord Lieu-
tenant, whom he warmly panegyrised, and generally in the
Government declaration of their policy, that he supported the
bills. So did Sir J. Newport, Mr. Calcraft, and Colonel Davies.
George Lamb voted, 25th April, 1822, for Lord J. Russell's
motion in favour of parliamentary reform.   William Lamb
neither voted or paired.

As a minimum of concession Canning, on the 30th April,
moved for leave to bring in a bill to enable Roman Catholic
peers to sit and vote in Parliament. His elaborate speech on
the occasion was listened to with feelings of mingled delight
and sadness by Huskisson and Lamb and many more, who

had reason to regard it as a farewell offering on a shrine where the high-priest of their political faith and hope was but too likely to minister no more. Contrary to the usual practice, even at this preliminary stage the proposal encountered vehement opposition, and the first reading was carried in a House of near five hundred members by a majority of only five. On the 10th of May the second reading was peremptorily opposed by Mr. Secretary Peel, who deprecated earnestly the success of the bill in proportion to the probability of the success of the general measure of emancipation. Lord Londonderry supported the concession, and it was carried by a majority of · twelve. The Duke of Portland moved the second reading in the Upper House. Lords Erskine, Grey, Grenville and Holland supported, Lords Colchester and Eldon opposed. The measure was lost by 171 to 129, including proxies; and the disheartened friends of toleration learned that its distinguished author was about to quit the scene of his ineffectual struggles, for the Golden East. The Directors of the East India Company had chosen Canning for their next Governor-General, and the Government, too glad to be relieved of his presence in Parliament, with effusion ratified their choice. His small but brilliant staff of adherents was disbanded, and at the end of the session he went to take leave of his constituents at Liverpool.

On the day after the prorogation, Lord Melbourne entertained at Whitehall a distinguished party, at what the Court Newsman designated "a grand turtle dinner." It was the last of the banquets given during the season to please Lady Caroline and Mrs. George Lamb, rather than to gratify any lingering fancy of the aged host for luxurious display. A few days after, Lady Holland made it a point that the familiar circle should once more meet around her table, before the world went out of town ; and so it happened that they had not separated for the autumn, when tidings of a deplorable event became known, which it was felt by all must inevitably lead to consequences of the greatest moment. The minister who for ten trying years had led the House of Commons and guided the foreign policy of the empire, in a paroxysm of mental aberration had fallen by his own hand. Nothing else was thought or spoken of for many days. Irrespective of party, Lord Londonderry had many attached friends; and a still more numerous circle who admired his courage and equanimity in public life, and delighted in his amenity, gentleness, and absolute freedom from affectation or pretension in private intercourse. The intrepid champion of reactionary views abroad and at home, he had long been pre-eminently hated and feared by the friends of constitutional progress; but no provocation could ruffle his parliamentary temper, and no threat of revolution bend or break his resolve that England should adhere to the policy agreed upon at the Congress of Vienna. Personally, few men exercised a greater power to charm, when he had time to be at the trouble; and in the interchange of courtesies and hospitalities he seemed wholly unconscious of the prejudices arising from differences of opinion. Without eloquence or wit, he possessed extraordinary influence in Parliament, and retained to the last the friendship of not a few opponents, and the affection of every friend who had known or trusted him. To Lamb he had invariably shown kindness and consideration; and it seemed but yesterday that they had parted at Westminister with mutual expressions of good-will, signifying little at the time, but recalled by the survivor in a deep sense of melancholy. The unchecked ebullition of satisfaction with which the deplorable event was received out of doors moved him only with a shudder of disgust, and made him all the more outspoken in paradoxical apology for faults, and exaggerated praise of good qualities.

In the funeral cortege which followed Londonderry's remains to the Abbey were the carriages of Lords Sydney, Melbourne, and Listowel, with those of many of his political friends. But popular hatred was too much concentrated upon one object to distinguish whose liveries were there. It was a dreadful scene, the passionate and implacable rage, such as before or since has not desecrated the portal of the cathedral. In Jerusalem Chamber assembled many who had served under the deceased statesman, some whom he had promoted, others whom he had befriended, in order to pay the last tribute of respect; and there were gathered also, Lords Grenville, Althorp, Bective and Gower, Alexander Baring, Sir Walter Stirling, and William Lamb. It was not possible that his mind should not turn to the imminent consequences of an event so startling; and he shared the curiosity of the Duke of Devonshire, whom he saw on his way through town from Paris, and of Lord Holland as to what would happen to Canning and what he would do.

While staying at Seaforth, the residence of Mr. John Gladstone, one of his influential supporters at Liverpool the disappointed statesman under sentence of viceregal banishment, received the tidings that the rival who had so long held the Foreign Office against him was no more. "Not gone yet," was the irrepressible thought of every friend of Canning, who was tardily preparing for exile. George IV. received the news at Edinburgh when about to commence a royal progress through Scotland. Instinctively he drew the same inference as they had done; and wrote urgently to the Premier that no steps should be taken with regard to the vacant post until he should have an opportunity of conferring personally with him. In point of form Lord Liverpool obeyed the interdict; but he needed no time to consider what must be done. The Duke of Wellington without hesitation arrived at a similar conclusion, that in the Foreign Office Canning was now inevitable. The Congress of Verona was to meet in October, and England had agreed to be represented there. Some of the last official papers which the deceased minister had taken with him to his seat at North Cray related to the proposals about to be submitted by Russia to the Privy Council of Europe for the more effectual suppression of representative aspirations in Italy and Spain. What he had meditated saying or doing at the approaching conclave was still to a certain extent doubtful; but having long had the conduct of English diplomacy completely in his hands, his colleagues had grown accustomed to rely mainly on his judgment, and the King on his disposition. Now all was changed; and the man whom the Court and Cabinet regarded with misgiving, must be the builder if not the architect of a new foreign policy, unless indeed they could make with him beforehand reassuring terms. But how and by whom was this to be done? Canning was too subtle and astute to squabble about the length of the reins or the colour of the ribbons to be placed at first on the horses' heads. Give him only the power, and he would use it as opportunity served. It was not till after a long interview on the 11th of September that his old and attached friend Lord Liverpool shook him by the hand cordially and congratulated him on renouncing the governorship of India, to be Secretary of State and leader of the House of Commons. How greatly this event was to influence the career of the subject of this biography he himself assuredly did not know.

Various and opposite were the feelings which Canning's sudden change of fortune caused in the ranks of the Opposition. Hobhouse and Lambton and nearly all the extreme men of the party had been congratulating themselves that they should hear his merciless jeers at their expense no more. Plunket and Lamb and most of the moderate Liberals were glad, on the contrary, that he should remain. Canning offered the third under-secretaryship (then incompatible with a seat in Parliament) to Lord Binning; and on his declining, to Mr. Ward, who consulted everybody he knew on the subject, and for more than a fortnight could not make up his mind what to do. His father was all against it, unwilling to forego the fond expectation that he would one day cut a great figure in Parliament. Copleston, who knew his weakness best, and grieved to see his fine understanding slowly drifting to ruin for want of active occupation which might compel him to cease thinking of his real or imaginary ailments, urged him to accept. Tierney said he ought to refuse, because he hated Canning, and because to his mind, wounded and worn with pecuniary embarrassments incurred in a long struggle to keep his position, the notion seemed absurd of a young man with vast expectations relinquishing his seat to drudge in an office at fifteen hundred a year. William Lamb wrote from Panshanger :

> I received your letter this morning alone, destroyed it as soon as I had read it, and have considered its contents as I rode over here from Brocket; and upon the whole, putting myself in your place, I have little doubt that you should accept the offer. It is one of the pleasantest places under Government—necessarily gives an insight into all that is going on, and would be rendered to you particularly agreeable by your cordial agreement and intimacy with your principal—add to this that it would have the effect of supporting and assisting Canning at this moment —that it might lead to more—that it would give you what you want in occupation and employment—and that, without flattering your abilities and knowledge of the world at home and abroad, it might enable you to be of essential service to the ministry and the country. These are considerations sufficient, in my mind, to induce you to accept; at the same time do not take it unless you can make up your mind, in the first place, to bear every species of abuse and misrepresentation, and the imputation of the most sordid and interested motives; in the second place, to go through with it if you undertake it, and not to be dispirited by any difficulties or annoyances which you may find in the office, and which you may depend upon it no office is free from. I write in a great hurry, and with a bad pen, but if you can read it you will understand me as well as if I had written three times as much.   Yours very sincerely, W. LAMB.*

From day to day the mind of the hypochondriac oscillated

* To the Hon. J. W. Ward from Panshanger, September 29th, 1822.

between conflicting doubts as to what people would think, and as to what he ought to think himself of the proposal. It ended in his refusing, and the post was offered to Frederick Lamb, whom he describes as just of his own age, but his superior in talents. He likewise declined, whereupon Canning, desirous of pleasing the King, appointed Lord Francis Conyngham.

Lady Caroline cared little for politics for their own sake ; but she liked celebrities of every sort, and politicians amongst the rest. Youth and age, wealth and poverty were of small account with her, and in her drawing-room were to be met critics and poets, philosophers and dramatists, promising wits from Cambridge, and veteran book-makers from the Row. She had made the acquaintance of Godwin soon after her ineffectual effort to get his vote for George Lamb at Westminster. He made himself agreeable, and she was delighted with the eccentricity of his opinions. Her husband had read without being much struck by his ' Theory of Political Justice' ; of ' Caleb Williams ' and ' St. Leon ' he thought more highly. Hobhouse considered him a bore ; but the son of an old friend in Herts, fresh from the University, and with his head full of Bond Street and Lord Byron, asked as a special favour that her ladyship would present him to the father of Mary Wollstonecraft, whose art as a novelist filled him, as the style of Hume did Gibbon, " with admiration and despair." The name of the youth was Edward Lytton Bulwer. In a letter without date, but evidently about this period, she wrote :

My brother, William Ponsonby, is so much delighted with the two books you left with me, and I am so enchanted with the letter of advice to the young American, that we both request you to send us a list of all your publications for the use of young people. Send also to St. James' Square, Hon. William Ponsonby, ' The Advice to the American,' ' A Roman History,' and ' The Pantheon.' I forget my brother's number, but it is next door to the Duke of St.

Albans'. Mr. Lytton Bulwer, a very young man and an enthusiast, wishes to be introduuced to you. He is taking his degree at Cambridge; on his return pray let me make him acquainted with you. I shall claim your promise of coming to Brocket; would your daughter or son accompany you? Hobhouse came to me last night; how strange it is I love Lord Byron so much now in my old age, in despite of all he is said to have said; and I also love Hobhouse because he so warmly takes his part. Pray write to me, for you see your advice has had some effect. I have been studying your little books with an ardour and a pleasure which would surprise you; but what has vexed me is that the two children and four young women to whom I endeavoured to read them, did not choose to attend. . . . After all, what is the use of anything here below, but to be enlightened and try to make others happy? From this day I will endeavour to conquer all my violence, all my passions; but you are destined to be my master. The only thing that checks my ardour is this: For what purpose, for whom should I endeavour to grow wise? What is the use of anything? What is the end of life? When we die, what difference is there here between a black-beetle and me? . . . The only thoughts that ever can make me lose my senses are these,—A want of knowledge as to what is really true— A certainty that I am useless—A fear that I am worthless —A belief that all is vanity and vexation of spirit, and that there is nothing new under the sun. The only prayer I ever say besides the sinner's, and the only life I shall ever leave written.

William Ponsonby—who was nearest to her in age of her brothers, and, throughout her wanderings and troubles, was ever ready to listen patiently to her complainings and to turn aside gently the querulous and fitful thoughts with which it was in vain to reason—tried to pique her sense of dignity. Her quarrel with Byron was now of long standing, and was generally known: and on this, as on most other subjects that fascinated her wandering imagination, she was ready, on brief acquaintance, to speak unreservedly to any one who would listen to her. It was to no purpose that her brother hushed her into silence on such a theme. In a placid mood she would promise to be more reserved, because he wished it, not because she was convinced she had been wrong. But at the first allusion to a sardonic fling of the poet in conversation or correspondence, whereof stories were seldom long wanting, she would break out, as formerly, in a torrent of reproach and lament, wildly recounting passages which had, or which she dreamed had occurred between them; and generally ending in an invective against nameless wicked ones who had poisoned his mind against her. Before they left town for Easter, she wrote—

By desire of her husband, to remind Godwin of his promised visit to Brocket, where they meant to stay a week. We are, and shall be, entirely alone until I have seen my dear father, who returns from Italy in May. Your room will be always ready, and a quiet day in the country may not displease you; and, as I said before, a person with your mind can, I am sure, encounter all the dulness of a mere family party without fear. You have only to choose a fine day, and let us know the night before; you will be sure to be welcome. I am, with respect and truth, yours,

C. L.

Melbourne House. Actually four in the morning.

From Brocket, some weeks later, in a fit of gloomy egotism, she warned her correspondent not to imagine that there was anything, after all, marked, sentimental, or interesting in her career:—

All I know is, that I was happy, well, rich, joyful, and surrounded by friends. I have now one faithful, kind friend in William Lamb, two others in my father and brother—but health, spirits, and all else is gone—gone

how ? Oh, assuredly not by the visitation of God, but
slowly and gradually, by my own fault! You said you
would like to see me and speak to me. I shall, if possible,
be in town in a few days. When I come I will let you
know. The last time I was in town, I was on my bed
three days, rode out and came off here on the 4th. God
preserve you.　　　　　　　　　　　　　Yours, C. L.

　　　Brocket Hall.

She delighted in the woods and gardens at Brocket — a
paradise, full of flowers and fruits, only wanting inhabitants. Her invalid boy and her venerable father-in-law
divided her attention; but the alternate spectacle of the
infirmity of youth and the infirmity of age added only to
the deepening habit of despondency.

　　Sir Charles and Lady Morgan, on their return from
Italy, stayed some time in London, and were frequently
guests at Whitehall. Lady Caroline's early predilection for
the Wild Irish Girl had not lessened with years; she admired
the courage and originality of her friend, and spent a good
deal of time in her company. Lamb was seldom of their
coterie, but he liked talking about books with Sir Charles,
who had wandered a good deal off the beaten tracks of
reading; and he enjoyed still more a dish of foreign politics
with his wife, the abuse of whom in certain journals he
condemned unsparingly. In this, as in many other instances, he seemed to make it a point to be attentive and
kind to those who were favourites of Lady Caroline: and
long after her death, when unexpected power had come to
him, he availed himself cheerfully of the opportunity it gave
to confer upon the authoress an important benefit.

CHAPTER X.

*Domestic Life—Augustus Lamb—Letters to Godwin —Huskisson—
Reply to Mackintosh—Refusal of office—Death and funeral of
Byron—Alienation.*

AUTUMN glided by more tranquilly than usual. Harvest
ripened plentifully, and was early gathered in. Employment grew once more abundant, disaffection gradually gave
place to reasonable hopes of progress, and the name of
Government was less unpopular than it had been. Instead
of unattainable projects of organic change, men's thoughts
turned to the prospect of substantial improvements in the
laws affecting industry and trade. Murmurs and reproaches
at our support of the Holy Alliance gave place to glad
expectation that England was about to point the way, if not
to aid the nations of the West in gradual self-emancipation.
The whole tone of administration was softened; and while
Canning was preparing his colleagues in the Cabinet, and
the mind of the King to recognise the independence of the
South American States, and warning the Porte that if the
Greeks were not humanely and justly governed Christendom would recognise the rending of their thrall; while
Huskisson was elaborating measures for the liberation of
trade, and Peel preparing mitigations of the criminal code
that Romilly would have rejoiced to see—moderate Liberals
were drawing slowly but steadily towards the Government.
Lamb found every day less and less in which he differed

from Palmerston and Huskisson; and altogether he was politically inclined to be more hopeful and better content.

Lord Melbourne dozed placidly in the sunshine, withdrawn altogether from the bustle of the world, and satisfied if he saw those around him healthful and happy. Even the troubled spirit of Lady Caroline partook of the general temper of content. Alluding to a contrary surmise in a recent review of her novels, she said she would not be judged by what she had written in ' Ada Reis,' as if it had been meant descriptively :—

I am satisfied with all I have. My husband has been to me a guardian angel, I love him most dearly; and my boy, though afflicted, is clever, amiable, and cheerful. Let me not be judged by hasty words and hasty letters. My heart is calm as a lake on a fine summer day; and I am as grateful to God for His mercy and blessing as it is possible to be.

Unhappily the placid surface was but too easily ruffled. The son of so many hopes and cares was nearly seventeen, well-grown for his age, and in features not ill-favoured; delicate in health, and of languid temperament, but uncomplaining, easily amused, rather of a reading turn, courteous, tractable, and fond. There was no indulgence his mother would not give him; no boyish whim of curiosity his father would not gladly gratify, if he would only ask it, or take it without asking. But he asked not, or asked for so little suitable to his years; and when provided by the yearning forethought of affection, it called forth no ejaculation of surprise or joy. His lips did not forget gentle words of thanks; but his eye kindled not, and his hand did not grasp the new fishing-rod or the new pony's bridle, as if it was his own. He could play cards with his grandfather, and was ready whenever the old lord was in the humour, but he hardly cared whether he lost or won, and was content to give over at the slightest hint of weariness. He did not revoke, and was even shrewd in his play, but it was too like tho cleverness of the automaton. When those about him talked he listened, and when they laughed he smiled; but he rarely caught tho contagion of their mirth, and seldom joined in the conversation. The impetuous mother strove in her erratic way to rally him into activity, or pique him into self-assertion, but all to no purpose. It was not in him to contend with her about anything, and as to the future, it was a region far beyond his ken or dream. And when she gave up the effort in despair, and was unable to hide her vexation, he would take her hand in his as though he thought he ought to soothe her if he knew how. But the cause of her grief and its intensity were as incomprehensible to him as its remedy was to her. In her perplexity she turned from physical to mental science. Medical skill could do nothing; but a metaphysician—a man who had made the mind's workings, the strength and weakness of brain power a study—who understood, or professed to understand, the difference between genius and learning, aptitude and dulness, passion and phlegm, reserve and incoherency, in all their strange varieties—might not he have insight into the great affliction of her life, and minister to a mind diseased? She would consult Godwin—have him down to Brocket, where he could observe the symptoms of the mental case under all circumstances, and form his diagnosis of the malady, if malady it were, and then advise, or mayhap, cure. Lamb did not share her fond anticipations. He knew tolerably well all that psychology had done in the way of opening new shafts into the depths of the great enigma of existence, what strata of curious rubbish it had drawn forth and cleared away, and what small residuum of precious things it had to show for its laborious delving. He knew that when the owner of one pit died another was opened by some new speculator in the wealth of the unseen world, to be neglected and superseded in his turn by some yet more confident adventurer. But for comfort, light, or even for termination of controversy, he had come to the conclusion that all their metaphysic learning and logic was but vanity and vexation of spirit: and he groaned as he said within himself—they cannot kindle mind, not ready to be set aflame; or tell us how and why it will not burn.   He did not object, however, to the renewed invitation to Godwin, whom he rather liked. Lady Caroline's letter, as usual, touched on a good many other subjects than the one uppermost in her thoughts—her own unappeasable discontent with herself and her destiny.

From the moment when I saw you last under such excessive agitation, until the present moment, I have been—you said I might be if I would—calm and perfectly well, and tolerably happy.   Is it not strange, then, that I can suffer my mind to be so overpowered, and mostly about trifles? Can you think of me with anything but contempt?   Tell me, would you dislike paying me a little visit?   I will not allure you by descriptions of a country life.   If you come, I imagine it is to pay me a friendly visit, and if you do not, I shall feel secure you have good reason for not coming.   The whole of what passed, which set me so beside myself, I forget and forgive; for my own faults are so great that I can see and remember nothing beside.   Yet I am tormented with such superabundance of activity, and have so little to do, that I want you to tell me how to go on.   It is all very well if one died at the end of a tragic scene, after playing a desperate part; but if one lives, instead of growing wiser one remains the same victim of every folly and passion, without the excuse of youth and inexperience: what then?   Pray say a few wise words to me.   There is no one more deeply sensible than myself of kindness from persons of high intellect, and at this period of my life I need it.   I have nothing to do—I mean necessarily.   There is no particular reason why I should exist; it conduces to no one's happiness, and, on the contrary, I stand in the way of many.   Besides, I seem to have lived five hundred years, and feel I am neither better nor worse than when I began.   My experience gives me no satisfaction; all my opinions and beliefs and feelings are shaken, as if suffering from frequent little shocks of earthquakes. I am like a boat in a calm, in an unknown and, to me, unsought-for sea, without compass to guide or even a knowledge whither I am destined. Now, this is probably the case of millions, but that does not mend the matter, and whilst a fly exists, it seeks to save itself. Therefore excuse me if I try to do the same. Pray write to me, and tell me also what you have done about my journal. Thank you for the frame; will you pay for it, and send me in any account we have at your house? I am very anxious about my dear boy. I must speak to you of him. Every one, as usual, is kind to me; I want for nothing this earth can offer, but self-control. Forgive my writing so much about myself, and believe me most sincerely yours.

It may be easily imagined that the writer of a letter like this to a comparative stranger was little suited for the intimate companionship of wedlock with any man of exigeant and fastidious nature, however gentle and generous he might be. The confidence that gave her unlimited freedom in the disposition of her time and choice of friends, her husband would indeed have conceded as easily to any woman that he loved. Distrust was not in him, and his pride would not accept compulsory devotion. Proofs of affection touched him deeply when they were spontaneous, and given as though unconsciously, and without profession or explanation of purpose. But he winced at a caress that insisted on exacting acknowledgment there and then; and chafed at the notion that any sacrifice made for him, whether great or small, imposed an obligation. He was ready to deny himself many things he liked, to please or gratify his wife; and he wished for nothing in return but the unclouded look and simple accents of her love. He was delighted when he saw that she on her part gave up in trifles her own way, as she was sometimes ready to do, to humour or amuse him. But all was marred by the insatiable longing for the romance

N 2

rather than the reality of fondness. She did not upbraid
him with occasional absence, but she mourned over it as
evidence unmistakable that she was forgotten and might be
done without. She was very proud of his attention, and of
the admiration of others for him; and she had too much
discernment not to see, though she had too much delicacy to
show, how much she felt chagrined at her share of social
celebrity being less than his; but it grieved her ambition,
which was boundless, and her avarice for distinction, which
was unappeasable; and, worse than all, she fretted herself to
death because she was not thought an indispensable part of
his being. Could she have only persuaded herself of that,
and that he felt it to be so, she imagined she would have
been happy, and failing this, her misfortune and his misery
was, that she was for ever brooding over her lot, explaining
her unhappiness to him, and telling her story to the whole
world in prose and verse. His forbearance by the testimony
of all who knew them was unspeakable; but his very
equanimity and self-control occasionally aggravated her
vexation. After spending a week in the country, with no
other society than hers, humouring quietly every whim, and
letting every little petulancy pass without remonstrance,
she would get into a paroxysm at his impassibility, declare
that he treated her like a child, and that she was the most
solitary of women. The fountains of the great deep of his
impatience were then broken up, and it rained a terrible
tempest of rebuke and ridicule, intermixed with reasoning
harder to bear than either, for the space of half an hour.
But he soon relented, and his irritation passed away.

It is hardly necessary to say that Goodwin was unable
to afford any consolation during his visit to his friends,
respecting the condition of their child, for child he still
remained in all but outward form. The philosopher appeared
occasionally among the crowd of notabilities, political and
literary, at Melbourne House, and Lady Caroline always made
him welcome.

The first significant proof of Canning's power, and his

determination to use it, was the introduction of Mr. Huskisson into the Cabinet.* His services in subordinate office were well known to Lord Liverpool, but the liberality of his opinions on questions of taxation and trade, and those connected with foreign affairs, had hitherto stood in his way. Up to this time he had never voted for the removal of religious disabilities or for any concession of electoral reform, yet he was looked upon as an unsafe man; and the Chancellor's consent to his promotion was so little to be expected that it was not asked.† At first Lord Liverpool did not venture more than to offer him the Presidency of the Board of Trade, with which was then associated the Treasurership of the Navy. Difficulties, he said about making the Cabinet too numerous, alone prevented his immediate admission; but the earliest opportunity would be taken of giving him the rank which he had fairly earned. With this Canning and Lamb advised him to be satisfied, and in January he accepted the offer accordingly. But when the session of 1823 had passed without the promise being fulfilled, Canning, who felt the ground growing firm beneath him, told the Premier that if, with his hands full of foreign affairs, he was to lead the Commons, as the times required they should be led, through the series of fiscal and financial changes that could no longer be postponed, he must have by his side in Council as well as in the House some one on whom he could absolutely rely to think with and for him. The mere consumption of time in the work of the Foreign Office rendered it impossible for him to gather and collate the masses of fact necessary for the elucidation of various and complicated subjects. Palmerston could not render the same sort of assistance, and was even less acceptable to the King. On Huskisson he could thoroughly depend, and his presence in the Cabinet was therefore indispensable; the Premier himself was already well-disposed, and before ministers separated in August, Huskisson was included in their

* January 21st, 1823.
†. Lord Eldon's letter to Lord Stowell, January 1823.

number. The announcement was received with no little satisfaction by Lamb. There had of late been more of approximation and confidence between them. From opposite sides both had become more and more identified with the middle policy of Canning. Huskisson was preparing to concur in the demand for complete religious liberty ; Lamb, for the sake of obtaining that liberty, to support, irrespective of party antecedents, any Government by which its advent might be hastened. Lord Granville, connected by early friendship with Huskisson, and by the ties of family·with Lamb, enjoyed peculiarly the confidence of the Foreign Secretary ; while Lord Palmerston, and other members of the Government who had always voted with him on the Catholic question, daily looked with strengthening hope to the time when he should be at the head of affairs.

From this period may be dated the slow but gradual undoing of the fiscal policy originating in the exigencies of the American War, and elaborated by Mr. Pitt and his successors, to supply the means of supporting the prolonged struggle with France. With its provisions were curiously and subtilely intertwined those of preference and prohibition, which it took a quarter of a century to eradicate completely from the statute book. It was a system of elaborate intricacy and ingenuity that covered like a net-work every field and store of the realm and its wide dependencies. Affecting every act and relation of life, from the cradle to the altar, from the play-ground to the grave, it weighed down every energy of commerce, and all the elasticity of invention. Every class except the landed and the official class chafed beneath its yoke, or pined under its pressure. The income tax had been flung off in 1816 in a spasm of popular impatience, against the protests and prophecies of administration ; but no such concentration of the resentments of suffering could be anticipated for the summary removal of any other impost. The schedules of articles paying custom, or excise duties ; the diversities of charge and the anomalies of exemption ; the riddles of drawback, and the multiplicity

of penalties for breach of equivocal or·half-repealed enactments, made up a code of hindrance and impediment which
drove industry often to despair. To gnaw away the fringe of
this web of oppression, and to curtail here a little and there a
little its all-embracing folds, until better days should come
and productive labour be set free, was the avowed purpose of
independent thinkers like Mill and Ricardo—the esoteric
purpose of Canning and Huskisson. Well-born Whigs, with
the exception of Lords Lansdowne, Althorp, Milton, and
Radnor, scoffed at political economy as useless for party
objects; and feared the application of its rules to the produce
of the soil, as likely to prove fatal at elections and ruinous to
rents. The mind of Lamb in this as in most other things oscillated between opposite theories. He was too candid not to own,
and too just not to condemn, the enormities of the existing
system. Prohibition of every kind he was ready to sweep
away, and competition in all branches of production he was
ready to facilitate. What might or ought to come afterwards,
he did not pretend to calculate. The remedial measures
brought forward by his friends in office from 1823 to 1826
were practical and humane ; cordially, therefore, he supported them all. He was rather proud of Huskisson being
in the Cabinet, and rather liked him at a quiet dinner;
if he would but hold himself better, and dress better, and
not be so confoundedly deferential to blockheads he must
in his heart despise, merely because they dined oftener at
Brighton, or had two or three borough seats in their pockets.

Lamb, receptive and discerning, looked into the heart of
the man with interest and sympathy. Glad of his gladness,
and proud of his pride, he could not help quizzing him a
little on his occasional ponderosity and tapistical reserve.
Huskisson's equanimity took all in good part ; and sometimes
he was too much pre-occupied with his own computative
thoughts to heed or hear the badinage of his kinsman.
But was he not worth a score of the ordinary talkers and
voters in St. Stephen's Chapel to the right or left of the
chair ? And was not Canning better worth following than

anybody else whatsoever? Day by day, in common with
several of his Whig friends, he drew closer to the eloquent
and enlightened minister. Canningism was hardly yet
a positive or distinctive creed, but among all parties it made
proselytes and had devoted believers.

The Huskissons were from this time more frequently
at Brocket. Lady Caroline was to him a puzzle and a
marvel; the aged peer was to her an object of gentle deference and regard. The more the friends talked politics,
the more Canningite Lamb became; and, as unreserve had
grown with him to be a social habit, he began to be suspected by out-and-out Whigs in the county of wavering in
his party allegiance. This would not have so much mattered
had it ended there. But when in the course of the parliamentary fray, ranks were broken and old rallying cries
disregarded, from the desire to save the progressive section
of the ministry from defeat, the name of the county member
in the opposite division list to that which contained Althorp,
Russell, and Brougham, set staunch Nonconformists and
hitherto lenient Liberals by the ears. Dogmatic Bentham-
ites, of which there were few, and incoherent Cobbetites,
of which there were many, half-ossified Whigs, and Radicals
of imperfect formation, cast their respective shells on the
heap of reproach; but with so little of clamour or combination that it widened and rose high without his noticing
the fact.

Fiscal and legal reforms occupied chiefly the attention of
Parliament during the session of 1824, and Lamb took little
part in their discussion. He listened with interest to the
first remarkable speech of Mr. Stanley, then in his twenty-
seventh year, who grappled vigorously with the arguments
of Mr. Hume against maintenance of the Irish Church, and
thus undertook, as the favourite and special duty of his life,
a defence which, after five and forty years, he was compelled
by his own followers reluctantly to abandon. In the effort
of George Lamb to introduce the principle that counsel
should be allowed to address the jury on behalf of persons

on trial for their lives, his brother took much interest; but, the debate having been prolonged to a later hour than was expected, he was accidentally shut out of the division. His only reported speech of any interest this year was against a motion of Hobhouse, on the 23rd of March, who, with the approval of the more advanced Liberals, endeavoured to prevent a renewal of the Alien Act. Recent attempts at insurrection in Italy and Spain had been loudly encouraged at popular meetings and in the press; but in the substantial form of contributions the aid offered had been small, and the only proof of continued sympathy with those who suffered for their premature devotion to the cause of freedom was unmeasured abuse of the rulers who had stamped out revolt. England was almost the only secure asylum for the fugitives who had escaped at the end of each abortive struggle, and there was no real danger that any Secretary of State would listen to demands for their surrender: Lord Grenville had been firm and haughty in repudiating any suggestion of the kind even in the anti-Jacobin days of Pitt; and under a Foreign Minister like Canning it was not alleged that any unhappy exile had cause to fear betrayal. But Lord Liverpool was apprehensive lest the right of asylum should be abused by reckless or desperate men, and the good faith of our national pledge of non-intervention compromised: and the Foreign Secretary, who had more difficulties with the Court and in the Cabinet than he dared confess or explain, thought he might be safely trusted with a deadly weapon of old-fashioned form which he could not be suspected of willingness to use. There was no statute law of asylum to whose reservations of control he could appeal on any sudden emergency; and the Alien Act was in truth a clumsy device to enable the executive summarily to send any foreigner out of the country whose presence should have become mischievous or dangerous. Mackintosh objected to an expedient so out of joint with his philosophy of freedom; Althorp, because he distrusted the plausible and devious ways of the minister.

Lamb took a different view. Replying to Mackintosh, he said :—

Nothing was so unsafe, nothing so uncertain, as analogy ; but if any one thing could be more unsafe or more uncertain than another, it was historical analogy. It was impossible to know the circumstances as they had previously existed. It was very easy to depreciate what was done at this or that former time, and to scatter sarcasm and invective on affairs that possibly were entitled to be very differently treated. He deprecated the indiscriminate language of vituperation lavished on various foreign governments. Lamenting as much as the honourable gentleman could do that civil and religious liberty did not flourish as he could wish it (and he undoubtedly wished that every nation should obtain liberty suited to its own habits, manners, and character), he would ask if the existing situation of certain countries of Europe, degraded as it was described to be, ought to be attributed solely to the sovereigns now reigning, and their ministers, or to the impracticable designs of that very Radical party who now lamented over the evils by which these countries were afflicted? Surely those who wished the people to resist their governments ought to know that to attempt to relieve a country from arbitrary power without the least chance of success was in fact a folly. He lamented to be obliged to say that injurious efforts abroad had been seconded by the violent and indefensible language used towards foreign governments in that and the other House of Parliament. Such language could do no good ; it might be productive of much mischief. There was, besides, no courage in it. Tyranny and oppression were not confined to absolute monarchies ; republics, whether democratical or aristocratical, had ever exhibited a spirit of great domestic tyranny, of much greater foreign aggression than monarchies ; nor was the abuse so freely bestowed on certain foreign rulers in the British Parlia-

ment, in his opinion, more wise than it was brave. Seeing
the state of Europe at the present moment, recollecting
that some individuals had thought proper to interfere with
the internal concerns of foreign states, recollecting what
had fallen from the Secretary for Foreign Affairs as to the
policy which the Cabinet of England wished to pursue,
and recollecting that there was an evident disposition on
the part of some persons in this country to mix themselves
up with the affairs of foreign powers —a disposition, he
doubted not, which arose from the noblest motive, from
the warm love which Englishmen bore to liberty, from that
superabundance of talent and activity which so eminently
distinguished this country, a disposition which he admitted to be praiseworthy, but which was not therefore
the less dangerous, the less embarrassing to this country,
or the less offensive to foreign powers—feeling very strongly
on these points, he should vote for the bill as a proper
and necessary measure. He did so the more readily
because he believed that the Secretary of State for the
Foreign Department would never countenance any act that
was calculated to tarnish the honour of the country ; and
that he would be as far from giving up any principle
which appeared to be beneficial to mankind as any
minister that had ever gone before him.

About this time Lord Liverpool offered him, through
Huskisson, one of the junior offices in the Government, and
he is believed to have communicated on the subject with
Canning. The views of the flexible and aspiring statesman
tended palpably towards detaching moderate men from the
old standards of party and combining them under his own.
But the Whigs showed little disposition to change sides
individually, and so long as Lord Eldon was Chancellor and
Lord Liverpool Premier the acceptance of office would only
be regarded by the world in that light. Lamb declined the
offer, saying only to the few intimates who knew of its
having been made that he preferred freedom to enjoy his

books and pleasures, which in a certain sense was true ; for, whatever confidence he may have had in the eventual aims of Canning, or his power to impress his reconstructive image and superscription on the policy of his own depart- ment, the position of a sincere Liberal in any subordinate office of the Liverpool administration could not be otherwise than compromising and humiliating.   Huskisson would have gladly hailed his enrolment among the friends of Canning ; and Stafford House already leaned that way.   But the Duke of Devonshire, whom he always consulted, approved of his resolution to remain independent and to bide his time.

With the luxurious establishments, almost his own, at Whitehall and in Hertfordshire he might well be content. But the profuse expenditure of his wife, though capriciously chequered at times with odd fits of self-denial, had for a good while far exceeded his allowance ; and though he did not play or bet to any amount worth noticing, he found him- self often without a balance on which to draw for sums the world believed he might easily throw away.   It is a curious illustration of his condition, that on one occasion Francis Place, who had given him credit for some years, and who found it impossible to get a settlement of his account, had him served with a writ ; instructing his solicitor at the same time " to see what that would do ; but, d—n it, nothing further."   Other mortifications arising from his easy-going unthrift followed ; the old Viscount, who had long outlived the taste for squandering, thought Lady Caroline too profuse, but except in passing vows of retrenchment, forgotten as soon as made, her " Lavishship," as he sometimes called her, cared for none of these things.   Her husband tried in various ways to persuade her to curb her taste for fantastic outlay ; and perhaps the vexation arising from her failure to do so tended to generate in his own disposition a certain degree of inconsistency regarding money, of which, when he came at last to have abundance, he was alternately generous and the contrary.   An allusion to the subject occurs in one of her earlier letters to Lady Morgan :—

Would I could be useful! I did write a book about stables
and domestic economy, upon a new and beautiful plan; but
unless some one saw it and thought it good, I would not
venture to publish it; yet I wrote it while I was writing
'Ada Reis.' My laundry and stables I conduct upon
that plan to save myself trouble, but it is more difficult
to put it into practice in a house, although it was done,
and with success one year. I mention this to show you
I, too, have been a good housewife, and saved William
much; but he says, What is the use of saving in one place
if you squander all away in another? Alas! what is the
use of anything? We may go on saying what is the use,
till we really puzzle ourselves, as I did as to why we exist
at all.*

Byron's death was known in England early in May, and
on the 12th of July his remains were followed out of London,
on the way to their last resting-place at Newstead, by
Campbell, Rogers, Moore, Hobhouse, Leycester, Stanhope,
and other attached friends. After most of the distinguished
mourners had returned to town, the sad procession took the
north road through Hertfordshire, and was met by an open
carriage, one of whose occupants inquired whose funeral
passed by. The questioner was Lady Caroline Lamb.
The effects of the shock were in every way lamentable.
For a time her health seemed to sink beneath it; and she
lay as one who had been stunned, and could not be recalled
to mental sensibility or interest in the ordinary concerns of
life. By degrees the *ennui* of solitary grief grew irksome;
she resumed her pen, and occasionally her pencil; then her
favourite books and music; until hopes were entertained
that the dark cloud had passed over her, and that she might
yet return to fill the place in society where she was certain
of welcome. But it was not so to be. Her disregard of
conventional opinion appeared to be more complete than ever,
and her wayward indulgence of irritability on the slightest
cause, more reckless and unaccountable. Caprice, to whose
freaks she had childishly given way long after they had

* Letter to Lady Morgan, Brocket.

grown to the dimensions of wilful unreason, had gained the
upper hand, and held her enfeebled understanding captive to
its will.   There was no whim of gesture or attire, no inconsistency of manner, no breach of conventional rule regarding
time or place which those about her could feel confident that
she might not commit.   There was neither mischief nor
malice in her vagaries ; and it was never whispered that she
sought deliberately to do harm to any one.   Sometimes they
were only ludicrous ; sometimes calculated to create alarm
for her own safety.   One day when numerous guests were
expected, she entered the dining-room when the servants
were laying the table ; and, after surveying its decorations,
told the butler they were too level and too low ; there was
no character about them, no feature to give expression : there
ought to be something picturesque or elevated ; a group of
figures, or at least of flowers, high above all the rest.   The
well-trained man of method and observance looked at my
lady and wondered, assented mildly, but went on spreading
the treasures of his plate-chest, while he thought within
himself, " Worse than ever."   Incensed at the contumacy of
his passive resistance, she peremptorily ordered the centre
piece to be taken away, and then without disturbing the
surrounding garniture stepped lightly into the vacant place
and stood in a graceful attitude to illustrate her idea.   The
butler rushed from the room, and finding Lamb in the library,
begged him for God's sake to come to the rescue.   The moment he saw her, he said only in the gentlest tone of expostulation " Caroline, Caroline ! " then took her in his arms
and carried her out of doors into the sunshine, talking of
some ordinary subject to divert her attention from what had
happened.   That evening she received her friends with as
calm a look and tone as in happier days ; but what an ordeal
for him to pass through !

Other incidents as strange lingered long in the memories of those who lived in the neighbourhood at the time.
A visit was to be returned at Danesbury, and having no one
to accompany her, she chose to occupy the seat beside the
coachman, instead of her wonted place in the carriage.   On

arriving at the door of the mansion, the footman waited to hand her down, when to his horror she exclaimed, " I am going to jump off, and you must catch me ;" and before he could expostulate, she had made good her word, and compelled him to perform that unusual office. But her hostess observed nothing particular in her manner during her visit, and heard nothing of the strange prank until after she was gone.

At other times, unfortunately, she gave way to fits of irritability and excitement unutterably painful ; and while the paroxysm lasted it was in vain trying to tranquillise her emotions, or appease the querulous impetuosity of her temper. While at table on one occasion at Melbourne House, her demeanour was so petulant and affronting, that when she had left the room Lamb quietly ordered horses and in half an hour was on his road to Brocket, glad to escape from the renewal of domestic strife. He sat up late enjoying the stillness of the summer night, and had not long betaken himself to rest when he was disturbed by some unusual noise in the corridor. As it did not cease, he rose, and on opening the door of his chamber found his wife lying at the entrance convulsed with what she took for grief. The absurdity and scandal of such incidents wounded his sensibility to the quick. He writhed beneath a yoke that after twenty years had grown intolerable. He could not persuade himself that she was insane ; on the contrary, he came to the conclusion, sadly but sternly, that if she found him really resolved to separate from her, she might, and perhaps would, be brought to comprehend how much she was to blame in making all around her miserable, him most of all. There was, between affection and resentment, a long and bitter struggle in his bosom ere it came to this. At last he told her quietly that his life was unendurable, and that they must part. He quitted her, and went for a time to Melbourne, where Mr. and Mrs. George Lamb resided. He would come to Brocket frequently as a matter of duty and respect to its venerable owner ; as an act of duty and of love towards his afflicted son, and as an unreproachful friend, who did not wish to keep alive the memory of unkindness, if his wife (no longer wife) would so receive him; but he would be the sport of her fantastic whims no more. It was then that she addressed to him the lines, which when they failed to move him, she sent for publication to one of the periodicals of the day :—

If thou could'st know what 'tis to weep,
　To weep unpitied and alone,
The livelong night, whilst others sleep,
Silent and mournful watch to keep,
　Thou would'st not do what I have done.

If thou could'st know what 'tis to smile—
　To smile whilst scorned by every one,
To hide, by many an artful wile,
A heart that knows more grief than guile,
　Thou would'st not do what I have done. ·

And, oh, if thou could'st think how drear,
　When friends are changed and health is gone,
The world would to thine eyes appear,
If thou, like me, to none wert dear,
　Thou would'st not do what I have done.

Members of the family were made aware of the reasons that had tardily and reluctantly led him to a determination, in the sad necessity of which they concurred. Their friendship for him continued unbroken to the end, especially that of her eldest brother, Lord Duncannon, with whom he ever continued to associate on terms the most confidential, both in public and private affairs.

Too late convinced by her husband's absence and the unwelcome watch over all her movements which had been prescribed as necessary, the sad consciousness came over her that she had wantonly let fall the reins of passionate whim and lawless temper. Instead of curbing the morbid impulses of discontent and self-idolatry, she had suffered them to subvert the darling privilege she so much valued of irresponsibility for her words and actions. Truly has it been said by a great analyst of human motives, that the gradations are infinite and impalpable between self-deception and voluntary fraud. Few persons know where the unfenced demesne of reason ends and the tractless wild of aberration begins. No one loved more to palter with the fiend than Byron. He delighted to climb the dizzy height of speculation and dance upon the brink of madness; these were among his favourite devices for making the world stare and for gratifying his insatiable vanity. And of the frail natures dazzled by his example and bewildered by the witchery of his verse here was one. In her admiration and enthusiasm she drank but too deeply of his cup of morbid egotism. Warned by every true friend that in its fragrance and its sparkling there was deadliest poison, she grew impatient, angry, even resentful; she would drink on until at last to all except herself the effect became only too palpable.

In more than one set of verses addressed to her husband, soon afterwards, she describes the bitterness of her humiliation. But the ineradicable sin of Byronism clings to every line. It is all importunity for pity from the man whose devotion she had worn out by her waywardness; and we find them duly given to the public in the Annuals of the succeeding year.

> Though all at once unheard, reprove me,
>   Left alike by friend and foe,
> I will not shrink, if thou but love me,
>   No hand but thine can strike the blow.
>
> *   *   *   *   *
>
> And say'st thou that I dare not face
>   The storm that bursts above my head?
> The proud must keenly feel disgrace,
>   And 'tis disgrace, alone, I dread.
>
> I fear not censure's bitter sneer,
>   I heed not envy's venomed tongue,
> Nor hadst thou seen one woman's tear
>   If my own heart had known no wrong.
>
> And even though wrong, if thou canst love me,
>   Or friend, or foe, may frown on me;
> Their barbarous rage shall never move me,
>   If blest by one kind word from thee.

Arriving in England, after a sojourn of some weeks in Paris, she wrote from Dover to the most attached of her literary correspondents in Ireland :—

It would be charitable in you to write me a letter, and it would be most kind if you would immediately send me Lord Byron's portrait, as more than six weeks have expired and I am again in England; if you will send it for me to Melbourne House, to the care of the porter, I shall be most sincerely obliged to you. My situation in life now is new and strange. I seem to be left to my fate most completely, and to take my chance on rough or smooth without the smallest interest being expressed for me : it is for a good purpose, no doubt; besides I must submit to my fate, it being without remedy. I am now with my maid at the Ship Tavern, Water Lane, having come over from Calais. I have no footman, page, carriage, horse, nor fine rooms. The melancholy of my situation in this little dreary apartment is increased by the very loud, jovial laughter of my neighbours who are smoking in the next room. Pray send me my invaluable portrait, and pray think kindly of me. Every one in France talked much of you, and with great enthusiasm. Direct to me at the Hon. William Ponsonby's, St. James' Square.

Then, in the twilight of seclusion, humiliated in the vital point of all her pride, and penitent for the error of her ways, she tried earnestly and with tears to regain her husband's love, though she dared not ask his confidence again. In the retrospect of years wasted in phantasy and frenzy, did any clue enable her to retrace her wanderings through the treacherous intricacies of self-worship ; or did the past seem all but one confused and calcined heap of disappointments? Who shall tell? We only know that he who had borne and foreborne beyond belief until it was no longer possible, as soon as he was told that she was really calm and

wished to see him, came to her again with looks and words
of the old genial and gentle time; and that thenceforth all
bickering and reproach ceased between them. Her shattered
health was a sufficient reason for her living chiefly at
Brocket, while his occupations led him to remain for the
most part in town. Infinite care was taken to disguise from
her the melancholy distrust of the abiding nature of her
equanimity by all around her, while by him the part was
acted to perfection in every glance and syllable of undoubting confidence in her self-possession. When absent he
wrote to her continually in terms that could not be distinguished from those he had formerly used: for, besides
the instinct of kindliness which thus prompted him to
gratify her susceptibility, he was too keen a metaphysician
not to know that the sympathy of sanity continually tendered
and received is the subtlest and best medicine to a mind
diseased.

CHAPTER XI.

PROGRESS AND REACTION.

The Catholic Association—Repression and Concession—Failure of proposed compromise—Giving up the county—Contest for Hertford.

GEORGE IV. had in 1825 become as averse from any measure of religious or political liberty as his father had ever been. He resisted to the last the policy of recognising the independence of the South American States because they were founded in successful rebellion, and because their forms of government were republican. He would gladly have sanctioned the offer of Russia to assist Spain in a prolonged effort to reconquer her misgoverned colonies; but Canning began to feel his power in the country, and therefore in the Government; and when all his arts of suasion in the closet failed, he threatened to resign unless his policy were adopted. His heart was likewise set on seeing the Greeks freed from the Turkish yoke; but as an English minister he felt himself bound to wait until they had fairly won by persistent valour and endurance, the rights of a separate people, before according their government national recognition. While occupied with these noble aims, and with the important measures of commercial freedom brought forward by Huskisson, he did not think it expedient to press with equal urgency for the settlement of the question of religious liberty. He believed that settlement could not be long delayed, and that public opinion would inevitably overbear the tottering prejudices of class and creed. His accession to the leadership of the Commons had raised the hopes of the Catholics that some legislative effort would be made effectually to abate the rigour of exclusion ; and when he was reluctantly compelled to own that in taking office he had made no actual stipulation on the subject, their disappointment was proportionately keen. The many sacrifices he had made in common with Plunket and Wellesley for the sake of consistency on the question were not indeed forgotten in Ireland; but the confessed inability of these statesmen to make their sentiments prevail in council, wrought silently but steadily a perilous change in the minds of thoughtful men on both sides of the Channel. Writing in England and for Englishmen, Sidney Smith declared that,

Looking to the sense and reason of the thing, and to the ordinary working of humanity and justice when assisted by self-interest and worldly policy, it might seem absurd to doubt of the result. But looking to the facts and the persons by which they were surrounded, one was constrained to fear greatly that these incapacities never would be removed, till they were removed by fear.*

Brougham and Tierney gave utterance to the same vaticina-tion in debate. The Catholics themselves after many feuds began to unite and consolidate their strength. Shiel, who had for years incurred the distrust and anger of O'Connell for his persistent advocacy of the more moderate courses, waived all difficulties and differences, and agreed to join in organised agitation. How sharp and bitter their enmity had been was hardly credited by their common adversaries at the time, or for many years after. But on the eve of a public meeting not long before, O'Connell wrote to a trusty henchman :—

I am just told that Shiel has prepared an address for the aggregate meeting full of the worst politics, re-joicing at the downfall of the spirit of democracy, a kind of ode in prose in favour of the Pitt system. I

---

* S. Smith's ' Works,' vol. iii. pp. 12, 13.

entreat of you to exert yourself to bring as many honest men as possible to the meeting to enable us to control any political rascality. Perhaps we are in more danger than you imagine.*

They met at the house of a friend in Wicklow in May 1823, and interchanging admissions of despondency, agreed to appeal to all classes of their communion in an address, which they jointly signed, adjuring them to unite in a general confederacy for emancipation. The response came slowly, but it came. The Catholic Association from this mustard seed grew apace, and in the course of the following year attained a magnitude and importance of which its sanguine authors hardly dreamed. The Catholic nobles and landed proprietors, headed by Lords Gormanston and Fingall, and the Catholic clergy headed by Bishop Doyle, gave in their adhesion; members of the bar and wealthy merchants joined the ranks; and many Protestants of influence and distinction enrolled themselves likewise as members. To show the power of the organisation and to confute at the same time the idea that their aims were subversive of order or law, a commission was publicly sent into the disturbed districts of Tipperary to interpose between the classes there engaged in deadly strife regarding rents and tithes; and to offer those who thought themselves aggrieved the aid of counsel and advocacy in the established tribunal, or, if both sides would agree, the speedy settlement of disputes by arbitration. The standing text from which these missionaries preached speedily passed into a proverb,—"The man who commits a crime gives strength to the enemy." Like other proverbs, it was destined to be too often disregarded; but it indicated with epigrammatic force the whole policy of O'Connell. While the energies of discontent were wasted in fierce acts of revenge for individual wrong, the moral sympathy of mankind was paralysed or alienated. But if political hope could be

* MS. letter, July 18th, 1821, to J. D. Mullen.

infused into the people, the waters of bitterness might be drained into one mighty stream capable of being regulated and directed. To make good the offer, and to carry on the costly business of systematic agitation, steady supplies were indispensable. The donations of opulence would soon have fallen short, and the middle classes would it was feared grow weary of contribution. O'Connell invented a device which solved the difficulty. Membership of the association was founded on the payment of one penny a month or one shilling a year. In every parish collectors were appointed to gather from the humble and the well-to-do their common quota and to enroll the subscribers.

The pence of the poor will do more to emancipate the peer than the pounds of the peer will do to emancipate them; for wherever a man gives his money he gives his heart; and whenever ascendency finds that enough of hearts are beating together it will give way.

The Catholic rent was the fruit of this sagacious counsel, and by the end of 1824 it had reached £500 a week. Government became seriously alarmed. Lord Wellesley wrote to the Premier that if something were not speedily done he could not be responsible for the preservation of authority, the reins of which were slipping from his hands. Despair of redress had worked a miracle of union in the people. A bill might be framed to prohibit political societies continuing their meetings for more than fourteen days, and thus the association might be put down; but peacefully this could not be attempted unless a measure of comprehensive relief from disabilities were carried at the same time. The restrictive measure was accordingly framed by Plunket as Irish law officer of the Crown, and it led to fierce debate. Lamb and many of the Opposition forbore to interpose obstacles to its introduction, in the persuasion that it would only serve to clear the way for the measure of concession which was to

follow. Others objected to shutting down the valves of
popular complaint before raking out the fire of intolerance
that burned beneath. Brougham, never so irritable or
impetuous, as when upon his legs, started at an ironical
cheer from the member for Herts, on whom he turned
ruthlessly as though they had never been comrades or
friends, upbraiding him with all manner of tergiversation
and abandonment of the old faith as it was in Whiggery.
Lamb without losing temper firmly replied :—

That he would not have intruded himself upon the House
were it not for the observation that had been so pointedly
directed against him by the honourable and learned
gentleman. The cheer to which the honourable and
learned gentleman alluded had been drawn from him for
no other reason but this, that he thought the honourable
and learned gentleman's language somewhat too exaggerated when speaking of the effect that would have
been produced in the times of those preceding Charles II.,
if any persons dared talk of scruples in a high quarter.
This, he thought, had tended to weaken the honourable
gentleman's argument; and that was his only motive for
expressing what he felt, in the usual manner, by a cheer.
The honourable and learned gentleman was pleased to
observe that he had tried all parties and opinions. He
was not aware on what facts this assertion was founded.
As he had never been one of those who despaired of the
resources of the country, even when most depressed, so he
did not wish to encourage a too sanguine feeling with
respect to the extent to which our prosperity was likely
to go. In the one case, as in the other, he would recommend moderation, both in action and in expectation.
With respect to the Catholic Association, he begged to
observe that he conceived a case was likely to be made
out against it, sufficiently strong to induce him to
vote for its regulation if not suppression. There were,
it was true, other associations of nearly a similar descrip-

tion ; but they differed in this, that they did not interfere
in political subjects.   If any assembly of persons met,
and, under the pretence of seeking redress for particular
grievances, proceeded to discuss the whole political affairs
of the empire, then he maintained that such a society was
a fit subject for legislative interference.   Again, subscriptions for particular public purposes were perfectly legal;
but if he found that the Roman Catholic clergy were
actively engaged in collecting what was called Catholic
rent, he should say that it was a symptom to be viewed
with great alarm.   When it was considered that the
Roman Catholic clergy claimed the power of absolution—
the power of totally forgiving sins—then he maintained
. that their operations ought to be looked to with great
caution, and only to be approved when directed to
purposes purely spiritual. Notwithstanding these opinions,
however, he was now, as he had ever been, the staunch
friend of Catholic emancipation.   Let the conduct of the
Catholic Association be what it might, still he felt that
all religious distinctions ought to be removed.   Whenever
the question came forward he should be found its firm
supporter ;   but he could not help observing that the
success of it was in a great degree endangered by the
imprudence, if not the violence, of some of its advocates.
It should not be forgotten that there were in this country
deep and well-founded objections to that question, and
that however time and circumstances might have quieted
or removed those prejudices, they ought not to be aroused
by any injudicious conduct on the part of those, or the
friends of those, who seek for emancipation.

On the second reading of the Suppression Bill, Plunket
argued that the permanency of the Association, its assumption of representative character, its activity in recruiting
members, its levy of contributions, and above all its
exercise of the duty of public prosecutor, rendered it a
complete usurpation of the functions of executive govern-

ment, without the check which the constitution had
imposed upon the authority exercised in the name of the
Crown, or the direct responsibility which Parliament was
accustomed to enforce.   This view he urged with his accustomed earnestness and energy, taking care, however, to
combine with it pleadings equally forcible for the pressing
need of that great measure of redress whose delay had
called into existence so formidable a body.   Tierney and
Brougham scoffed at the policy of open questions in the
Cabinet, and urged that the agitation should be allowed free
scope so long as intolerable grievances were not removed.
Canning argued that the duty of Parliament was to get
rid of both, and to do so simultaneously.   Words of
revolutionary import used by O'Connell were quoted with
effect in the debate in justification of the exceptional
provisions proposed; but Mackintosh ingeniously essayed to
extenuate the import of his daring language, which he
described as the rhetoric of just impatience, not the logic
of dangerous conspiracy.   Lamb deprecated the Jesuitical
casuistry which had been employed by his honourable and
learned friend :—

One thing with respect to the Catholic Association was
   certain,—whatever might be their intentions, they had
   not performed a single act which was not calculated to
   place all the sentiments of England in array against them.
   If the effect of particular expressions was to be argued, it
   must be considered who the parties were by whom such
   expressions had been uttered.   Let it be remembered that
   the learned gentleman whose words had formed the
   subject of so much discussion—that he was a man
   accustomed to public speaking, and, from the very
   nature of his profession, used to maintain a command of
   temper.   Such an individual had no right to plead that
   warmth which sometimes led an inexperienced orator
   beyond his real meaning; that which he had said, be the
   effect what it might, must be assumed to have been said

in earnest and with deliberation. He had never intended,
in anything he had ever uttered, to introduce discussion
or parallel as to the merits of the two contending faiths;
his objection was to associations like the Catholic Association, and to the principles on which they proceeded.
Was it to be endured, that any assembly should take it
upon itself to open an account for the redress of grievances,
and to give itself, in such a character, a permanent existence? Some honourable gentlemen were fond of
metaphor, and perhaps a lively illustration did sometimes hit harder than an argument. Some gentlemen
had invented a simile for Catholic associations, calling
them safety-valves by which the dangerous ebullitions of
public feeling were wont to escape. But were honourable
gentlemen sure that they had not mistaken the office of
societies like these; were they sure that, instead of the
safety-valves which let the public feeling out, they were
not the furnaces that raised it into fury? There was
already too much disposition among the lower orders,
even in England, to litigation. Everybody knew that of
the indictments and causes which were tried in courts—
if half were entirely omitted, it would be for the benefit
of all the parties concerned in them. But, if people
would go to law and prosecute each other needlessly, at
their own expense, and even to their own ruin, where
would be the end of petty ill-blood and dissension, when
they were enabled to do it free of cost? What, he
asked, could be more likely to effect all the mischief
apprehended from the " Constitutional Society" than that
very Catholic Association which gentlemen were defending?
Over and over again it had been argued, by those who
were the advocates of liberal principles, that it was
objectionable even for the Houses of Parliament to order
prosecutions, because it sent a man to his trial with an
opinion in some sort already pronounced upon him. And
here was a body, assembled by its own authority, taking
upon itself to order people to be prosecuted, and its

existence was defended! He (Mr. Lamb) looked at the conduct of this society, subject to the condition of the country in which it existed. Here was a confederacy, of its own motion, causing persons to be put upon their trial, and before juries taken from among a people on the very brink of rebellion: or if they were not on the brink of rebellion, they were smarting under restrictions likely to inspire them with anything rather than impartial spirit or good-will.

By a majority of 145 the House passed the Suppression Bill. The day after it was sent to the Lords* Sir Francis Burdett moved the second reading of the Relief Bill, which, supported by Plunket and Canning, was carried by a majority of only twenty-one. The numbers on both sides were, however, greater than had ever divided before upon the question, and the majority included, in addition to old friends, many who now for the first time voted, and of these several who hitherto had uniformly voted the other way.†

Along with this, wrote Plunket to Lord Wellesley, there is a general admission that the measure must ultimately be carried. The prospects now opening of a peaceful and prosperous administration of government in Ireland are of the most gratifying and hopeful character. In order to realise these prospects it is most essential that you should have the means of holding continued and cordial intercourse with the principal persons, whether lay or ecclesiastical, of the Roman Catholic persuasion. I mean this not merely with a view to the present measure, but to the effectual and tranquil administration of the general business of the country. I have heard much of the present opinions and sentiments of the Roman Catholic leaders, and I have seen something of them. I believe they are, at present, sincerely disposed to support Government, and to express their confidence in, and to afford all

* February 28th, 1825. † Ward to Bishop Copleston.

the facilities in their power to the carrying of the present measure. It appears to me to be obvious policy to encourage these feelings and not to let the Suppression Bill assume a character of triumph over them.[*]

These views Plunket expounded in conversation at Lansdowne House, in presence of Lamb, Holland, Tierney, and Spring Rice, about the same time. The whole Liberal party concurred with one or two exceptions in supporting the two supplemental bills called The Wings, by which it was hoped that emancipation might be borne at last over the obstacles that had hitherto impeded its progress. The one was the abolition of forty shilling franchise, which had been deplorably abused for the creation of multitudes of dependent voters; the other the payment from the Treasury of £1000 a year to every bishop, £200 a year to every parish priest and £60 to every curate of the ancient faith in Ireland. Lord Francis L. Gower undertook the charge of the latter; and, as soon as the Relief Bill had passed through its various stages, succeeded in obtaining leave to bring in a bill for the purpose. Lamb and Dudley were zealous in its favour, and hopeful that the end of controversy was nigh. But the end was not yet. The declaration in the House of Lords, of the Duke of York, as heir presumptive to the throne, that "in whatever situation he might be placed he would never forsake his father's principles, so help him God," suddenly quickened the dying embers of intolerance into flame, and put an end to all the sanguine hopes entertained of amicable compromise.

George IV., with all his resentment at the espousal by the Whigs of the cause of the Queen, and their vituperation of his own inconsistency to early promises and professions, was anxious to keep well with many of them individually, and especially those whose social ambition had its centripetal movement round Devonshire House. Lamb continued to be a favourite, and in the midst of the excitement of the

[*] March 2nd, 1825.

Catholic question we find him dining at the palace with Lord and Lady Cowper, Lord Anglesey, and the Dukes of Devonshire and Wellington.*

Agitation in Ireland burst forth anew. O'Connell redeemed his promise of driving a coach and six through the Suppression Act by devising a new association for charitable purposes such as were not forbidden by the statute. In 1826 simultaneous meetings to petition were organised; the Catholic rent was collected more amply, and expended more boastfully than ever; moderate men, exasperated at the fatuity that had thrown away the last chance of gracious concession, joined the movement, and the executive was defied openly to put it down. In England there was upon the surface no ruffle of the calm that denotes the return of industrial prosperity. The panic of 1825 gradually passed away. The middle classes had betaken themselves afresh to the cumulating of profits, and capitalists to the rebuilding of fortunes. In the late eventful struggle it was felt by both political parties that they had put forth their utmost strength, and that the issue must be decided by an appeal to the people. Parliament was six sessions old; and it would be useless to re-try the cause of sectarian liberty before the approaching dissolution. The speeches of Canning and Plunket would, it was believed by their admirers, work a potent spell upon the younger minds of the community wherever access was general to the luxury of dear newspapers. The believers in Lord Eldon and the Duke of York were equally sanguine that in the counties and small country towns a fresh election would show a retrocession in the tide of liberal sentiment. The patriotism and Protestantism of the majority in the Commons were gravely impugned, and members were so pelted with reproach and taunt that some were deterred from attempting to keep their representative position, and several who ventured to do so lost their seats.

---

* This was shortly after the Duke of York's memorable speech, which his Majesty loudly complained of as disrespectful to himself, and shortly before the decisive vote of the Lords rejecting the Relief Bill.

By many in Hertfordshire who had hitherto supported
Lamb he felt, after his votes in 1825, that he was condemned
past all forgiveness :

> For the same thing that's righteous in
> The one in t'other is a sin.
>
> Is't not contemptible and nonsense
> That bigots should be slaves to conscience?

He would not temporise or palter; and the only question
was whether, disregarding much defection, he ought to prepare to stand another contest, which would certainly be
expensive and as certainly doubtful. Apart from the
Catholic Question, now complicated with that of concurrent endowment, he had disappointed some earnest Liberals
by what they deemed lukewarmness in the cause of parliamentary reform. And though the Whig interest was still
believed to be preponderant, his best friends could not
conceal their apprehensions as to the consequence of his
standing in the face of such alienation. For the borough it
was said he was certain of being returned, if he would consent to change places with Mr. Calvert, who was personally
popular in the county and against whose votes no objections
had been raised. The subject was discussed in all its bear-
ings by those who had his interest at heart. While pondering
what to do, symptoms of increasing feebleness in Lord
Melbourne threatened to relieve him from further responsibility as a representative, and warranted urgent recommendations by other members of his family that he should free
himself from even the contingent liability for a great expenditure of money which might prove almost if not altogether
useless. When a dissolution did not seem so near at hand,
a deputation had been sent to the metropolis in search of a
Radical candidate for the town. They applied to Mr. T. S.
Duncombe, a man of family and fashion, who was tired of
routine duty in the Guards, and ambitious of a seat in
Parliament. He had some time before, at much trouble
and expense, tried to win the confidence of Pontefract, and,

though unsuccessful, he took expensive lessons in the art of canvassing, of which eventually he became so accomplished a master.　He agreed to pay a visit to Hertford, where he quickly won his way by a charm of manner which in electioneering oftentimes goes further than more solid qualifications.　This was in 1823, and he had in the interval confirmed the favourable impression then made, giving a pledge to hold himself in readiness whenever occasion should arise.　On the first rumour of Mr. Calvert's intention to retire, urgent messages were sent to him recommending a resumption of his canvass, and on the 5th of September his address appeared, " assuring the constituency of his unalterable determination to give his aid at the next election in support of the sacred cause of their independence."　This, it was felt, rendered a counter-declaration necessary.　Mr. Lamb was then in Derbyshire, but was daily expected to return.　A requisition from many of the most respectable electors of the borough awaited his arrival at Panshanger ; and he sent next day the following reply :

Panshanger, September 10th, 1825.

MY DEAR SIR,

I beg leave to acknowledge having received from you yesterday morning, a letter numerously and most respectably signed, inviting me to become a candidate for the representation of the borough of Hertford, at the next general election. As this was the first direct intimation which I had received of such a proposal, it was but natural that I should wish to take a few hours for deliberation upon a step of considerable importance both to the inhabitants of Hertford and to myself.

With respect to the county, I have every reason to expect that were I to persevere in offering myself, I should meet with a support, at least as powerful and effectual as that with which I have been honoured upon former occasions ; but at the same time the reasons stated in the letter transmitted by you yesterday are of such weight as to induce me to decline a contest. Under these circumstances, and

feeling strongly how desirable it is in every point of view
that the borough of Hertford should maintain its deservedly high character, by continuing to be represented
by gentlemen resident in the county, I cannot hesitate to
accept the offer which has been made me; and I beg you
will have the goodness to communicate to those by whom
the letter has been signed, as well as to all others who
have expressed themselves favourably towards me, how
deeply I feel this mark of their kindness, and how much I
am flattered and gratified by this testimony of their good
opinion.   Believe me, my dear Sir,

Yours faithfully,
WM. LAMB.

His committee then commenced a canvass in favour of the
retiring county member, and it might have been successful
but for the signal popularity rapidly gained by his rival,
and the adhesion of many influential supporters of Mr. Byron,
the Tory member for the borough.

The position was indeed anomalous, and naturally provoked bitter taunts and lively ridicule. Family influence
had hitherto divided the representation of the town; the
house of Cecil usually nominating one of the members, and
that of Cowper the other. The arrangement was denounced
as "unconstitutional and unjust, odious and tyrannical,"
which had privately prepared the transfer of Mr. Calvert to
the county, and of Mr. Lamb to the borough. The latter, it
was insinuated, was moreover intended as a *locum tenens* for
Lord Fordwich, who would ere long come of age. Obviously
it was requisite that he should renounce at once all future
claim as a candidate for the county, and this he did by
issuing the following address :—

*To the Gentry, Clergy, Freeholders, and Inhabitants of the
County of Hertford.*

The certainty of an approaching dissolution of the present
Parliament renders it my duty to inform you that I shall

not present myself as a candidate for the honour of representing you at the ensuing election. I am induced to
come to this determination solely by personal and private
considerations. What would have been the event of a poll
it is impossible to determine with perfect certainty, but I
have every reason to think, that had I persevered in soli-
citing your suffrages, I should have found the course,
which I have pursued in Parliament, sanctioned by the
approbation of a great majority of my constituents ; and
amongst many reasons for deep regret at dissolving the
connection which has subsisted between us, there is none
which I feel more poignantly than that my opponents will
thereby lose the most legitimate opportunity of arraigning
my public conduct, and I the fairest occasion of defending it.

At this moment you will allow me to recall to your recollection
the address which I published after the last election in
the year 1820, in which I ventured to express a confident hope that the fortitude and courage which had
surmounted the difficulties and perils of the war would
carry the country safely through those heavy embarrassments, which the war had left behind it. This expectation has not been disappointed ; and, though well aware
that elation in prosperity is to the full as dangerous as
depression in adversity, I cannot abstain from remarking
to you, that the House of Commons, which is now called
upon to render up its trust, delivers the public affairs into
the hands of its constituents in a different situation from
that in which it received them ; in a state indeed so improved, that even three years ago the most sanguine mind
would hardly have ventured to hope for the amendment.

At the same time such are the vicissitudes of human affairs,
such the magnitude, complication, and diversity of the
interests of this widely extended empire, that it is impossible to say how soon difficulties may embarrass or
calamity fall upon us. Whensoever that hour shall arrive,
I trust that the nation will be found to have learned from

late experience that safety is to be sought in patience,
spirit, and resolution; in a firm adherence to sound principles and good faith; not in measures of spoliation; not
in ill-considered and desperate projects; still less in
timidity and despondency, exaggerated complaint, and
undistinguishing crimination,

With the warmest gratitude to my friends, for the firm
support and the liberal allowance, which I have ever experienced at their hands; with the acknowledgment to my
adversaries, that from them I have met with nothing but
fair political opposition,—I bid you farewell, and remain,

With great respect,

Your most obedient and devoted Servant,

W. LAMB.

Panshanger, September 22nd, 1825.

Meanwhile canvassing on both sides went on briskly.
Duncombe's gaiety of manner, readiness at repartee, transcendent dandyism and lavish expenditure made him the idol of
the crowd.   His faults were forgiven and his foibles forgotten
in the vehemence of his vows to abolish negro slavery, repeal
the corn laws, and obtain a sweeping measure of parliamentary reform.   He quizzed unmercifully his competitor
in the race as being unsound in both fore-legs; and the
usual interchange of taunts and recriminations was kept up
for some weeks during which the county town enjoyed all
the excitement that usually precedes an election.   But no
election loomed as yet in sight.   Parties in the Government
were so balanced, and it was so difficult to estimate the
probable strength of their respective adherents in the new
Parliament, that Lord Liverpool resolved to defer the
dissolution until the end of another session.   A truce in
electioneering was therefore agreed upon, a fact which
Duncombe announced to his staff early in November by
declaring that the enemy had gone into winter quarters.

Towards the end of February, Hertford was astir once
more with preparations for the election, which could not be

much longer postponed.   Duncombe rallied his partisans
by a characteristic manifesto :—

GENTLEMEN,

Mr. William Lamb, the county member, having, with
that consistency which is so peculiarly his own,
renewed those "scenes" the "heat and agitation" of
which he had so strenuously deprecated, it becomes
necessary for me once more to address you.   Your firmness,
energy, and courage in support of our common cause,
excite in me feelings of the warmest gratitude and
admiration.   Believe me, your reward will not be an empty
one; you may possibly have to encounter the frowns and
petty persecutions of the squirearchy, who seek to enthral
you; you may, it is most likely, forfeit the condescending
protection of noblemen, whose parliamentary influence
your votes have formerly contributed to increase.   But
you will also have the pure and delightful satisfaction of
knowing that you have raised yourselves from the ranks
of slavery to those of freedom.   Cast off with indignation
your unworthy fetters, and raise aloft the noble and gallant
banner of British independence.   I am too proud of the
honourable office of leading you in this glorious cause, not
to feel determined to leave no effort unattempted, and to
spare no exertion that can contribute to such a result,—
united as we are, by the powerful ties of liberty and independence, our success is certain, and we shall, on the
day of the election, read a severe lesson to those who would
trample on your rights, and make you the victims of family
arrangements and unconstitutional compromises.*

Dead walls and wooden gates were decorated, as usual on
such occasions, with every variety of electioneering literature,
and many amusing and ill-natured things were said in speech
and print by heated partisans on either side. Attacks on what
was declared to be his political inconsistency, Lamb did not

* To the truly independent electors of the borough of Hertford.
Queen Street, Mayfair, February 26th, 1826.

seem to mind ; but when it appeared to be part of the tactics
of his adversaries to drag before the hissing crowd the griefs
and troubles of his private life, his pride and sensibility
dissuaded him from continuing the contest.*   Having made
up his mind to retire, the terms in which he announced
his withdrawal confessed frankly his disappointment and
mortification :—

> Driven from the representation of the county by the advan-
> tage taken of my peculiar situation by a minority of the
> freeholders, it would have been very grateful to my feelings,
> and as I view it not injurious to your character, if I had
> found support from you at such a period, and under such
> circumstances.   Such an employment of the elective
> franchise would at least have had in it something of a
> lofty and generous nature.   When, however, I perceived
> that a difference of opinion greater than I had anticipated
> prevailed amongst you, I took the earliest opportunity of
> informing my friends that it did not suit with my views
> to run the slightest risk of failure,—that your suffrages,
> if spontaneously bestowed, would be received with thank-
> fulness, and ever acknowledged with gratitude ; but that
> they were not to me so precious an object as to be sought
> and struggled for against difficulty, ill-will, and opposition.

Looking round amongst his old supporters for some one
eligible to take his place, his choice fell on Mr. Henry
Bulwer, who had already shown that he possessed capability
and ambition to win distinction in a different sphere from
his elder brother.   Two years before he had volunteered to
go out to the Morea, as one of the representatives of the
Greek Committee, confidentially to report to them the actual
state of affairs, and to advise the bondholders in England
with respect to the loan raised to carry on the war.   On his
return he published an amusing volume of letters descriptive

* One of the most malignant attacks of this kind alluded openly to his
wife, and was subscribed " Glenarvon."

of his sojourn in the classic land of conflict; and, on the whole, gained credit by the good use he had made of his powers of observation and judgment.   But his repute as author or envoy went for little with a constituency by this time thoroughly demoralised by rancour, money, and beer. Rather effeminate in appearance and voice, and with more fine appreciation of sarcasm than capacity for rough-and-ready humour, he was never able to overtake the headway made by his dandy competitor.   For a good while he was satisfied with the assurances that in the long run people would lean to a son of their own county in preference to a fancy foreigner from Yorkshire; and what youth of political inexperience ever doubted that his first contested election might after all be won?   So he went on, reporting progress in delicate little notes to Panshanger and Knebworth, till most of his money was spent, and a good deal of the confidence of his discerning friends.   Still it would never do to give in on the eve of the battle, and he persevered to the end.   The Radicals pelted him with imputations of secret help from Hatfield; and the Tories were half afraid to split their votes in his favour, lest with similar help from ultra-Liberals their own man might go to the wall.   In such a triangular duel he was sure to be worsted; and ere the writ came down Whiggery knew it was beaten, though it said nothing about it.   Bulwer's family had long been connected with the county, and he had already given proofs of taste and talent as a writer; but these went for little in the heat and passion of a general election like that of 1826, and notwithstanding all the influence that could be brought to bear in his support, he was distanced at the poll by both his competitors.   A day or two before a creditor to whom a considerable sum was due threatened to arrest Duncombe; and thus prevented his showing himself in the town.   A handbill appeared, containing merely the words "Where is he?"   His friends all the more resolved that he should be ahead early in the day, and having succeeded in placing him there before noon, a triumphant placard was issued, "Where is he now?"

The battle won, he came forth to receive more than the customary meed of gratulation. His unfastidious biographer lauds the exertions he made to win the wavering affections of the constituency throughout this protracted courtship, and then records with a brevity of candour that "Mr. Duncombe having bribed handsomely, secured a majority at Hertford."[*]

The results of the general election were less favourable to the progress of toleration than its supporters had been encouraged to expect: Lord J. Russell was beaten in Huntingdonshire, Mr. Brougham in Westmoreland, Lord Howick and Mr. Beaumont in Northumberland. But in Ireland the revolt of the Forty-shilling Freeholders, till then the electoral vassals of the landed proprietary was signalised by the return of Mr. Villiers Stuart for the county of Waterford, where the influence of the Beresford family had been regarded as supreme.

Lord Melbourne had for some time wished to dispose of a pension of £1200 a year, purchased by his father not long before his death from Lady Gower. It was the moiety of a grant in perpetuity, charged on the revenue of the Duchy of Cornwall, and, in default, on that of the Excise, by Charles II. in favour of the first Earl of Bath, son of Sir Bevil Granville, who fell at Lansdowne fight in defence of the royal cause. It was divided on failure of heirs male between his daughters, one of whom married Sir W. Leveson Gower, the widow of whose grandson sold it for £36,000 to Sir Matthew Lamb. In 1826 Consols stood at or about 75; and the Treasury offered to redeem it at five-and-twenty years' purchase. £24,000 was paid to Lord Mansfield, who held a mortgage for that amount, and the balance, £6000, to Lord Melbourne.

---

[*] 'Life of T. S. Duncombe,' vol. i. p. 86.

CHAPTER XII.

CANNING'S ADMINISTRATION.

Rise of Copley — Coalition — Treatment of Plunket — Dissenters Marriage Bill—A Chief Secretary's Office—Death of Canning— Goderich and Lansdowne.

THE year 1827 was an eventful one in the personal history of those with whom these memoirs are concerned. Early in January the heir presumptive to the throne was borne to the tomb; and a few weeks later, the Premier who had held office nearly as long as Mr. Pitt was laid aside by illness from which he never rallied. The brilliant and versatile chief of the middle or transitional party had likewise in the inclement spring of 1827 threatening notice of his end; but he could not bear to put away the ambitious cup at length so nearly brimming to the full; he owned to Knighton that he had lain awake for many nights without ever losing consciousness, and felt his nervous system quivering from head to heel through the effects of calomel; yet he refused to devolve on Robinson or Huskisson the task of bringing in the promised Corn Bill; and by an effort greater than he could sustain, he performed that difficult duty to perfection. On the 3rd of March Sir Francis Burdett moved for leave to bring in the Catholic Relief Bill. Lord Elliot, for many years an opponent of concession, avowed himself a convert to its necessity. Copley, lately appointed Master of the Rolls, until he entered Parliament had been known as a Radical, and something more. To the surprise of all, he now broke forth as an enthusiast for the policy of "No Surrender." Stirred by his Nisi Prius zeal, Smithfield's

embers glowed again ; the Armada hove in sight; Charles
IX. and his plotting mother were conjured from the dead
to gaze from Louvre windows at Huguenots shot down;
plots to murder Elizabeth ; plots to blow up the Parliament
of James; were made to explode in historic order; the trial
of the seven Bishops was rehearsed; and the charter of
Magdalene College put again in jeopardy; the rebellions of
1641 and 1798, and the dispensing power of royalty with
the pretended air of the Stuarts, were each in turn made to
pass in dread array by one who had in early life professed
himself a Jacobin, and in maturer days a hater of intolerance.
But in March 1827 the Great Seal was visibly slipping from
Lord Eldon's hand; Lord Liverpool was sick unto death;
and the rumour gained currency, that whether Peel or
Canning succeeded him, George IV. had averred that the
keeper of his delicate conscience must be a Protestant.
Whichever way the scales inclined, the Master of the Rolls
meant to be Chancellor. If he could but persuade the King
of his being sound in spiritual things, Canning must know
well enough how flexible and facile he would prove in council.
The *rôle* of bigot was a part worth playing for one night
only ; fastidious critics might condemn, and old companions
stare, but he had made up his mind that it was the way to
win ; and so it proved. His speech drew down many plaudits,
although by not a few the framework of his argument and
most of his historic illustrations were recognised as identical
with those of a recent pamphlet from the pen of the caustic
Prebendary of Durham.* Canning, in reply, could not resist
the temptation of taxing him with plagiarism ; and sought to
blunt the point and dim the glitter of his hastily furbished
fanaticism by the long-remembered travesty of the lines—

> Dear Tom, this brown jug that now foams with mild ale,
> And formerly plighted to Kate of the Vale,
>   Was once Toby Philpotts', &c.

Peel defended warmly his learned and unlooked-for ally

* Dr. Philpotts.

in the policy of resistance. Plunket, on the other hand, grappled fearlessly with the law and the logic of Copley, and by anticipation showed how readily his ill-fitting bonds might be broken asunder, and how quickly he might cast away such cords of conscience from him. In truth it was a memorable wrestling for power. The life of Lord Liverpool hung in the balance; and no man knew for certain who would succeed him, or which policy would prevail. The Master of the Rolls had shortly before delighted the Liberals by his proposed reforms of the Court of Chancery; and he now won the confidence of the wavering monarch by his timely trifling with "No Popery." Plunket, who had spent his best abilities and best days in hewing down intolerance, saw that its wide-spreading branches were at length trembling to their fall; and raising his axe for a final blow, he struck as none but he could strike, even at the root. No man who heard his invective against the short-sighted folly of exclusion, his denunciation of its suicidal selfishness, his malediction of the cruelty of prolonging the fearful tantalisation of a people certain to be eventually free, ever forgot his burning words. They were his last in the Commons. For us they are unfortunately lost; but were gratitude in the world, their worth and courage, uttered as they were in that supreme hour of national fate, would not have passed away. In a House of 548, religious liberty was negatived by a majority of four.

For some weeks George IV. tried by various expedients to withhold from Canning the long-coveted prize of life, which now he claimed as his by equitable reversion. He had served under Lord Liverpool upon the understanding that the removal of religious disabilities was an open question, and that he and those who thought with him sat in the Cabinet in all respects upon a footing of equality with those who thought differently. He would not compromise that equality by admitting their opinion on this vital point to be a disqualification for the first office in the State. His Majesty had in writing assured him that in all other respects he was not only eligible, but pre-eminently qualified in his estimation. If then it was the royal will, that an anti-Catholic must be the future head of the administration, he must ask to be excused from forming a part of it. But no one would venture to try the experiment of governing with only a majority of four.

By Canning's nomination to the Premiership, Brooks's would be rent in twain from the top to the bottom. Lords Landsdowne, Carlisle and Holland, Tierney, Burdett and Mackintosh listened to the suasive voice of Brougham, and one by one agreed to enter into coalition. The Duke of Devonshire and other Whig magnates took the same view, and confidentially aided in promoting the design. Earl Grey, on the contrary, denounced the proposal as compromising the honour of the Whigs, and with him stood inflexibly Lords Althorp, Tavistock and Milton, Lambton, Hobhouse and Lord George Cavendish. Lord Althorp assembled his friends around him at the Albany, and Lord George at Burlington House, where they agreed to remain in opposition to any new Government that might be formed; placing in abeyance the removal of religious disabilities, and Parliamentary reform. Brougham, however, carried the vote of an influential meeting at Brooks's in favour of coalition, Sir Francis Burdett backing him with a paradoxical but amusing speech against the evils of over-tenacious consistency. Throughout the controversy Lamb sided with the coalitionists; but not having a seat at the moment, his opinion had less weight than many of less wit; and the public, though listening eagerly for every informing rumour, knew little of what was going on.*

The suspense lasted to the 12th of April, when the King was at length persuaded to desire Mr. Canning to form a new administration. The Duke, the Chancellor, Mr. Peel, and four other members of the Liverpool Cabinet declined to act under him, and their places were thereupon filled by the Duke of Clarence, made Lord High Admiral, Duke of

* 'Memoir of Earl Spencer,' p. 174.

Portland, Lords Dudley, Palmerston and Harrowby, Mr.
Sturges Bourne, the Marquis of Anglesey, and Copley as
keeper of the Great Seal. Canning's letter offering the last
characteristically ended with the words, *Philpoto non obstante.*
Out of the Cabinet were the Duke of Devonshire, Lord
Chamberlain; the Duke of Leeds, Master of the Horse; Mr.
Tierney, Master of the Mint; Marquis Wellesley, remaining
Viceroy; Plunket raised to the peerage, and designated
as Chancellor of Ireland. The King was as glad to get
the great tribune of the Catholics out of the Commons as
Canning was to have him in the Lords. But no sooner was
his patent of nobility signed, and the seat for Dublin
University vacated, than his Majesty was seized with a spasm
in the Irish side of his conscience, which neither vigorous
nor soothing treatment could allay. He "commanded the
Archbishop of Canterbury to write in his name to Lord
Manners, signifying his desire that he would continue to
hold the Great Seal of Ireland for another year, in order
to afford time for placing it in proper hands."* And his
Lordship at once informed the Lord Lieutenant of the
communication and of his resolution to comply with what
he regarded as a command of the sovereign. After the
Primate's missive had been despatched with instructions to
make it publicly known, its purport was intimated to Mr.
Canning, who needed not this unconstitutional warning how
hollow was the ground on which he trod. Without reflection
or consultation, he forthwith named Plunket Master of the
Rolls in England. The office, being for life, would have more
than compensated his friend in point of emolument for the
loss of higher dignity. The bar, however, murmured at the
intrusion of one who had never practised amongst them,
and that so openly and angrily that, although the Premier
was unwilling to give way, Plunket declined the office, not
being able to reconcile himself to act in opposition to the
feelings of a great number of the profession against the
appointment of an Irishman, or rather an Irish barrister, to

* Marquis Wellesley to Plunket, April 19th, 1827.

a judicial seat in England.* Canning did all that in him lay to retrieve the consequences of a disappointment so undeserved. There was reason to believe that the octogenarian chief of the Irish Court of Common Pleas was not unwilling to resign. Mr. Doherty, a kinsman of the Premier and a favourite with him, undertook to negotiate the change. But it was not so easily accomplished; and during the doubtful interval, Croker, an old antagonist at University election, gave out that Plunket had been made a lord-in-waiting. At length the concession of a step in the peerage secured Lord Norbury's acquiescence; and the worst judge that Ireland ever saw was replaced by one of the most upright, able, and humane.

Althorp, willing to waive his own predilections, and yielding to the judgment of the friends he loved and trusted, was ever governed by the practical desire to shape the ends of party to good purpose. He intimated accordingly his readiness to give the new administration a fair trial, though he declined to cross the floor. His father of late years seldom mingled in debate, but stirred by a sense of the importance of the crisis, he went down to the House of Lords and emphatically expressed, a few days after, his resolve to support Mr. Canning; partly in recognition of his adhesion, but influenced, no doubt, still more by personal estimation. The Duke of Clarence named Lord Robert Spencer, who had gained a high character for efficiency as a naval commander, his private secretary; the Premier requested Lord Althorp to be chairman of the promised Finance Committee.

It seemed as if the occasion that filled his party with exultation and hope was to be for Lamb one only of tantalisation and chagrin. Personally he believed that he was liked by the new Premier, and if he had kept his seat he might fairly have counted on being deemed as eligible as other men of the moderate Whig section who had experience in Parliament, good connections, capacity for affairs, and who were not distasteful to the Court. But what

* Plunket to Mr. J. Lloyd, April 20, 1827.

could he expect, standing as he did outside the lists on the
eve of the race being run? Knowledge, aptitude, courage,
coincidence with the Premier in opinions more than many
of those who were likely to bear office,—what did all avail if
he had neither a following to bring, or a vote of his own to
give? In the middle of the first session of the new Parliament vacancies were not likely to occur; and if they did,
who would secure him a nomination? There was in the
new Cabinet one whom self-interest and good-will alike
prompted to further his desires, and who had the power of
so doing. His relative Huskisson was indeed more powerful than ever. There was little in common between the
personal tastes and habits of the cautious financier and the
frank man of fashion: but there was much in their political
tendencies that since 1822 had drawn them towards each
other. Huskisson, timid and irresolute by nature, had
none of the accomplishments that in public or private life
help to conceal defects and to make knowledge and ability
go far. Beside a leader of superior genius he was invaluable. Full of information, clear in his figures as in his
logic, indefatigable in research and ever ready with illustration, now that Peel had left the Treasury bench he was
second only to the Premier in general estimation. He had
few personal adherents, and might legitimately wish to add
to their number. In the last Parliament Lamb had generally voted with him; and the exclusion of his connection
from the existing House was a source of disappointment
and sincere regret. If he were there again he might with
confidence be relied on as a staunch supporter: if he were
there again, why should he not have office? In a ministerial
crisis a few earnest words frequently determine the future
course of a career. Canning, who was said to have eyes
all round his head, hardly needed reminding that he should
direct a seat to be found for the near connection of the
houses of Cavendish, Spencer Ponsonby, and Howard.
Thus it came to pass that before the writ was moved for
Newport, vacated by his elevation to the chief place in the

Government, arrangements had been made for returning in his room the ex-member for the county of Hertford. At the general election in the preceding year, Lord Eldon's son, the Hon. W. Scott, was returned with Mr. Canning, who had had enough of the onerous distinction of representing a great constituency like Liverpool, and who wished to end his parliamentary career where it had begun. But in the altered condition of affairs the same influence which had returned him in July 1826 could not be depended on in April 1827; and, beset with difficulties on all sides, it was thought imprudent that he should expose himself to the needless risk and trouble of a contest. The Hon. A. F. Ellis readily agreed to make way for him, and he re-entered the House as member for Seaford. Lamb thereupon offered himself for Newport, and on the 27th of April was returned by a small majority. A petition was threatened, but before it could be presented he was appointed Chief Secretary for Ireland.

On Canning's proposal of the newly returned member for Newport as Minister for Ireland, the King said, "William Lamb, William Lamb,—put him anywhere you like." It was in fact one of the appointments that pleased him most; and on coming to kiss hands the felicitations of his Majesty were particularly gracious. Rather than contest Newport again, he availed himself of a vacancy made for him by Mr. William Russell at Bletchingley, for which he was returned without opposition on the 8th of May, while Mr. Scott found a congenial colleague for the Hampshire borough in Mr. Spencer Perceval.

Sir James Scarlett, who up to this time was thoroughly identified with the Whigs, became Solicitor-General; and a further pledge of an altered policy in domestic affairs was given to Ireland by the appointment of Mr. Spring Rice as Under-Secretary for the Home Department. For several years the latter had represented the City of Limerick. His intimate acquaintance with Irish business and great facility in debate had rendered him one of the most trusted and

influential members of his party. His private correspondence shows how highly his judgment and advice were regarded by the most distinguished men of his time on both
sides of the Channel. A better choice could not have been
made, under the circumstances, by a minister desirous of
daily information on all that was thought and said regarding
the Government in that portion of the kingdom, whose long
alienated confidence he wished to conciliate, but whose
hopes and demands he was not yet in a position definitely
to satisfy.

Canning at first offered Palmerston the Exchequer; but
Croker having suggested that he might escape a contest for
the University if he waited until the end of the session, it
was decided that he should remain Secretary at War with a
seat in the Cabinet. He knew, however, that George IV.
hated him. Why (in his Autobiography) he does not say;
but the royal dislike soon made itself manifest in a somewhat curious way. Mr. Canning sent for him, and, with
evident embarrassment, explained how he feared he would
be unable to fulfil his intention of promoting him to be
Chancellor of the Exchequer. He said he was content with
his old office, and there for the moment the matter dropped.
Soon afterwards the First Minister, to his surprise, informed
him that his Majesty had had reason to know that the
vacant Governorship of Jamaica was just the thing he
would like; at which he laughed so heartily that Canning
seemed annoyed, and did not repeat the proposal. Determined to be rid of him at any price, the King then authorized the Premier to offer him the Governor-Generalship of
India, but this also he declined, as he had done when the
splendid post had been suggested as a tempting object of
ambition by Lord Liverpool.*

The new administration was fiercely assailed from the
outset by opposite extremes. Lord Grey in the Upper
House and Hobhouse and Lambton in the Lower headed
the irreconcilables of their party; while Sir R. Peel and the

* Autobiographic Sketch.

Duke of Wellington lent their sanction to the bitterest
attacks on the personal character and conduct of Canning.
The King stipulated that the heads of the law in both
England and Ireland should be men professing sentiments
avowedly opposed to concession. Lamb, who understood
Canning's difficulties, thought he would have been wrong
had he refused to acquiesce. It was something to get
Copley out of the Commons, where, with a seat for the
University of Cambridge and a judicial place worth £8000 a
year for life, he might have become a formidable malcontent
and obstacle in the way of reasonable progress: while in the
Upper House he might more easily recant all he had said
in the Lower, when the proper time came. Nor was he
long in justifying this estimate of his versatility. Even
in the brief remnant of the session of 1827, he threw
Lord Eldon into hysterics by the philosophic radicalism of
his defence of the Dissenters Marriage Bill. All that was
needed to secure the nuptial tie was publicity and certainty,
and the observance of some decorous form. For the rest,
one religious service was as good as another; for the
Established Church only did itself harm and made itself
odious by imposing its sanctions legally on persons professing
other creeds. With such a Court to deal with as that of
George IV., and with a House of Commons still unreformed,
it might well seem Quixotic to refuse the aid which
Lyndhurst had ready to give any premier or party that
wanted him. Canning persuaded his facile colleague
Robinson to take a peerage and the leadership in the
Lords, which he held just long enough to incur a signal
though undeserved defeat on the Corn Bill. His amiable
manners, conscientiousness, veracity, statistical knowledge,
and familiarity with Virgil, admirable accomplishments
as a subordinate debater, were worth just nothing at all
for the defence of a beleaguered position and the chieftain-
ship of an outnumbered party. Enemies he had none ; but
the figure he cut as leader was simply pitiable; and as
generally happens in such cases, the only pity he got was

his own; for his friends were justly provoked beyond measure at his irresolution. Sir Denis le Marchant says: "Even upon an attack from Lord Londonderry I recollect his once bursting into tears." *

Canning sent for Lamb on the eve of his departure for Ireland, and expounded to him the views he entertained of the transitional policy to be pursued. Emancipation was inevitable, and even imminent; but until a government of toleration should be consolidated, it were simple fatuity to attempt its legislative enactment. The way for it must be prepared by administrative changes high and low, so that men's minds might become gradually accustomed to see the friends of toleration and, as far as a bigoted code allowed, the victims of exclusion brought into posts of influence. The Premier spoke with the unreserve of great confidence in the discretion of his new lieutenant; and Lamb bade him farewell not without a certain sadness as he gazed upon his worn features and felt his feverish hand, but still with hopeful anticipation that after the recess he should find him renewed in strength and reinvigorated for the struggle manifestly in store for them. He little dreamed that he should see his face no more. After an hour spent at Lansdowne House he left town for Brocket, where he spent the evening, and then set out upon his journey, travelling by night in consequence of the excessive heat of the weather.†

Ill-health was the sufficient cause assigned for Lady Caroline's remaining at Brocket; but it was his wish that Augustus should accompany him to Ireland. Change of scene might possibly be useful, and any break in the monotonous round of secluded life in which he had latterly spent his days could not be other than beneficial. Stronger even than these considerations was the feeling that he could not bear being long separated from the youth, whom every day he regarded with more tenderness and fondness. To no one did his unuttered thoughts turn in solitude or sleeplessness

* 'Memoir of Earl Spencer,' p. 41.   † July 4th, 1827.

so yearningly or so devotedly; and from no one did he receive wistful looks of affection and confidence so undoubted and undoubting. What would he not have gladly given to be able even to hope that the mysterious cloud might yet pass away from the face of the glass wherein he had been looking for twenty years in vain, to see his own mental image reproduced! And who but himself would take the pains to comfort and cheer the still immature mind that imperfectly seemed to grow more and more sensible of its captivity? Poor Lady Caroline's desultory fits of endearment and paroxyms of solicitude, though natural and touching, were anything but calculated to mend her son's condition, which medically required the avoidance of sudden cause of emotion, whether pleasurable or painful. It was therefore with the strong approval of his physician that Lamb took his son, as he said, to keep him company at Dublin, and to show him a number of things and places he had never seen before.

From the day he took his seat in the Secretary's Room at the Castle access thereto never was denied. His intuitive sense of what he was there to do and how it should be done prompted every look and action without formal preface, programme, or apology. Canning, who knew him well, and who, with longer and larger experience, was a still more consummate discerner of spirits, had placed him there to work out a policy of gradual change, preparatory to the ultimate enactment of justice for all. The way had to be cleared of innumerable prejudices and superstitions of misrule, which though separately small and mean, collectively served to impede the way towards the reconstruction of society on a just and solid basis. There cannot be a doubt that ere his sun went down, the ambitious minister saw the day of justice afar off and was glad; and into the receptive ear of William Lamb he poured from time to time thoughts and imaginings, and hopes and plans which he dared communicate to few. Without ostensibly subverting the outworks of ascendency, he wished to see them gradually dismantled; without forcibly

removing the old land-marks of exclusion, he would have
them quietly overpassed. No written instructions could
have explained all he meant should be done, and no official
power of prophecy could vindicate the times and opportunities
for effecting it. Disciplehood was indispensable for the
purpose; and among his many personal adherents Canning
had none more deft or devoted than his new Minister for
Ireland. From the outset he resolved to see and hear for
himself everybody and everything. The prescriptive reserve
which haunted the Secretary's office he put aside with no
other notice than a hearty laugh. Peel had encircled the
department with an arctic zone of distrust which, save by a
few adventurers, was impenetrable : Goulburn was the centre
of a mere fog, without light or sound or motion. His successor came to bring brighter and more hopeful weather.
The staff of the department viewed his proceedings with
surprise at first, and then with sorrow. Some hinted doubts
as to whether he was quite aware of the sort of persons he
consented to see, and inwardly they deplored the obstinacy
of his imprudence in seeming to talk to them just as he
would to old acquaintances. Old Mr. Gregory groaned;
melancholy Mr. Mangin sighed; the sententious Attorney-
General, Mr. Joy, kept his mind to himself except when asked
point-blank for an opinion, and then flavoured it with a sneer.
The versatile Solicitor-General, Mr. Doherty, who had fought
for his kinsman the Prime Minister at Liverpool elections,
and hoped that he would now have his reward, was all
things to all men; and finding that Lamb loved a joke, plied
him with specimens innumerable of Celtic fun. But the
Secretary went his own way, and kept to it. If agitation
would not go to bed, he would like to have a chat with it;
and when his disposition became known some very queer
people tried how far they could presume on his accessibility :
they found it was not very far. When disposed to be saucy
or disrespectful, he good-humouredly but firmly pulled them
up; never snapping or bullying, but gravely rebuking or
merrily laughing them out of " their damned nonsense." In

a word, he had made up his mind that if he could not take care of himself, it was not worth while getting others to take care of him. His desire was to know if possible what discontents were uppermost in men's thoughts, and what vexations pressed hardest for removal. He would hear what anybody had to say, believing only as little of it as appeared to him to have reason. The messengers of the office used to say long after his time, "When Mr. Lamb was here the only orders were, Show him in :" and though he could not promise to grant one in fifty of their requests, they invariably went away in better humour than they came, and muttering as they passed the sentry at the gate, "Not a bad kind of man that." At the end of an early letter to the Home Office full of details of business he says : "I have a dozen fellows talking to me whilst I write this letter, which will account for its incoherence,"*. in regard to official formalities; for there was none as to substance and sense.

Plunket went to Ireland to enter upon his judicial duties; and he saw Canning no more. They parted with feelings of mutual· dissatisfaction. Lamb, who was the confidant of both, when recalling these circumstances some time after, wrote : "You are of course well aware that Canning was discontented with Plunket, and of course *vice versâ.*"† The minister, who knew best how insecure was still his hold of power, and whose hourly care was to avoid or postpone questions which might afford pretext for quarrel to the King, feared to press anew Plunket's unsatisfied claims, and thought him unreasonable in expecting it. On the other hand, it was not the first time unhappily that Plunket thought he had been let down, where the maintenance of his interests was in the balance. Canning, with all his great and noble qualities, had the character of being shifty and devious in his course; most frequently by being mute where his outspoken aid was

---

* August 22nd, 1827.
† MS. private and confidential to T. S. Rice, September 21st, 1827.

confidently reckoned on. It had been so in 1822, when
Plunket's position and credit were at stake, and when he
was indebted solely for his vindication and triumph to his
own undaunted eloquence. And now, when he had irre-
vocably given up the great position he had in twenty years
established for himself in the House of Commons on the
explicit assurance that he should have the Great Seal of
Ireland as his just reward, he found himself sacrificed to
the very principle of exclusion on account of opinions, by
refusing to acknowledge which in his own case, Canning
had become Premier. Had it it only been a question of
delay, the disappointment might have been easily assuaged.
But Canning did not venture to hold out expectations which
must speedily be dissipated. Lord Manners's stay in Ireland
could not be indefinitely prolonged, and already his successor was resolved on. The choice was certainly a strange,
and even by its object an unsuspected one. Before leaving
London

I told Lansdowne that I knew whom Canning destined for
  Irish Chancellor, and that I thought it an appointment
  which he would approve. He told me that he intended
  Alexander, but that it was a profound secret, known only
  to himself, Lyndhurst, and me; that he had not communicated with Alexander, and did not know whether he would
  accept the office.*

Alexander was known as a sound equity lawyer and an
upright judge, but his translation from Westminster to
Dublin was not contemplated on these accounts alone.
Canning hoped to tempt Brougham, by the offer of the
chief seat in the Exchequer, to quit Parliament, where
formerly he had been an enemy, was latterly a supporter,
but was certain to be always troublesome either as an ally
or a foe. Brougham declined without a peerage, not choosing
to be shelved at forty-nine, and preferring the enjoyments
of popularity and the sort of power it gives to doubling his

* Confidential letter to T. S. Rice.

income, with judicial repose. When Lamb met Plunket for
the first time in Dublin on his return from circuit, he was
secretly embarrassed by knowing what was in contemplation, and fearing the chagrin its announcement would occasion to his friend; but he bears cordial testimony to his
steadfastness during the period of suspense which ensued
on Canning's death :—

> Plunket has been most firm and decided in his language
> during the whole of the late uncertainties, although he
> cannot feel otherwise than dissatisfied, and although, as I
> am informed, great efforts have been made to excite and
> increase that dissatisfaction. Pray mention this to Aber-
> cromby when you see him, and tell him I should like much
> to hear from him.*

Parliament was prorogued on the 2nd of July. Canning
breathed more freely, and set about consolidating his long-
planned edifice of power. Lord Lansdowne assumed the
office of Home Secretary, Mr. Sturges Bourne being content
with the Commissionership of Woods and Forests. Lord William Bentinck was named Governor-General of India. His
nephew, Lord George, being private secretary to the Premier.
A beginning was promptly made in breaking down the
system of sectarian exclusion in the dispensation of patronage and the distribution of honours. In Ireland especially
the change was regarded as significant, and to the Viceroy
and his new Secretary it was the performance of a welcome
duty. Huskisson, advised to go abroad, called to take leave
of Canning on the 18th of July, and struck by his altered
looks, observed that he seemed like the person most in want
of change of air and rest. Canning, who was still in bed,
replied gaily that it was only the reflection from the yellow
lining of the curtains. Huskisson sailed on the 19th,
and landing at Calais, entangled his foot in a cable and
lacerated it so seriously that he was unable to walk for

* Confidential letter to T. S. Rice.

several days. Lady Caroline received frequent letters from
Ireland from her son, full of fondness; and from the
husband, in whose new career she took no little interest,
descriptive of his unaccustomed ways of official life. He
had early intimation from Whitehall of the uneasiness entertained regarding the Premier's condition; but, with his
habitual caution, dropped no hint of it in his letters to
Brocket, lest through that quarter alarm should spread.
Mr. Canning's removal to Chiswick was noticed in the newspapers without particular comment, and it was not until the
6th of August that even in private letters any serious fears
were breathed of his being in danger. A note without date,
probably written on the 7th, is thus explained :—

Brocket, Wednesday.

I have just heard to my excessive horror that Mr. Canning
is dying or dead. I am coming to town in consequence to
know the truth, and if I can to see the Duke of Devonshire.
In the meantime will you call on me to-morrow the
moment you are up, and pray let it be early, I have two
or three notes from William, evidently not knowing this
disastrous news.*

At Innspruck, on the 12th of August, letters from England
informed Huskisson of Canning's convalescence. He went
thence to the Tyrol in better health and spirits. On the
15th, as his party were setting out for Coire, an *estaffette*
from Sir Brook Taylor, Minister at Munich, brought him
a letter from Lord Granville at Paris announcing the
alarming turn which the Premier's illness had taken. As
fast as he was able he returned to Paris, and on the 20th
of August reached the English Embassy. On the way he
heard the fatal news. The funeral had already taken place,
and Huskisson, prostrate with fatigue and grief, remained at
Paris for some time. He there received letters from Lord
Goderich, urgently desiring his return, and offering him the
readership of the House of Commons; this he was assured

---

* To Lady Morgan, who was then in London.

was especially desired by the King. Why he was not placed in the Exchequer, for which he was pre-eminently qualified, does not distinctly appear. Tierney preferred the leisure and comparative obscurity of the Mint; most of the other offices remained as they were, the Admiralty continuing under the presidency, or rather the command, for so he treated it, of the heir presumptive to the throne. The Duke of Wellington consented to be Commander-in-Chief, declaring at the same time that he had never considered the office one which pledged the holder to agreement with ministers of the day on subjects of general policy. Lord Harrowby made way for the Duke of Portland as President of the Council. Lord Carlisle became Privy Seal, and Lord Holland was made Chancellor of the Duchy of Lancaster.

Canning's death caused no alteration in the policy on which his colleagues were agreed. The Duke of Wellington, by accepting the command-in-chief of the army, would, it was supposed, be somewhat mollified in his opposition; and Lord Grey would, it was hoped, be propitiated by the peerage promised to his son-in-law Mr. Lambton. Lord Grenville and the Duke of Buckingham sent their proxies to Lord Goderich, and the appointment of Copleston, the friend of Dudley, to the see of Llandaff gave ministers another vote among the spiritual peers. The country during the autumn was tranquil and prosperous; the revenue promised well; and except in the Levant there was no symptom of disturbance in foreign affairs.

George IV. persuaded himself, when he reluctantly accepted Canning as head of a coalition government, that he would be able to exercise more directly than probably he had ever done before, personal influence and control in nominations to office. In the instance of the Irish Chancellorship he had signally prevailed; and believing Goderich to be far less capable of resistance than his predecessor, he took the occasion of a visit to Windsor to inform him that he desired the appointment forthwith of Herries as Chancellor of the Exchequer. His new minister made no objection, and communicated to Herries, on his return to London, the wishes of the King without, apparently, considering that before doing so he ought to have consulted his Whig colleagues. His Majesty thus lost no time in beginning to humiliate in order to divide the weakened Cabinet. Instead of waiting for Lord Goderich to recommend a new colleague at the Treasury, he had at once named Mr. Herries, reckoning astutely on submission on the part of the too compliant minister. The three Whig members of the Cabinet demurred to this departure from constitutional usage; but finding their remonstrance vain, Lord Lansdowne resigned. The question with him was not new or unconsidered. He was aware of the difficulties with which Lord Liverpool had to contend owing to this disposition of the King. In 1822 Charles Grant had been summarily dismissed from the Chief Secretaryship of Ireland without any assignable cause, and with protestations by Lord Londonderry and by Lord Liverpool himself of the Cabinet's satisfaction at his conduct and regret at his removal, solely because he had been found impracticable in matters of patronage, where the nominees of the Court were concerned.* Such nominees were in those days a numerous brood; and the Irish establishment had long been treated as an outhouse, where they could be conveniently reared. But the Treasury, after all, was the seat and centre of patronage; and his Majesty needed little prompting in his wish that the second as well as the first Commissioner should feel that he owed his place directly to him. Lord Lansdowne therefore upon constitutional grounds refused to sit in a Cabinet whose advice was not previously taken in the filling up of the greater offices. If the Premier had consulted some of the colleagues with whose opinions he had theretofore been more closely agreed, omitting all communication with those who, like himself, had entered into coalition upon a footing of equality, that only made the matter worse. He disclaimed all private or unconfessed objections to Herries, but he refused to aquiesce

* Letter from T. S. Rice to Lord Lansdowne, January 28th, 1822.

in a precedent so destructive of the principle of cabinet responsibility as the independent nomination of Finance Minister by the Crown. The other Whigs were prepared to follow his example, and for some days all was suspense and doubt. At length the King protested that the whole affair was a misconception, and left it to be inferred that whatever mistake had been made was altogether on the part of the Premier. He proffered the Home Secretary an assurance that he had no idea of creating a precedent, by an appointment of the kind, and made it a personal request that he would withdraw his resignation; Lord Lansdowne only yielded, at the end of a long interview, upon condition that he should be at liberty to state to whomsoever he thought fit the reasons why he consented to resume office. The circumstances drew forth warm expressions of satisfaction and confidence from various independent quarters, and tended to establish him in a position of influence with his party, which he ever afterwards maintained.* Brougham was especially effusive in his praise, and more than ever sanguine of the permanency of the Government, and exultant by anticipation at the part of unofficial Coryphæus which he believed it would enable him to play in legal reform. In his other function of self-appointed mentor to the administration he took care to mingle his meed of encouragement with confidential admonitions to prudence, and pliability to the Court, sufficiently amusing :—

What an excellent, honourable, and useful end all this has had. I am sure Lord Lansdowne does far more good to his principles and party by giving way when the matter is so pressed, and on such grounds, than by gaining a victory dangerous to the victor and galling to, and never to be forgotten by the vanquished. Nothing can be better, and I look forward now to amity and courtesy, and I hope kindness, prevailing with the King and our friends. They should not be outrageously proud and dignified, but think

* Letter from T. S. Rice, September 3rd, 4th, and 5th, 1827.

how much good on momentous questions they may do by gratifying the King and his friends in trifles. All other modes seem resorted to of furthering great objects, this alone we always neglect. I rejoice in the prospect before us for the next session. I shall have some half-dozen reforms in our law and policy well matured, for I must avail myself of the influence my singular position gives me in the House to do permanent good; viz. all the weight of being out of place (both weight with the King and country) and the favour of the old Tory opposition, who I do not think will quarrel with me rashly.*

His vituperation of Herries was equally exaggerated; and the *Times* having taken a similar tone, while the *Courier* defended the favourite of the King, a polemic ensued between the oracles of the two sections of the Cabinet. Lord Goderich, much disturbed thereby, sent his private secretary, Mr. Drummond, to the Home Office to expostulate against what he supposed to be Whig instigation. The Under-Secretary disavowed any personal knowledge of the writer in the *Times*, or of any influence which might have swayed him; but he promised, through a third party to suggest the cessation of the strife as injurious to the stability of the Coalition; and thereupon communicated through his friend Empson with Mr. Barnes. The *Courier*, on the other hand, was persuaded to moderate the rancour of its pen, and for a time there was peace between the journals.†

Lord Lansdowne did not consent to form part of the re-organised administration without making terms for his friends; these are best told in his own words:—

I have arranged, I will not say insisted, that an arrangement should immediately be made for bringing Mackintosh and young Stanley into office, so that there is respect for the past and hope for the future. Lord Darlington is to be a marquis, likewise my friend Lord Camden; the Chan-

---

* From H. Brougham to T. S. Rice, September 4th, 1827.   † Idem.

cellorship of the Exchequer has been pressed again upon
Sturges Bourne, also upon Huskisson. It is essential
that all this should be made known to justify an acquiescence which I think requires a little propping up in
the public eye.

Mr. Stanley spent a few days at Bowood early in September,
upon the intimation of his appointment as Under-Secretary
for the Colonies, with which he was much pleased; and his
official life commenced in October.

After a visit to Panshanger, Huskisson returned to
Eartham, where his physicians thought he must remain for
the quiet and repose indispensable to his recovery. He was
subsequently reported to be very low in bodily health and
much depressed in spirits; and among the apprehensions
which his state occasioned was the effect which his continued debility might have in the approaching session by
giving greater scope and prominence to words and works of
supererogation from their irrepressible patron Brougham.*
Huskisson's health did not improve. The Home Secretary
was alarmed at the accounts which reached him on the subject—"It is unnecessary to proclaim it to the profane, but
we cannot disguise from ourselves that he is *l'homme neces-
saire* for this administration."†

* Letter from T. S. Rice, September 14th, 1827.
† From Bowood, September 16th, 1827.

CHAPTER XIII.

DUBLIN CASTLE.

Dublin Corporation—Assistant Barristers—Police Force—Subsidising the Press—Jobbing—Post Office Abuses—Agrarian Combinations.

It had been usual to vote the honorary freedom of Dublin to each Chief Secretary on his assuming office; but in the bitterness of party, the compliment was now for the first time withheld. At a meeting of the Common Council early in August, the proposal to follow the usual precedent was rejected upon the specific ground that the Goderich Cabinet were not to be trusted, and that their newly appointed representative in Ireland had disentitled himself by his votes and speeches in Parliament to the confidence of the Protestants of the realm. The Board of Aldermen were more nearly divided in political opinions; and on a subsequent day they agreed to atone for the affront thus offered by appointing a deputation to wait on Mr. Lamb with a copy of an address which they desired on a convenient day to present with civic formalities. He received the deputation with due courtesy, and said he would intimate to the Lord Mayor when he should be ready to receive the address in form. It would not have been easy to give a public answer, such as would satisfy the Corporation in its querulous mood, without seeming to compromise the policy of the Government; and as nothing was to be gained by entering into controversy with a public body daily losing influence and repute, it was thought most prudent to defer the formal reception of the address *sine die*.

In July appeared the first of a series of articles entitled ' Lessons for Lamb,' written by Mr. Stanton, the proprietor of the *Morning Register*. Their object was to direct his attention to the abuses in local taxation long admitted by successive holders of power. Promises of reform had frequently been made by Mr. Goulburn and others; but these had been forgotten as soon as uttered, and the citizens of Dublin, then oppressed with assessments to the amount of over £250,000 a year, had too much reason of complaint against Government. One of the most crying of these grievances was the corrupt and oppressive mismanagement of the impost levied on house property under the name of "pipe water and metal main rates." The new Chief Secretary was counselled to make no hasty pledges of redress, but to set about the work in a workmanlike manner, and wait for popularity till the thing was done. A Select Committee had recommended all that was desired in 1822, and another in 1825 reported to the same purport; yet still the overtaxed and tantalised householders waited for a cheap and good supply of water. In reply to remonstrances often urged previously in vain, the Irish Secretary gave an unconditional pledge that all the details of local disbursements should be in future open to investigation. This was received in Dublin with a degree of satisfaction that reads to us now as painfully strange. Yet it is quite true not only that the irresponsible local officials had up to this time contemptuously refused to publish annual accounts but that gross instances of wholesale malversation were brought to the notice of the executive without convincing them that ratepayers were entitled to have cognisance of the way in which their money was expended.

Nowhere did the ill effects of misused patronage manifest themselves more mischievously than in the demoralisation of the constabulary. Needy and incompetent men were frequently appointed to sub-inspectorships, and sometimes to higher posts, in districts where their antecedents were too

well known.   Abuses, both in the nature of partiality and
corruption, grew apace.   The chief constables were generally
above their business; they lived expensively, ran in debt,
and then were at the mercy of their inferiors.   Spring Rice
transmitted the copy of a note he had just received on the
subject, omitting names, which he did not venture to insert
owing to the existing state of the Post Office :—

It is reported that —— is dismissed.   At all events he
owes more than he can ever pay, and of course cannot
appear; he is now *at Paris.*   —— is also in debt beyond
his means, and I believe —— is as deep as either.   The
police horses, after being fed for some time on grass cut in
the hedgerows, are turned out to grass where they are
useless for the public service, as they are kept by the
farmer in pledge for their grazing.   There are now ten or
twelve persons paid as inspectors and chief magistrates.   If
they were all changed into superintendents of districts of
three or four counties it would be much more efficient
with *half the number* of chief constables than the present
establishment.   This would create a clear saving by the
reduction of the chief constables, and it would save the
expense of paymasters in Dublin and pay-clerks in the
counties, as the inspector's clerk could pay in every
district.   Many other savings might also be effected.

Lamb thought the improved condition of the country would
allow of a reduction of £10,000 a year in the estimate for
the mounted police, and he so reported to Whitehall.   But
ere the winter closed, his hope of lasting tranquillity vanished,
and Tipperary became as turbulent as ever.

The Irish Secretary frequently thanks his indefatigable
correspondent at the Home Office for his confidential suggestions on practical topics connected with Ireland, on many
of which he confessed himself to be wholly uninformed; but
it was easier to receive and read than to answer or act upon
these recommendations Some of his terse and thoughtful
observations of what was going on around him are curious :—

I am worried by magistrates, assistant barristers, &c., for the statutes; but the printer assures me that they are not yet printed in England. Pray let me know how this is. Nobody in England ever, I believe, thinks of a law till about a year after it has passed; but here they are so busy and eager for new laws that there is no satisfying them.

Disregarding precedent of failure in 1806, Plunket had advised the appointment in 1824 of a Roman Catholic, Mr. Richard Farrell, to the office of Assistant Barrister. Lord Manners and Mr. Goulburn did not approve; but they did not actually refuse to comply. There was a good deal of grumbling among the privileged majority of the outer bar at the ominous infraction of a system hitherto strictly observed. But the intruder was personally unexceptionable; and with a shrug and a sigh the deviation from orthodox rule was allowed to pass. No further attempt was then made to go beyond the pale of sectarian monopoly, or to show six millions of people whose allegiance was claimed, and whose taxes were levied by law, that their ordinary disputes in a court of justice were triable without respect of creeds: and Lamb found in Ireland but one county-court judge professing the ancient faith. His sense of right and of policy revolted at the continuance of this needless aggravation of injustice, and he recommended strongly that it should be gradually swept away.

It would take me some time to collect and digest the materials necessary for answering your letter of the 31st ult. as fully as I could wish. But I prefer noticing imperfectly the various important suggestions made in it to the appearance of delay and neglect. It may be proper in this place to inform you that most, if not all the points to which your letter adverts, have been already considered by the Lord Lieutenant; and that I have already discussed with him the propriety of preparing the necessary documents, with a view to their early discussion in the

next session of Parliament. Before, however, I advert to
those subjects which you have enumerated, I will shortly
mention other matters, some of which have been already
brought forward under the Lord Lieutenant's direction,
and all of which are intended to be introduced in the
next session, entirely agreeing with you and the Lord
Lieutenant that it will be wise to employ the present
time in maturing and preparing measures, so as to have
them actually in readiness by the meeting of Parliament.
1. Jury Bill.—I have received some suggestions founded
on the differences between the law and the practice of the
two countries, to which it appears to me that it will be
necessary to advert. I have submitted the bill to the
judges, and am assured by the Chief Justice that he will
consider it, and give me his opinion upon it; and I will
take care that any alteration which it may appear wise to
adopt shall be communicated to you at a period sufficiently
early to enable you to form your own judgment deliberately, and to obtain upon it the opinion of others. 2. The
General Paving and Lighting Bill.—This bill, as well as
the Jury Bill, was brought in *pro formâ* and printed in
the course of the last session, and the same course shall
be pursued with it. 3. The bill for the renewal of the
Insolvent Act was left by Mr. Goulburn in a complete
state of preparation; but as it is a subject of great importance and great interest, on which opinions are a good
deal divided, and as great abuses are said to prevail in the
administration of this branch of the law, I wish to call
your particular attention to it, and to beg that you will
suggest any alteration which you may find calculated to
obviate inconvenience and prevent fraud. 4. The bills
for the consolidation and amendment of the criminal law,
the prevention of malicious outrages, are in a state of for-
wardness; but they require great care and consideration,
the law of Ireland being in many points essentially
different from that of England. Similar acts have been
in operation in England during the late assizes, and it

would be desirable to have the benefit and advantage of the experience which has now been had of their actual working in practice. With respect to any reformations of the law generally, it appears to me not unadvisable that this country should follow England at a certain interval of time, for the sake of experience and greater maturity of legislation. These are the principal measures not mentioned in your letter, which are at present under the consideration of the Lord Lieutenant, and I now proceed to those which you have enumerated. 1. The statutes which relate to public works.—Whatever may be the decision upon the general principle of these measures, which is a large and important question for every Government, and more particularly for the Government of a country placed in such peculiar circumstances as Ireland, it is evidently expedient to reduce to some order the statutes which prescribe and regulate this system, and which appear to be extremly confused—so much so, indeed, that I own myself unable to understand them, and to provide, as you suggest, for some methodical arrangement in the execution, and some frequent and strict audit of the expenditure. At the same time, the difficulty of effecting this object will be considerable, and will form the main ingredient in the considerations of the wisdom of the general principle, and certainly one of the strongest objections to the adoption of it. The advancing of public money for such purposes in Ireland as a general measure originated in the severe distress of 1822. Unquestionably the works then undertaken in Ireland have been highly beneficial to the country, and have greatly relieved local distress. The extreme pressure of that crisis, however, and the great solicitude of Parliament for the immediate application of the grants to the relief of the suffering population, prevented the possibility of applying such effectual checks on a systematic plan against the danger of mismanagement and abuse, as may be provided, if it should be determined to establish a system of

this description for the future benefit of Ireland. It
would be well to know with certainty what has been done
in England on this subject; what abuses may have been
practised, and remedies applied or suggested for the future
regulation of such expenditure. 2. The civil bill process
is under consideration, and I am in hopes of soon having
a bill in such a state of preparation as to be able to submit
it to the judges for their consideration. 3. A bill has
been prepared for the reformation of the abuses pointed
out by the report on the office for the registration of
deeds. This bill is now also under consideration, and no
exertion shall be spared in order to have an efficient
measure in preparation by the opening of Parliament.
I cannot find that this report has been referred to the
judges, certainly no opinion has been given, nor do I
believe formed by them upon the subject, but before the
bill is transmitted to you their opinion shall be taken.
4. Tolls and Customs.—This is a large, and as affecting
the rights of Corporations, a delicate position, upon which I
confess myself uninformed; but attention shall be paid to
it, and I shall be thankful for any suggestion or information on the subject. 5. Grand Jury presentments.—It
is unnecessary to expatiate on the magnitude, the importance and the difficulty of this subject, connected and
interwoven as it is with all the transactions and with the
whole system of the local administration of this country.
Plans of reformation may be suggested by others, but it
would only be deceiving you, and subjecting myself to
the charge of presumption, if I were to hold out any
expectations of being prepared myself to bring forward
any general measure on this subject in the next session of
Parliament. I am well aware that a bill has been re-
peatedly called for; but you are well aware that those
measures which are the most loudly demanded are often
found the most difficult to get adopted, and that the plan
which receives the most general assent is apt to be
subjected in detail to the most serious objection and

opposition. I do not mean to say that some beneficial amendments may not be devised immediately, but with respect to the general question, I should apprehend that the renewal of the committee of last year would be found the preferable mode of proceeding. It is proper here to state that Mr. Goulburn, with the Lord Lieutenant's approbation, intended to have submitted the matter to a committee of the House of Commons in the last session of Parliament as a preliminary step to the introduction of any new law. 6. The Corporate Magistracy in both countries requires serious consideration, and will, I am convinced, soon press itself inevitably on the attention of the legislature. You are of course aware of the 7 Geo. 4 c. 61, which has given the Lord Lieutenant the power of applying a remedy in cases of necessity. 7. Tithe.—The Tithe Composition Act passed in 1823, has been carried into effect in 940 parishes. The total parishes in Ireland are 2600, and at the present time the Act is preparing to be carried into effect in about two hundred parishes. This is a copy of a return which I obtained from the office here upon my first arrival. Some further progress has been made since that time, but nothing very material. It would undoubtedly be highly beneficial to establish a still more permanent system, but considering the great progress this measure has made and is still making, and the extensive and increasing advantages resulting from it, together with the consideration that the earliest of these compositions have still eighteen years to run, induce me to submit to you that it would not be advisable to interfere further at present with this subject, which we know to be so pregnant with jealousy and alarm. An extension of the leasing powers of the Church would be highly advantageous in both countries, but the agitation of such a question at present, especially in Ireland, strikes me as liable to all the prudential objections which I have hinted at above. 8. Sheriffs.—A bill has been prepared on this subject. The abuses stated in the report are admitted still to prevail in some parts of Ireland; but those who are best informed on the subject appear to conceive that there will be considerable difficulty in devising such legislative measures as will obviate these abuses without running the risk of introducing and encouraging others. 9. Education.—This question is, as you observe, far too large for incidental discussion. It is one of great delicacy and difficulty, particularly in the point of view in which it is placed by your letters; but it has received and will receive the most anxious consideration on the part of the Lord Lieutenant. In a matter in which religious jealousy is so strong, and religious feelings so highly excited, and so many conflicting interests and passions are to be conciliated, it is impossible to proceed otherwise than with the greatest caution and deliberation. I have thus gone through very generally and very imperfectly the several heads of your letter. I will write more particularly upon each of them, according to the information I collect and the views which open themselves. No exertion, depend upon it, will be spared on the part of the Lord Lieutenant for the purpose of enabling his Majesty's Government to bring forward in a mature and perfect shape such measures as they may deem it expedient to propose; or to give a full statement of their views and intentions upon any subject to which the attention of Parliament may be directed by others. The Lord Lieutenant has seen this letter, and entirely approves it.*

A kindly and confiding rejoinder from the Home Secretary expressed his

Satisfaction that nearly all the measures on which he had written connected with Ireland, respecting which it was desirable that some decision should be taken previous to the ensuing session, as well as others not immediately adverted to, had engaged the attention of the Lord Lieutenant and his Chief Secretary. He need not repeat that

* From W. Lamb to Lord Lansdowne, September 19th, 1827.

while he felt it his duty to dwell occasionally upon those points connected with the local administration of Ireland which had led to discussion in or out of Parliament, he felt persuaded they had not been overlooked in Ireland, and that Lord Wellesley and he were best able to judge of the nature of the difficulties which interfered with a remedy where the present system should be considered defective. Upon several of the measures under consideration, Rice's experience as a magistrate and a grand juror would enable him to furnish useful suggestions, and he had requested him to write fully as to details.*

Throughout the whole period an active correspondence was kept up between Whitehall and the Castle; the vigilant and suggestive Under-Secretary being full of practical information as to men and things, which he seems to have been always ready to impart to his friend. Some of the cautions and commentaries interchanged regarding the disposal of patronage, and projects of all kinds for effecting jobs are sufficiently amusing. After a long disclosure of the local abuses existing in the constabulary force, Spring Rice says :—

I received a letter this morning that is so comical, but so instructive, that I cannot resist giving it to you. Dick Martin caught hold of Goulburn and Copley (last session) and, under pretence of assimilating the law, obtained their support of a bill abolishing the functions of coroners in civil matters, they having immemorially enjoyed a power concurrent with sheriffs in execution of civil process. I warned Goulburn of the mischief he was about to sanction; but he was suspicious, I inexorable. I divided the House, but of course was beaten, and the bill was carried. What has been the result? Look at the report of the Commissioners. A monopoly of injustice being given to the sheriffs, the difficulty of recovering debts has been augmented tenfold; and to complete the whole argument by one illustration, I received a letter from

* Lord Lansdowne to W. Lamb, October 4th, 1827.

a magistrate and a grand juror, a late high employé of the Government, and a near relation of a noble friend of yours and mine, of which I now give you a literal copy :—
" I have this moment heard that the Commissioners of " Inquiry recommend that coroners should be employed " as before, in the execution of civil process. Have the " goodness to drop me a line to say if this is to be the case, " for if it be so, all poor gentlemen who unfortunately " happen to be in difficulties must fly the country. God " forbid that it should be so." *

Among other subjects discussed in the confidential correspondence of this period was the pecuniary relations existing between the Government and the press. An annual vote was regularly taken, nominally for the expense of publishing proclamations in certain Irish journals; and another for printing the Dublin Gazette. Both had from time to time been questioned in Parliament, the latter as being excessive in amount, and the former as wrong in principle; but the Liverpool administration had defended the outlay as a legitimate and necessary means of influencing public opinion, and in committee of supply were always successful on division. In point of fact, the prices paid for the insertion as advertisements of royal proclamations yielded a sufficient profit to the conductors of certain favoured newspapers to sustain them with a very limited sale. One of these was the *Hibernian Journal*, which it was admitted had no circulation worth mentioning,.and no contributions worth reading. The patronage of the Castle had been withdrawn from it by Mr. Charles Grant, when Chief Secretary, and the following week it ceased to appear. Other newspapers made a better show of independent existence, and continued to be recipients of Treasury pay. Spring Rice urged strongly the policy of reforming the system of Government advertisements, and of renouncing openly the idea of guiding or controlling opinion by a method at once wasteful and indefensible.

* T. S. Rice to W. Lamb, September 27th, 1827.

Is this mode of influencing the press worthy or honourable, or even effectual? Does a good Government require this aid? Can it support a weak one? And, above all, does it not contain within it mischiefs infinitely greater than any it seeks to avert? The best answer to these questions is to be found in the actual condition of the press. The influence of these proclamations is so well known and admitted that the papers writing under this retaining fee have but little weight with the public. The editors, in place of thinking of the public only, worship the Castle, and then generally repay the favours they receive in adulation, base, unprincipled, and tasteless. On the other hand, the papers excluded from a participation in these profits are driven into furious discontent. The favoured few, being monopolists, consider they have a right to do as they choose, charge what they like, and the result has been a general system of jobbing and corruption. In Limerick, for example, the Commissioner of Accounts for several years reported fraudulent and unreasonable charges against a particular paper, and yet to the present time it has received the patronage of the Government. If not right, can all this be useful? The whole has produced the degradation of the press without contributing to the power of the Government. If retrenchment is to be practised, is not this one of the points on which economy and sound policy run together? The Dublin Gazette is one of those jobs which, producing no benefit at all commensurate with its cost, which either the carelessness of the Local Government or the ignorance of the Treasury has allowed to continue. The most effectual remedy would be to reduce the duty on advertisements, and to throw upon all papers the necessity of inserting proclamations gratuitously. In an Irish paper of twenty or thirty years back you will find the advertisements greater than at present, though the lands, &c., to be let or sold, and the commercial transactions of the day were then less important in all Ireland than they now are in a single province. Duties on advertisements operate as a tax on the transfer of commodities, and as such are objectionable on every principle by which taxation ought to be regulated. If this be impracticable, let the proclamations be inserted only in the Gazette, and such as are locally interesting will be gratuitously reprinted in the newspapers. All this applies to Government notices in every civil and military department.[*]

The letter containing these suggestions was first sent for approval to Lord Landsdowne, who replied next day :—

I shall forward your letter to Lamb, with a line from myself. I entirely concur in your view of the course which it would be most dignified, and ultimately most useful for the Government to pursue ; but we must hear what he feels and thinks on the subject.[†]

His individual assent was cordially and promptly given to the views thus enunciated, and in his reply he fully expressed his concurrence in the propriety of withdrawing the subsidies from the press.[‡] Nevertheless, he found the opinions even of the best among his local advisers adverse to a sudden change of system :—

Plunket when he heard of our scheme about the press laughed loudly, and said, "Oh, this is Utopian." I only mention this to show you what strong possession the idea has of minds here. I am not apt to be very positive about future measures, but if I feel confident of anything, it is that taking away all the payments would not in the least diminish the strength of the Government.[§]

He had not been long in Ireland before he conceived

* From T. S. Rice to William Lamb, September 12th, 1827.
† Lord Lansdowne to T. S. Rice, September 13th, 1827.
‡ From Lord Lansdowne, September 23rd, 1827.
§ Letter from W. Lamb, not dated, but probably towards the end of September.

the idea of making a personal acquaintance with some of the leaders of agitation. Sir Philip Crampton, with whose conversational talents he was especially charmed, undertook to gratify his wish by asking Shiel to meet him at dinner. The only other person invited was Mr. Blake, the Chief Remembrancer, who, though a Catholic, had long enjoyed the confidence of Lord Wellesley and Lord Grenville, and was the intimate friend of Lord Plunket. The Chief Secretary threw aside all reserve of tone, and invited equal candour. Shiel depicted as few could so graphically do the chronic sources of predial disturbance, which he argued were aggravated and heightened by the sectarian character of the administration of justice. While combating stoutly for the indispensability of maintaining order at any cost, as the first condition of legal liberty, Lamb was involuntarily moved by the touching recitals of wrong and oppression which daily drove the peasantry to madness; and he disdained to hide his disgust at the manner in which criminal justice was administered by exclusive juries and a partisan bench. He began to understand for the first time in his life whence arose the anarchic sympathy with agrarian outrage which was not shown to mean or mercenary crime. Involuntarily yielding to the force of new conviction, he asked numerous questions, and listened with increasing curiosity to the details of cases illustrating internecine war between the many and the few. It happened that several of these were instances of lawless vengeance dealt out by the peasantry on process-servers, tithe-collectors or small proprietors themselves. "And why," he asked, "don't they go at the big ones?" Absenteeism answered the question in part, and for the rest the habit of going armed after nightfall, which at the time prevailed in many counties. A well-known landlord in Tipperary was commonly called the "Woodcock," because he was so hard to hit; and other examples were supplied by Sir Philip to prove, as he said, that there was no especial tenderness shown to rank or fortune. But the significance of the question, and the tone

in which it was put, were not to be forgotten.   Ten years
afterwards, when the minister had reached the height of
power, it was recalled to his memory by Shiel.

Lamb spent but a few months in Ireland, and it cannot
be said that he accomplished great changes during his
stay.   To him it was not given.   But he did what he could.
He visited the Four Courts Marshalsea, then the Dublin
Debtors' Prison, which was at the time singularly unhealthy
and ill-regulated.   Spendthrifts who had lost caste in society,
speculators who had gone half crazed with their schemes,
bravos of old descent and ruined fortunes, who were fond of
boasting of the real or fabulous deeds they had done, and
litigants whose pertinacious seeking for justice had brought
them to beggary, with a crowd of obscure and wretched
victims of misery, dwelt together, each as he chose, or could,
in every variety of defiant jollity and wan despair.   Certain
reforms had been not long before carried into effect ; and he
expressed himself satisfied with the improved discipline and
cleanliness which began to be visible ; but he thought the
whole system bad and requiring thorough change.   One
thing he did accomplish, namely, to abolish the weekly
rent paid by debtors for their miserable unfurnished rooms ;
" this, as well as being a great relief to poor persons, would,
independent of its consideration in a pecuniary point of view,
compel the authorities to classify the prisoners."

From the time of Lord Cornwallis, jobbing in every
department of the public service had continued to be
regarded as a perquisite of nobility and gentry, which it
was a mere vulgar affectation to disguise or deny.   Church
dignities, judicial appointments, cadetships in India, places
in the excise, post office, and police, formed the recognised
staple of the wholesale and retail traffic carried on with
Government.   Peers and members of Parliament, prelates
and ladies of fashion partook the richest fruits of the field
of patronage ; country gentlemen of influence, advocates of
note at the bar, and trusted officials of more or less weight,
gathered the gleanings and found them ample.   Not only

the prevalent feeling, but the almost invariable tone of application for employment and promotion implied the absolute belief that nothing was given away except by favour. Fitness or unfitness was hardly worth talking about. To carry the Union the country had been drowned in corruption; and the pestiferous flood, though gradually subsiding, still overspread the land, and stifled the growth of self-reliance, of merit, and of industry. Demands of the audacious magnitude which Lord Castlereagh was instructed to grant, and Sir Arthur Wellesley somewhat later thought it expedient to palter with, had become rarer in the days of their successors in office; Government in a certain sense had bought up the privilege and power of many great families to be troublesome; the market had grown flat, and only now and then, or here and there, booty on the old scale could be wrung from economising imperialism or irresolute viceroyalty. Lord Wellesley had striven at the outset to assert his right to the more valuable appointments civil and ecclesiastical, and when his peculiar domain was encroached upon by Downing Street he tried hard to preserve a veto. Towards the end of his pro-consulate even this was frequently infringed; and the place-hunters of high and low degree learned more and more to look to London as a true and higher source of all quarterly blessings. Lamb was not long in Ireland before he felt the pressure of influence thus exercised or attempted through his colleagues in England. Unacquainted with the personal character of nineteen out of twenty applicants for favour, and indisposed by temperament to think ill of persons without specific cause, he would have easily become an assenting party to many bad appointments, had the Home Office been in other hands. One of the best consequences, however, of his intimacy with Spring Rice, and his confidence in Lord Lansdowne, was that from time to time he was kept aware of predatory designs upon the Irish executive ere they came ostensibly before him. A confidential letter from the Under-Secretary on the 15th of September contained an intimation that Lord —— wanted a piece of preferment of more than ordinary distinction ; and as he was an hospitable, busy, talkative, and not very scrupulous individual, who had no other claim on the consideration of Government than the vague fear that he might be able to exercise some power of annoyance in case he was refused, Lamb laconically replied, " I have never heard of the application, and you may depend upon it, if I can help it, it shall not be done.   G—— indeed ! not if Lady G—— should," &c.*   Far greater was his consternation on receipt of the further warning which his brief epistle had evoked.   To the Irish Secretary, hitherto incredulous as to the system of espionage carried on, Spring Rice wrote without reserve, " What would Lady G—— say if a copy of your letter was sent to her ?"†   Certain information had reached the Home Department that the Post Office was not to be depended on, where letters to or from official persons were concerned.   The local staff in Ireland consisted almost exclusively of the dependants of the party theretofore in power ; and a common instinct inspired them with apprehension, lest in the consolidation of the new Government not merely the empire should be ruined, but their special monopoly should be broken up.   Fresh indications that letters from the Castle were tampered with, early aroused the suspicion of the Under-Secretary, and at length on the 24th of September he wrote privately to his chief, who was then at Bowood :—

It is quite clear that the seals of Lamb's last three letters have been broken at the Irish P.O.   This I knew to be suspected ; but the appearances of the last speak for themselves, and I have written to Lamb on the subject.   I shall direct three or four small boxes to be prepared for the Irish correspondence, as it would never answer to have the correspondence between this department and the Castle, examined by the Orange clerks at the Post Office.

* T. S. Rice, September 19th.
† T. S. Rice to W. Lamb, September 1827.

At length even Lamb's good-nature could no longer keep its eyes shut to what was going on around him :—

You frighten me out of my wits about my letters, not so much for what may have been in them of a public as of a private nature. Did you get a line in answer to yours about G——? I hope they have not sent a copy of it to her ladyship. When I first came here I was told that malpractices took place at the Post Office ; but my letters seemed to go so safe, and yours to come, that I gradually lost all distrust, and, I must say, I have never observed anything in the appearance of the letters from England to excite the least suspicion. By asking at the Irish Office you may see our keys; they are quite different from those of the Cabinet. When I got your letter yesterday morning, I sent for Lees, but, upon second thoughts, I considered it best to say nothing to him about the matter, as it would give alarm and induce caution. If such things are done it is best that they should go on in order that they may be detected.*

Later on he was again assured from the Home Office that the seals of his letters were tampered with frequently ; luckily, the one about which he was most uneasy had escaped. On examination, the locks of the Irish Office boxes had been pronounced worthless as a preventive against furtive prying ; the new ones, it was hoped, would prove more reliable. How to effect a discovery was the puzzle.

In the old times the practice of opening letters at the Post Office was adopted, I believe, for the convenience of the Government, and, like every other bad measure, it recoiled on its authors. Forbes, one of Grattan's friends, wrote during the critical times of the Regency, and concluded by saying: "I would tell you much more, but, at this moment, that old rogue John Lees is reading every word of the letter." The prudent course is the one you have

* W. Lamb to T. S. Rice, September 27th, 1827.

taken, to lie by and watch. Send the letters you despatch
from the Castle or Park in some *safe* person's keeping. It
has been suggested that it is in that part of the journey
that the mischief occurs.*

Later on renewed uneasiness was felt at Whitehall owing
to the renewed proofs of malpractices in the Post Office ; and
various suggestions were made for detecting the offenders :—

Have you any police person you can rely on? If not, shall
we send you a Bow Street officer ? Turn this in your mind,
for be assured treachery is somewhere latent about you,
and presents an example of the entire Irish system.†

But the Irish Secretary was not to be easily scared or drawn
into departing from the characteristic bearing and demeanour
by which through life he was distinguished. Keenly susceptible of reproach and femininely sensitive to misconstruction,
his sagacity and his pride equally concurred in forbidding
him to betray the pain or uneasiness he suffered. What
casual observers set down for indifference was in truth but
the consistent adherence to his notion of what became a
public man, in whatever circumstances he might be placed.
To wince when hurt in presence of the crowd was in his
view weakness unpardonable ; to countervail artifice and to
baffle attack he would listen to any suggestion, and resort
to any legitimate means ; but to show uneasiness, or to
confess being out-witted, was in his mind to prove incapacity
for the conduct of affairs. In great things and in small he
pursued the same line of what seemed to be *insouciance*,
sometimes haughty, sometimes jocose, but always perplexing
to adversaries and reassuring to friends. His reply to the
recommendation above noted was in this vein :—

With regard to the letters you suspect to have been opened,
recollect the absolute necessity of precision upon such
points ; the extreme difficulty of proof, and the manifest

* Letter from T. S. Rice, October 2nd, 1827.
† Letter (secret) from T. S. Rice, October 29th, 1827.

absurdity of stirring in such a matter with the least chance of failure. Recollect that these letters have passed through both Post Offices. The letter dated the 28th, though it bore the post-mark of the 29th, I wrote here late at night, and sent it into town in the morning by the messenger, which accounts for that circumstance. You say that the seals and covers establish beyond all possible doubt the fact that both seals had been broken. Now upon inspection it does not seem to me that there is the least appearance of either of them having been *broken*. They have been torn and cut round, but neither has been broken; and if I produce these covers and seals, all they will have to say is that they know nothing about it, and considering the variety of hands they have passed through since they were in the Post Office here, it will be quite impossible to fix anything in the shape of proof upon any individual belonging to that establishment. I will send by the post to-morrow two letters to you and two to Landsdowne—that inside with a cross × on the outside. Observe in what state they come; do not open them unless they appear to have been untouched; return them in the state in which you receive them. If you do not receive them at all let me know.*

Next day he wrote:—

It is impossible for me to judge by the state of the covers after they have been opened, whether they have been meddled with or not. It is a strong circumstance that you who see them as they arrive think that they have. But are you sure, after all, that it is not the badness of the sealing-wax, and my careless manner of folding and sealing a letter, for which I was always famous? Do you judge by the crease across the seal; and if you do, may not that have been occasioned by my tearing a sheet of paper for a cover, and in folding it, allowing the rough

* From W. Lamb, November 2nd, 1827.

torn edge to remain outwards ? The person who manages the English (branch of the) Post Office here is Mr. Homan, who was connected with Sheridan,* professes himself a great Whig, and is always trotting about the office with plans of economy and amendment. I know if I mentioned the matter that the blame would very probably be thrown upon him, . . . I do not at present think that there is sufficient evidence to make it prudent to stir. All the letters from England have reached my hands with the utmost punctuality and without any appearance that could create the least suspicion.†

Curiously enough, at the very moment that his sense of fairness was desiring that it should be borne in mind how many hands each confidential letter passed through on *both* sides of the channel, Lord Lansdowne was expressing serious doubts whether his communications between Wiltshire and Whitehall were secure from furtive inspection :—

I have thought it right to write to the Chancellor (as he sent me all sorts of civil messages about it) to thank him for the Lord-Lieutenancy, and I have inclosed my letter to you, with an address to the King to be sent in by you, as I am not certain whether, if I sent it into the post here, it would go properly.

On the 17th October, being public quarter-day, it was proposed by Mr. Jno. W. Pasley (Coroner of the County of Dublin) that the freedom of the Guild of St. George should be presented to the Right Hon. W. Lamb, which motion was carried unanimously; and that the Master, Mr. Alderman Harty, the Wardens and Committee of five, should wait on him.‡

Towards the close of his term of office Lord Wellesley took less and less share in the details of administration; yet

---

* His private secretary in 1807.
† From W. Lamb, November 3rd, 1827.
‡ 'Freeman's Journal.'

his habitual susceptibility, ever on the watch for neglect or slight, occasioned him much unnecessary pain, and kept him in a state of nervous irritability he could not conceal from those around him; sometimes, not even from strangers, when guests at his table. The activity of his Chief Secretary, his readiness to hear all species of complaint and to discuss openly any fair means of redress, still more, the value set upon his ability and discretion by members of the Government who corresponded with him, aggravating the besetting infirmity of the Viceroy's character, which was undoubtedly the envious greed of official fame. Lamb saw through and through his weakness, and being as much exempt from it himself as any man of high ambition ever was, he strove to avoid, as far as he was concerned, giving him any cause for jealousy. When despatches came from the Home Office, implying by their language that his independent opinion and advice was desired by the Cabinet upon matters of importance, he privately remonstrated at their erroneous form, and offered to send them back in order that they might be re-written.

The words "and of yourself" should, I apprehend, be omitted. There is, I believe, no such thing as an original public correspondence between the Chief Secretary to the Lord Lieutenant and the Secretary of State. Everything that the Chief Secretary writes is commanded and directed by the Lord Lieutenant. Some jealousy has already been excited upon this point, and I am afraid of more. If you agree with me in this, and think it absolutely necessary, send other letters. But, perhaps, as the man is so near his end you may let him expire in peace ; and, if his office could expire with him, so much the better. He talks of leaving before Christmas, and has written to Lord Anglesey to know when he means to arrive.*

Soon after the failure of the ill-advised attempt to

* Letter, November 11th, 1827.

prosecute O'Connell for his allusions to the triumph of Bolivar, Plunket, writing confidentially to the Duke of Buckingham, accompanied his regret at the violent language of the Catholic leaders in Ireland with expressions of his belief that they had little less effect in stirring the popular mind than in exciting hostile prejudices in England. One of our great misfortunes is that we have not any regular and safe channel of communication with the Roman Catholic body through whom admonition and private remonstrance might effect a useful purpose. This is one of the principal reasons why I have always been so anxious for a settlement with the Roman Catholic clergy.* The memorable attempt to realise that favourite dream of all the Liberal statesmen of the time failed, and a new penal statute was passed in 1825 to suppress the Catholic Association. The bitterness of tantalisation was added to that of hope deferred; and the Government did not venture to put to proof the metal of the new weapon they had forged. The business of agitation went briskly on, and alarmists grew hourly more convinced that a sanguinary insurrection was meditated and that the forfeited estates were in jeopardy. How little such designs were harboured by the chief demagogue is evidenced in a letter addressed by him to the Attorney-General under the seal of confidence :—

I regret that I feel it a duty to inform you that the accounts from the country by those who are well-acquainted with the people are terrific. The Ribbon connection has assumed a new form. There is now no oath, nor any very distinct assertion of object. It is spreading fast through Leinster—in the southern counties almost as much as in the northern. It has got extensively into Connaught and Munster. It has its origin in the north. The Orangemen of Cavan and Fermanagh have armed themselves with daggers of about fourteen inches in length in the blade, or, what is nearly as bad, the lower

* 'Memoirs of Court and Cabinet of George IV.,' vol. ii. p. 194.

orders of Catholics have been made to believe that they are
so armed, and in consequence of such report the Ribbon-
men are getting similar arms. It is sought not to involve
the married men in this society, but *all* the unmarried
peasants are expected to be in it. One priest assured me
that no less than seven youths in his parish, of regular
habits, left his confessional rather than renounce the
system, or abstain from supporting it. I have no remedy
to suggest save the increase of the King's troops in
Ireland. The exhibition of such a force may alone do
good. The Yeomanry are worse than useless. I have
done my duty in communicating these facts to you.
Those who gave me this information cannot be deceived,
and are themselves greatly horrified. The diminution of
the currency in both countries will certainly create still
greater distress among our landholders, and, of course,
increase the tendency to Whiteboyism of every species.*

There was in his mind at all times a detestation of secret
societies and acts of violence against life and property.
Political exclusion and religious outlawry he was fearless to
denounce and deride ; but those who knew him best, best knew
how powerfully and how sincerely his influence would have
been exercised on the side of order and law, had not authority
spurned his service and impugned the loyalty of the creed
he held. It was, in theory, the maddest of mistakes ; in
practice, the most impracticable of impolicies.

The new Chief Secretary had been thoroughly imbued
with these views by Plunket and by Canning. Like the
latter, he appreciated the tenacity of the prejudices to be
overcome before emancipation could be carried ; but, unlike
the latter, he was hardly fitted to realise the fact that every
year's delay in conceding what was inevitable, lessened the
chance of its producing peace, or eliciting gratitude when
it came. Plunket confessed, when asked his opinion by
Canning, late in 1826,

---

* Letter from O'Connell to Plunket, March 7th, 1826.

He was not as sanguine as in 1825 of the efficacy of the
Roman Catholic measure in tranquillising Ireland, and
every year more of postponement made him less so. He,
at the same time, seriously believed that the measure, if
soon carried and honestly acted on, would give a fair
chance of tranquillity. And until it took place the task
of governing Ireland and administering its laws would
become every day more difficult. The new Catholic
association completely identified itself with the old,
and daily violated the recent law for its suppression.
Not to prosecute its leaders was a mark of weakness; to
prosecute them would be very indiscreet, and probably
unavailing; it would be in truth to prosecute the Roman
Catholic people, who from head to foot made common
cause with them. So long as there was profound peace
things might drag on in that way; but, come war,
or rumour of war, and who could answer for the
consequences? *

It was not surprising that a man of fashion, hitherto unused to business and wholly unacquainted with the perplexed
and troubled country he was sent to aid in governing,
should not easily be persuaded of the intensity of the evils
thus depicted with the power of a master whose life had been
spent in the study of them. His admiration of Plunket's
abilities, and sympathy in his scorn of vulgar applause, led
him to rely upon his judgment more than that of any other
man. As for himself, he was open-eyed and open-eared to
the complaints of the weak and the expostulations of the
unprivileged, candid in admission and outspoken in rebuke
of domineering wrong, as none of his predecessors had been.
The banter and even *brusquerie* of his manner rather tickled
the fancy of a people with whom raillery and quizzing is
an habitual condiment of thought and speech. They hated
Goulburn as much for the melancholy literalism of his talk
as for the sentiments it conveyed. They thought Mr. Lamb

* Letter from Plunket to Mr. Canning, October 10th, 1826.

a jolly sort of fellow, who looked as if he was given to mirth and took real delight in laughter. The Celts, moreover, are apt to be taken with a fine face and fine person; and if they must be ruled by some one from the other side of the channel, it was a comfort to think that he was not afraid to ride at his fences, and that he was an uncommonly handsome man.

CHAPTER XIV.

THE IRISH CHANCELLORSHIP.

Plunket—Sir Anthony Hart—Catholic Magistrates—Schools and Asylums — O'Connell's position — Perplexities of patronage — Agrarianism—Retirement of Lord Wellesley.

In Plunket's disappearance from the scene of his triumphs —the greatest triumphs of argumentative eloquence won by any man of his time—the cause of religious liberty sustained a heavier loss than any it had suffered since the death of Fox, just twenty years before.   Grattan, Mackintosh, Burdett, and Brougham had each and all laid splendid offerings on the shrine; but the shrine was the shrine of party, and they made no sacrifice in what they brought there.   It is no disparagement of their wisdom or their worth to ask what else as party men they could do.   Whig traditions and Radical theories, the interest of opposition, and popular expectation out of doors, all alike pointed the same way and promised the same ready, constant and inspiring applause.   Plunket had from first to last little feeling as a party man; and probably no man of eminence had so little of party sympathy or party support.   An adherent of Lord Grenville, he sometimes co-operated with the Whigs and sometimes differed from them; but during his five years' Attorney-Generalship he was alternately brought into antagonism with the followers of Eldon and the admirers of Grey; and neither spared him in the vehemence of their attacks. Without a relative or connection in Parliament, without a

house in London, and without leisure or opportunity to
cultivate social intimacies or disarm personal misapprehen-
sions, he held his own undauntedly against all odds, and
wrung simultaneously from adversaries and allies tributes
of homage unlike those paid to any other man. Peel, from
whom he differed daily and differed sharply as to the whole
course of Irish administration, stated that his speech for
Catholic emancipation in 1825 was the highest display of
reasoning and declamation which he had ever heard. And
Mackintosh, when asked who had done most for the cause of
religious freedom, answered, unhesitatingly,

Plunket; for all the rest, Grattan, Sidney Smith, O'Connell,
spoke what enthusiastic sympathisers already felt and
were eager to applaud, while he wrestled with the
strongest prejudice in its strongest hold, and by dint of
his resistless power left it weakened and prostrate so that
it never was the same again.

The late Lord Fortescue, when asked what he thought
of him as compared with his eminent contemporaries, said,

The difference was one not of degree but of kind; it seemed
as of the very nature of the man; all the others made
you feel that they were doing their best—with him it
seemed as if he was taking no trouble, and could do even
better if he liked.

A friend quoted this fine criticism in conversation with
Lord Russell, and asked if he thought him so transcendent
in debate?

That, he replied, is the only phrase that properly conveys
my impression of his power : he was not measurable by
other men, he was above them all.

It may easily be conceived how desirous the new Chief
Secretary was to have the benefit of Plunket's long experience in Irish administration; and how anxiously he
looked for occasions to consult him confidentially in the

progress of affairs.   But the opportunities did not readily
present themselves.   During the autumn, Plunket betook
himself to Old Connaught, his favourite residence on the
confines of Wicklow, not far from Tinnehinch, where his
illustrious master in politics spent the evening of his days.
In the enjoyment, hitherto untasted, of leisure, competency,
and freedom from professional anxiety, the new Chief Justice
might be pardoned for resigning himself to repose ; and
except during ordinary visits they saw little of each other.
When winter came the business of the judicial bench did
not so absorb time or attention as to prevent Plunket
affording Lamb the benefit of his experience on various
questions which the former had left ripe for legislation.
But symptoms of creeping paralysis were already felt in
every limb of the doomed administration.   The Home
Secretary was well-disposed towards every suggestion of
remedial legislation ; and the Viceroy was willing as ever
to forward and enforce a policy of progress.   But in Mr. Joy
the Irish executive had a law-adviser-in-chief who cared for
none of these things ; and in Mr. Gregory, an Under-Secretary whose capacity for obstruction nothing less than the
indomitable zeal and determination of Plunket had been
able to overcome.   When the Chief Secretary asked why a
measure could not be framed to remedy some practical
grievance of tithe, church-cess, sub-letting, or education,
he was encountered with a blinding shower of difficulties
and doubts which he knew not how to meet or to escape.
In answering deputations his natural quickness and sagacity
showed him the way to conciliate irritable complainants, and
his frank admission of what he felt to be practical wrongs
won for him golden opinions at the time, and laid the
foundation of personal esteem and liking not without subsequent results.   But in conclave at the Castle he soon
found himself at helpless disadvantage.   Ignorant of details innumerable of law and fact, he was surrounded by
officials exulting in their riddance of him, who was so
long their plague,—and chief adversary in maintaining

intact the old order of things : while from Lord Goderich he could get no exposition of an Irish policy, for policy he had none to expound.

The idea of promoting Alexander had not been laid aside. The first reliable intimation of its probability was conveyed to Plunket by Lord Holland :

The present Government, I believe, means to name Alexander Chancellor of Ireland. I need not tell you that no appointment to that office *but one* can give me any perfect satisfaction or real pleasure; but I suppose the impracticability of that one being granted, and the reasons of it being known and submitted to, one must consider Alexander as something better than one had a right to expect. His opinions are *bad*, but his age and habits disqualify him, and his character, temper and moderation, rescue him from becoming either the leader or tool of any active faction. At least he is better than Saurin, and I believe a great push was made by Lord Manners to secure the seals devolving on him, a true descendant of the Orange line.*

Lamb's sagacious perception of the susceptibility of others, and his freedom from the vanity of being thought better informed than his departmental chief regarding the views of the Cabinet, is indicated in a short note written on the first appearance in print of Alexander's probable appointment :

Pray remember my hint about informing Lord Wellesley of it a day or two before it actually takes place, or rather before it is known from authority ; also a line to Plunket, and that from as high authority as possible, would I think have a good effect. Plunket, as you know, has behaved very steadily and handsomely.†

The Home Secretary suggested accordingly that Lord Goderich should write to the susceptible Viceroy on the

---

* To Lord Plunket, August 23rd, 1827.
† To T. S. Rice, September 4th, 1827.

subject of the Chancellorship; but he thought it as well that it should be known in Ireland that the appointment was offered to the Chief Baron by Canning before his death, though no answer was received from him till afterwards : so that Plunket was set aside before, and not as the act of the new Government.*

Plunket made no secret of his chagrin when communicating confidentially with Spring Rice :

I was not aware till very lately, and that long since Canning's death, in consequence too of a letter from a private friend not a member of the Government, of any application at all having been made to the Chief Baron, nor had I any reason to suppose that he was in contemplation. When the place of Master of the Rolls was offered to me, it was accompanied by a distinct declaration that my claims, whatever they were, were to remain unaffected by that appointment ; and the same assurance was distinctly repeated when I was appointed to the situation which I now fill. I was fully apprised of the difficulties which stood in the way of my appointment to the Great Seal. I have not the slightest doubt that when Canning made the proposal to the Chief Baron, and when the present Cabinet adopted it, he and they acted under an impression that those difficulties were insuperable. I need not assure you that even were my conviction on this point less decided it should not make any difference in the cordiality with which I regard the interest of the present administration, and with·which I shall support them as far as the duties belonging to the office I fill are not incompatible with any interference in politics.†

To the Home Secretary he wrote,

Earnestly deprecating the appointment of any person on that side (of the channel) but himself, which made the case

* Marquis of Lansdowne, from Bowood, September 9th, 1827.
† From Lord Plunket to T. S. Rice, September 16th, 1827.

of the Irish Seal sufficiently embarrassing to those that had to determine upon it.*

The Chief Baron finally made up his mind that he was too old for transplanting if he was to bear any further fruit, and another occupant of the Irish Woolsack had to be sought for in Lincoln's Inn. An announcement of the fact appeared upon authority in the morning papers :

> We can state on the most undoubted authority that the chief Baron Alexander does not proceed to Ireland as Lord Chancellor of that country. An objection is known to exist to Lord Plunket in a certain high quarter, arising from his strenuous advocacy of a cause with which the name of that eminent man is inseparably associated. The present probability as to the person who is to be appointed the successor of Lord Manners is, that the important office will devolve upon Mr. Burton, a Puisne Judge of the Court of King's Bench. The character of this gentleman is, that he is " learned in the law," and *præterea nihil*. He is neither a bigot nor a liberal, but in such a country as Ireland occupies the insipid station of a neutral.—*Morning Chronicle.*

Lord Goderich could not make up his mind, on the refusal of Alexander, to whom the Irish Chancellorship should be given. Late in October nothing had been settled. Feelers had been thrown out in semi-official journals that Mr. Justice Burton might be advanced to the Woolsack; but Lamb, who was in constant communication with Plunket, wrote saying that he would take the promotion of any of his colleagues on the common law bench as a great aggravation of his own exclusion. In England his jealousy on this score does not seem to have been appreciated. His objection was in fact ascribed to a morbid desire that if he could not himself have the chief prize in his profession it should be given to an Englishman, as it had generally been, in order that his

* Letter from Lord Lansdowne, October 16th, 1827.

exclusion might ostensibly rest on national, but not personal grounds. The question was pointedly asked, " Why did Plunket feel so utterly averse to an Irish appointment? Does he ever regret his decision respecting the Rolls? Could he be induced to reconsider it? The bar here are thoroughly ashamed of themselves. He would be hailed with acclamation. He would be truly in his own country. Being placed here he could most advance her interests, and his summers might still be spent at Old Connaught as before. Pray give me a line *in secrecy* on this subject, which is most material." * By return of post he received a reply that Plunket was by no means confiding or communicative regarding his own affairs.

Though he always speaks very favourably of me, he always appears to be peculiarly distant and reserved. This may possibly be my own fault ; but however that may be, the natural consequence is that I know very little of his views, objects, and intentions, except from others, which mode of information is always liable to error and misconception. I understand his present language to be that he trusts that whosoever they appoint they will not insult him by the appointment ; and that his explanation of what he should consider as an insult is the appointment either of an individual of the local bench or bar, or of an individual of the same political opinions as his own ; meaning, of course, by political opinions the Roman Catholic question. Now it seems to me the first of these objections is absurd ; and the second something worse. In the first instance, it would be impossible to conclude that any one who was placed in this situation was therefore considered to be of inferior character and ability ; and in the second, he prefers his own personal feelings to the furtherance of that cause which is identified with his best thoughts. However, it must be recollected that I have not heard these sentiments from himself, and

* Letter from T. S. Rice, October 20th, 1827.

therefore I may be in error respecting them. About a week or ten days ago the Lord Lieutenant, who, as I have already apprised Lansdowne confidentially, is extremely discontented and anxious for anything that would make a general move in which he might possibly find a place, wrote to me, certainly under the influence of one of those sudden accesses of violent feeling to which he is particularly liable, that he was in the highest degree alarmed at the report of the Irish Seal being intended to be bestowed upon Mr. Anthony Hart, that it was an insult to the bar and the nation, &c. At the same time he sent an express to Lord Plunket, who went down to him immediately. After this interview he wrote to me, in a comparatively calm tone, that Lord Plunket did not feel himself peculiarly hurt by the appointment of Mr. Hart; and that though he himself thought it most objectionable, and that it was miserable weakness in the ministry not to insist upon the nomination of Plunket, still, under the whole of the circumstances, he should not now feel himself called upon to interfere, and there the matter ended. I quite agree with you generally, that it would not be justifiable to hazard the existence of the Government upon the point; besides, it having been conceded by Canning, it appears to be hardly fair now to press it, if the objections continue. It is almost superfluous to say that it is necessary to have a man of stability and who knows his business, and one of whom it is possible to say something beforehand, and to feel secure how he will turn out. Unfortunately, most persons are very sure at the present moment that the claims of the individual in question are in point of ability paramount, and form an exception to general rules; otherwise, I should say that the reasons in favour of Hart preponderate very strongly; and this must, I believe, be the opinion and feeling of the most able and best judging here. I am aware that that opinion is very much encouraged by the state of parties here. One party hates the other so cordially that they had rather see a negro promoted than one who is opposed to themselves upon the politics of this country. I think, if you consider, you will feel it to be almost impossible that Plunket should ever alter his decision with respect to the Rolls—to take it once, to give it up, and then to take it again, would be such a series of vacillations, and would expose him to such ridicule, that I think he could hardly do it. I am going down to-day to the Lord Lieutenant's, to stay with him at his country-house until Wednesday; and I shall probably hear from him all that passed at the interview which I have mentioned in the former part of this letter. After all, if Burton is the individual the Government have in view, I do not think much objection would be felt in any quarter; but do you not think it would be better if I were to communicate openly and distinctly with Plunket upon the subject? To do that with any effect I must of course be fully informed of the intentions of Government, and the course which is intended to be taken.*

Sir Anthony Hart, who for some time had been Vice-Chancellor, was actually appointed before this letter reached London. He stipulated expressly " that he was to have no politics, general, local, or religious; and that of Papists or Orangemen he was to know nothing."† The Under-Secretary at Whitehall tells his colleague at the Castle that he got Lord Dudley's signature to the letter of appointment to save it a journey to Bowood; and forthwith forwarded it to Windsor, requesting Lord Conyngham to obtain the King's signature without delay in order that it might be transmitted by the next post to Ireland. Thus at length he writes:—

The dice are uncovered, and I hope that the new Chancellor may be met somewhat more cordially than Alexander would have been.‡

* W. Lamb to T. S. Rice, October 22nd, 1827.
† Letter from T. S. Rice, October 23rd, 1827.
‡ Letter to T. S. Rice, October 26th, 1827.

The royal apprehension of Plunket being over, Lord Manners was allowed to relinquish the Great Seal of Ireland and Sir Anthony Hart was appointed to succeed him. When George IV., some months later, asked Lamb why a person had been chosen whose name was unknown in public life, he replied, " Because he is a man without either religion or politics, and therefore safe for Ireland." Without showy talents or a spark of humour, Sir Anthony got on very well. He was a sound lawyer, a painstaking judge, and utterly unswayed by the fits of prejudice and passion to which all concerned in Irish administration were liable.

Upon the whole Lamb received the intelligence of his appointment with a feeling of relief from uncertainty which had become painful :—

Undoubtedly it would have been more satisfactory to every one connected with this Government to have had Plunket; yet it is to a certain degree an advantage that it is arranged without occasioning any move at this bar. At present the Lord Lieutenant is so hampered by promises made to Lefroy, when Torrens was promoted to the bench, that there would have been some difficulty in parrying his appointment, which although the individual is, I believe, a good man, would have been in point of political impression one of the worst that could be made. Otherwise, if the appointment of a Solicitor of our own way of thinking could be secured, it would be undoubtedly desirable to promote Joy, who is, as far as the politics of this country are concerned, a most decided and inveterate enemy. I presume you have written to Plunket. You never informed me of the communication you had last with the Master of the Rolls, nor of the manner in which it had been disposed of.*

Sir Edward Bellew, an old Catholic baronet of good estate and estimable character, had applied for the commission of the peace, and had been refused by Lord Manners. Like other

* From W. Lamb, October 26th, 1827.

men of his creed and station, he had taken comparatively little part in politics, contenting himself with giving a yearly subscription to the Catholic rent, allowing his name to be enrolled as a member of the Association, and taking the chair occasionally at an aggregate meeting. These disqualifications, as they had hitherto been considered, ought not in the judgment of Lamb to have any weight with the new Chancellor, and the Home Office left the question absolutely to his discretion.*

I am not at all acquainted with Sir A. Hart, but from his age and habits I should fear that he would hardly be equal to the taking of a step that I should think most advisable, but which would, it must be felt, be one not deficient in boldness, and which would cast a strong reflection upon the conduct of his predecessor. I will, however, converse with him upon the subject, and see what can be done. With respect to the plan proposed that a book should be specially kept and accessible in which the names of all magistrates and the persons recommending should be entered, do you not think it objectionable in this point of view, that it seems to imply a right in persons to recommend for the commission of the peace, and to have their recommendation attended to, and also that it will afford an opportunity to those whose recommendations are refused of comparing their claims with those of the persons whose recommendations will appear to have been complied with? This matter of the appointment of the magistrates I have never thought satisfactorily managed in England. There they are recommended by the Lord Lieutenant; they are selected according to the peculiar notions and circumstances of each Lord Lieutenant. In some counties he has election interests to serve, and nominates none but persons in his own interest; in others he is identified with the representation either of the county or borough, is anxious after popularity, and nominates anybody who can

* From T. S. Rice, October 26th, 1827.

be considered in the rank of a gentleman. In the first case the magistracy is perfectly close; in the latter it is too much diffused and too indiscriminate; both of which are great evils.

In what I wrote of O'Connell I must again repeat, that I spoke from what I had heard of his feelings from others, and had had no opportunity of ascertaining this from himself, so that it is very possible I may have been entirely mistaken, but I rather suspect that my report tallied pretty well with what he himself had expressed to those with whom he communicates. As to the reception of the new Chancellor, depend upon it, it will be very good, and so would that of Alexander have been. The bar is so divided by the politics of the country that they never can act with any concert, and each party is so rejoiced with the disappointment of the other, that all will accept with the greatest satisfaction a man in whose election neither have any peculiar interest. As to the press, it appears to me to be entirely insignificant and contemptible. With respect to the other matter, the letter which has been written has had the most astonishing effect. Pray keep them up to it, and make them write again. I know it is a great bore, but it is necessary. Attention will do much; I believe everything. There is essentially a perfect agreement in views and principles, and a natural leaning towards them. Attention only is wanting, and it is worth while to bestow it.*

The Chancellor's frank and fearless impartiality, and his unaffected zeal in the discharge of his duties, won for him the good opinion of nearly all who came into personal contact with him. Lamb "could not sufficiently express " when writing to one of his colleagues in England, "how much he liked him, and what expectations he had that he would do much good."† And yet the same letter contains incidentally a curious cropping-up of the primary formation

* To T. S. Rice, October 28th, 1827.
† Private letter from W. Lamb, November 15th, 1827.

of the pettifogger amid all the generous and genial super-incumbent strata. The Chancellor represented to Lamb that when Ponsonby was in his situation twenty years before he received his letters from England free, and wished that he should have a like privilege.

Sir A. Hart dealt from the outset with the question of eligibility to hold the commission of the peace with a frankness and fearlessness with which his colleagues were equally surprised and pleased. Lamb felt that it was necessary for the new Chancellor to do nothing, more especially at the commencement, " which should appear like a reflection and censure upon Lord Manners, who, though detested upon the one side, had left a host of powerful and warmly attached friends amongst those whose friendship, as you well know, is worth having. He would not say this to Sir Anthony, because he did not fear that he would be too dashing and imprudent, and it would not be wise to utter any suggestion that might add to the caution of an Equity lawyer." * Even Saurin and Joy must see the advantage of having so open-minded and plain-dealing a man, and one so thoroughly master of his business. All the members of the Government were more than satisfied with him, and Lamb's expectation was that he would do much good.†

Hart personified, in point of fact, the principle of negation on which the Cabinet was founded. Neither hot or cold, aggressive or obstructive; progressive at the full pace of public opinion, or subservient to the crapulous bidding of a despotic Court, he tried honestly, but unavailingly, to let wrong die out, without daring to call right into existence. He hoped that by slow degrees the ways and habits of rule might be so changed and the permanent official staff so re-organised as to render impossible a resumption of Sidmouth's and Eldon's abortive system of repression. Every move in the Goderich game of chess had to be played without explanation beforehand, even in whispers to the backers who

---

* Letter, November 3rd, 1827.
† Letter, November 10th, 1827.

stood nearest wistfully looking on ; and eventually with any number of inconsistent explanations, to turn the edge of conflicting criticisms. Chancellor Hart was sent to Ireland, very much as a *podesta* in the Middle Ages used to be commissioned to administer justice in an Italian State torn by internecine feuds. He understood thoroughly why he had been chosen, and he resolved to act the part without fear, favour or affection. By all parties he was sure to be suspected at the outset ; for colourless impartiality was hitherto unknown ; and its inscrutable features were regarded only as a mask sooner or later to be dropped. Sir Anthony's firmness, probity, and temper lived down these misgivings. In court, diligent, patient, upright, learned, and clear, he made an excellent judge; in council, ignorant of men and things, and unsympathetic with the views and aspirations of his colleagues in administration, he was unimpressive, unhelpful, useless, and at length almost dumb. With all his industry and integrity, his knowledge of Equity, and his clean-handedness, his nomination was wholly indefensible. If the bar of Ireland cannot furnish men fit to preside in courts of supreme jurisdiction these tribunals ought not to exist, but should be made provincially subordinate to the Courts of Westminster. If, on the other hand, men have never been wanting in the ranks of the profession competent to fill these exalted stations, the interests not only of the profession, but of the community, demand that the highest prizes should be given fairly amongst them. But the Chancellorship is a political as well as a judicial office, and his special functions can be adequately performed only by one who, as each local question arises, does not need to be crammed for the occasion with bits and scraps of personal or party information. If the Viceroy or the Secretary be a stranger, he ought to have a chancellor to consult confidentially at any and at every moment, who can tell him without prompting who is who, and what is what. Lord Wellesley needed no adviser of the sort, for he had known the country from his birth, and knew all its byways like the walks in his garden. But he was then about to give place to a successor utterly unacquainted with the idiosyncrasies of that troubled land; and as a political, ecclesiastical or social privy councillor he might as well have consulted one of his aides-de-camp, or his German private secretary, as Lord Chancellor Hart.

Here is a specimen of the troubles of ecclesiastical patronage :—

By-the-by, I do not know what can be done about Clare, he has chosen to feel grievously ill-used, and both he and Gort have written the most violent and offensive letters, both to me and the Lord Lieutenant. I did not promise him the living, nor had I power to promise it; perhaps I did use language which might be a little too much calculated to encourage him in the expectation that he would have it. But I found the Lord Lieutenant very anxious to give it to Dr. Wallis. I also found Dr. W. already in possession of a cure which is annexed to Kilmurry, and which is in the gift of the Bishop, and which it appeared to me very inexpedient to separate from it. I also found that in point of character there was every reason to give it to Dr. W.; that the father of the gentleman for whom Clare applied was already in possession of two large benefices within the diocese; that Lord Limerick and the Chief Baron had both applied as well as Lord Clare; and under the circumstances I did not feel justified in pressing upon the Lord Lieutenant the application of Lord Clare, to whom, by-the-by, he was as anxious to attend as I was.*

It must be owned that at this period he was incredulous regarding the possibility of establishing a neutral system of primary instruction in Ireland. He prognosticated accurately many of the consequences which the attempt was certain to entail; and too truly foreshadowed the irreconcilability of jealous churches on the subject. But he underrated the

* To T. S. Rice, October 28th, 1827.

desire of the people, of all grades and persuasions, for
elementary education ; and overlooked the glaring injustice of
leaving the impoverished majority to provide schools for their
children out of their own means and substance, while all the old
endowments remained in the hands of the wealthier sect :—

The more I think about education, the more difficult and
doubtful I consider the question. Are the Government
prepared for the expense of it ? Are they prepared to
establish a board to manage it according to the recommendation of the Commissioners, and do they consider what
influence such a board, with the management of such funds,
the nomination of so many masters, the building of so
many school-houses, will possess in the country? Is it
not certain that the moment the matter is undertaken by
the Government, all private education will at once cease,
and all the greater part of the schools which at present
exist will be put an end to? The price of masters will be
raised, as also will the nature of the recommendation
necessary; and, in short, the old *rôle* of educator will be
deserted. These are objections which strike me independent of the formidable obstacles which arise out of the
difference of the two forms of religion, and the Ninth
Report. The latter appears evidently intended for the
purpose of escaping from their former concession in the
recommendation of the First Report, and of laying the
ground of opposition to any general plan that may be
proposed. The Roman Catholics also on their part
think to intimidate us by stating that if the Government
does not do something, they will themselves call upon
their flocks for contributions, and establish a fund by the
Association for their own people. I myself do not see the
danger of this, and should be disposed to desire them to
try the experiment. Everything of this sort is better
done by private exertion than by public institution.*

A report of the Education Commissioners, four years

* To T. S. Rice, October 28th, 1827.

previously consigned what were called the Charter Schools to extinction. These institutions had been established in several county towns, and elsewhere, for the avowed purpose of proselytism to the ascendant creed. For purposes of education they had proved lamentably deficient in most instances; but the annual grant had been continued notwithstanding. The Chief Secretary wrote on this as on most other topics, to his ever-ready correspondent at the Home Office for information as to what had taken place in the time of his predecessor :—

I see that the first report was ordered to be printed on the 3rd of June, 1825. Pray, was it almost immediately declared in the House of Commons by Goulburn, that the Charter Schools were to be given up? You can probably give me the history of this transaction, and point out the details which took place upon it. I find myself much puzzled, and a good deal of labour imposed upon me in consequence of my never having paid the least attention to any of the reports or debates upon Irish subjects. I wrote to the Incorporated Society, informing them that the first grant for 1828 could not exceed £12,000; for 1829, £6,000, and that after that year no further grant would be made for that service. This I thought was giving them time enough; but they remonstrated vehemently, and represented that the reduction ought to be more gradual. They also claimed superannuation for their officers.*

His correspondence on this subject continues :—

I have communicated confidentially with the managers of the Belfast Institution, through their secretary, and I now inclose to you a letter which I have received, and which contains the whole of the views of the Board upon the amount and distribution of the proposed Parliamentary Grant. You will observe that the suggestion of the

* From W. Lamb, October 30th, 1827.

establishment of a professorship of theology for students of the Established Church meets with their unequivocal approbation. At the same time, it is impossible to say how the Church may be inclined to view this proposition, and it has been hinted to me that it may possibly excite some jealousy in Trinity College, as being calculated to diminish the number of their students. Under these circumstances, I think the best course that I can pursue is to converse confidentially with the Primate on the subject, when he comes to Dublin—which of course he will do, for the discharge of his duty as one of the Lords Justices, upon Lord Wellesley's departure. You will perceive that the Board of Management objects to the manner of making and distributing the grant recommended by the Commissioners (Fourth Report, p. 25). As far as I have considered the subject, I am induced to agree with the Board of Management; but it may be a material consideration how far it may be prudent to omit any check or control the adoption of which the Commissioners have advised. I should be glad to hear your opinion upon this point, as well as upon all the others, which are touched upon in the inclosed letter, and upon the whole subject generally.[*]

I am very much afraid about the Divinity Professor at Belfast. In the present temper of Church and State, and religious feeling in this country, it is impossible to say how a proposition of that sort may be viewed. Nobody is acquainted with the intention of making any such proposition at present, but as soon as it is made the Primate will of course consult the other Bishops. The Archbishop is too cool and wary a man to be preoccupied. At least, I apprehend so. Somehow or other, I have no predilection for this Belfast business; I never had. I think you exaggerate its importance, and do not see that it does not stand upon the same principle as other grants which you condemn; or, at least, how capable it is of being confounded

[*] From Phœnix Park, December 16th, 1827.

with them, and how difficult to be distinguished from them. These people forget everything else in their own particular object. The Kildare Place Society have sent me in an estimate of £40,000.*

Popular objections had been raised for some time to the increased grants annually voted by Parliament to the Kildare Place Society, and the Society for Discountenancing Vice, both of which consisted exclusively of members of the Established Church, and had for their avowed object the spread of Protestant education among the humbler classes. Considering the then undiminished sources of the ecclesiastical endowment, and the uninfringed monopoly of office and employment enjoyed by members of the Anglican communion, Lamb could not recommend the continuance of such partial appropriations of the public revenue, and strongly urged ministers to consider and decide the question of their reduction or abolition during the meetings of the Cabinet in November. The questions of policy involved were too important, he thought, to be settled by those who prepared the estimate of Irish Civil Contingencies; and he therefore hoped Lansdowne would not let ministers separate without coming to some decision.† About the same time, Sir John Byng was appointed Commander of the Forces in Ireland, superseding Sir Colquhoun Grant, to whose judgment and temper in managing the garrison of Dublin he bore cordial testimony, and whose removal, therefore, he viewed with regret. "This of course cannot be helped, but one is sorry to stir anything that is quiet here." ‡

The law about foundlings requires serious consideration. Nothing can be done with the Foundling Hospital but by Act of Parliament, for by the present Act they are bound to receive every child sent according to the provisions of the Act. I do not know what you mean by the "Local

---

* To T. S. Rice, December 25th and 28th, 1827.
† Marked "secret," from W. Lamb, November 18th, 1827.
‡ Idem.

Foundling Establishments," but will inquire respecting them. What do you think of considerably raising the price to be paid upon the admission of a child into the Foundling Hospital? A law doing away with admission altogether would be too strong, would it not? *

Great complaints had from time to time arisen in the execution of the office of sheriff; the underlings of which were not only partial, but corrupt. Lord Lansdowne desired that steps should be taken to reform the whole system ; and the Chief Secretary endeavoured to master the question with a view to legislation :—

Upon the sheriff question, it will never do for us to attack the Corporation of Dublin according to the recommendation of the Committee, still less all the other corporations in Ireland. We should have that whole interest in England against us. Goulburn's bill carries into effect all the recommendations of the Commissioners with respect to the county sheriffs. I doubt if they are of any use. The idea of changing the whole nature of the office and assimilating the practice to that of Scotland may be good, but it is difficult in execution, and will require very serious consideration. It is a total change of the whole law.†

As an instance of the inveteracy which characterised the spirit of administrative exclusion even in matters the most unpolitical, it may be mentioned that till this time Catholics were silently treated as ineligible to act as governors of county asylums. The members for the city of Limerick addressed a formal application to the Government in favour of the appointment of three respectable persons of that persuasion to be commissioners of the lunatic asylum of the place, no petition or remonstrance having hitherto been of any avail on the subject.‡ The gentlemen recommended were forthwith appointed.§

* To T. S. Rice, December 25th and 28th, 1827.　　　† Ibid.
‡ From T. S. Rice, November, 1827.
§ From W. Lamb, December 2nd, 1827.

O'Connell remained during the autumn at Derrynane, and abstained from any public expression that could embarrass the course of the new Government. In his private correspondence he did not conceal his just expectation that the denial of his rank at the bar, which Lord Manners persisted in to the last, would now be remedied, as had been done in England in several instances, by a patent conferring on him pre-audience after the law officers of the Crown. Without any opportunity of ascertaining this from himself, Lamb represented strongly to the Home Office what he had learned of his feelings from others on this subject.* O'Connell felt bitterly his continued exclusion from the place he had fairly won above his fellow-practitioners of the law, and wrote to Spring Rice remonstrating against its continuance under a government professing principles of sectarian impartiality. He had no objection, he said, to appeal directly to the new Lord Chancellor, and to refer him to the chief judges of assize of the Munster Circuit, who must bear testimony to the fact of his unequalled amount of business, both civil and criminal; while every half-employed competitor of the privileged creed took rank in court before him. The Under-Secretary inclosed his reply, which had been approved by Lord Lansdowne, to Lamb, and suggested a conference with Sir A. Hart, from whom he anticipated no objection. He wisely recommended that if a patent of precedency were conceded it had better come with the grace of a voluntary gift than as if yielded to complaint or negotiation; and wishing that his friend should have the credit of the concession, he begged that no allusion should be made to his advice in conversation with the Chancellor.† Lord Lansdowne authorized an intimation to be conveyed to the Irish Chancellor that "there would be no indisposition, but the contrary, to make a communication from the Home Office on the subject of O'Connell's claim to precedency should he consider such a step expedient. But it would be on every possible ground better that the matter

---

* W. Lamb to T. S. Rice, October 28th, 1827.

† T. S. Rice, December 1827.

should be strictly considered as it affected the profession, the business of the courts, and the interests of suitors and the public." The Under-Secretary sent Sir A. Hart a private letter from himself to O'Connell, endeavouring to dissuade him from making the request, as likely to embarrass the party; but he admitted frankly that they had no claim upon him to follow their advice, and that he wished the Chancellor to consider and decide the matter on strictly professional grounds.* The Home Secretary approved of the dissuasive letter, but would not sway the Chancellor's decision;† and Lamb was left free to form and give his own opinion on the subject. O'Connell replied with some bitterness, reproaching the Whigs with their indifference to individual claims for justice, all the harder to bear when, for the convenience of Government, the general demands of their communion had been put in partial abeyance—"The previous administration had at least the virtue of sincerity; the grace of hypocrisy was now employed to mitigate the exclusive system." Spring Rice rejoined that this was neither candid nor kind. When O'Connell had first proposed to apply for a patent of precedency with reference to the judges, regarding his forensic position, he had been supposed to contemplate a public and official proceeding; and this had been deprecated in confidence as one in every way unwise. But when he explained that he meant to follow only precedents at the English bar, and to conduct the correspondence on a private footing, the objection disappeared. In spite of what he had said to him in private, he had really urged upon his colleagues the justice of his professional remonstrance against denial of his rank at the bar. Not fifty such letters should "deter him from labouring still to serve him, as an act of justice, and as a debt due to his profession and his country. Whatever his correspondent's feelings might be, he would endeavour to do what was right, to serve him in spite of himself."‡ O'Con-

* To Sir A. Hart, December 6th, 1827.
† To W. Lamb from T. S. Rice, December 8th, 1827.
‡ To O'Connell, December 14th, 1827.

nell was touched and gratified by a circumstantial proof placed before him at the same time of a sincere desire to serve him in another matter. He acknowledged his mistake, and the correspondence closed with mutual expressions of good-will. But the opportunity was lost, and nothing was done.

The new Chancellor did not think much of Saurin :—

After hearing his first argument, he asked a friend to whom he was accustomed to speak without reserve, "Is this the gentleman who has made such a sensation in this country ?" " Yes," was the reply; " I am rather surprised at it," the rejoinder. The great means by which the Orange gentry have drawn over every one who has come here was by assuming that their set were the only persons worth associating with, quite the first company ; and you who know Almack's, know that this is supposed to be one of the strongest, if not the very strongest passion of the human mind. Now to this Hart is completely inaccessible, he does not care one damn for one society more than another; on the contrary, he rather prefers the lower. I do not believe Leach, with all the polish of London fashion upon him, would have been above this feeling here, and from what I hear of Alexander, I think he would have been much more likely to have been overcome by it.

With respect to the Drogheda business, the very course which you have recommended to A. Dawson, is that which I had settled with Wallace should be pursued. The Bishop of Limerick, and the persons whom you propose for the Directors of the Limerick Lunatic Asylum, are very proper, and I have ordered them to be appointed forthwith ; but we have added that the Bishop of Killaloe should also be appointed, and that he should be requested to name such gentlemen as are fit for the office in the county of Clare, which is a contributory county and does not send any directors at present. I could not of course refuse to make the offer to the Bishop, and also to mention to him the suggestion of the Bishop of Limerick, but I shall wait a reply from you before I do anything further in it.*

Of the difficulties of a position commanding official patronage he was deeply sensible. He had never been in office in England, and therefore did not know that it might not be the same there. But in Ireland he could not give away a place of fifty pounds a year without making fifty enemies.†

Players at chess who carry on their game by correspondence are liable to make odd mistakes through inadvertence, which could not otherwise occur. A comical blunder appears in letters between the friends, who understood each other in general so well. The Under-Secretary inclosed an epistle addressed to him regarding the state of the country by a distinguished individual, whose initials he supposed the Secretary for Ireland would recognise at a glance. Lamb only made out that the surname was Doyle, and with a judgmatical comment on the style, which he thought very good, returned the letter of Sir Charles.‡ Great was his amusement at discovering by return of post that he had exchanged heedlessly a bishop for a knight.

I must say that you do not acquire experience rapidly: only imagine your blunder; you mistake Dromio of Syracuse for Dromio of Ephesus, a general for a bishop; the awful I. K. L. for an innocent K.C.B. I sent you Bishop Doyle's letter more as a curiosity than anything else; for as to his reasoning, I do not by any means admit its applicability as a general expression for solving our Irish problem. In Ireland we are all given to admit the mischief but to shift the burthen of responsibility, we fling ours north to Greenland, Nova Zembla, or the Lord knows where. Thus the Protestant denounces the Papist, the Papist the

* Letter to T. S. Rice, December 11th, 1827.
† From W. Lamb, December 2nd, 1827.
‡ Private letter, December 6th, 1827.

Proctor; the Proctor the Policeman, the Policeman the
Country Justice; the resident the absentee, the latter the
Pope, the devil and I regret to add the Irish Secretary.
The latter takes his revenge on all classes in turn, and so
the vicious circle ends as it began.   Whether Peachum
and Lockit "we are all in the wrong," or the old song,
"They were all of them rogues in their turn," describes
the case most accurately, I stop not to ask.*

I agree, however, with much of Doyle's letter, and I do
believe the people are monstrously aggrieved by rent and
tithe.   He mentions ——.   Now if one-half of what is told
me of him be true, and it comes from many different
quarters, if he had had forty thousand lives, there could
have been no wonder if they had all been taken.   I have
no doubt it is Lady Clare who has influenced Clare.   No
man could be so wrong-headed; at the same time, I
observe that those who have been in England, are more
craving and unreasonable than those who have lived here
all their lives, particularly those who have formed anything of an English connection.   It exalts and influences
their ideas of their own consequence (always a feeble
point) to an astonishing degree.   I wrote to Lansdowne
about the yeomanry here not long ago; the sooner they
are all got rid of the better; at the same time, you are
aware that the measure is one of a too delicate nature, and
which will produce considerable sensation.   I believe that
if the Militia staff were sent after the yeomanry, it would
be so much the better, not any country gentleman in
Ireland would be against this.   To-morrow the Archbishop of Dublin takes the chair at the Rotunda for the
new reformation, and news is just brought that O'Connell
and Shiel have both taken tickets, so fun is expected.†

The most valuable piece of patronage in the staff of

* From T. S. Rice, December 10th, 1827.
† To T. S. Rice, December 13th, 1827.

each of the Common Law Courts was the office of Protho-
notary, in which a vacancy occurring, Plunket asked the
appointment for his second son.   A day or two after, tidings
were received that difficulties in the Cabinet were likely to
lead to its overthrow.   Lamb wrote merely a few lines
saying he was unable to collect distinctly what had happened.
To him it was entirely unintelligible; all he hoped was
that his correspondent would give all possible speed to the
appointment of David Plunket.

A fellow said to him the other day, speaking of the termination of Lord Plunket's career, "For a failure, for a complete failure, it must be admitted that it was not so bad."
There was justice in this observation.*

He learned that his advice was acted upon without hesitation or delay. "A pretty good hedge for a losing player.
£1500 salary, and patronage to a greater extent, is a
tolerable appanage for a younger son.   You are strong,"
adds his correspondent, "to be able to part with so much."†

In the first place, Plunket begs that I will desire you to
express to Lord Lansdowne how very much he feels the
manner in which he has received the appointment of his
son. And secondly, I have sent you by to-night's post
some papers upon the subject of the Linen Board, which
I beg you will forward to Lord Lansdowne as soon as
you receive them, and request his attention to them. As
to Æneas M'Donnell it would be highly unadvisable to
interfere. The latter wants to get off his sentence, and
therefore represents to Blunt that great dangers are impending, &c. &c., all of which, I have no doubt, he would
represent as sure to be averted 'by his being pardoned.
The whole plan on the part of the Roman Catholics is to
act by menace and intimidation. I quite agree with you
that what has taken place in politics is awkward and

* From W. Lamb, December 21st, 1827.
† To W. Lamb from T. S. Rice, December 24th, 1827.

untoward, but it does not surprise me in the least. I will write again to-morrow, but am tired now.*

As had frequently happened before, the discontinuance of political agitation was followed by the revival of wild schemes and plots among the peasantry in the more restless localities. Ministers grew uneasy at frequent reports of agrarian disturbance, indicating the renewed activity of secret societies banded together for local rather than general objects. As early as the 20th of October a letter from Lamb reached Bowood conveying information so "unsatisfactory that, although marked private and confidential, it was by the Home Secretary's direction forwarded in circulation to the other members of the Cabinet. The Under-Secretary was desired not to let the letter out of his own hands."† As time went on, matters continued to grow worse :—

As to the state of Tipperary, you see what it is. Donoughmore, Llandaff, Glengall, Prittie, all agree that it is worse than it ever was, and that the system of combination and terror is more completely established and organised than ever before. What this arises from you know better than I; at least, I hope you do. It has got to its present head from the inactivity and relaxation of the police in that province, which is mainly owing to the supineness, &c., arising in a great degree from ill-health, of the inspector, General Wilcocks, whom we are going to change immediately. We are also about to get rid of Wilson, but the roots of the evil of course lie far deeper, and if we could ascertain them, there would still remain the task of eradicating them. With respect to D'Arcy's report, I am not aware that you alluded to it in your official letter. I remember it appeared to me upon the whole favourable, but I will look over it again to-morrow. I will send an experimental despatch to Lansdowne to-morrow. I knew it

* To T. S. Rice, December 24th, 1827.
† From Lord Lansdowne, October 21st, 1827.

was no use to write to him until he came to London. I
have now written some letters of considerable consequence
upon questions which must be decided upon by the administration. Lord Wellesley talks of leaving before
Christmas, about the 15th of next month. I have written
to Lord Anglesey to know when he means to arrive.*

Lansdowne thought it to be his duty, even at the risk of
disturbing the equanimity of the Viceroy, whose term of
office now drew near its close, to call serious attention to
the flagrancy of insubordination in parts of Munster, and
to inquire what measures, repressive or remedial, the Irish
executive were prepared to recommend. Lord Wellesley
waxed more and more impatient to be relieved of his
office. His successor had been some time announced, and
men's eyes were turning to the new Viceroy, whose influence
was already discernible in the horizon. The position of
superseded satrap did not suit the conqueror of Tippoo
Saib. Early in December, he wrote to the Home Office
naming for Lords Justices the Protestant and the Catholic
Archbishops of Dublin, and the Lord Chancellor, and requesting that the necessary documents should be forwarded
forthwith to enable him to quit the scene where he lagged
superfluous. Lord Lansdowne wrote him a soothing letter
of gratitude on behalf of the King, and of appreciation by
the Cabinet of his distinguished viceregal career. Spring
Rice asked Lamb why the two Chief Justices, Plunket and
Bushe, had been left out of the commission. No wonder he
replied:

It is quite impossible that Plunket and Bushe could have
been in the commission as Lords Justices; you must mean
the commisioners for holding the Great Seal. Three
Lords Justices are too many, five would be the Devil.†

From Huskisson's private communications, though neither

* Private letter from W. Lamb, December 11th, 1827.
† From W. Lamb, December 15, 1827.

numerous or unreserved, he had gathered truly how little confidence was felt by his colleagues in the new Chancellor of the Exchequer. Without his advice Tierney had been authorized to ask Lord Spencer if the Chairmanship of the promised Finance Committee would be accepted by his son. Althorp was disposed to comply, but told his father he did not believe the King would consent to his nomination ;* and so it proved. Herries declared that in a matter affecting his department he ought to have been consulted, and that if the arrangement were insisted on he would resign. Huskisson, on the other hand, refused to yield upon a point which touched so nearly his authority as leader in the Commons; and the Premier and Home Secretary supported him.

Before Christmas private letters gave mysterious hints that a break-up in the Government was at hand. Paragraphs appeared more or less obscurely indicating that the First Lord of the Treasury was about to retire. On the 16th, the bow-window at White's already declared the resignation of the Premier to be accepted, and named Lord Harrowby as his successor.† This was premature, but not wholly unfounded. A king's messenger had been, in fact, sent to the ex-Lord President, but had brought back no answer of which the public were destined to be informed.

Lord Goderich had begun to realise thoroughly the perplexities and pains of a situation for which, better than any one else, he knew himself to be unfit. By an unaccountable caprice of fortune he had been allowed to sit undisturbed in the dressing-gown and slippers of power during the recess; and if the wherewithal to fabricate a policy of any distinctive kind had been in him, there was time and opportunity enough for the purpose. But as another session drew nigh he was constrained to own that except secondary measures of administrative reform he had none to present to Parliament. In foreign affairs, Lord Dudley, with all his

---

* Lord Althorp to his father, November 24th, 1827.
† From T. S. Rice, December 16th, 1827.

naivete and talent, was unable to get beyond the point of saying clever things about events that had happened; but he was wholly incapable of pre-determining what ought to happen, or how that which ought not, might be averted. The Premier felt more and more his inability to lead the Cabinet, to satisfy the King, or to face Parliament. He would be examined and cross-examined about Navarino and Catholic Emancipation; and he was utterly unable to make up his mind as to what was to be said or what was to be done. The Duke of Clarence was becoming hourly more unmanageable by his bearers at the Admiralty; and after the fate of the Turkish fleet, nobody could feel sure what ally's squadron we might not next send to the bottom. Canning had risked the consequences of his Royal Highness's appointment as Lord High Admiral, relying on his own personal ascendency to prevent mischief, or to supersede the impulsive Duke, should necessity arise. But his timid successor would have died of palpitation of the heart before he accomplished such a feat; and when, in addition to all other perplexities, he learned that many leading Tories, including Lords Eldon and Bathurst, had offered to concert plans of opposition with Earl Grey sooner than allow him to enjoy his position of chief minister in peace, he began to persuade himself that his health was giving way, and to prepare his Majesty for the contingency of a possible change.* George IV. readily divined the truth, and carefully dissembled his satisfaction. Lord Goderich returned from Windsor on the 18th, delighted with the more than cordial assurances of unabated confidence on the part of royalty, and for a few days more, emphatic contradictions were given personally and in the press to the rumours of his resignation. Even Spring Rice seems to have been lulled into security. He told Lamb there was little doubt of their going on as before. There was no denying that the report and the cause which produced it increased the difficulties very considerably. But those difficulties must be met and

* Confidential letter from T. S. Rice, December 19th, 1827.

overcome.   To succeed there must indeed be spirit and manliness equal to integrity and good intention.   "The knights must come into the lists with a flourish of trumpets and kettle-drums, and not with lutes and harps.   Lord Goderich would continue in for the present.   All this it must be admitted was devilish unlucky, as it would give the notion of timidity and irresolution; and the world, which is always cowardly and easily bullied, pardons a crime more easily than a weakness.   The mass of mankind hate the feeble.   The King has expressed himself with the utmost determination, and there does not seem to have been one thought of the Tories." *   Lamb, however, knew better than his correspondent with whom they had to deal; and from this time he ceased to feel any reliance on the stability of the Government.

* A confidential letter from T. S. Rice, December 19th, 1827.

CHAPTER XV.

THE WELLINGTON ADMINISTRATION.

*Illness and death of Lady Caroline—Resignation of Goderich—
Commander-in-Chief sent for—Eldon left out—Huskisson and his
friends remain—Eastern Question.*

THE Lords Justices took little part in the business of
Government, and its responsibilities for the time being
devolved chiefly upon Lamb. His correspondence with
Whitehall continued daily to embrace exceptional topics
of local or individual interest and the large questions
awaiting legislative attention:—

You have never returned me Baron Pennefather's report
upon the case of Mary Doran. The circumstances are
most distressing; but what can be done in the case of
a barbarous murder? It appeared to me that the case of
the Chelsea Pensioners, though not within the letter, was
within the spirit and principle of the order respecting the
payment of the troops, and that it was safer to have the
payments made in notes of the Bank of Ireland. You
will perceive that the Roman Catholics have-fixed on the
15th instant for their simultaneous meetings after Mass.
Nothing can be more unfair or ungenerous than that they
should assume a sterner tone towards us than they did
towards the former Government. However, I am clearly
of opinion that they should not be interfered with in any
way. If any breach of the public peace takes place it is
upon their own heads. Considering the various causes of
disturbances which are abroad, I am only surprised that

the tranquillity of the country is maintained, and of course I should not be the least so at its being disturbed at any moment. Pray return me Baron Pennefather's report. I am harassed to death with domestic calamity, but I feel that it would be awkward that I should leave this place at this moment.*

The later period of Lamb's sojourn in Ireland was overcast by the gloom of family affliction; from which he sought relief in the varied details of official work. In the beginning of November the health of Lady Caroline invisibly declined. Lady Morgan notes in her diary, 27th November, that though the Chief Secretary came to dine with her to meet Lord Cloncurry, William Curran, Evans of Portran, and A. R. Blake, he was in the lowest spirits from the bad accounts of poor Lady Caroline; her life they feared was fast ebbing but she had tried friends around her. A fortnight later he inclosed a note from Dr. Goddard, the physician in attendance, saying that medicine knew no effectual cure; and that the expedients resorted to for temporary relief were necessarily trying in their painful nature even to temperaments more happily constituted. She showed, however, little of impatience in her suffering, and there was hardly a word of petulance or complaint. From the first she evidently felt the seriousness of her condition, and gradually accustomed herself to contemplate the event which at no distant time she knew to be approaching. Her letters to her husband might have been written by one who had never known a troubled hour. They were full of affection, fortitude, and tenderness; not a word of recurrence to sad memories, or of repining at her actual lot. It seemed as if the unquiet spirit which so long had lamentably possessed her was at length cast out; and that she reverted calmly to the days of early love and admiration for the man to whom in girlhood she had given her heart and hand. They were frequently inclosed by him to Lady

* To T. S. Rice, January 4th, 1828.

Morgan, towards whom to the end she evinced strong feelings of attachment; and there are many brief but touching
proofs of the solicitude he felt on her account as time wore
on and no indication of amendment appeared :—

Phœnix Park, December 3rd, 1827.

DEAR LADY MORGAN,
I send you the letters which I received by yesterday's mail.
They are very melancholy. The firmness and distinctness
with which her letter is written shows how strong she is
both in mind and body. Send these to the Castle when
you have done with them. I have got a bad cold and sore
throat, which prevents my going into town to day.

Yours faithfully,
WM. LAMB.

The following is the letter inclosed :—

DEAREST WILLIAM,
This is the first time I can write. I have suffered much, and
I hope patiently, since I wrote last. Tapping is by no
means an agreeable sensation. It does not give pain like
a tooth drawn, but it turns you deadly cold and sick. The
operation was more troublesome than usual; this is the
first day I feel easy. All the county have been to see me.
My dear brother has read to me and soothed me, and
is coming back. I never met with such affection and kindness as from all persons of both our families, and dear
Emily and Caroline; but what pleased me most was your
dear letter saying you loved and forgave me. God bless
you, dearest. My love to Augustus. All here doing well.

Ever yours,
CAROLINE.

Dublin Castle, January 11th, 1828.

DEAR LADY MORGAN,
I inclose you the letter which I have received this morning.
The natural strength of her constitution shows itself, but

I am afraid fruitlessly.   I am sorry that I cannot accept
your invitation for the 14th inst.   Yours faithfully,

WM. LAMB.

After the departure of Lord Wellesley and before the
arrival of his successor, a new movement in the strategy of
agitation, originating with Mr. Shiel, had marked the opening of the new year.   Simultaneous meetings throughout
the whole country were summoned for the second week in
January.   Two thousand assemblages around the altars of
a people.   More than six millions in number uttered as if
with one voice the passionate prayer for equal justice ; and
the response which loudly came from every organ of liberal
opinion in Great Britain was followed by tokens of sympathy
not to be mistaken, from France and other continental states.
The lull in threatening excitement caused by Canning's accession to power, and prolonged till the close of the year,
ended with the Goderich administration.   The meetings of
the Central Association in Dublin were resumed, and larger
contributions than   ever   from   the   United   States augmented its revenues.   Whatever ministerial changes might
take place, it became more and more plainly inevitable that
the removal of religious disabilities must at least be recognised as an open question among the advisers of the
Crown.   Until a settlement could be come to, and while the
irritation and mischief caused by its postponement were prolonged, it seemed to the Chief Secretary peculiarly necessary
to show diligence in preparing and carrying remedial measures
of subordinate but substantial importance :—

Only let not too many be attempted at the same time.   Let
me implore you not to attempt too many things at once.
There is the Jury Bill, an alteration of considerable importance, and which deserves to be well weighed.   Let
one measure be adopted and settle down a little before
you bring on another.   If you dash at the whole at once,
you run the risk of producing confusion and discrediting
your own reformations.   Pray let me know what is going

on. I have written fully to the Lord Lieutenant upon the simultaneous meetings of the Roman Catholics, and have desired him to communicate with the ministers upon them.*

Some of his despatches refer to personal jealousies about the shrievalty in counties, and to general recommendations for reforming the manner of filling the office in corporate towns. Others are occupied with discussions relative to plans of primary education, for the consideration of which the Home Secretary proposed that he should move for a select committee. But what, he asked, were they to do when they got into the committee? Were they prepared for the plan of the Commissioners, to establish non-sectarian schools in which lessons in the Bible should be taught without exposition or comment?

There appear to me to be innumerable difficulties in the way of carrying it into effect, in constituting the Board, in the question of the Scriptures, &c. But if it is thought wise to have a committee upon it, I have no objection, but it must be done upon mature consultation, and with some determinate object.

Lord Goderich, in the audience on the 18th of December, had recommended the addition of Lords Wellesley and Holland to the Cabinet. This would not have changed the proportion of parties as originally settled, while it would have given great additional strength to the Government in debating power, and political weight in the eyes of the country. The King gave no reply. A few days later the same proposal was submitted by the Premier in a letter which was seen by Mr. Huskisson and Lord Lansdowne, but to which a post-script, which they did not see, was added to the effect that domestic circumstances affecting the health of one most dear to the writer rendered him sometimes incapable of continuing

* To T. S. Rice, January 7th, 1828.

to perform the duties of his station. Lyndhurst, who had
adroitly offered to be the bearer of the letter, was asked by
his Majesty who should be sent for; and, as had doubtless
been pre-arranged, he named the Duke of Wellington. He
shared the dislike of Peel which he knew was felt by the
King, and he could not be unconscious of the distrust and reserve with which he himself was regarded in return. Under
the great soldier, his position would be very different from
that which he could hope to occupy under the strait-laced
and exacting formalist, whose value as Home Secretary and
leader of the Commons was indisputable, but whose " fitness
to be at the top" he never would admit. "Remember," he
said to a colleague long afterwards, when Peel had gained
and lost that high position, "I never thought him a great
man." Differ as they might, they had one thing in common,
weariness of the obstinacy and imbecility of Lord Eldon.
George IV. liked what he had seen of the new Chancellor,
and he was accordingly retained. It was perhaps the only instance in which within twelve months the Great Seal had
been confided to the same hands by three different Premiers.
Huskisson consented to remain Secretary for the Colonies
and leader of the House of Commons; Palmerston, Dudley,
and Grant retained their respective positions, while the
places vacated were filled by Bathurst, Peel, Goulburn, Aberdeen, Ellenborough and Melville; Herries being transferred
to the Duchy of Lancaster. It is said that Lord Wellesley
had reason to believe that he would be named as the most
fitting Premier by his brother, and that the Duke's acceptance of the post himself caused an estrangement that was
never subsequently healed.[*]

Lord Eldon, though seventy-seven, felt aggrieved at being
passed over. The Duke paid him the compliment of a
friendly visit, to talk over matters, the day after his own appointment, but the ex-Chancellor saw no more of him until
the administration was complete; he then paid a second
visit—one, it would seem, of explanation. He had found it

* H. Bulwer, 'Life of Palmerston,' 213.

impracticable to put together such a cabinet as Lord Eldon would like to join. The component elements were freely discussed—the firmness of some, the flexibility of others, and the infirmity of the whole. The field-marshal was too proud to ask the ancient judge in so many words whether it would do, but he evidently had a curiosity to know what his old friend thought of it; and he told him : " I said I thought it a damned bad one." Before they parted the confidence of the soldier seemed shaken, and the grief of the lawyer for his own fate and that of the British constitution broke forth in tears.

For a period of six months the Duke had been Commander-in-Chief, a proud and independent position which by universal assent he might have continued to hold for life, but which the ambition of being a political leader induced him to exchange for the uncertainty, anxiety, and, as it proved, unpopularity of the Premiership. That he lived to look back upon this part of his life without pride or satisfaction, is indicated in a memorandum which he wrote ten years later, on military administration :—

In the winter of 1827–8, Lord Goderich having reported to George IV. that the Government was defunct, I being at that time Commander-in-Chief of the army, the King sent for me ; and, I conclude for my sins, I was told I was to form a Government for his Majesty. I acceded, and very shortly after the Government was formed, it was intimated to me by my colleagues that I ought to resign my office as Commander-in-Chief of the army. I resigned accordingly, and Lord Hill was recommended to the King to be my successor. I, at the same time, declared my determination never to interfere from that time in any military affair or arrangement, and particularly not in one of a personal nature, such as the promotion, rewards, appointment to offices, grant of commissions to officers or recommendations to the sovereign of gentlemen for commissions, unless I should be called upon for my advice or assistance by the general commanding the army in chief, by the sovereign, or his ministers.*

The most singular feature in the statement perhaps is the incidental admission that, when sent for by the King, it did not at first occur to the great soldier that if he assumed the powers and functions of chief minister he must renounce those of Commander-in-Chief. Their union in the same person probably never occurred as a possibility to the mind of George IV., who was especially jealous of the extent and degree of authority conceded to any one. But it would be incredible, if we had it not thus frankly confessed under the Duke's own hand, that he waited to be told by his colleagues (probably by Lyndhurst and Huskisson) that the functions of the two great offices of state could not be concentrated in the same individual; whereupon, as he declares with characteristeric simplicity he not only laid down his military power, but thenceforth scrupulously abstained, whether in or out of office, from attempting to exercise any personal influence with his successor.

The Duke wrote to Ireland without delay, expressing his hope that Lamb would retain the situation he had hitherto filled with so much credit to himself and satisfaction to the King. Consistently with the course he had formerly pursued, he resolved to act in concert with others whom he politically trusted, regarding the reacceptance of office, and until he knew their determination he would give no definite reply. His answer to the new Premier's letter courteously intimated this resolve:—

I have just received your letter of the 12th inst., and feel sensibly the friendly terms in which it is expressed. Both on account of your public character and the uniform kindness which I have ever experienced at your hands, there is no man either with whom or under whom personally I should be more happy to serve than yourself; but the

* MS. memorandum on Military Patronage, in the collection of original papers at Apsley House, dated March 13th, 1839.

reply to your proposal depends upon so many considerations, that I trust you will think it prudent that I should
delay making it until I have the opportunity of conversing
with you upon the whole of the intended arrangements and
upon the proposed course of measures. For this purpose
I shall leave this country as early as I possibly can, and
hope to arrive in London by the end of the week at latest.

His departure was unavoidably delayed for some days, and
at length, on the 23rd of January, he left Ireland after six
months' residence, to return no more.

On reaching Melbourne House, he was shocked at the
change which had taken place in Lady Caroline during his
absence. She had been removed to town for the benefit of
medical advice soon after Christmas; and whatever skill and
care could do was done to soothe her sufferings and preserve
the attenuated thread of life. Conscious of her approaching
end, her chief anxiety seemed to be that her husband should
be with her at the last. Long used to her exaggerated tone
of despondency, he had not fully realised the imminence of
her danger until within a few days of quitting Dublin; but
no syllable of reproach for his seeming delay in coming
escaped the dying lips. The fever of that troubled soul had
ceased, her warfare with the world was over, and her feeble
accents were of the old love only, the first great triumph of
her life, and her last. She lingered only a few days longer,
for the most part in a state bordering on unconsciousness.
Her brother William, who throughout her illness had been
unremitting in his care, warmly expressed his sense of the
solace which her husband's frequent letters had afforded
her, and the tenderness of his demeanour when he came.
"William Lamb behaved throughout as I always knew he
would."

In the still fresh grave, all conjugal fret and feud was
buried; and memories of the earlier days of mutual attachment and admiration seemed to fill his mind. He did not
care to look back into the long account between them of

faults and shortcomings. It was closed for ever in this world; and even among his adversaries none was found ruthless enough to endeavour to reopen it.

A bequest to her old friend Lady Morgan was the miniature of Byron painted in 1813 by Saunders. It was accompanied by a letter from Lamb, February 1828, expressive only of generous and manly sorrow. The portrait was kept by Lady Morgan in a small ebony cabinet until her death. It was finished with exquisite care, and considered by many of the poet's contemporaries a more faithful likeness than those with which the world is generally familiar. Less masculine and more refined, it resembles rather in expression the statue by Thorwaldsen in the Library at Cambridge. With other pictures it was sold at Christie's, and is now in the possession of a gentleman residing near Carshalton.

In spite of all her waywardness and folly, Lamb was beyond all doubt passionately fond of his wife. She retained to the last a strong influence over him, and years after her death he used to speak of her with tears, and ask moodily, "Shall we meet in another world?"

On communicating with his late colleagues, he found that Lansdowne, Carlisle, Spring Rice, and Mackintosh had not been invited to remain; but that Dudley, Palmerston, Grant and Tierney had been asked to do so; Huskisson continuing to be leader of the Commons. Should he stay or go? Intimacies and friendships pleaded opposite ways; for a day or two he hesitated; but finally determined to hold on. Was he wrong? Judging by the event, it may be said, as it was said at the time, "Undoubtedly." But it is worthy of observation that by none of those who for the next three months sat on the opposite benches was his course regarded otherwise than as a venturous attempt on his part to reinfuse the tolerant and modifying element of Canningism into Government. It was an unsuccessful coalition; and if any one could have foreshown Huskisson and his friends where and why it would fail, none of them would have joined the Duke. But such wisdom aforethought was not possessed by any one concerned at the time. George IV. expressed personally his satisfaction that Lamb retained his office; but he had given, and was soon to give again, proof that his mind was not to be swayed in such matters by the personal liking or flattery of the King. He liked his office, irksome and onerous though he often felt its cares to be. But it gave him for the first time fit occupation. After waiting during half a lifetime for the opportunity to prove his capability of usefulness as an administrator, he might well be pardoned a feeling of reluctance to cast the opportunity away. He was conscious that in opposition he could never hope to assert his place among statesmen. Enthusiasm for abstract principles was not in his heart, or the demagogue's greed of applause in his head. His capacity was that of a minister, not of a rhetorician; and when he was told that as Secretary for Ireland he could still speak and vote for Catholic Emancipation, and a lessening of prohibitory duties on foreign corn, he resolved to remain with Huskisson, Dudley, Palmerston, and Grant in the new administration. How long he would have been able with satisfaction to himself to have retained his post without a seat in the Cabinet, and subject to the control of a Home Secretary like Peel, conjecture must be vain. He was not called upon by Lord Anglesey to alter or forego in any respect the administrative policy pursued under Lord Wellesley; the popularity he had acquired did not seem to abate; and when Mr. Hyde Villiers visited Ireland somewhat later he learned that as Chief Secretary he was generally liked beyond all precedent. But he soon found the difference in his position caused by the retirement of Lord Lansdowne and Spring Rice, with whom he had hitherto worked in uninterrupted confidence and cordiality.

Lord William Bentinck in terms sufficiently flattering asked the late Under-Secretary to accompany him in a confidential capacity to India: and the prospect of office at home having come to an end, Rice felt disposed for some days to entertain the proposal as one which opened fairly to him a new career of usefulness and ambition. The term of the East Indies Charter was approaching its end; a growing disposition already manifested itself in the public mind to impose new conditions, on its renewal, favourable to free principles of trade, of discussion and of local rule; the new Viceroy was a man with whom, personally and politically, it would have been agreeable to act; and the pecuniary inducements were not inconsiderable. But subsequently to his first expression of conditional acceptance "a bar had been put to the project by the feeling of one whom it was his primary duty to consult."[*]

Great irritation was expressed by Canning's immediate friends at Huskisson's retaining office under the Duke. A few days after his return to England he assured Mrs. Canning that " no power on earth should ever induce him to unite in office with those whom he considered as the destroyers of his friend." When assailed in Parliament his explanation was received coldly. His vindication of himself and his friends rested on their number and the importance of the offices they retained, six of the Cabinet out of thirteen having been appointed by Mr. Canning. He was thus entitled to say that they had obtained guarantees that the principles would be respected which they had always upheld. The Duke, when taunted with having made terms of compromise, repudiated as derogatory to himself and Huskisson the idea of any compact or bargain; but frankly recognised the confidence which might be reasonably felt in the policy of a Government that comprised so many friends of the deceased Premier.[†] Lamb, though not in the Cabinet, was especially concerned on account of the situation that he filled. To suppose that he entertained no doubts or misgivings when severing himself for the time from the Whig friends with whom till yesterday he had been confidentially acting, and who thenceforth resumed their old attitude in opposition, would be to misread

* Lady Theodosia, daughter of Lord Limerick, whom he had married. Letter to Lord William Bentinck, January 3rd, 1828.

† Debate in the Lords, February 1828.

the whole character of the man. He had never expected to find himself so placed ; and not all his liking for Huskisson, Dudley, and Palmerston could reconcile him to antagonism in public with Lansdowne, Holland, and Spring Rice. In private their friendship was never marred, and if he lived less with them during the few months that followed, it was in some measure owing to the bereavement which necessarily withdrew him from general society. But as they had not quarrelled with Lord Grey in the previous year, though vexed by his pitiless attack on Canning, so there was not a trace of ungenerous comment on the course now taken by Lamb. He was able to point with satisfaction to the omission in the King's speech of any threatening allusion to the Catholic Association. The knowledge he had recently acquired of the actual condition of things in Ireland taught him to regard that body, not indeed as innocuous, but rather as constituting a specific danger so formidable that no sacrifice could be too great to effect the removal of the intolerable grievance that was its cause. He had not been many days at the Irish Office when the question was raised in Parliament by one of his late colleagues regarding the policy to be pursued towards Ireland ;—was it to be one of repression or reconciliation? On the 13th of February he wrote a confidential note to the new Premier :—

Spring Rice gave notice yesterday in the House that he would on Friday next ask whether it was the intention of ministers to continue the 6th of George IV. c. 4, being the act against the Roman Catholic Association. It would of course be better to be able to give him a decisive answer, as the matter being kept in suspense occasions agitation.*

The Cabinet on being consulted agreed that no new measure of coercion should be brought forward, and he was directed to reply to the question accordingly.

On the expiration of Lord Wellesley's term of office, the

* MS. correspondence at Apsley House.

Goderich Cabinet had agreed to recommend the Marquis of Anglesey to be his successor. Personally a favourite with the King, an idol with the army, and known to be far-going in liberality on sectarian questions,* his appointment was deemed a politic stroke, which the Duke of Wellington saw no reason to disapprove. On the 27th of February he was gazetted Lord Lieutenant of Ireland, and his public entry into Dublin was marked with demonstrations of popular good-will.

The most notable paragraph in the speech on the opening of the session of 1828 "lamented that the conflict at Navarino should have occurred with the naval force of an ancient ally; and hoped that this untoward event would not be followed by further hostilities, and would not impede the amicable adjustment of existing differences between the Porte and the Greeks." Angry criticism was directed against the language thus applied to a transaction which, though certainly not contemplated beforehand by the Goderich Cabinet, had never been censured by them, and which it was strenuously contended was the legitimate consequence of the tripartite treaty of July acknowledging Hellenic independence. Lamb, though he had nothing departmentally to do with the matter, never shrank from defending the foreign policy of his colleagues as substantially just and wise. Huskisson and Dudley could not be mistaken as to the real views entertained by Canning of Russian designs south of the Danube. And from these they knew that there was no substantial difference in the sentiments of the Duke. The Porte was, if possible, to be withheld from attempting the reconquest of the Morea, whose allegiance she had forfeited, and whose possession she had lost; but because her councils were obstinate and rash it was not our interest that her territory should be appropriated by a neighbour already too powerful and aggressive. To the French Ambassador the language of the new Premier was clear and emphatic.

* Sir W. Freemantle to the Duke of Buckingham, February 25th, 1828.

We are all interested in the continued existence in a state
of independence of the power of the Porte in Europe. We
are not prepared for its destruction. We ought to direct
our efforts steadily to attain our original object, the pacification of Greece without injury, or at least as little injury
as possible, to the power of the Porte, according to the
plan upon which the allies have acted.*

At the same time Dudley, with whom Lamb was more
intimate than ever, reminded Prince Lieven that in the
judgment of the British Cabinet the Ottoman Empire was
not like some of those whose example we might cite within
our own times, which, after having been invaded, resumed
their domestic tranquillity and their political existence
upon the retreat of the invaders; once broken up, its capital
taken, and its provinces in rebellion, the recomposition of it
as an independent state would be a work scarcely within the
reach of human capacity or human skill. A new order of
things must arise in those countries of which it now consists.
What that order might be it was vain to conjecture; but we
might venture to foretell that a final adjustment would not
take place till after a series of troubles and disasters, for which
the greatest benefits that could be supposed to arise from
it could not for many years afford a sufficient compensation.†
If the loss of her fleet enabled a Muscovite army to overrun
Bulgaria and to threaten Constantinople, that was a danger
to the peace of Europe, and to the freedom of our trade in
the East, to which no administration could be blind; and
Lamb contended always that Canning's policy which led to
the Treaty of London was inflexibly to control the separate
and selfish aims of the Muscovite without encouraging the
Porte in its vain dream of reconquering a people whom its
misrule had driven into successful revolt. Had he been living
he would not have hesitated to place in the lips of royalty a
plain intimation that England would continue to stand fair

* To Count La Ferronays, February 26th, 1828.
† To the Russian Ambassador, March 7th, 1828.

between the rival empires, offering aid to neither, but letting
the world know that she could not behold with indifference
any approach to the subjugation of the weaker by the
stronger state.

It was not long, however, before a question arose which
revealed the incongruity of the elements whereof the Cabinet
was made up, and which, though summarily settled by the
Premier's good sense, presaged disruption at no distant day.
Lord John Russell moved for a committee of the whole
House to take into consideration the propriety of repealing
the Test Act, by which dissenters would have been excluded
from municipal and other offices were it not for a bill
annually passed suspending the penalties for its infraction.
The retention on the statute-book of a penal law affecting
conscience, long after its purpose and its provisions had
become obsolete, admitted of no constitutional defence. But
the newly formed administration were afraid to begin to
give way; and Huskisson had no better plea to offer for
resisting the change than the invidious one that the removal
of statutable disabilities from the dissenters would make the
sense of grievance on the part of the Catholics all the more
intolerable. The conclusive answer, if any were needed, to
this half-hearted excuse lay in the fact that the Catholic
Association had warmly recommended petitions for the
repeal of the Test Act. But the case was too clear for
argument. Palmerston, Grant, and Lamb, felt bound by
the obligation of official loyalty to divide with their leader;
but most of the Canningites out of office left the House
without voting, and the motion was carried by a majority of
fourty-four, in which were included Duncannon and George
Lamb. It being clear, from the numerous defections in the
ministerial ranks, that the old spirit of exclusion was gone,
the minority in the Cabinet urged that the opportunity
should be taken of yielding gracefully and betimes to public
opinion. The Duke wisely and promptly agreed to a change
of front, difficult and awkward as the proceeding might be;
and Huskisson was authorized to state, on behalf of the

Government, that, bowing to the decision of the House of Commons, they would cordially support the bill. It passed through all its stages with little controversy, and was supported in the Upper House, to the horror of Lord Eldon, by his versatile successor on the woolsack.

One of the last measures of importance carried by the Liverpool administration was the Sub-letting Act, applicable only to Ireland. For many years a constant theme of censure by economic writers and reports of select committees had been the excessive partition of the soil for the purpose of creating forty-shilling freeholds. Crowds of sub-tenants were yearly multiplied, not only impoverished by usurious exaction, but who were subjected to the risk, and often to the loss, of what little they possessed by process of distraint for default in payment of rent, by the middle-man under whom they held. Nothing but a disabling law would, it was supposed, check this fertile source of disquietude and misery; and in 1826 an enactment was passed rendering null and void sub-leases or sub-assignments of land, without regard to the depreciation of the interests for which fines had frequently been given by the primary lessees. Unable to enforce the payment of rent from the small occupiers, the middle-men began, wherever they could, to serve ejectments; and agrarian suffering and disturbance were thus rendered greater than before. Petitions couched in terms of bitterest complaint continued to pour in from the central and southern Irish counties, and Lamb was appealed to by Hume, H. Grattan, and others to bring in an amending bill, which should mitigate the hardships complained of, if not to remove them altogether. Good Irish landlords like Lord Milton and Mr. Brownlow deprecated, on the other hand, any sudden reversal of recent legislation, as tending still further to unsettle the respect for law in the minds of the people. The Chief Secretary admitted the inconsiderate and improvident rigour of certain provisions in the statute of 1826, but declined to encourage the demand made by the Catholic Association for its absolute

repeal. He had in contemplation an amending bill, which
he hoped might in a great degree assuage the evils which
had been pointed out; and with this assurance the discussion
was allowed to drop. Before an opportunity was afforded
for the consideration of his remedial measure he had felt it
his duty to quit office ; and nothing further was done until
four years later, when, as minister for the Home Department, he carried through the Upper House an amended
Sub-letting Act, introduced in the Commons when Mr.
Stanley was Chief Secretary for Ireland. *

Sir Francis Burdett had charge of the Catholic Relief
Bill upon the last of many occasions on which it was
presented by an independent member. With the exception
of Brougham, the great orators were gone who had formerly
pleaded in its favour, wisely, but in vain. The Ministerial
bench was still divided on the question, Peel manifesting
more than his former skill and tact as a debater, and
successfully disguising his conviction that the cause was
lost, which he still incited those who believed in him,
persistently to defend. The Secretary for Ireland felt it
due to the position he held not to remain silent or
acquiescent after the statements of principle and of fact
that had fallen from the Home Secretary. On constitutional
grounds he must controvert the maxim that laws deemed
fundamental in the settlement of the kingdom at the
Revolution could not be changed without endangering
the stability of the throne, and fatally altering the historic
unity and character of Parliament. It was impossible
to believe that the active intelligence of a great nation
would submit for any lengthened period to be bound by
the edicts or enactments of a distant and dissimilar age.
Adaptation to new circumstances and modification of old
provisions were inevitable in the current of national life ;
and it was misleading and mischievous to teach the
unthinking and the timid to look with dread on mutations
that were inevitable. Fears of this kind had been in-

* 2 & 3 William IV. c. 17.

dustriously excited previous to the union with Scotland. It was said that to admit a body of representatives brought up under a different system of jurisprudence, and zealously devoted to a different creed and method of church government, would destroy the homogeneous nature of the legislature; but experience had speedily dissipated these apprehensions, which were now entirely forgotten; and so it would be when they had admitted, as sooner or later they were certain to do, a reasonable number of Catholic members from Ireland. If the temper of the community, disabled from holding political rank or performing political service, were as bad as had been described, and as inimical to the constituted Government of the realm, that was but another reason for bringing to an end the anomalies and absurdities which put a whole people out of temper and alienated their affections from those whom they should be led to honour and obey. But the great measure was still unhappily delayed. The last opportunity of yielding to considerations of national justice and generosity was lost; and the fatal notice to the people of Ireland was given, that until they could exact redress by the open threat of force they had no chance of obtaining it.

The cause of Parliamentary Reform seemed just then to have as little prospect of success. Sweeping proposals were no longer brought forward, but Lord J. Russell and Mr. Tennyson brought in bills to transfer respectively the seats forfeited by Penryn and East Retford, by reason of proved corruption, to Manchester and Birmingham, neither of which at that time possessed representatives. The Commons passed the former measure, but the Lords postponed its adoption, and were understood to be disinclined to pass it. The Cabinet, at the instance of Peel, resolved that the seats for East Retford should be conferred on an agricultural district consisting of the hundreds around the delinquent town; but Huskisson had declared in his place that if but one borough only were disfranchised, Birmingham should have the seats. On the 19th of May, when the

East Retford bill was pending, Lord Sandon, as a moderate
reformer, claimed the fulfilment of this pledge, which would
have left the Upper House the option of conferring the
seats for Penryn on a rural district.   Huskisson, who had
acquiesced in the Cabinet in Peel's view, was in a dilemma,
and sat during the debate wavering and perplexed.   Before
he could make up his mind what to do the division was
called.   Peel gave him a reproachful look when he saw that,
without explanation, he was about to break his word given
in council; and the irresolute minister, tormented by self-
distrust and the obvious discontent he had provoked among
his colleagues, went home, and ere he slept wrote to the
Duke, offering to resign.   His Grace thought he had
behaved ill, took him at his word, and forthwith forwarded
his letter to Windsor.   Palmerston laughed at his over-
scrupulous friend next morning, and with Dudley undertook
to rectify the error.   They saw the Premier, who coldly
intimated that the resignation might still be withdrawn;
but this was a humiliation they could not recommend, and
further parleying proved in vain.   With Huskisson all
Canning's friends, including Lamb, retired from the administration, and Lord F. L. Gower became Secretary for
Ireland.

Jerden called on him and persuaded him to resume his
contributions to the *Literary Gazette*.   They had previously
been casual, but now became more frequent, being chiefly
criticisms on theological or ethical works.   Some of his
reviews were of plagiaristic or platitudinarian volumes of
sermons, and are spiced with keen, though not irreverent
humour.

CHAPTER XVI.

Fifty years gone by—Catholic Emancipation—William IV.—Change of Government.

PENISTON, first Lord Melbourne, died on the 22nd of July, 1828, in his eighty-third year, leaving his estates in Derbyshire and Hertfordshire to William Lamb. A note to Lady Holland announced the event, which took place without suffering, his sister Emily having been for some days in close attendance with him upon his father.

A sense of sadness crept over him as he paced The Dell, where he had so often loved to linger in the indolent enjoyment of summer life. The unfallen foliage of the oaks and beeches on either side made it still a spacious shelter from the winds of the outer world. But the voice of spring was long since mute, the golden gladness had passed away, and the hue of autumn seemed to presage the darkening season of decline and of decay. Youth and maturity were passed. The lot had fallen to him in pleasant places; and though late, he had come into possession of a goodly heritage. Honour, love, ambition, troops of friends, he had all; and if he had not always made good use of opportunities, he could not reproach himself with having idly or wilfully neglected them. He had read thoughtfully as much as, or more than the majority of men of his day; he had loved, how fondly, and endured how patiently, and forborne how tenderly, none living knew. The hope of posterity had not been denied him;

nor a place in the first assembly in the world. Yet what did all avail to quench the unslaked thirst of sympathy, purpose, occupation? Learning, criticism, and philosophy might make men listen to his talk, but they had not given him the energy or perseverance necessary to build up even as much as Sallust built to keep in memory his name. The partner of his youth, with all her faults and errors, he loved better than any woman he had ever known. She had survived his confidence, though not his affection; and had worn herself out with waywardness ere she was old: and the son she had borne him, now come to man's estate, remained childish still, and without giving any hope of mental manhood. For five-and-twenty years Lamb had been a member of the House of Commons, a favourite there, seldom refused a hearing; the intimate of its greatest men, and for a season the occupant of a difficult post; yet he had not made a speech worth remembering, and the Cabinet—the crown of parliamentary strivings—had never been conceded him. In full possession of faculties the world called excellent, with health and strength unbroken, his time his own, with fortune ample, and a name which, though new and hitherto undistinguished, he might yet ennoble,—public life lay open to him as ever, and with his dislike of trouble and contention, the more tranquil region of the House of Lords was not distasteful. But he was lonely and listless, disdaining to repine, yet haunted by regrets. Half a century spent and gone, and how little to show for it! He would have given a great deal to have had a fervid, even a fantastic faith in anything worth working for. He had been born a Whig, bred a courtier, drawn by conviction into Canningism, and persuaded to retain office under the Duke of Wellington. But Whiggery was said to be worn out. There was no longer a Court genial, generous, or gay; Canning was dead, and the great soldier's administration seemed tottering to its fall. Utilitarian levelling like that of Bentham he regarded as nonsense. State parsimony like Joseph Hume's he thought a pettifogging blunder. Radicalism after the manner of Hunt and Cobbett he called mere ragamuffinism. He envied Stanley, as he said, the equal pleasure he took in fighting a main of cocks and defending the abuses of the Established Church. He coveted Palmerston's light-heartedness and india-rubber temperament, and Lansdowne's delight in the arts and in the duties of hospitality. Althorp's devotion to his wethers and short-horns, and Holland's happiness in his great dinners and amusement at my lady's whimsicality, were alike to him marvels of contentedness. He was inactive, yet he was not at ease. He felt that he had as keen an insight into motives and as firm a grasp of the tendencies of things as any of them, and he could not reconcile himself to subsiding at fifty into a country gentleman that did not hunt, or a peer that voted by proxy. The forecast of Charles Fox and the estimate of Castlereagh, repeated in her last days by his mother, recurred to him in his solitude and recalled him from despondency. He would try again, try on; but how? While he pondered an unexpected shadow fell upon his path that looked like the realisation of hope long deferred. It proved illusory, and vanished into nothing, as out of nothing it almost seemed to come; but it changed the whole condition of the man, and served undoubtedly to hasten his advancement to the first rank in his party.

Late in August Mr. Greville mentions a party at Stoke, during which he asked the new Viscount if the rumour was true that he had been offered the Admiralty. "He said he had never heard of it." Yet the rumour had its significance. The Duke of Clarence had just been compelled to relinquish the post of Lord High Admiral; and for every reason it was of importance that a return to the usual mode of administering the naval department by a board of commissioners should be justified by the character of efficiency, its members, and more especially its president, enjoyed. That the ex-Secretary for Ireland, who had never been in the Cabinet, should hear himself talked of as a probable First Lord of the Admiralty in a circle closely associated with the Court could not but sound like an augury of things to come.

Irish affairs were fast drifting near the rapids. O'Connell's election for Clare, in defiance of his legal ineligibility, seemed to have dazed his adversaries and crazed his friends. It was a moral *coup d'état*, which proved irreversible. His opponent, Vesey Fitzgerald, the most popular man in his county, had all his life been an emancipator; yet, because he had become a member of the now distrusted Cabinet, he was driven from the representation by an overwhelming majority. O'Connell himself had hesitated to make the experiment, and when it succeeded, hardly knew how to turn it to account. Parliament was still in session, but he did not demand admission to St. Stephen's to claim the seat. He contented himself with franking letters and delighting the multitude by allowing them to call him "The Member." All the autumn lively debate arose at every dinner-table as to whether he would attempt to take his seat. In one of these convivial discussions Plunket asked Chief Baron O'Grady what he thought. His learned brother replied, "I think he will, although he said he would." The Catholic Association, freed from even the nominal inhibition of a statute never put in force, revelled in the enjoyment of unbridled power, and served notices to quit on all county members whose names were not found upon its roll. Adhesions and subscriptions poured in from Nonconformists in England, and from not a few fugitives of 1798 settled in America. The spirit of ascendency for the first time seemed fairly daunted; and, to crown all, Canning's memorable question became practical and pressing—"What is to be done when the extinguishers take fire?"

Lord Anglesey, who had been chosen Viceroy because George IV. had "implicit confidence in his dash and devotion," began to feel the ground going from under him. He sought counsel from the Chancellor, but found him very much in the mood of Macbeth when he exclaims, "There is nor flying hence nor tarrying here." Trusting him without reserve, he imparted to him his own deepening sense of the untenableness of the position he had been instructed to hold.

The Chancellor had the same wish as Lamb to meet the agitators face to face, and hear for himself what they had to say. Lord Cloncurry, in accordance with his wish, invited O'Connell to meet him at Lyons, the residence of his lordship in Kildare; and Sir Anthony was much interested and amused on the occasion. If the incident was not formally noticed as a matter of reproof from Downing Street, it was probably because the Viceroy himself had become the absorbing object of royal suspicion. He, too, had been a guest of the malcontent Lord of Lyons, an indiscretion not to be mutely endured. The Premier "could not conceal from him that his visit and those of the Lord Chancellor to Lord Cloncurry, and the attendance of his lordship at the Roman Catholic Association immediately subsequent, were not circumstances calculated to give satisfaction to the King."* Lord Cloncurry's account of how he came on a single occasion to be present in the dreaded assembly was, that multitudinous marchings in Tipperary had been announced for a day then near at hand, and that the authorities were full of apprehensions of a serious breach of the peace. He offered, with Mr. William Curran,† to remonstrate with the popular leaders upon the danger of allowing these demonstrations to proceed; and, there being barely time for interposition, they had waived all scruple and sought an interview, which proved successful. When it was concluded in one of the committee-rooms O'Connell naively said, "While you are here you may as well come in and see our meeting." The mediators thought they could not refuse, and were of course cordially received; but neither of them appeared on the scene again. The Viceroy replied with warmth that the fidelity of his life to the person and government of his Majesty ought to have shielded him from mistrust or misgiving; and he continued his invitations to Lord Cloncurry as before. His presumption in seeming to anticipate the inevitable, and the extreme imprudence of his language in public and private

---

* Duke of Wellington to Lord Anglesey, November 11th, 1828.

† The son and biographer of the celebrated orator.

led to his recall. Some of his letters to the Duke had been laid before the King, who was highly indignant at their dictatorial tone; and his Grace, though personally attached to him, was heard to complain of his insolence to himself. Vesey Fitzgerald, being asked about his removal by Melbourne, said "he had done remarkably well, but the rock on which he split was his vanity."* On receiving the intimation of his recall Lord Anglesey showed the Duke's letter to Mr. George Villiers, who communicated its contents to Shiel, with whom he called soon afterwards on O'Connell. The Liberator seemed greatly cast down by the intelligence; anticipated nothing but a policy of arbitrary repression; and altogether caused them so much uneasiness as to what he might be impelled by the unlooked-for incident to say or do, that they insisted on staying to dine with him, partly in order to discuss all possible contingencies, and still more to prevent his being left to less cool-headed companionship during the evening. When they parted they fancied that they had persuaded him to refrain from comment in his speech at the Association on the morrow. But such tidings could not be kept secret, and he had no choice but to give utterance to the sense of disappointment that everywhere prevailed. The revolution already planned and matured by the Government was inaugurated by the sacrifice. The Duke of Northumberland, a moderate partisan of resistance, was named Viceroy. Lord Anglesey's departure was marked with every demonstration of popular sorrow. Accompanied to the place of embarkation by many persons of distinction and a vast multitude, his parting words to O'Connell were, "Agitate, agitate, and you will succeed."

At the opening of Parliament on the 1st of February, 1829, "William, Viscount Melbourne, took the oaths and his seat in the House of Peers."† The royal speech on the same day recommended both Houses to take into consideration the expediency of settling the Catholic question.

* Greville, 'Memoirs,' i. p. 150.
† Lords' Journal, lxi. 5.

The interval between the announcement of the great measure and its formal introduction was spent in conjectures as to how many would avow themselves converts; whether O'Connell would take his seat for Clare, or whether he would be excluded by a special clause of the bill. He arrived in London on the 9th, and was immediately called on by Ellice, Burdett, Ebrington, Hume and others, most of whom urged him to dissolve the Catholic Association, and so take away all excuse for the threatened measure for its suppression. He told them that until the bill was carried he would not propose to break in pieces the instrument which had compelled the offer of surrender. He could not tell what the Lords might do, sinister rumours being afloat as to the Duke's failure to enforce compliance with his right-about-face policy.

A stringent Act to put down the triumphant Association was made a condition precedent of the Relief Bill. It passed rapidly through the Lower House, with brief and formal protests, but without serious let or hindrance. In the Upper House, Anglesey, who could not forgive his recent recall, indulged in eulogy *ad invidiam* of the tact and talent displayed by the Catholic leaders; and Lord Longford taunted ministers with not having executed the former Suppression Act or come to Parliament betimes for greater powers. Melbourne replied:—

It is impossible that I can allow the observations which have been made upon the conduct of the last two Governments in Ireland to pass, without troubling your lordships with a very few words upon the subject. The noble lord says that the Government of 1825 having determined on a bill for the purpose of putting down the Catholic Association conducted itself extremely ill, because it did not, when it found the act prove inoperative, come to Parliament for further powers. I beg to tell the noble lord that the bill in question was introduced, not only on the responsibility, and by the advice of my noble

friend,—the then Attorney-General for Ireland, and now
a member of this House (Lord Plunket),—but that it received the sanction, generally, of his Majesty's ministers,
at that time forming the Government, and particularly of
the noble and learned Earl (of Eldon), who at that period
was the adviser of the Crown, and Lord Chancellor of
England. That learned peer bears as much of the responsibility of what was then done, or omitted to be done, as
can by possibility be placed to the account of my noble
friend the late Attorney-General for Ireland. The noble
lord says the second Government was still more culpable
than the first, because powers were placed in the magistracy of Ireland, who were members of the Association; and
he argues that Government were altogether responsible
for such appointments. The noble lord has undoubtedly
great experience as respects these appointments in England, but he is wholly ignorant of the practice which is
pursued in Ireland. The Lord Chancellor, there, appoints
the magistrates solely and entirely on his own responsibility, and an appointment is no way to be considered as
the act of the Government; but at the same time, I must
say, that when there were so many individuals in that
country,—persons of character and property,—who were
eligible to those offices, whether they were Catholics or
Protestants, to adhere to any rule of exclusion would have
been vain. I readily admit the insufficiency of the law
of 1825, and the causes of that insufficiency have been
very ably stated by the noble duke. That bill was
designated by one of the first lawyers in Ireland, the
"Enabling Bill," inasmuch as it gave to the Catholic
Association a power that it did not before possess. And
what was the consequence? Why, no sooner were the
provisions of that bill known in Ireland, than the Association advertised meetings to be held as under that
Bill—under the sanction of that very law, by the passing
of which it was intended to effect the demolition of the
Association! I have heard it asked in this House—and

I was astonished at the question—what was the reason
that the law of 1825 had proved inefficient for the
purpose for which it was intended? I will answer that
question in two words—Catholic disabilities were the
cause which rendered that act inoperative. It is impossible for any Government to act with proper energy,
when it finds its arms borne down by a sense of injury
and injustice in respect of those over whom the power
of that Government extends. I beg leave to say that the
present measure will, in my opinion, share the same fate
as the former Acts, if it be not followed by one of grace
and concession. It may have the effect of putting down
this Association and similar Associations; but it will be
perfectly ineffectual to stay the tide of public opinion in
Ireland. It will be impossible to preserve order and
security to the Protestant Establishments in that country,
unless his Majesty's Roman Catholic subjects are admitted
to the enjoyment of the blessings of the British constitution. With respect to the Roman Catholic Association,
I am one of those who do not think it has contributed to
the success of that cause which, we hope, is now arriving
at consummation. On the contrary, I think—though, I
differ in opinion from very many noble lords—that its
uncontrolled violence, and its unguarded conduct, have
rather impeded than advanced the great cause of Catholic
emancipation. I shall give my cordial support to the
bill as it at present stands, upon the understanding and
expectation that it will be followed by a measure which
shall have for its object the relief of all classes of his
Majesty's Roman Catholic subjects.*

This was not the popular line to take, but it was the way to
render effective aid in securing the great benefit of religious
liberty too long deferred. For its sake he was ready to
concur in the propitiatory offering to the wounded pride of

* 'Mirror of Parliament,' February 24th, 1829.

authority; and to bear his part in the sacrifice. The
juncture was critical.

The Duke of Rutland and other Tory friends of Government, piqued at not having had any hint in time that would
have enabled them to keep up their county repute of being
in the secret of what was designed, had announced their
intention of withdrawing to their country seats, and taking
no further part in the controversy. Lords Eldon and
Winchelsea, Kenyon and Roden prepared to rally round the
Duke of Cumberland for a last stand in the trenches of
the betrayed citadel. Plunket made impromptu one of his
best historical speeches in rebuke of the constitutional wail
of the ex-Chancellor.* But the Duke of Cumberland was
frequently at Windsor, where he at last wrought upon the
royal convert so effectually that serious misgivings were
entertained as to his fidelity in redeeming his promise to
give his assent to the Disabilities Bill. Peel's defeat at
Oxford gave new energy to reactionists, and George IV. told
his household that they might if they pleased vote against
ministers. The Duke sought an audience to remonstrate
and reassure himself in his position; but six hours, with
occasional intervals, were spent in bringing his Majesty to
reason. The Premier, at length satisfied, took his departure for Strathfieldsaye to receive the judges, who
were on circuit. There, long after midnight, while he still
sat clearing his arrear of correspondence, the Chancellor
appeared, to tell him that he had been sent for, and told
by his Majesty that certain clauses of the bill as brought
in by Peel had not been previously explained to him, and
that he could not give his assent to them if passed by Parliament. Before breakfast his Grace was on his way to
Windsor, and Lyndhurst had set out for town. George IV.
used every argument to excuse his vacillation, but the
minister who had staked his reputation upon carrying what
Pitt, Grenville, and Canning had been unable to carry was
not to be talked over at such a moment, and he quitted the

* 'Mirror of Parliament,' February 19th.

royal presence with a declaration that unless the sovereign would continue his promised support upon the question he must forthwith resign. The fear of being left to the Duke of Cumberland's party, or to the Whigs, finally determined the wavering monarch. Peel, upon his defeat at Oxford, hired for the session the seat for Westbury at an extravagant price, and introduced the Relief Bill on the 5th of March. Its liberality and completeness won hearty praise from the Opposition; its only serious flaw being the unworthy contrivance which, by a certain turn of phrase, excluded O'Connell until re-elected. No second opinion existed among the Whigs on this point; it was regarded by them as sheer infatuation abortively to endeavour thus to shut out the man by whom confessedly the door had been broken in. Spring Rice, who loved him not, said truly that instead of excluding him, they should pay him to come into Parliament, and rather buy a seat for him than let him remain out. Though disheartened, the opponents of the measure did not yet despair. The Duke hesitated to accept the resignations of holders of office like Lord Lowther who voted against him; he feared to add to the exasperation prevalent among old supporters, or to rely too much upon the Whigs, who when he had done their work would, he believed, desert him. He knew that there was no depending on the King, whose irritability and caprice were the misery of all about him. Out of doors opinion was still divided. On the second reading Mr. Sadler, who had been brought in for the purpose, delivered a speech which produced a great impression against the bill. No man at sixty-seven had been ever known before to begin a parliamentary career successfully. It was said, probably with truth, that had he spoken as long and as well on any other question he would not have been one-half reported, or the following week asked out to dinner as a rising man. This did not change the significance of the fact that in him a deep national feeling found a voice to which, willingly or unwillingly, every one paused to listen. The instinct of eloquence consists, after all, in knowing when, quite as much as in knowing what to say. Sadler had the credit of adding some votes to the minority; on the other side, the person who did best, to the delight of Melbourne and the surprise of those who knew him not so well, was Palmerston.

On the 28th of March, Lord Eldon had an audience of the King which lasted for four hours; it was the forlorn hope of the party of resistance, and when it failed the long struggle was over. Sir Robert Peel's version of what passed differs materially from that of the Earl. In the Lords the Chancellor formally recanted all his vaticinations of three years before, while Grey and Plunket had the proud satisfaction of witnessing a triumph of the great principle in the advocacy of which they had spent their lives. Some one congratulated Lord Grenville that the great measure he too had fought for so long and so unselfishly was at last about to be carried. He replied sadly that he could feel no exultation at what was called a settlement, but which in reality would certainly settle nothing. " You are not going to pay the priests;" he said, "and therefore you will do more harm than good by giving them mouthpieces in Parliament." *

An action brought against Melbourne early in the year came on for trial on the second day of Michaelmas Term in the Court of King's Bench, putting him to no little expense, and causing him still more annoyance. He had been a frequent guest in Ireland of Lord Brandon, who had married Elizabeth, daughter of Colonel Latouche and granddaughter of the Countess of Miltown, afterwards Lady Cloncurry. To many charms of person Lady Brandon added those which a lively disposition and an unusual degree of culture were calculated to afford. Her house was one of the most agreeable at the time in Dublin, and many persons of congenial sentiments were there to be found, whom in the rigid severance of political parties then prevailing, the Chief Secretary did not meet elsewhere. Lord Brandon was gouty, and spent the autumn at Buxton and the winter abroad; his life had not

* Archbishop Whately in Senior's Journal, November 13th, 1858.

been the most domestic, and the ill-assorted marriage proved unhappy. Mutual complaints led in the following year to a separation, and to an attempt by him to obtain a divorce. With this design in view, he was, unfortunately for himself, advised to sue Lord Melbourne for damages on the alleged ground of improper intimacy with his wife during her residence in London. Mr. Gurney, with whom were associated Mr. Brougham and Mr. Charles Phillips, stated the case for the plaintiff; but the evidence given was so valueless that Lord Tenterden refused to call on Mr. Scarlett, who was counsel for the defendant; and telling the jury that " nobody could give one word of proof against Lord Melbourne," directed a rule to be entered for a nonsuit. In the ecclesiastical court, soon afterwards, Lord Brandon equally failed in the proceedings he had instituted against his wife. It is said that the array of witnesses ready to be called on the other side scared him from proceeding, and prompted his counsel to withdraw the case. Dr. Lushington decided that such a proceeding could only be allowed on condition of the plaintiff's paying the costs, and this being done the miserable affair ended.

At the commencement of 1830, the breach seemed as impassable as ever between ministers and the ultra-Tory party, who still looked with desperate devotion to the Duke of Cumberland and Lord Eldon as their faithful but hopelessly baffled chiefs. The Premier and his Royal Highness were hardly on speaking terms, and few, if any, of the seceders had returned to the ranks of the party. The debating strength of the Treasury Bench was unexpectedly weakened by the sudden illness of Mr. Vesey Fitzgerald, whose place as President of the Board of Trade was but indifferently filled by Sir Frankland Lewis, a careful and accomplished man, but formal, verbose, and dull. Palmerston rather disparaged Fitzgerald, whom he called fluent, but rather vulgar. Spring Rice estimated more accurately his worth to his friends and the detriment caused by his loss:—

I grieve at his illness; his conduct at the Board of Trade

was in all respects admirable, and his zeal for the interests of Ireland was equalled by a knowledge of the actual condition of the country not possessed by any other member of the Cabinet. We Irish change so rapidly that the Duke of Wellington, Peel and Goulburn are already as much outrun by events as if they had studied no later authority than Spencer and Sir John Davies.*

The little section then led by Mr. Huskisson had been raised in importance by the speeches of Palmerston on foreign affairs. But they were all officers, and had no soldiers, or any extensive field of opinion to recruit from. The Whigs were not gaining influence, and there were rumours of defections among some of the great families. Yet after all the Duke's difficulty lay in devising measures big enough to engage attention without exciting serious antagonism, and in finding colleagues, when he wanted them, who should be at once docile in the Cabinet, efficient in office, and unprovocative of jealousy in the House. It was to this desire of personal government that Huskisson alluded when he said to a friend, the very day before his death, "The Duke will find out at last that he cannot govern England with men only who will move at the word of a drill sergeant." But for the present he was resolved to try. Peel had submitted to be shorn of his personal influence with clergy and squirearchy, and he felt that he had no power of resistance till it had time to grow again. Lyndhurst was too easygoing and self-indulgent to differ about any matter of mere opinion; his sole conviction was that the best thing in life was to be Keeper of the Great Seal. Aberdeen and Ellenborough could hardly be said to occupy as yet a space in the public eye of leading importance; and the rest were what Brougham used to call eleventh-rate men.

As the meeting of Parliament approached, reports thickened. His faithful correspondent kept Lord Lansdowne informed at Bowood of such as were most believable.

* To J. Abercromby, January 9th, 1830.

Edward Ellice had come to town bringing Lord Grey's last word, that "if the Duke conceived an union of all parties unconnected with the Government was impossible, he never was so wrong in his life." Melbourne was of course one of the most available, because one of the most many-sided and most popular elements of such a projected combination. In one way or another he had intimacies, if not relations, with each of the sections whom it was thus hoped to combine, and his personal influence to that end Lord Grey well knew was all the more likely to be effective because his air and tone were more than ever those of banter and indifference. Huskisson was said, on the score of health, to be desirous that Palmerston should take his place during the session as spokesman of the surviving remnant of the Canningites. This was obvious policy with respect to the ultra-Tories and to the Liberals, many of whom felt a distrust of Huskisson not entertained towards the ex-Secretary at War. To enlist rank and file, Palmerston was put forward as recruiting sergeant.

Before the meeting of Parliament, Lords Cleveland, Grosvenor, and Darnley had given in their adhesion to ministers; and the names of the Duke of Bedford and Lord Jersey were included by the gossips in a list of moderate Whigs who were ready to rally to their support against royal reaction. But these were fitted, as Spring Rice said, rather to serve as reinforcements for the back than the front bench, where everything depended on the Home Secretary's encyclopædic power of talk. Brougham made people laugh at Brooks's by announcing that the session would open with a change in the standing orders, allowing Peel to speak any number of times (not exceeding thirty) on all questions.* The rank and file of Opposition were ready indeed to be led to the attack on any point that might appear exposed; but if the Premier had any legislative policy he was inflexible in his resolve to keep it to himself; and even the newspapers could suggest nothing more tempting of topics for adverse

* Letter to Sir John Newport, January 18th, 1830.

criticism than *ex officio* prosecutions of the *Morning Journal*, than neglect of agricultural distress and the want of vigour in our foreign policy in the Levant. Not a muttering was heard, however distant or faint, of the storm already threatening in the horizon and soon to sweep into comparative forgetfulness all the common elements of parliamentary fret and fume. Lord Althorp and his friends, Parnell, Graham, Thompson, and Baring, were full of economics and busily engaged with subjects of retrenchment, about which the politicians proper cared not a jot, as ministers were believed to be ready to outbid them in paring down, provided always the Windsor and Whitehall pension lists were not touched. But in the diaries and letters of the period scarcely a word is said about Parliamentary Reform.

The two Houses met on the 4th of February, and the temporary break-up of party ties caused by late events was more strikingly displayed than ever. Sir Edward Knatchbull moved an amendment to the Address, declaring the prevalence of distress to be general, and not, as ministers had advised his Majesty to say, only partial. Brougham and Sadler concurred; and O'Connell had the gratification, of which he had dreamed so long, of hearing his own voice in the Chapel of St. Stephen. Curiosity, dislike, sympathy, and at length admiration of his suasive tone and fine delivery secured him breathless attention, and at the conclusion ungrudging praise. Who will venture to say that he understands or can realise the intoxication of that hour? Many triumphs had been his before, and many awaited him, of which the world took more heed. There was nothing peculiarly apt or telling in the speech itself; nothing he did not far surpass on subsequent occasions. But no occasion could for him have the exquisite satisfaction of this. He had been shut out, and he had broken in, assuring ingress not for himself only, but for his race and creed. And there he stood alone, their leader, representative, chief, the welcomed by many, courteously received and recognised as worthy to be there by all.

Lord Holland made an amusing speech on Greek affairs, quizzing the "Athenian Aberdeen" with effacing the inscription by Canning of national sympathy on the ruins of ancient freedom. Melbourne backed his friend with vivacity and vigour. The "travelled Thane," as his poetic namesake called him, made a poor defence, but the Premier covered his retreat in his own fashion. Robert Grant, listening on the steps of the throne, though his sympathies were the other way, whispered to Greville, "He speaks like a great man."*

A few days afterwards Melbourne was less fortunate. Frederick Lamb, whose abilities began to be recognised in diplomacy, had published, on the eve of the session, a pamphlet on Portuguese affairs, denouncing what had been done in favour of Don Miguel by the advice of ministers and their immediate predecessors; and Melbourne fraternally undertook to urge the same view in the House of Lords. Not having been in the Goderich Cabinet he felt himself free to disapprove of Lord Dudley's language in the affair of Terceira as well as that of Lord Aberdeen. But his temerity drew down on him severe chastisement. The Duke and Lord Lansdowne concurred in excusing our tacit acquiescence in the acts of the usurper; and Lord Goderich spoke better than usual in support of both. Mr. Greville, who heard the debate, condemns Melbourne for not having got up his case better, and says that his manner was confused and his tone indiscreet. It was perhaps the only instance in a parliamentary life of forty years in which he severed himself on a question of importance from his political friends. They all regretted his failure, which was ascribed by some to passing indisposition, by others to want of judgment. The experiment of privateering he never tried again.†

The first public meeting of the Birmingham Political Union took place on the 17th of May, Mr. Muntz in the chair. The council recommended petitions in favour of

* 'Memoirs,' February 13th, 1830.
† Greville, 'Journal,' February 19th and 21st.

Lord Blandford's bill to expel all'placemen from parliament, abolition of rotten boroughs, repeal of the Septennial Act, and adoption of household suffrage. Their advice was accepted by an excited assembly, who went, however, much further, denouncing the Pension List and the flagrant abuses and jobs in all public departments. The keynote of complaint thus struck was re-echoed far and near. The allegations of distress were reiterated and intensified, until men esteemed for their knowledge and judgment, and who were supposed to have the best means of obtaining information, were led to believe that a state of anarchy was imminent.

Such was the condition in which George IV. left the realm. Unhonoured and unloved he passed away, and the folds of oblivion fell rapidly and silently over the recollection of his worthless name. Yet of many acts of hospitality and kindness Melbourne could not be unmindful. From boyhood he had been to some extent a favourite with the King; and though painfully conscious of his faults and weaknesses, he shrank from joining in the censure unsparingly pronounced upon them.

In appearance, habits, and demeanour, his successor was in every particular his opposite; and for a season spared no pains to win the smiles and salutations of the crowd. He did not understand that princely clap-trap goes for as little with hard-driven artisans as with coxcombs of quality.

It was well known that the Duke of Clarence had little of that peculiar pride which is called dignity; that he was at times half crazy, and at no time fit to be left to his own guidance. He had made these things more than sufficiently notorious during the time he held the office of Lord High Admiral, from which it become necessary to remove him. As king, his deportment was just the reverse of that of his late brother. Instead of shutting himself up and excluding himself from the sight of the people, he went about challenging popularity. He walked in the

streets, he rode in an open carriage with his queen, and
set the crowd shouting and vociferating, waving hats and
handkerchiefs like parish school children at a holiday
show. These were joined by the other royalists, no longer
a majority of the people. The rest stayed away or took
no heed of the folly; and, as Burke had said of the same
sort of people in his time, indulged in the gloom of their
discontent. The King nodded and laughed and lifted his
hat to the silly people, and was exeedingly delighted.
The Queen was just the contrary of her husband as well
in appearance as in conduct; and the mob soon began to
take a dislike to her.*

One of the first acts of the new sovereign was to direct
that the Duke of Norfolk should be named a Privy Councillor. The compliment to his Roman Catholic subjects was
not the less appreciated because it was paid to the first
noble in the realm, whose exclusion was a relic of intolerant
rule, abrogated in law, but not yet in fact. Melbourne took
means for conveying to the King how cordially he and
others approved of the spontaneous exercise of royal favour,
and family estrangement did not prevent him from congratulating his Grace on his taking the seat at the Council
Board so many of his ancestors had occupied.

Administration had escaped defeat, and with a new sovereign and a new Parliament they might hope that the
bitterness of late resentments would gradually die away.
The Premier had unbounded confidence in his own power
of managing the Upper House; but he was not at ease regarding the deficiency of debating power in the Lower,
which was indeed palpable to all. Palmerston thought
Ministers wretchedly weak, and that they would be out-
debated in a moment if questions were to arise in which
the Whigs chose vigorously to attack them. Peel was their
sole reliance, and he had lost weight by his recent change of
opinion. Vesey Fitzgerald was a good fighting speaker, but

* 'MS. Political Narratives,' by Francis Place, 1830, i., p. 32.

not a favourite with the House. Goulburn was very indifferent. Murray could hardly say a word, and Herries
was absolutely mute. But where could they look for reinforcements? The Duke would hardly like to take back
the Canningites as a party, and individually none of them
were disposed to join, lest they should be too far outnumbered in the Cabinet to be able to make their opinions
felt on any question of importance. Palmerston thought
the Duke would like better to get in some of the rising
Whigs, who would help in debate and succumb to the weight
of his authority in council. But Lord Rosslyn's appointment had made more enemies than friends.* Nevertheless
in July 1830 overtures were made to Melbourne to ascertain
if he with Palmerston and Grant would join the Government. Without Huskisson and Lord Grey he said it was
impossible for him to take office. To Huskisson the Duke
did not object; but Lord Grey had spoken of him both
publicly and privately in terms that must prevent their
acting confidentially together. After Huskisson's death
the proposal was renewed, this time through Palmerston.
Lord Clive was authorized by the Duke to ask him to return to the Cabinet and to inquire who were his friends.
He replied Melbourne and Grant; but that they would be
unwilling to join without Lansdowne and Grey. The Duke
was ready to assent to the three first-mentioned, but not to
the others, and instead of these suggested Goderich. Palmerston declined to regard him as any sufficient substitute;
and left town for Paris, considering the affair at an end.
On his return at the end of a fortnight the Duke asked him
to call at Apsley House. The interview lasted six minutes;
he said he could make room, he thought, for Grant and Melbourne; but further he was not prepared to go. Palmerston maintained a reconstruction of the Cabinet to be indispensable if any fusion was contemplated. He had by this
time begun to estimate the great changes that were taking
place in public opinion respecting Reform; and invited a

* Letter to the Hon. Wm. Temple, June 14th, 1829.

conference on the subject to meet at Stanhope Street, to which came Melbourne, the Grants, Denison, Binning, Lyttelton, Graham, Warrender, and others. They were not all agreed, but he and the Grants and Lyttelton had made up their minds to support the motion of which Brougham had already given notice on his return for the West Riding of Yorkshire. When J. W. Croker was therefore sent to persuade him to reconsider the Duke's offer a few days afterwards, Palmerston asked what the Duke meant to do upon the question, which was rapidly becoming the dividing line between parties, and on hearing Palmerston's resolve Croker said " good-bye," for it was clear they would never sit together in office again. Melbourne, always apt to take less sanguine views of public affairs, gravitated somewhat more slowly to the conclusion that parliamentary reform was peaceably attainable ; and his mind was imbued with all Burke's horror of violent revolution; but when he found not only Holland House and Woburn, but Lansdowne House and Broadlands half inclined to accept Brougham as a standard-bearer on the question, he came to the belief that to help to guide the inevitable was the most conservative part that he could play.

The death of Huskisson, in September, ripened the tendency of the Canningites to absorption in the Liberal party. Melbourne thought him more highly qualified than any of his rivals ; for he understood profoundly the true principles of trade, and was yet so free from dogmatism or asperity as to be able to mollify the prejudices that beset their adoption. His yielding temper and versatile disposition created doubts of his being governed by high principle ; and his consenting to retain office in January 1828 under the Duke of Wellington was a mistake the effect of which Melbourne thought irretrievable ; such, however, was not his own opinion, and to his over-anxiety to pay court to the Duke on the fatal occasion of their meeting at the Manchester Railway, the accident was generally ascribed which caused his death. Bereft unexpectedly within two years of their greater and their lesser leader, the Canningites were now not a sheep without a shepherd, but as sheep-dogs without a master. By official standing and experience, Palmerston may have thought himself entitled to the vacant position of chief. The repeated proposals of the Duke were fairly calculated to encourage such a pretension; Melbourne's indolence, Grant's timidity, and the friendship of both tended to foster its development. But events were at hand that speedily swept into oblivion any schemes of the kind, causing Melbourne definitely to resume his place among the Whigs; Dudley, Binning, and Wynn to fall back into the ranks of the Tories; and Palmerston finally to break with the latter, and cast in his lot with the former.

In the autumn of 1830 the Home Office was no place of rest. Throughout the autumn an uneasy feeling as to the future pervaded all classes. Political associations in the manufacturing towns were multiplied, their objects varying with the complexion of local suffering or the humour of local leadership, but all betraying a wild hope of social redemption by means of political change. The spirit of disaffection in the rural districts took less organic form. In the darkness of ignorance that might be felt, its hand was uplifted against property. Machinery of various kinds tending to dispense with unskilled labour was assailed with curses and with blows. The harvest was no sooner garnered than the ricks were set on fire; and threatening notices signed with the ominous pseudonym of "Swing" were affixed to the gate of the farmyard and the forge, none would tell by whom or why. Decrepit officialism ascribed all to the Paris revolution of July; Birmingham patriotism set all down to the want of little shillings and one-pound notes; Manchester and Glasgow politicians ascribed it all to prohibitory duties; and the Benthamite Radicals thought every man a fool, or worse, who did not see in it the want of universal suffrage, annual parliaments and vote by ballot. Sir Robert Peel had grown daily more dejected at the state of the country and more dissatisfied with the want of determinate policy in the Government. Dining with a small party at Apsley House early in August, he somewhat abruptly asked the Duke, "In the event of a rising here, similar to that in France, what steps should be taken at the outset to resist it?" His Grace replied, "If wide-spread, and in anything like force, it would be a very difficult thing, and must depend entirely on circumstances." The results of the general election were not reassuring, and the attempts made to obtain strength for the administration ended in disappointment. The Home Secretary waxed more and more desponding as rural crime and urban agitation grew apace. He believed that the existing fabric of Government was doomed; and he told his old tutor, Bishop Lloyd, that if once the break-up of traditional authority began, he did not think the monarchy would last five years. Almost every day he found at the Home Office letters threatening his life, or putting him on his guard against some dreadful conspiracy, and it is said that at last he had hardly resolution to open any of which the address was at all suspicious.* Outward appearances were kept up till Parliament met; but with the announcement that ministers would not suffer the King to visit the City in the month of November, the mask of executive self-possession dropped. In the words of Lord Wellesley, it was "an act of intrepid cowardice;" and it proved irretrievable.

Ministers admitted severe distress, but said its pressure was partial. Sir E. Knatchbull moved an amendment to the Address declaring that the sovereign had been misinformed, and that the suffering of the people was general and beyond description. One hundred and five voted this; and its rejection, after the language used in debate concerning it, spread additional alarm.

Here was enough, and more than enough, coupled as it was with declamations out of doors, to make those who take

* Sir D. Le Marchant was so informed when under-secretary in 1847. 'Memoirs of Earl Spencer,' p. 208.

opinions on trust believe that the country was on the
verge of bankruptcy.   Here was enough to alarm the timid
and to excite the working people, to whom no change,
as they thought, could do any harm.   In consequence a
persuasion, to a greater extent perhaps than ever before,
prevailed that a break-up was at hand, though many who
held this faith did not know what they themselves meant.
Many persons whose station in society and whose general
knowledge ought to have convinced them of the absurdity
of entertaining such notions spoke to me on the terrible
state of all trades, and prophesied that the time was at
hand when the stoppage of trade, commerce, and manu-
factures would be complete and a great and terrible change
would be effected ; some went so far as to name the month
of June beyond which time it would be impossible to go
on; and when such men could talk in this sort of way, it
may be easily imagined that the same opinion was general
throughout the country ; that great alarm prevailed, and
that men really did persuade themselves that there was
only one preventive, and that was parliamentary reform.
No such remedy was prescribed by either Whigs or Tories
in Parliament, but the people saw no other, and their
reiterated demands soon gave the tone to many members
of both Houses ; and this, coupled with the notices of distress and the dread of the consequences, were the cause
of the change which, on the accession to power of the
Whigs, compelled them to propose the Reform Bill.*

All the zealots of the propagandism of Atwood and
Cobbett occupied themselves in forcibly depicting the incoherent demands of the agriculturists who wanted new
"laws to make corn dear and other commodities cheap, and
the manufacturing people who wanted high profits and high
wages with cheap (farming) produce :—as absurd and unintelligible a state of things as had ever perhaps existed."†

* 'MS. Political Narratives,' by Francis Place, 1830, i. p. 24.
† B. M. 27,789.

It was popularly expected that the speech from the throne would intimate at least a desire for peace abroad and a willingness to reform at home. It wantonly ran counter to both anticipations. The Belgians were scolded roundly for their ingratitude in insisting on a repeal of the union with Holland, whose sovereign was described as an impartial and paternal ruler; and lest the analogy should be missed, royal threats of chastisement were held out against all who should abet seditious schemes or foster hopes of organic change in any portion of the realm. Place dined with Bentham in the evening alone, and when a copy of the King's speech was brought to him the old philosopher imagined that such expressions would not have been hazarded without some previous soundings of temper of the Peers at all events, and a reliance on their support of the policy forthshadowed. He augured ill for the future at home and abroad, and his forebodings seemed to be confirmed by the unanimous vote of the Upper House in favour of an address in reply, which, according to custom, was a mere echo of the speech. Great was his surprise and glee next morning on reading the memorable commentary of the Premier, who in answer to some measured words of Lord Grey about Intervention and Electoral change, declared the existing system of representation to be as nearly perfect as human wisdom could make it, and that so long as he was minister no alternative would be proposed. "He has thrown away the scabbard," said Dudley as they left the House : "No," rejoined Melbourne, "the sword with which he might have parried attack, and maintained the position for a good while." Place was in ecstasy. He urged Hume and others to keep the Duke in office by all means, until the irresolute Whigs should have made up their minds to a comprehensive and practical measure of reform; for his Grace could no longer do any harm, and the worst to be feared was from their too cheaply winning the personal game of office. Writing to Hobhouse, who had asked for his opinion, he said : "Pray do all you can to prevent the unwise conduct of your friends in resisting ministers in such a way as may compel them to resign. Abuse their proceedings as much as you please, but beyond that do nothing to prevent them from sinking as low as possible; aid them then to work themselves out of office, and it will be quite soon enough. I fear and abhor a premature change." * In the same letter he says, that should the Duke go in procession with the King to the Mansion House, there are many who would not shrink from shooting him. Hunt's threat of heading 20,000 petitioners for redress of grievances he disbelieved; but "Thomas Atwood, the most influential man in England, proposed in writing to enrol an association not to pay taxes, if ministerial interference should produce the probability of a war with Belgium; and I believe something of the kind will be done.† Many rich men are willing to take part in it. Every shop in London would be closed, and bank notes would not be taken. A violent revolution would inevitably ensue." Atwood's language was clearly indictable. Place framed a declaration in hypothetical terms pointing in the same direction, but postponing any resolution until Government had done some specific act tending to commit the country to war; and this many respectable traders signed. But the Opposition in Parliament pressed ministers on Sir Henry Parnell's motion to reduce the Civil List, and after a brief resistance, conducted so languidly that several near friends and adherents were not brought down to vote, they were left in a minority of twenty-nine. Lord Worcester, who was too late to vote, brought the news to Apsley House, which he had heard on his way, that *they* had twenty-nine in the Commons; and till the party broke up, none of the guests were aware that "they" were the Opposition, nor was it until some of them met again at Princess Lieven's later in the evening that they learned the truth. In better times a hostile vote snatched in this way might have been rescinded; but no attempt of the kind was made. Peel was supposed to be glad of the

---

* To J. C. Hobhouse, November 8th, 1830.   † Idem.

opportunity to shake off a weight of responsibility, without either compensating popularity or power, and when the Cabinet met next day they decided at once to resign.

Retrenchment was generally desired; and some species of parliamentary reform was deemed inevitable, but there was nothing like an agreement among the half-dozen sections of Opposition as to where reform should begin or where it should end. Had Peel been allowed an unfettered discretion in dealing with the motion of Brougham, he would possibly have succeeded in setting Whigs against Radicals and Scotch Covenanters against Irish Catholics, thus deferring for a season the settlement of the question and a change of Government; but the Premier, like all his predecessors and nearly all who have succeeded him, was impelled by some inscrutable impulse to commit official *felo de se.* Mr. Pitt, after eighteen years' experience of the incoherency and intolerance of George III., picked a quarrel with his Majesty about religious disabilities, and threw up his office when he could not prevail. After three years' self-exile, he discovered that his *sine quâ non* might with honour be waived; and he came back without being able to give any logical account of why he had quitted. Lord Grenville, with a majority to back him, tried, in miniature, a similar experiment, and sought to oblige George III. to concede the eligibility of Catholic officers to promotion in the army. On being resisted summarily he abandoned the project he had advised a few weeks before as indispensable, and thus tempted the King to demand from him a pledge which, as a man of constitutional loyalty and legislative honour, he could not give. Perceval and Canning were cut off by death; but Goderich had dug a shallow well in his garden for no other purpose except for that of extinguishing his own existence; and now Wellington, when nobody wanted it, came forth with a new confession of Conservative faith full of damnatory clauses against all who did not believe in the divine right of borough-mongers to name half the House of Commons. It is far from clear that he could have been put into a minority on any great question, had he acted with his habitual prudence, and waited for the development of Brougham's project of reform, which there was good ground for believing was far from being matured.　His anathema by anticipation against all change, however moderate, sealed the doom of his Cabinet, and saved the impetuous but perplexed member for Yorkshire from the grave responsibility his electioneering promises involved.

CHAPTER XVII.

*The Grey administration—Home Office—The Duke in Hampshire—
Anglesey and Stanley—State of Ireland – First Reform Bill.*

ON the 16th November Earl Grey was sent for by the King;
he took counsel first with Lansdowne and Holland, and with
their concurrence sent for Althorp, and told him that unless he would undertake the leadership of the Commons as
Chancellor of the Exchequer he would at once decline the
task of forming a new administration.   Not without difficulty
did he prevail on his reluctant friend, who had been warned
by Lord Tavistock the night before that the responsibility
was likely to devolve upon him ; but he was unable to overcome his unaffected misgivings as to his own fitness, and
his genuine antipathy to the restraints and burthens of
office.   He looked forward to a continued residence in town
with aversion ; and no feeling of ambition or desire of
power weighed in the opposite scale.   Palmerston, now the
ostensible head of the Canningites, was ready, and indeed
so eager for the post that he waited on Earl Grey in the
course of the afternoon, and offered himself for it.[*]   But
though it was universally felt that without him, Melbourne,
and Grant no Cabinet could be formed, Grey was im-
movable in his resolution, and the recluse of the Albany was
compelled to yield.

There was hesitation for some days about the disposal of

---

[*] Le Marchant, 'Memoir of Earl Spencer,' p. 212.

the Great Seal. Melbourne, who had sat in Cabinet with Lyndhurst, and understood his flexibility, thought he might with advantage be retained. He had never found any difficulty with him; he stood well at Court; he was ambitious, fond of luxury, and in debt: why not keep him on? Brougham coveted the Rolls; but this would have made him over-ruler of Whigdom. The Attorney-Generalship was offered instead. This would have left him but an out-door servant of the Cabinet: "The Great Seal or nothing," was his angry reply. The Duke of Bedford, who was consulted confidentially, took his part, and deprecated the scandal of throwing over a faithful and energetic friend for the favour of the compliant Lyndhurst, who was consoled, however, with the office of Chief Baron, it being understood that the holder should not be conspicuous in party warfare. Lady Lyndhurst thought he had been trifled with by the new Premier, and she refused to speak to him when they met, though they had been intimate. It is certain that Melbourne, Althorp, and the majority of their colleagues thought it desirable that Brougham should be got out of the Commons, and lulled, as they imagined, to repose on the Woolsack. The bar laughed, Mr. Sugden sneered, and William IV., who had occasional glimpses of political forecast, assented not without reluctance. On the other hand, the *Times* pronounced the appointment admirable, and the London University was exceeding glad.

A very general expectation prevailed that Mackintosh would be included in the new list of ministers. Holland, who appreciated justly his marvellous attainments and true elevation of political thought, much desired it, as did Lansdowne and Althorp. But Grey entertained a decided prejudice against him. "He thought him a time-server, and rather a flatterer. He did not do him justice, and avowedly did not like him."* The friends of Sir James had consequently to be contented with his appointment as Judge Advocate, in the hope that eventually he might be more

---

* Lord Lansdowne to the author.

suitably rewarded. The philosopher was too honest to affect indifference to the disparagement he did not deserve; but he could not afford to be left out altogether when his party was coming in. Too proud to complain, he chafed in silence, and tried to forget among his books the injustice that attends unequal conditions of birth and fortune. Disappointment, however, preyed upon him, and ere his vaguely promised turn came he had ceased to pine. Even in sarcasm to compare him with men, who by dint of acreage, effrontery, or complaisance, from time to time won their way into Cabinet office, would be to trifle with the dignity of a truly noble reputation.

It was not long before the discrimination of the Duke in his estimate of the men whose aid was best worth seeking, and whose adhesion betimes might have prolonged his ministerial existence, was fully vindicated. While Lord Anglesey's impetuosity and imprudence inflamed agitation in Ireland, unexpected diligence, promptitude, and vigour was from the first shown by Melbourne in dealing with a state of turbulence and crime in England long unexampled. To follow the ablest minister of the evicted party, in the Home Office, he was chosen at a crisis the most critical in domestic affairs. The popular cauldron was already seething with social discontents, and the additional ingredient of organic change was in the new Premier's hand ready to be flung into it. If it should boil over, and conflagration follow, he well knew that for him all the high hope and lofty pride, and historic aspirations, and condescending patronage of the country, with whose fate and fortune the master-thought of his life was to associate his name would be swept away beyond a chance of retrieval. For the credit of the incoming party, for the safety of the realm, and specially and emphatically for the safety and the credit of a Prime Minister at sixty-nine, it was all-important to place at the head of the daily administration of domestic affairs a man who understood them, whose good sense would tell him without prompting what to do, and in

whom courage and good-humour would not fail in the day
of trial. It is impossible to believe that, having to choose
from a crowd of associates and aspirants of every degree
of talent, influence, rank, and fortune, Grey would have
perilled the splendid chance for which he had waited half a
century by giving the Home Department to any but the
man he deemed most fit for it. Why did he regard
Melbourne as most fit? Not because he brought to the
performance of its duties technical knowledge of tape-istry;
for he had not held during twelve months the secretaryship
for Ireland, and he had never been in any other office. Not
that he had a knack in spinning the staple or weaving the
web of Acts of Parliament; for in four-and-twenty years he
had never framed a clause or moved to bring in a bill. Not
that he was a prize-fighter of renown in St. Stephen's ring;
for it may with confidence be said that not half-a-dozen
persons could recall an instance wherein a speech of his had
produced any remarkable effect. It was certainly not because
he pressed his claims to prominent and important office; for
there never was a man more given to make little of the gifts
that he possessed, or to exaggerate more his own shortcomings. Want of regular occupation from the time that
he had left the bar had begotten in him desultory habits of
all kinds, calculated to render the punctual discharge of
multifarious official duties peculiarly laborious. He would
probably have been satisfied with the Duchy or Privy Seal,
and would certainly have preferred one of the other offices
whose walls are not of glass, and whose occupants are
consequently left unobserved to perform their functions at
their own time and in their own way. The distinctive
qualities which marked him out as fit to be placed at the
head of the civil executive seemed from the first to have
struck Holland, who probably knew them best, and who
was himself beyond compare the finest judge of character,
and, on the whole, the most impartial and disinterested man
of whom the First Minister took counsel. His clear blue
eyes rested fixedly on Melbourne, and if any doubt had

previously existed in the mind of the Premier it would have
been dispelled by his advice, and the recollection that no one ,
would be more acceptable personally to the King. What,
then, were those distinctive qualities which recommended
their possessor so irresistibly? William IV. liked him
because, as he used to say, " he was a great gentleman;"
by which he meant that under all circumstances he felt
that he could appeal not only to his sense of honour,
but to his generosity and genuine loyalty to the state.
Lansdowne valued him for his veracity and highmindedness ;
Holland, for the wisdom of his wit and good-nature of
his candour; Grey, for his indomitable spirit, which he
knew would quail neither under the displeasure of the
Court or of the multitude. With Palmerston and Grant
he had been bound up for three years, and they were of
course more than satisfied to see high distinction accorded
him, and to know that so large a share of the government
patronage would be dispensed by hands like his. With
the personal tastes and theoretical opinions of Althorp he
had little sympathy; and with the impetuosity of Stanley,
the impatience of Durham, the inappeasable restlessness of
Brougham, he was constantly amazed, sometimes amused,
and often very angry. But they all grew to liking him and
trusting him for the transparent frankness and directness of
his dealings, whether in great affairs or small; and while
among themselves there were occasional jealousies and
squabbles, none of his colleagues during the time they
served together ever had a difference with him, or a
misgiving with regard to him. To the outer world with
which he came in contact personally the charm of his
manner was its perfect unaffectedness. Instead of making
speeches to deputations, he talked matters over with them;
instead of ceremonious bows and mysterious nothings, in
answer to complaints of hardship or injustice, he would set
them at their ease by a friendly chat, and without pledging
himself to do what they asked, promised to look into it and
see what could be done. The pomp and platitude of office

were to him an abomination. Where resistance and rebuke were required, he pronounced it with earnestness and
emphasis, in simple words, and in accents grave but gentle.
Sometimes he would read the unreasonable a lecture, and
sometimes adjure the misguided not to be led astray by evil
counsel; and when he deemed it deserved he would heartily
commend and praise, and whatever he had to say, he would
say it exactly as the impulse moved him, for he never officially
intoned the service.

On assuming the duties of the Home Office, he found
a state of things beset on all sides with social perplexity
and political alarm. The respect for property, which for
generations had been an almost unbroken rural tradition,
seemed to be suddenly melting away. Incendiary fires lit
up the darkness of the hungry night throughout thirteen
of the southern counties. The Duke of Buckingham wrote
from Avington to the ex-Premier :

Nothing can be worse than the state of this neighbourhood.
I may say that this part of the country is wholly in the
hands of the rebels. There are two troops of dragoons
and a few marines in Winchester. The 42nd started
from Southampton at nine o'clock this morning. But
they are already separated in different divisions, in consequence of different riots. 1500 rioters are to assemble
to-morrow morning, and will attack any farmhouses where
there are threshing-machines. They go about levying
contributions on every gentleman's house. There are
very few magistrates, and what there are are completely
cowed. In short, something decisive must instantly be
done.*

By the same post the Duke of Wellington received from Sir
William Heathcote a letter equally alarming, and both were
forwarded without delay to Whitehall.

One of Melbourne's first acts was to issue a circular

* November 22nd, 1830. MS. at Apsley House.

calling on the magistracy, in the then disturbed state of
the country, to act with promptitude, vigour, and decision.
The open acts of violence and the secret and malicious
destruction of property daily taking place demanded that
the powers intrusted to the magistracy should be exercised with a firmness and vigour which are not required in
ordinary times. Measures which might strengthen the civil
force of the country, by uniting and bringing it together,
and giving it the power and efficiency which arise from
communication and union, were loudly called for ; and for
the purpose of assisting them in obtaining this object, in
maintaining the authority of the law they might rely on
the most steady and effectual support of Government. The
Duke acquainted Melbourne that he was going at once into
Hampshire, and would report as soon as it was possible to
dispense with the services of the troops, which he knew
were called for elsewhere. At midnight he wrote from
Strathfieldsaye :

It appears that yesterday a mob of three or four hundred
persons did a great deal of mischief in the neighbourhood
of Kington. They went this morning to Mr. Chute's,
about five miles from hence towards Basingstoke. They
were returning towards Wolveston, an estate recently
purchased by me from Sir Peter Pole. They had levied a
contribution at the time. The magistrates of Berkshire
and Hampshire had removed a detachment of Guards
from Reading to Aldermaston, which followed the mob.
The magistrates at Basingstoke moved the Lancers from
that town as soon as they heard of the approach of the
mob. They were thus inclosed between the two detach-
ments, and the whole were taken. I am informed that the
pressed men were allowed to go away ; the ringleaders, to
the amount of seventy-one, were detained and brought into
Basingstoke this evening, the amount of troops employed
being small, twenty Guards and twenty Lancers.*

* To Viscount Melbourne, November 23rd, 1830.

In other counties the work of pacification was not so
easy; and to stimulate the organisation and concert, without
which the scattered resources of authority must prove inadequate, a confidential letter was sent from the Home
Office on the 25th of November to the Lord Lieutenant of
each county, of which the copy addressed to the Duke of
Wellington ran as follows:—

In consequence of the acts of outrage and violence which
have taken place, and still continue to take place, in
different parts of the country, I am commanded by his
Majesty to urge upon your Grace in the strongest manner
the necessity of taking, with the least possible delay, such
measures as may be effectual for the repression of tumult,
the preservation of the public peace, and the protection of
the properties and lives of his Majesty's subjects. For
these purposes I am assured that your Grace will feel that
the utmost diligence and energy should be exerted in
concerting measures with the gentry and yeomanry of the
county, in assembling and strengthening the civil force,
and in disposing and arranging it in such a manner as
may secure its general union and co-operation. In order
that your Grace's efforts may receive the most effectual
support and assistance, I have the honour of inclosing the
copy of a letter which I have addressed to all justices of
the peace, mayors, and other magistrates having jurisdiction in the county over which your Grace presides.
Reposing the firmest reliance upon your Grace's zeal, it is
unnecessary for me to recommend the most prompt and
immediate personal superintendence of those parts of the
county in which insubordination and disorder may unfortunately prevail; but it is my duty to represent, that
if any circumstances should prevent your actual presence
in such disturbed districts, it is greatly to be desired
that your Grace should lose no time in appointing a Vice-
Lieutenant, under the provisions of the 46th of George III.
c. 90, s. 45. Under the present circumstances I shall

wish to hear from your Grace as speedily as possible after the receipt of this letter.*

On the following day Melbourne wrote privately to the Duke, to whom on this as on every other occasion he was careful to pay the highest consideration and deference:

I have just received your letter of yesterday. If your letters are not acknowledged officially, or as punctally as they ought to be, you must attribute it to the great pressure of business. We are to have a Cabinet to-day at four, but perhaps I shall be so hurried as not to be able to write to you after it. We shall send down a special commission as speedily as possible, and a very able and active solicitor, Mr. Talents, will go to-night to Winchester to consider the cases, and to obtain and arrange the evidence. We intend the commission to be for Hampshire and Wiltshire, but I apprehend, upon consideration, Berkshire would be included, as I apprehend a good many have been taken in that county. It should, however, sit at Winchester first. With respect to yeomanry and volunteers, the course I have taken hitherto is to supply those who have actually embodied themselves with arms; I am a little afraid of being hurried by the vehemence of the moment into the adoption of any expensive and comparatively inefficient system, which it may not be easy afterwards to get rid of. However, I am fully sensible that the spirit of the gentry, &c. &c., must be excited and encouraged in every way, instead of being chided. Any proposition of this nature which you will send me I will sanction. And perhaps you will favour me with your opinion upon the subject, and will try to direct the spirit of the country into the most useful channel. What do you think of the measure of calling out the pensioners, the magistrates' writ or order to be issued to direct them to be sworn in as special constables? The magistrates

* To His Grace the Lord Lieutenant of Hants, November 25th, 1830.

have this power at present, but they think it might be strengthened by such an order.*

Early in December a special commission was issued to try the offenders, with whom the jails were full. In the towns the working classes, though they condemned rick-burning, sympathised with the blind despair of the farm labourers, whose abject plight and bitter penury they well understood.† The artisan and working classes knew that from the gathering-grounds of poverty in the surrounding districts the influx of want and labour into the towns was increasing, and in bad times swamping. Some were for baling out the tide by emigration, some for damming it up in its well-head by a more stringent poor law, some for drying it up by free imports of foreign corn; but all agreed that hanging for arson, or transportation for agrarian cabals to raise wages, could not reach the core of the evil. The new Home Secretary saw this clearly, and while he felt obliged to maintain the authority of the law, he bethought him of an expedient never before tried in England in like circumstances, namely, to make confidence with some of those whom the despairing multitude trusted, and induce them to offer wise and temperate counsel, dissuasive from violence, and pointing to relief, if time were given for its legislative realisation. He sent his brother George to Francis Place, whose ability and honesty he had long appreciated, both as a supporter and an opponent at elections; and who he there-fore felt sure would not abuse the confidence thus reposed in him. "We are of opinion that you can write to them with more effect than any one else;" and then he went on to explain how his friends thought they should be spoken to.

This is always the way with men in office: they tell you what a clever fellow you are, and then they patronise you and instruct you, and show by their instructions that they think you may be a clever fellow—only—then, it is

* November 26th, 1830.　　† Place, i. p. 84.

by being their tool that you will be a clever fellow. I never show any symptoms of dislike to any such persons, but let them talk on until they say all they have to say: this was the case with Mr. Lamb; and when he had done speaking I gave him my reasons for thinking any writing addressed to people at the present moment must be mischievous, and he was satisfied the best way would be to refrain from making any address to them just now. After a rather long conversation with him on the state of the people and their opinions, I took the opportunity of speaking to him respecting reform of Parliament. I found that he knew very little of what was really passing The information he had received appeared to be very vague and defective. I told him much that was new to him, and my views as to the future. I said that the right course for his friends to pursue was straight and clear, but that I feared they would not take it, and so did all the men whom I knew whose information was extensive, and whose opinions were likely to be correct, but at any rate were such as ought to command attention. That Lord Grey had on the preceding Sunday told a friend of mine " that whatever proposition for reform might be made by ministers, it must be such an one as the House of Commons would entertain;" and I observed if this rule were adopted, nothing but mischief could result from it. That if the people were thus handed over to the borough-mongers, there would be a tremendous outcry against ministers; and their popularity would be destroyed, their present small majority would become a minority, and they would be thrust out with ignominy. That if, on the contrary, they proposed a plan of reform which would destroy corruption, by which the borough-mongers would lose their control, and the members be returned by the great body of the people having any sort of property, so that they might recover their just influence over their representatives, ministers would be lauded and supported far more than any administration ever had been. That it seemed almost

certain, if they did so, that they would be out-voted and
compelled to resign, but that they would fall back upon the
people, the whole of whom would make common cause with
them, and compel the King to restore them to office, with
full power, as far as his influence and power went, to accomplish a thorough reform in the Commons House. That
if they were driven out of office for having introduced such
a measure as that described, no ministers the King could
appoint would be able to keep their uneasy seats, and
remain in their hateful offices for six months, probably not
six weeks ; and when they were ousted by the people, and
their friends restored, they might carry any measures of
reform they pleased. Mr. Lamb assented to this, but cau-
tiously and properly refrained from giving any distinct
opinion except on one point. I said, clear as was the
course ministers ought to take, and easy as it would be
found if it was courageously followed up, I did not think
his friends had the courage to take it and resolutely to
pursue it ; to this he replied *" he feared they had not."**

Mr. Stanley's appointment was generally approved. His
courageous defence of the Church Establishment in Ireland †
could hardly be forgotten by the Protestants, nor his votes
in favour of emancipation by Catholics. His management
of an extensive estate in Munster was painstaking and
popular; and his personal energy, love of work, and love of
humour would, it was supposed, certainly make way. Qualities
of mind and temper which tended to countervail his many
talents and advantages were then unknown, and under other
circumstances might have less early become conspicuous, or
have never retained predominance in popular estimation.
But at the outset the auguries were all favourable ; troops of
friends were loud in felicitations, and some whose experience
gave them a right to counsel tendered their advice. Old Sir
John Newport told Lord Althorp that what he most desired

---

* MS. Political Recollections, &c., part i.
† Speech on Mr. Hume's motion, 1826.

was, that Stanley should have an under-secretary at the Castle uncommitted to the evil ways of past rule, and fit to be trusted implicitly to carry out the policy of his chief; and when he thought it seemed likely that the old permanent staff would be left unchanged, he went the length of saying that his support could not be given to his friends in office unless Gregory were removed. Spring Rice told this next day to Stanley, backing it with the expression that it was the only point on which he would volunteer advice.*

The Secretary of the Treasury, who understood the wants and perplexities of Ireland well, and who feared the impetuous and imperious temper of the new Chief Secretary, endeavoured to induce Melbourne to take from the outset a guiding as well as controlling part in legislation for that portion of the realm. " He had a long interview with him on the subject of Irish measures, and he gave him in the shape of a memorandum all that occurred to him on the Grand Jury Laws, with the heads of a plan which he undertook to lay before the Viceregal Government, and on other subjects the full and frank results of his opinions." He likewise endeavoured to impress Althorp with his views, but he " felt disposed to fling all the responsibility on the Lord Lieutenant. This, he adds, will never do ; the failure will be complete." † Never was forecast more quickly or literally verified. Just in proportion as the Home Secretary was induced to forego the guidance and control of Irish affairs, they became a source of disappointment and disrepute to the administration. The sound principles advocated by him when previously filling subordinate, and destined to be developed fully when he afterwards gained supreme executive power, were forgotten during the next three years, and the result was in every day deplorable.

Lord Anglesey's appointment a second time to the Vice-royalty of Ireland had been hailed with general satisfaction, and if Melbourne and Lansdowne estimated more accurately

---

* Letter to Stanley, November 18th, 1830.
† To Lord Lansdowne, January 3rd, 1831.

than others his capacity for civil administration, they were
only too willing to hope that the zest for popularity which
in 1828 had led him astray would be countervailed by the
opposite tendency already discernible in his youthful Chief
Secretary. But ere quitting London the rare opportunity
which circumstances had unexpectedly afforded the Whigs
of conciliating Ireland was rashly thrown away.   In a long
conference at Uxbridge House, to which O'Connell had been
frankly invited, Lord Anglesey announced his intention of
retaining the law officers of the old Government, as well as
the Under-Secretary, and thus persisting in the same system
of religious exclusion which rendered Emancipation politically
a dead letter. O'Connell did not conceal his surprise and
indignation; and declared at once that such a course would
array against the new ministers the whole Catholic community, who had theretofore looked upon them as old and
faithful friends. It would moreover furnish him, he said,
with conclusive arguments in favour of his still undeveloped
project of Repeal. Were it left an open question he was
content not to make it a shibboleth at elections; and if
practically all distinction between Protestant and Catholic
were put an end to at once and for ever in the distribution of
office, the Irish people would begin to believe at last in the
law, and in the principle of equal justice. For himself he
asked no favour; and not a word was said about the Church
Establishment. But if partisans of ascendency were still to
be officially preferred, he could not do otherwise than raise
the standard of opposition. Expostulation, however, was in
vain. Lord Grey had unfortunately confided to the indiscretion of the gallant Marquis the choice of his subordinates
in the Viceregal executive; bereft of the hope that his personal reappearance in Ireland would reawaken the cheers
of the populace as they escorted him to the shore on his
recall in 1828, he sadly set out on his ill-starred mission.

O'Connell, he was convinced, was bent upon desperate
agitation. This, he adds, would produce no change in his
course and conduct. For the love of Ireland he deprecated

agitation as the only thing that could prevent her from prospering. He prayed for peace and repose. But if the sword
was really to be drawn and the scabbard thrown away ; if he,
who had suffered so much for her, was to become a suspected
character and to be treated as an enemy ; if for the protection
of the state he was to be driven to the dire necessity of again
turning soldier, why then he must endeavour to get back
into old habits, and live amongst a people he loved in a state
of misery and distress.* On the 19th of December Lord
Anglesey wrote requesting that no friend of his in Ireland
would think it necessary to meet him on his landing, and
thereby incur a share of his unpopularity, proofs of which
he anticipated. His mortification at the manner in which he
was likely to be received overflows in his letters at this time,
his sole offence being, as he avers, " a solitary law appointment."† This was the elevation of Mr. Doherty to the
Chief Justiceship of the Court of Common Pleas, which
O'Connell regarded as a wanton affront to himself. The reception of the reappointed Viceroy was not what his morbid
sensibility led him to fear. Many persons of distinction
met him at Kingstown and accompanied him to the Castle.

He encountered on his arrival all the evidences of popular
hostility. Agitation, which he himself had sanctioned as the
only effectual means of extorting justice, suddenly broke
forth anew. The Relief Act was declared to have been a
cheat which it was not meant to carry into operation ; and
as neither Whigs nor Tories, according to O'Connell, would
keep faith, there was nothing left but to insist on a separate
parliament for Ireland. Mr. Stanley, who had been made
the special object of vituperation by the great demagogue,
sent him a challenge, which he scornfully refused upon the
ground that he had already fought one fatal duel. A
proclamation was issued putting down public meetings, and
a criminal prosecution was commenced against O'Connell.

Had the law appointments in Ireland been filled up as

---

* Private letter to Lord Cloncurry, December 15th, 1830.
† Letter to Lord Cloncurry.

they had been in England, reparation would have been made
to the liberal bar for their long denial of fair promotion;
and law advisers would have been given to Lord Anglesey
who would have kept him from engaging in the deplorable
personal conflict into which he precipitately plunged.   But
while Brougham and Denman were placed in office in
England; in Ireland neither Whig or Radical was treated
with the semblance of confidence or fair play.   Lord Plunket
was indeed too formidable to be overlooked; but Holmes and
Wallace, O'Loghlen and Perrin were practically told to stand
by; and O'Connell, who in professional standing, ability, and
influence stood without a rival, instead of being named
Attorney-General, as he would undoubtedly have been had
the Irish Executive of 1830 been responsible to an Irish
Parliament, was not even offered a silk gown.   Practically
this was to proclaim not only that liberal opinions were a
disqualification for advancement, but, what was far worse,
that religious disabilities had not been removed, the statute
of the previous year notwithstanding.   Mr. Blackburn was
a man of learning and integrity in every way fitted to
advise an anti-reform Government; but their appointment
as Attorney and Solicitor General was under the circumstances equivalent to a declaration of want of confidence
in nine-tenths of the Irish people.   After five-and-forty
years its fatuity and folly stand out as clearly as they did
then, and how Melbourne and Plunket could have reconciled
themselves to such a selection must ever remain an enigma.

Within a fortnight Government declared war against the
discussion of Repeal, under a temporary Act passed in 1829
to prevent dangerous assemblages for political or religious
objects.   Lord Anglesey issued a proclamation prohibiting
a meeting of trade societies in Dublin, which had been
summoned to petition for redress of the grievances ascribed
to the Union.   O'Connell forthwith issued a manifesto calling
a similar meeting under another name.   The Viceroy over
trumped him by a second proclamation; and the ridiculous
spectacle was continued for many days of notice and counter-

notice, until at length a warrant was issued for his apprehension on the charge of inciting to sedition; and on his
being held to bail, the contest was transferred to the Court
of King's Bench, in which, as then constituted, the ultimate
decision could not be doubtful. After some weeks spent in
arguing pleas and demurrers which were overruled, O'Connell
resolved, instead of going through the form of a trial, which
must have been a mere useless humiliation, to let judgment
go by default, and throw upon the executive the responsibility
of putting him in prison.

It cannot be denied that both Melbourne and Holland
acquiesced in a course of proceeding which neither of them
would have advised; and Althorp expressed the feelings of
many of the best men of his party when he wrote confidentially: "I cannot say that I am satisfied with what is
doing in Ireland. Notwithstanding the unanimous opinion
of our law authorities there, I entertain some doubts of the
legality of O'Connell's arrest. But as our law appointments
are already censured by many, and perhaps approved by
none very much, we shall be considered responsible for any
blunders they may have made;" and he thought it very
possible that when Parliament met they might be turned out
in consequence.* The fatuity of the whole course of proceeding was proved in the humiliating sequel. O'Connell
had no mind to trust his fate and fortune in the decision of
a great constitutional question by the Court of King's Bench
as it was then constituted, and the right minded majority
of the Cabinet saw nothing but humiliation and defeat in
rendering inveterate a breach between the Liberal party in
England and Ireland. After a certain show of forensic skill,
a truce was tacitly agreed on, and by the first of March the
attention of all was riveted on the forthcoming scheme of
parliamentary reform, a statement of which by Lord John
Russell was fixed for that day.

In the Court of Queen's Bench, Mr. Perrin, the leading
counsel for O'Connell, withdrew his plea of not guilty, and

* To Earl Spencer, January 22nd, 1831.

the case was allowed to stand over until the first day of
Easter Term, to the delight of all who deprecated further
excitement, and the disappointment of equally unthinking
friends and foes.   Lord Anglesey was exultant because he
had   won   in   the   encounter;   the Attorney-General was
satisfied, because under his advice the authority of law had
not only been asserted, but was shown to be irresistible;
Lord Grey was glad, because he hated the agitator, and
because his defeat enabled him to tell the King that his
power to stir up discontent was now at an end.   This was,
indeed, the prevalent impression in political circles, and was
the staple of many well-turned periods in the daily press.
To say that O'Connell was not mortified at having to admit
himself checkmated for the first time in his life by the law
officers of the Crown would be untrue.   To imagine that by
this defeat he was likely to be disheartened or dismayed was
to wholly misconceive his nature; and to suppose that the
people whose feelings he embodied, and whose passions he
wielded at will, would suddenly lose faith in him was a
mere delusion.   Lord Duncannon's re-election for Kilkenny
was ostensibly opposed on the ground of his not being a
repealer; but the old popularity of his name did not
fail him, and as in the case of Sir Henry Parnell, just then
made Secretary at War, who was standing for the Queen's
County, agitation's guns were not shotted against him, and
he and O'Connell met a week after as if nothing had
happened.   They understood one another better from that
day.   The great debate on the introduction of the Reform
Bill was at hand; O'Connell's aid was wanted, and at the
critical moment it was not wanting.   The thoroughness of
his support evoked the hearty cheers of all on his side of
the House, his recent prosecutors not excepted.

Before the time arrived, however, for pronouncing the
sentence the statute was about to expire.   Ministers were
already engaged in the struggles of the Reform Bill, and
it was not convenient to detach a score or two of their
supporters on the question.

Melbourne had not forgotten the impressions made upon his mind, when Secretary for Ireland, of the hardships caused by the Sub-letting Act. His retirement from office in 1828 had prevented his attempting their legislative remedy; but now that he had the power to originate measures, he recurred to the subject; and with a view to gain correct information, addressed the Catholic Bishop of Kildare and Leighlin, whose evidence before the Select Committee on all that related to the condition of the Irish people he had studied with care.

Although I have not the honour of any personal acquaintance with you, I am sure you will forgive me for addressing you upon a subject which relates to the welfare of your country, and upon which you are capable of affording me useful and important information. You are probably informed that we are engaged upon a revisal of the law commonly called the Sub-letting Act, and for this purpose I am very anxious to obtain some certain and actual knowledge with respect to the real extent and effect of its operation. The perusal of your evidence before the Committee of the House of Commons in the last year proves to me that no man is more intimately or practically acquainted with the state of Ireland than yourself. In that evidence I find, that the disposition (viz., to consolidate farms, and eject the poorer tenantry) was encouraged and aided by several legal enactments, among which I may specify Sir John Newport's Act, next the Sub-letting Act, and afterwards the Act annexed to the late Relief Bill which disfranchised the forty-shilling freeholders. . . . . . What I wish to hear from you is, how many cases you actually know of, in your own knowledge, in which tenants have been removed by their landlords by virtue and force of that law; and whether you can communicate to me the form of the notices which have been served, and whether their validity has been disputed and brought to trial; and before what courts, and in what manner the questions have been decided. I have myself made much inquiry to this effect, but I cannot obtain authentic information of any single case in which prosecutions in ejectment have taken place under that law. This difficulty will, I feel confident, excuse in your eyes the trouble which I give you by this application ; and I remain with great respect, your faithful and obedient Servant, &c.*

Bishop Doyle's reply, which doubtless contained much useful information, led to further correspondence.   Melbourne wrote again :

I beg leave to acknowledge your letter of the 13th inst., and to return you my thanks for the promptness with which you have replied to mine.   Upon reading your communication, it appears to me that the effect which you ascribe to the Sub-letting Act is actually that which the legislature intended to produce.   The object of the law was to prevent sub-letting for the future ; an object which, according to your statement, is effectually attained by it. The objection generally urged against the law, and which it is intended by the new law to obviate, is, that its provisions have a retrospective effect ; but with the working of the measure, as far as it is prospective, no interference is contemplated.   Will you allow me to trespass so much further upon your time and intelligence, as to ask you whether you think the law, in this point of view, prejudicial or the contrary ; and what is the nature and character of the enactment pointed out in your postscript, in which you observe that a law going directly and not circuitously to prevent the sub-division of land is what this country wanted and still requires. †

His reply to the Home Secretary set clearly in moral and political apposition the twofold working of the Sub-letting

---

* From the Home Office to the Right Rev. Dr. Doyle, &c., February 9th, 1831.

† Idem, February 17th, 1831.

Act as originally passed. *A parte ante* it wrought uncompensated and unwarrantable confiscation. *A parte post* it might be a prudent economic restriction upon the infinitesimal partition of land. But so long as the rural population had no better employment or surer chance of subsistence than the possession of a potato-field, it was idle to expect them to submit to eviction from their miserable holdings. Intensely conservative in his love of order, respect for law, and conviction of the duty of deference to authority, he deplored the misery endured by the people, and felt bound to uplift his voice stern as that of the prophets of old, against sordid and shameful oppression. Again and again he staked his reputation as a patriot and his influence as chief priest of his diocese in dissuading the exasperated peasantry from engaging in illegal combinations, and by denouncing their resort to violence and crime; but he appealed both in private and public to the conscience of their rulers to make without delay a provision for the destitute poor, by a tax on land, equivalent to half the tithe, which he contended ought to cease and determine. His letter to Spring Rice expounding this policy as the true antidote to revolutionary agitation, and the indispensable requisite for national peace, won the assent both of the Viceroy and O'Connell. The former pressed its adoption on the Cabinet; the latter publicly declared himself convinced and converted.[*] But the Bishop well knew that such changes could not be easily or suddenly brought about, and that until Parliament should be reformed they were wholly unattainable; he readily, therefore, greeted and encouraged every improvement in detail of the existing law which might assuage bitterness of feeling or mitigate immediate misery. He strongly deprecated the rearming of the yeomanry to aid the police in the enforcement of tithes, and the persistent exclusion from administrative office of all who did not profess the ascendant creed. But the Chief Secretary resented passionately disaffection to the Union and the

* O'Connell to Dr. Doyle, March 29th, 1831.

Established Church; both of which he persuaded Lord Grey must be maintained at any sacrifice. The Premier listened to his impetuous and imperious counsel, and the predial war began which lasted many years. Isolated deeds of violence were perpetrated with impunity, and sanguinary conflicts, sometimes involving considerable loss of life, occurred in various counties. But to remove the causes of social or sectarian discontent little, if anything, was done. The state of anarchy in Ireland troubled Melbourne more than it surprised him. He used to say, "it is too bad that when the right thing was done it was done so tardily and insincerely as to falsify every reasonable anticipation, and to realise every evil augury. What all the wise men promised has not happened; and what all the damned fools said would happen has come to pass."

Plunket had at length attained the reward of his priceless services. No one any longer contested his claim to the Great Seal of Ireland; and no one felicitated him more heartily than Melbourne, who remembered well the tantalisation he had been forced to suffer under Goderich and Canning. "The whole aspect of the man," he said, "is changed since he has had his due. The look is iron still, but the old fine polish has come back, and the cancerous rust that was growing over it is gone." In social intercourse he again grew communicative: loquacious, or what is called chatty, he never was, but he was no longer moody or reserved. He dined out oftener in London, and at home saw more company; and seldom suffered an occasion to pass without the mark of his wit. One of the Viceregal aides-de-camp had written a book of travels, to which he prefixed the epithet of "personal narrative." Stanley, always fastidious in composition, quizzed him as to the reason for the superfluous phrase; and appealed to Plunket to say what a personal narrative meant. "We lawyers divide all things worth talking of into two kinds, and all that is not *real* we call *personal*."

· CHAPTER XVIII.

THE REFORM BILL.

Ten Pound Franchise—Schedule A.—Majority in the Commons—
• Bill rejected by the Lords—General Perturbation.

LORD J. RUSSELL, instead of claiming a seat in the Cabinet, had stipulated when taking office that to him should be confided the introduction of the ministerial measure of reform ; and with him were associated Lord Durham, Sir James Graham, and Lord Duncannon, as a committee to prepare the bill. " Durham proposed the ballot, and Graham assented from a feeling that the bill would all seem flat without it, rather than from choice. I was against it, said Lord John, and thought if adopted it would be necessary to modify our plans respecting the suffrage. Duncannon asked Althorp's advice as to what he should do, and the latter said by all means vote for the Ballot. The report to the Cabinet was accordingly in that sense, if there was to be a £20 franchise." On this point wide differences prevailed. Durham, Althorp, and Duncannon would have preferred a £20 franchise with the ballot to a £10 franchise without it. Brougham, Graham, and Russell preferred the latter. Melbourne said, " I am for a low figure. Unless we have a large basis to work upon we shall do nothing;" and this was the judgment of the venerable Premier, who forty years before had advocated household suffrage, but who never could endure the idea of secret voting.

During Lord John's statement Hobhouse sat next Baring

Wall, who exclaimed, when the long list of boroughs was read, "They are mad, they are mad." All the Opposition seemed delighted but Sir R. Peel, who looked serious and angry, as if he had discerned that the ministers by the boldness of their measure would secure the support of the country. "Burdett and I walked home together, and agreed that there was very little chance of the measure being carried. We thought our friends in Westminster would oppose the £10 franchise, but we were wrong."* Popular distrust held its breath, indeed, while awaiting the revelation of the ministerial plan. Place records how he sat alone in his house at Charing Cross, on the evening of the 1st of March, fearing to learn details of the scheme, which would dash the hopes strained nearly to snapping. At length a friend who had reported the first half of Lord John's speech came in, and gave him the chief points of the proposed measure :—

It was so very much beyond anything I had expected, that had it been told me by a person unused to proceedings in the House, I should have supposed he had made a mistake. We both were delighted, and we at once took measures to cause it to be known in the coffee-houses in the neighbourhood, whence it spread like wildfire. In less than an hour from the conclusion of the speech, the intelligence was spread all over the metropolis. Next morning the joy of the reformers was excessive. Nothing within my memory had ever before produced such general exultation. Lord John treated his difficult and complicated subject in a masterly manner; it was so well arranged, clear, and simple, that no one could mistake any part of it."†

Calling next day on Place, Burdett and Hobhouse found him delighted with the Bill, and were told all their supporters were equally pleased with it. The echo of

---

* Hobhouse Autobiography in 'Edinburgh Review.'
† Place, part i. p. 30.

satisfaction came quickly from all the great towns, and ere the day fixed for the second reading, petitions in favour of the measure poured in. Nevertheless, looking at the constitution of the Lower House as it then existed, it seemed difficult to comprehend how it could be brought to commit patriotic suicide. The enormity of the proposal was, in Croker's opinion, its redeeming merit : for, of course, it could never be carried. In point of fact it was only carried after two nights' debate by a majority of one. Even such a nominal success was more than had been counted on out of doors. It had come to this, that Reform was no longer out of the question. Illuminations were announced in honour of the occasion, and the windows of those who refused to affect rejoicing would it was feared be broken, according to immemorial usage. In the afternoon a gentleman called on Place from the Comptroller of the Household, requesting him to take measures to prevent mischief, and offering to provide any assistance that might be thought necessary. Place told him "any one who would spend money had the power to cause mischief to be done; but that no one had the power to prevent its being done." If any one had the power he said it would not be advisable to use it, for the reasons already given to his old acquaintance, Tom Young, who had just been with him. On many occasions men in power had permitted money to be distributed to vagabonds to break windows; clerks in office and understrappers had done as their masters wished them, to set the mob on to bawl for lights, that the exhibition of loyalty might be as complete as possible. He knew people whose windows were broken, and who complained to the magistrates ; but they were treated as disloyal persons, and told that a few farthing candles would have saved their windows ; and they were sneered at and laughed at in Parliament. If no one paid blackguards to do mischief, and there were no well-dressed rascals to hound them on, there would be no damage done, except perhaps to the windows of a few obnoxious lords. This was nothing compared to the destruction these fellows, and such as they, had perpetrated on more than one occasion within his memory; every vagabond expected that he should be applauded for the mischief he did, and would in no instance be prosecuted. The case was now wholly altered, and every one who broke windows did so in fear of being apprehended and punished. The Opposition, who pretended that the people were giving up the bill and the ministers, and that there was a reaction in favour of themselves, would, if no windows were broken, shout victory, and hold up the circumstance as proof positive of the fact. Sooner than recommence the old system of giving money to the mob, it was better therefore to leave them alone.*

Young had been recommended to the Home Secretary by the Duke of Devonshire as a shrewd, handy sort of man, whom he had found as purser of his yacht more serviceable than men of better breeding. To his surprise, and that of others, Melbourne named him private secretary, and, as he said, made use of him as a weather-gauge when nicer instruments were off their balance. Had he checked the habitual bluntness of the man, or winced at his innate vulgarity, he would have been no longer useful. "Through him," he would say, "I am able to look down below; which for me is more important than all I can learn from all the fine gentleman clerks about me." By long sufferance Tom Young grew too familiar not not only with his chief, but with persons who could brook it less good-humouredly. But he was devoted, indefatigable, had a keen discernment of the foibles and oddities of his master; and save on one occasion served him sagaciously and well.

Hopes of reaction rose high. It was clear that, without a working majority, ministers had not a chance of carrying their scheme through committee, and preparations were made accordingly to fight it clause by clause. It was not thought possible that the King would be induced to dissolve a Parliament scarce eight months old to try an experiment

* Place MS., vol. i. part ii. p. 52.

so novel and so perilous. Melbourne did not despond, like some of his colleagues, or believe that the country would fall into convulsion or ruin if the bill were lost or the Cabinet overthrown; but he thought they were bound to abide the issue they had raised, and prove to the country that they were steadfast and sincere. They must go on until they were stopped by a hostile vote. It came, on General Gascoigne's amendment, in the middle of April; and the Cabinet unanimously advised a dissolution.

Never were the two Houses simultaneously so excited as when the guns were heard announcing the arrival of the King to dissolve Parliament. Sir R. Peel in vain essayed to get a hearing, Burdett disputing the priority of audience. Althorp moved that Peel should be heard, but Black Rod cut short the intended protest. Sir H. Harding crossed the floor and said to Hobhouse, "The next time you hear those guns they will be shotted, and will take off some of your heads." Lord Goderich describes the scene in the Lords as even more disorderly. Lord Londonderry shook his fist at the Duke of Richmond, and the Chancellor was hooted by the Opposition peers when he left the Woolsack. Lord Tankerville said the angry lords would without scruple have voted off the ministers' heads that day.*

Lyndhurst was sitting in the Exchequer, when he received the tidings that without previous notice the King was coming down to prorogue Parliament in person. The House of Lords was already in disorder, several peers trying ineffectually to be heard, in the midst of which his Majesty entered wearing the crown awry and betraying many signs of haste and anger. As he returned to the palace he was vociferously cheered by the multitude; and the Chief Baron, seeing clearly the error that had been committed, whispered to one of his party, "All is now lost."

The general election gave ministers a decisive majority, and the struggle thenceforth became undisguisedly one between the two Houses.

* Hobhouse, vol. ii. pp. 103, 105.

Nearly all the large towns and most of the counties sent to the new Parliament supporters of the Bill; even smaller towns threatened with partial disfranchisement did so too. The rotten boroughs belonging to Whigs were likewise thrown into the scale. Their price, however, daily diminished from the fear of coming abolition. Lord Yarborough, as guardian of the daughter of Sir L. Holmes, sold to the Government for £4000 the next presentation to the eight political stalls in St. Stephen's appurtenant to her property in the Isle of Wight. The eight incumbents duly prayed for sudden death, and had the rare privilege of performing the part of chief mourners at their own funerals.

Reform was still a riddle, about the solution of which the Cabinet itself was not agreed; still less the legislature or the country. "The Whigs felt how feeble was their hold on the nation. They could count neither on the suppport of the Radicals nor the forbearance of the Tories. Some had adopted Reform from necessity, others from choice; that they should act cordially together in the accomplishment of their task was not to be expected."*

Elated with the success of the elections, and misled by his law advisers, Mr. Stanley introduced on the 1st of July a bill limiting, in Ireland, the privilege of having fire-arms, and punishing their retention without licence in a manner hitherto unprecedented in any part of the kingdom. Not only the Irish members, Whig and Catholic, and the whole body of the English and Scotch Radicals, but even some of his colleagues on the Treasury Bench disapproved of his proposals; his exposition of the measure was listened to with amazement not to be concealed. The Cabinet had some weeks previously acceded to his recommendation that the existing Arms Act should be renewed for three years: but he subsequently adopted a variety of suggestions rendering the law more stringent and penal, and these he proceeded to embody in the bill without consulting the Home Secretary or any other member of the Government. Althorp,

* 'Memoir of Lord Spencer,' p. 237.

writing confidentially to his father on the following day, says :—

I did not know that he had altered the bill and made it one of the most tyrannical measures I ever heard proposed. I was quite astonished, and so was Graham, for not one of us had ever heard that these alterations were to be made in it. We must stand by Stanley, but we must soften down his measure. It is a great scrape; for O'Connell will have the credit of forcing upon us any modification which is embodied in the bill.*

Melbourne first heard of the rash proceeding when he read the *Morning Chronicle* early next day in his dressing-room. He was very wroth; and wrote at once to the Premier his opinion on the subject. Various concessions were eventually made in committee, all of which were received in Ireland with scornful exultation. Confidence in the discretion of the executive was dangerously wounded, and Stanley's wild threat of disarming the disaffected population proved wholly vain. The second Reform Bill was introduced by Lord J. Russell, and on the 24th of June a majority of 106 approved its principle; the discussion of its details commenced on the 4th of July, and was not brought to a close until the 7th of September. A fortnight later Althorp, accompanied by two hundred members, appeared at the bar of the Upper House, where Lord John presented the bill which was to deprive the lords of the power they had long enjoyed of nominating a third of the House of Commons. In the memorable debate, which lasted five nights, Grey, Lyndhurst, and Brougham outshone all others; Plunket, Ellenborough, and Carnarvon, though each in turn eloquent and effective, failed to command the same degree of interest. The speeches of Lansdowne and Holland on the one side, and of Harrowby and the Duke on the other, though full of weight were still less striking. The Home Secretary took a course peculiarly his own. Others

---

* Letter to Earl Spencer, July 2nd, 1831.

had appealed to the remembrance of their continued advocacy of the same opinions, as entitling their earnest adjurations to be heard. His claim rested on the opposite consideration. He had argued against fundamental change as long as he could consistently with his sense of duty to the throne and the safety of the nation. No man had held out longer against lifting the anchors of the state; no man had oftener opposed reform when the nation did not want it; no man was more ready to admit the possibility of its being abused if conceded; no man would have been more contented to remain without the concession. But it was clear that the nation had set its heart on remodelling this portion of its institutions, and it was worse than idle to set at nought its irresistible will. His fearless candour in abjuring past opinions when they had become no longer practically tenable was better calculated to tell upon the minds of any who were wavering than the most specious apologies for inconsistency. But waverers just then were few. The notion had been carefully instilled into the minds of conservative peers, that some measure of reform having become inevitable, they had but to reject the sweeping proposals sent up to them by the other House in order to eject their fabricators from office, and to place in their room warier and wiser men, who would be able to find means for reconciling the removal of certain electoral anomalies with the retention of what was best worth preserving in aristocratic influence. Following Lord Harrowby, Melbourne said :—

My Lords, I am most willing to concur with your lordships in applauding the ability displayed in the eloquent but I must say miscellaneous and sometimes contradictory speech which we have just heard from my noble friend; indeed I cannot but think that much which has fallen from my noble friend would have been better suited to a committee on the bill than to a motion for its second reading. In what fell from my noble friend in an early part of his speech I entirely agree ; namely, that it is incumbent on the various members of his Majesty's Government to explain the grounds on which they support the measure, particularly those who were formerly unfriendly to Reform, and who have recorded their opinions against it; and being myself in this predicament, without that intimation, I should have taken an opportunity of stating the reasons which have induced me to vote for the second reading of this bill. Nay, my lords, concurring heartily with my noble friend at the head of the Government, in now proposing this measure to Parliament, I think it my duty to state át length my reasons for supporting it. To many of the arguments of my noble friend it was impossible for me to listen with any other than a favourable ear; for they are arguments which I have myself urged elsewhere. If ever there was an individual in the country more anxious than another that the affairs of the country might have gone on without being forced to incur the hazard and responsibility which must result from so great and fundamental a change in the House of Commons, I am that person. That great philosopher and statesman, Lord Bacon, says that the difference between civil affairs and the sciences is, that while in the latter there should be nothing but change and movement, the former should rest for support on authority and reputation. "Verum in rebus civilibus mutatio etiam in melius (even if the change were for the better) suspecta est ob perturbationem; cum civilia auctoritate, consensu, fama, et opinione, non demonstratione nitantur. In artibus autem et scientiis tanquam in metalli fodinis, omnia novis operibus et ulterioribus progressibus circumstrepere debent." Undoubtedly the perturbation arising from change is to be avoided; but then the other terms of the proposition must be observed. That which it is proposed to change must be supported by authority, consent, reputation, and opinion. If we find that the columns of that support are snapped and falling—if we find that instead of authority, there is a disrespect for all authority—if we find that

instead of *consensus* there is *dissensus*—if we find that
instead of reputation and opinion, there are aversion and
repudiation, it is then our duty to look about us and to
consider the dangerous situation in which we are placed ;
it is then time to propose some change, it is then time to
revert to the first principles of the constitution, that we
may repair the edifice which is tottering and crumbling
around us. My lords, we have been told by one of your
lordships that we ought not to yield to popular opinion,
that we ought not to be governed *arbitrio popularis auræ ;*
and that it frequently becomes the duty of legislative and representative bodies, and of all those having
authority, to resist the will of the people. I readily
admit the truth of that proposition. Else why have a
representative body at all ? The wildest democrat in
existence, those who assert that all power is derived from
the people, would hardly deny the proposition. No man
can suppose that it is the duty of a legislative body to
yield to every gust of the popular breath; no man can
suppose that in questions involving the immediate petty
interests of the people this should be done, much less
in making those fundamental changes which affect the
whole interests of a great country, and of which the
people are necessarily very incompetent judges. But, my
lords, although it may be our duty to resist the will of
the people for a time, is it possible to resist it for ever ?
Have we not in this case resisted it long enough ? I say this
the more freely, because I have on former occasions been
in the foreground in resisting parliamentary reform. Night
after night have I resisted it in another place, going far
beyond some of those who are now adverse to the present
measure. Wherever the flag of parliamentary reform was
hoisted, I ranged myself under the opposite banner ; if I did
not lift the standard of the constitution and call its supporters to the field, I was always ready to follow it, and
went beyond others in repelling every approach to reform.
I always opposed in the other House of Parliament the

extension of the elective franchise to Manchester and Birmingham. I look back with great regret to the period when a motion of that kind was brought before the other House of Parliament, because circumstances connected with that motion deprived the administration of that day of the services of Mr. Huskisson; I shall never cease to regret them, for I think, and shall, I believe, always think that he was not fairly treated; and that occurrence, I own, first shook my confidence in the noble duke opposite. On that occasion, however, I opposed the transfer of the elective franchise to Birmingham, because in my own heart I knew that if that proposition were adopted, it must necessarily lead to a large measure of reform, like that which is now offered to your lordships. For why, my lords, give the elective franchise to Manchester and to Birmingham? Because they have become great emporiums of commerce, daily increasing in wealth and importance. Because they are full of men of opulence, of spirit and intelligence, because they have arrived almost at imperial grandeur and metropolitan magnificence. Such of your lordships as oppose the Reform Bill, the noble earl who spoke last (Harrowby), and the noble earl who preceded him (Winchelsea), would give those towns the elective franchise because they have thus increased. But the whole country has so increased, my lords; and it seems to me, therefore, as almost all your lordships have given up the idea that there shall be no reform, to be impossible longer to resist the adoption of the large measure now proposed, or one equal to it. The noble earl recommended us to give time to the people; he said that on former occasions, when the wishes of the people on this subject have been resisted, when similar claims were made and denied, everything has returned to a peaceful channel. For a certain time that may be good policy; the argument is plausible, but all experience proves, when the wishes of the people are founded on reason and justice, and when they are consistent with the fundamental

principles of the constitution, that there must come a time
when both the legislative and executive powers must
yield to the popular voice or be annihilated.   Two of the
great arguments against the measure are, that Reform is
merely used as a weapon of party, and that the popular
demand for it is merely a temporary clamour that springs
up whenever any general calamity occurs, and subsides
when that calamity is at an end.   Admitting both these
arguments to be well-founded, would it not be desirable
to deprive party of so formidable a weapon?   But when
your lordships see that on every occasion of public
calamity and distress, from whatever cause arising, the
people call for an alteration in the representation, and
that the call is accompanied with a deep rankling sense of
injustice suffered and of rights withheld, can your lordships suppose that an opinion so continually revived has
not some deep-seated foundation, and can you be insensible
to the danger of continuing a permanent cause for angry
and discontented feelings to be revived and renewed at
every period of public distress and calamity?   Do not, my
lords, be parties to the continuance of this evil, if I must
not say this great injustice.   What constituted the great
dangers of the system formerly pursued towards the
Roman Catholics in Ireland?   That it gave opportunities
to those who, as it has been well observed, "were always
lying in wait to take advantage of the disasters of the
country."   It gave a handle to those who were always
ready to stir up sedition.   The same kind of danger that
the empire was exposed to by the refusal of Catholic emancipation, it is now exposed to by the denial of Reform, but
to a much greater degree.   The Catholics were comparatively a small body, whose strength could always be
seen and measured, but the spirit of Reform has been diffused through the whole population, and the whole people
may be said to be ready for commotion.   My lords, the
popular feeling on the subject of Reform extends, your
lordships do not know how far; it penetrates, your lord-

ships do not know how deep; and the great danger is that it will break forth with irresistible violence when your lordships are flattering yourselves that the country is enjoying general repose and perfect tranquillity, or when it is immersed in other dangers, and has no arms to resist a discontented people. I have already observed that my noble friend who has just spoken stated many things which would have been better stated in a committee. Why will he not allow the bill to go into that committee? I am sure my noble friend did himself great injustice when he said that his right hand had so far forgot its cunning, that he should be unable to adopt any amendments to the bill. But my noble friend has not stated one objection which does not apply only to the details of the bill, and which may not be obviated in the committee. Undoubtedly the measure is an extensive one. It does away with the nomination boroughs; it takes away one member from a number of other boroughs; it alters the constituency of boroughs; it proposes to add to the county representation—a measure which has always been proposed in every plan of parliamentary reform submitted to either House of Parliament; it proposes a general alteration of the qualification throughout the country; and it introduces—which is not the least important part of the bill—a great variety of regulations as to the conduct and management of elections, with a view to conducting them cheaply and bringing them to a speedy termination. I will not deny that these are great and important changes and alterations, requiring much deliberation, and I regret that so much misapprehension exists in the public mind as to the supposed delay in proceeding with this bill. I cannot concur in the censure which has been passed upon the House of Commons for the time and consideration they bestowed on this very important bill. That House could not have done otherwise and have done its duty, and no time has been needlessly consumed, no delay has been excessive, considering the great importance of the measure. But as this great measure is eagerly sought for by the country—as it is proposed by his Majesty's Government—as it has been thus deliberated upon and considered by the House of Commons, and as they, with a large majority pray your lordships' concurrence— will you, I ask, at once reject it? Will you, by a single night's vote, defeat the hopes of the nation, and cast away, as if it were idle and worthless, the fruit of so much care? Will you reject it on the ground that you may, perhaps, hereafter entertain some similar measure? If such, my lords, be the ground of your opposition—if you now oppose the bill, promising to give a better measure hereafter— consider, my lords, that such a promise is a condemnation of the present system, and the justification almost of that dangerous discontent which I have adverted to, and which your lordships will not in that case remedy; but your lordships will weigh and deeply consider the step proposed to you; and pause, I implore you, before you disappoint the wishes of the great body of the people. My noble friend has gone into the whole history of the question since the American War. I can only say that into all the considerations which that extensive and discursive survey embraces, I am not prepared to enter, as the question before your lordships is sufficiently extensive and im- portant in itself. Let us consider the circumstances in which we are placed and the subject as brought before us. Though all things may undoubtedly go well as long as the members of the other House act harmoniously together—supposing however, which may easily happen, that the members returned by the popular voice range themselves on one side, determined to carry this measure, and those who are returned in a manner which I need not point out, were to range themselves on the other, what, my lords, would be the result? Could such a contest be other- wise than perfectly ruinous? Or suppose, my lords, that we should range ourselves in continued opposition to the majority of the other House and the wishes of the people, must not that lead to consequences the most disastrous? My noble friend misinterpreted the language of my noble friend at the head of the Treasury, when he inferred that the bill must not be touched or modified, and that your lordships were to be no longer masters of the measure, and must merely register the decrees of the House of Commons. That is not the conclusion which I drew from what was stated by my noble friend, nor will his language bear such an interpretation. Nothing which fell from my noble friend can warrant the assumption that he wishes in the slightest degree to impede or control your lordships' deliberation. The noble lord has asked what is the basis of the measure, and whether it is not the population? Population is not the basis of the measure. It was necessary that we should have for the purposes of disfranchisement some practical rule, and therefore the want of population was adopted as the rule to disfranchise nomination boroughs. But there is nothing about population on the face of the bill. I do not mean to deny the statements by which the bill has been supported in another place; all that I mean to say is this—that there was a necessity for some strict rule both for disfranchisement and for enfranchisement, and population was undoubtedly chosen as the rule for determining the places which should continue to return members to Parliament: but that mere population was the basis adopted for the representation of the country I distinctly deny. We never intended that population should be the basis of the representation of the country. The whole measure goes to effect an extension of the present system of representation, and adapts it more completely to the circumstances and situation of the country; but it looks at property, at different interests, and at different classes, as well as at population. It is impossible, however, on the second reading of the bill, when the general principle of Reform is the only question for our consideration, when we have to determine whether there shall be a reform or not.

[No, no !] Noble lords are eager to disclaim hostility to
Reform ; every one is anxious to show that he is a reformer ;
and noble lords now as indignantly deny the charge of
being anti-reformers, as they some years ago would have
spurned at the imputation of being reformers. When
that is the case, I put it to your lordships, as reform is
the general principle of the bill, and as that is now the
question for discussion, I put it to your lordships whether
you can now refuse to read a bill a second time of which
you approve the principle. It is agreeable to the course
of your lordships' proceedings to discuss the principle of a
bill before going into a committee ; and if you approve
of that principle, to go into a committee. Or are your
lordships prepared to say that you approve of the reform,
and will not go into a committee ? I appeal to the noble earl
who spoke early in the debate, and who introduced a bill in
the beginning of the session, in which he took a considerable interest, but which I must say was of very trifling
importance as compared to this bill, and was as inconsistent
as a bill could well be, and the noble lord pressed your
lordships to allow him to go into a committee, merely on
account of the excellency of the object he had in view. If
your lordships oppose the principle of Reform, you will not
allow the bill to go to a committee, but as your lordships
are all reformers, and as the bill is made to your hand,
you will surely assent to the second reading, and amend
and change it in committee according to the reason,
the sense, and the justice of the House. If not, what
alternative is there ? What course will your lordships
pursue ? What do you propose ? If you will not allow the
bill to go into a committee, and there is no other bill,
what have you to offer ? If it is necessary, as is stated, to
appease the spirit of the people—if it is necessary to
propitiate them, your lordships will allow the bill to go
to the committee, and so spare yourselves the mortification of hereafter retracting, and of presenting some other
similar bill. The arguments which have been directed

against the details of the bill are fit only for the committee, and I should wish to spare your lordships' time by not now discussing them.   I will not go, therefore, into all the questions mooted by the noble earl.   I do not deny that this is a measure of great importance—that it causes great change—that it will be followed by other great changes; that other measures will be necessary to carry it into complete effect.   There must be a change in the constitution in respect to ministers having seats in another place. There are some defects which may lead to other changes. I would not exclude ministers from that House, nor allow them to obtain seats there by any other means than the voice of the people.   I should be exceedingly sorry to see such a change, but the bill will make other changes necessary to adapt it to the working of the constitution, and to the circumstances of the country; but to effect these changes, I rely on the elasticity of the constitution, and on its adapting power, which has preserved and improved it in times past, and will not fail, I hope, to preserve and improve it on future occasions.   I am departing, however, from the rule I laid down not to go into the details, which demand more discussion than I can now give them.   I must abstain, though that is doing the measure injustice, because it is not possible for me to go the length I wish.   I will only implore your lordships to consider the subject well, and not now to touch those subjects which will best be considered in the committee, but to reserve yourselves for the discussion of those details in which you are, I trust, determined to enter in another stage of the bill.   Your lordships are about to decide a great question—a question involving the peace and happiness of the empire in a far greater degree than that great question it was the glory of the noble duke's administration (the Duke of Wellington) to conduct to a successful termination.   There is, however, I beg leave to observe to your lordships, a great difference between this bill and that for the relief of the Roman Catholics, to which it has been compared.

That measure, my lords, had been frequently demanded,
and as frequently refused, till at length you were forced to
forget your own previous resistance, and grant that which
you before denied.   You are not pledged to any opposition
to this bill.   You have it now in your power to grant
what will be considered a boon, on which the repose of the
country depends, and which is looked for with impatience.
By this bill you are not bound in any manner.   You have
never rejected this or any similar bill.   Some of your
lordships may in the other House of Parliament have
expressed an opinion on Reform; but as a body—as a
House of Peers—you are unbound and uncompromised.
Your lordships have free liberty and power to decide as
you think fit, and you will come to the decision free
from the influence of fear, free from all apprehension, free
from all menace, free even from that fear ·by which a
noble and generous mind is sometimes led to rash and
untimely acts—free, my lords, from the imputation of
fear.   The noble duke stated at the beginning of the
debates on the subject of Catholic Emancipation, that he
did not consider that he was addressing himself to your
lordships' fears.   I am not of a different opinion.   It is
said that the great measure of Catholic Emancipation has
not accomplished all that was promised.   I admit that—
but I would beg leave to ask what would have been now
the state of Ireland had not that measure been passed into
a law?   If the want of complete success is to be ascribed
to the conduct of one man; if he has had the power
to oppose the beneficial workings of the measure, and
delay its advantages, I must say that the power of that
man is the creature of your lordships' hands; your
obstinacy gave him influence, and gave him the power
which he possesses to impede the healing effect of that
beneficial law.   That he should have had the power to
raise obstacles to the peace and tranquillity of the
country, is a circumstance which I deeply and seriously
lament; and I implore your lordships to raise up no such

other man, not to give a scimitar into the hands of many
such men, by making the people believe that their humble
petitions are disregarded, and that they must not look to
your lordships for redress.   Do not, my lords, arm a host
of demagogues with the discontent of the people.   Whatever other motives may actuate your lordships, I implore
you not to be guilty of the rashness of fear; I implore
you not to be guilty of the greater rashness of delay.   I
will remind your lordships of the address of the Roman
Consul to his council on going to war, when he planned
that masterly march which overthrew the Carthaginian
general before he could unite himself to other forces—a
march which, perhaps, changed the destinies of the world.
What that great man then addressed to his council I will
presume to repeat to your lordships.   He assured them
that their safety depended on the adopting his plan
immediately, and that there would be danger in delay.   He
exclaimed, " Only do not procrastinate—do not make that
measure which is safe, if adopted immediately, dangerous
by delay."   *Ne consilium suum, quod tutum celeritas fecisset
temerarum morando facerent.*

Lyndhurst was the soul of opposition to the Reform Bill,
but held back till the fifth night of the debate on the
second reading to answer Brougham.   He praised his rival's
eloquence, but charged him and Melbourne with inconsistency, quoting their former speeches against democratic
change.   Lord Grey replied that these had been utterances
against universal suffrage and annual parliaments, not
against the enfranchisement of thrift and trade.   But had
not the Chief Baron been in other days a far-going friend
of Reform?   Every one knew that the retort struck home;
yet Lyndhurst intrepidly assured the peers that it was not
true.   Denman whispered Le Marchant, " Villain—No, he
was a Democrat!"[*]—for he had gone circuit with him,
and frequently heard him advocate not only Reform, but

* ' Memoir of Earl Spencer,' p. 350.

the substitution for Parliament of a constituent assembly like that of France. The Lords, notwithstanding, believed in their judicial leader, who thought that, if beaten, ministers would resign. In point of tactics the blunder was irreparable; it consolidated the hitherto uncemented materials of the Reform party, and created for the first time a wave of excitement throughout the country, which even Melbourne, with all his incredulity and caution, saw must be headed, or it would overwhelm all.

By a majority of forty-one in a crowded house the ministerial bill was thrown out. Althorp wrote to his father next day:—

It appears to me that a majority of forty-one is not to be coped with. I am sure neither Grey nor myself can stay in unless we have a reasonable prospect of carrying a measure as large as the one we have lost; and I do not see how we can say that we have a reasonable prospect of doing this in the face of such a majority. By the ordinary rule we ought to resign. I am inclined to think that this is the only mode of carrying Reform. I think it will never pass the House of Lords unless it is brought forward by its enemies, as the Catholic Question was.[*]

Melbourne leaned at first towards the same conclusion. The Cabinet met in the afternoon, and decided nothing. But in the course of the next few hours tidings reached the Home Office from various quarters of the most alarming nature. The people, who had had in general no idea that the bill was really in danger, became suddenly exasperated by disappointment; and commotion on all sides grew imminent. Mobs assembled at various places; most revolutionary language was used by persons hitherto moderate and calm; even the leaders of political unions betrayed their anxiety lest they should not be able to guide or control the passions of the hour; and not a few of the

* 'Memoir of Earl Spencer,' p. 354.

lords who had voted in the late majority expressed their anxious wish that resolutions pledging their party to a large measure of reform should be forthwith moved in the Upper House, in the hope of thereby allaying the tempest. Upon consultation, however, no agreement could be come to as to the terms to be employed, and nothing was done. The King and the Commons concurred in desiring that ministers should not resign, and throughout the country a fierce demand was raised for the creation of peers. Durham, who was ever ready to outbid his colleagues for popularity, vehemently urged this course ; but the Premier, supported by Richmond, Lansdowne, Melbourne, and Palmerston, resolved to keep this expedient in reserve and until the last extremity.

The second Reform Bill was again rejected by the Lords at the instance of the Duke of Wellington, who was swayed chiefly by the advice of the Chief Baron.

Place writes in his diary, on the 9th of October :—" In the afternoon a journeyman bookseller named Bowyer called and introduced himself, and said he was in conjunction with an attorney's clerk named Powell to get up a great meeting of the working classes and others, to form a procession and present to the King at his levée an address that they should pledge themselves to stand by the King, his ministers, the House of Commons, and the bill." Place encouraged him all he could to proceed with it, and gave him a circular note with the names of many persons to whom he might show it, as well for pecuniary aid as personal assistance and reference to others ; and notes to every person conducting the daily papers, requesting them to insert paragraphs ; they did so, and the project was immediately made public. " I gave him a note to Mr. Young, Lord Melbourne's private secretary, and advised him to communicate freely with Young, but to tell him he did not come for either advice, approbation or disapprobation, as he had resolved to go through with the business, and to let him know that the whole of it would be conducted in an orderly, discreet way, so that no one need fear any disagreeable results. This was done ; and

when I saw Mr. Young I repeated what I had said to
Bowyer, and advised them to keep the police and soldiers
out of sight."*

Birmingham and Bristol led the way in revolutionary
projects. In the former town, a notice was issued for
public meetings by the council of the Political Union to
organise the non-payment of taxes until the Bill was
carried; and the people were told to come armed. It was
impossible for Government to allow such an assembly to
take place; yet an attempt to disperse it by force would in
all probability have caused a violent schism in the ranks of
their supporters, and thereby destroy their only chance of
peaceful triumph. Fortunately the council of the Union
had for its chief adviser Mr. Henry Atwood, who, whatever
his speculative errors may have been, had no sympathy
with appeals to violence or terror. One of his active colleagues, Mr. Joseph Parkes, a solicitor in good practice,
was personally known to Place, from whom the Home
Secretary constantly received information; and through him
a communication was unofficially made, pointing out the
folly and danger of the threatened proceeding. Parkes
executed his difficult task with fidelity and skill; and the
meeting was indefinitely postponed. At Bristol it fared
otherwise. No sagacious leader there held the reins of
popular feeling in hand; and because there was no regular
organisation, it was supposed that there could be no serious
peril. The entrance of Sir Charles Wetherell in a sort of
party triumph, when about to open the sessions as Recorder,
kindled the first sparks of turbulence, and ere many hours
the city was wrapped in its flame. The magistrates at
first treated the uproar with indifference, and subsequently
showed deplorable want of decision. Business was suspended; the inefficient constabulary were overpowered; the
houses of obnoxious politicians were set on fire, and the
work of pillage began. Upwards of £300,000 happened to

* Vol. ii. part i. p. 25.

be in the Post Office, which would have fallen into the hands of the mob, had not one of the clerks courageously undertaken to convey it without any guard to Bath. Destruction of property and life, accompanied with many circumstances of wanton cruelty, ensued; strangely at variance with the general character of the population. Vigorous measures of suppression were taken, however, by the Home Secretary; and at the end of three days order was restored, and the principal delinquents were handed over to justice. To guard against a similar outbreak in London, discretionary powers were conferred by Melbourne on Lord Hill, and in his absence on Lord Fitzroy Somerset, to hold the troops in readiness; and no breach of the peace in the metropolis occurred.

Melbourne, speaking of the Corporation of Bristol in reference to the riots, and comparing the conduct of the people of Bristol and Birmingham, the latter of whom had been unjustly impugned, said " he had no apprehension of mischief at Birmingham, where there was no corporation. He had no doubt at all that the very same description of persons who made the riots at Bristol would at Birmingham be employed to prevent rioting."[*] " The words last quoted," says Place, " are not in the published speech, but I was assured at the time, and this assurance has since been repeated to me, that the words were used."

Faith in the security of movable property had not received such a shock since Chief Justice Mansfield's library was given to the flames by Lord George Gordon's mob. Two generations had passed away since that outbreak of bigotry in alliance with ruffianism, and the old traditional belief had come to doze again in peace. Those who had something to lose were so much stronger in England than those who had nothing, that danger of plunder and arson was as much a thing gone by as peril from foot-pads on Hounslow Heath. Suddenly the lurid blaze in which half Bristol was threatened

[*] MS., vol. ii. part i. p. 124.

with ruin threw a ghastly reflection far and wide over the land. What town could tell whose turn might be next? The utter impotency of the effete system of municipal watch and special constables had been proved during three days of bloodshed and rapine in the most conservative community in the realm. What would become of free-spoken and free-thinking seats of manufacture, if ragamuffinism there should catch the contagion? And what would become of London, with its accumulations of realised property widely scattered? It must be confessed now that men came to think of it, their goods were wholly defenceless should the hungry multitude, whom no man could number, take it into their heads to have a raid and a general bonfire. It was a terrible question for those in power, and especially for a Home Secretary, to whom in emergency the entire community instinctively looked in their helplessness for the means of protection and orders what to do. Melbourne did not conceal his anxiety from those around him. He did not believe in the possibility of any serious injury being attempted to the dwelling of Royalty or the offices of the Government. The interchange of a few communications with the Horse Guards assured him that the chief places in Westminster might easily be protected from molestation. Nor did he think the City was in much danger, even though another Lord Mayor should prove himself as great a blockhead as Sir John Key. But for the rest of the metropolis he shuddered daily, for he knew how deficient in numbers and organisation were the New Police, as they were still called; and he felt that unless the "Haves" should volunteer to organise some method of self-protection, "the Have-nots" might rifle or burn any district they pleased, or any two or three districts simultaneously, if sufficiently remote from each other, before the glitter of bayonets could scare them from their prey. It was not without a groan and a certain amount of profane swearing that he read the bold but timely counsel given by the *Times*, that associations should at once be formed by loyal men who

were Reformers, for the purpose of constituting themselves a
volunteer constabulary for the defence of property and order
during the existing state of things. The improbability that
the busy and unarmed men of the middle classes could be
got together in such numbers, and induced to submit to any
sort of discipline or drill by any amount of newspaper suasion,
did not allay his fears that London might, like Paris, become
a hive of revolutionary sections. But he soon learned that
there were many and determined men who saw in the peril
of the hour an opportunity not to be neglected for fabricat-
ing a casting weight for the political scale. The men of
Birmingham had already their Political Union. The leading
Radicals of the metropolis quickly took the resolution of
forming a similar society; for the twofold purpose of
securing the passing of the Reform Bill and defending order,
property, and law. As politicians, they felt that if the
imputation of disorder and spoliation were not stamped out
by overwhelming demonstrations, the cause of progress was
lost; and they knew, as citizens, that after the expectation
which had been raised, the excitement and perturbation
which paralysed business would never cease until the
promised measure was carried. The steps by which during
November the new organisation was rapidly called into
existence are chronicled in the journals of the day; but the
reasons and explanations which led to each resolution, and
not unfrequently to its retractation or modification, are only to
be gathered from the letters and personal narratives of the
chief actors in the scene, most of whom have long since passed
away. One of the most graphic accounts is that contained
in the political narrative of the events of the period by
Bentham's friend at Charing Cross. He enumerates with
pride the active men, fellow-workers with himself, whose
energy and worth he lauds enthusiastically,—others who
were marplots, he scruples not to brand as fools or worse;
but who nevertheless took part in rocking the cradle of
the scheme of volunteering in defence of order. Among

the former were Major Beauclerc, Mr. Roebuck, W. J. Fox, Colonel Jones, and Erskine Perry. The Ultras distinguished by the name of Rotunda Men (from the place where they used to assemble), finding they could not have their way, appeared to have co-operated with the stronger and wiser majority. The general meetings of the Union were attended by several men of distinction, and drew vast audiences together. But its real work consisted in an active propagandism for the enrolment of members in separate local societies, all of them framed in exact accordance with the central model, but each being self-contained and distinct the from rest. The deputations sent to each district had strict instructions to excite their friends to organise a local union for themselves; but as soon as they saw it was about to be done they were to make it a point to withdraw; and thus to furnish no excuse for the accusation that they were infringing the statute of George III. enacted for the purpose of preventing the existence of corresponding societies. Nor was their caution superfluous. Various attempts were actually made at the time at rival schemes with the most revolutionary designs, which fell into the mistake of organising branches and appointing delegations in the hope of thereby effecting by combination of members and concentration of authority what they lacked in weight of character or position. Some of these openly attacked the transfer of property by inheritance or will; others affected to assert the right of appointing officers and constables whom all persons must be compelled to obey. So formidable did these beginnings of sedition appear that the Home Secretary, with the sanction of the Cabinet, submitted to the King for his signature a proclamation, which was issued on the 21st of November, and which warned the people against incurring the penalties of the law that forbade associations with affiliated branches, with grades, divisions, and subordination of officers, as subversive of the royal authority. At the next meeting of the Political Union the chairman thanked ministers for the proclamation, as calculated to do their society infinite service ; as they had taken care not to offend against the statute as the wild and wicked counter-schemes were safe to do. Melbourne was kept accurately informed from day to day of all that was going on : he believed that Place, whatever his views and opinions might be, would not deceive him as to matters of fact ; and in this he was not mistaken. In times of commotion no duty of a ruler is more imperative, yet none more difficult, than that of standing fast when sanguine or bewildered friends on all sides are shouting that something decisive must be done—they know not exactly what. During one of the not unfrequent paroxysms of the time the Home Minister was reminded of the many letters calling for some new and peremptory instruction as to the course to be taken in case of possible emergency ; but neither Chief Clerk nor Under-Secretary could point out distinctly what the novel direction ought to be : " Whenever you are in doubt," he said, " what should be done, do nothing."

CHAPTER XIX.

PARLIAMENT REFORMED.

*Correspondence with Bishop Doyle—Power to make Peers—Projects
of compromise—Second reading carried—Defeat in Committee—
Disturbed condition of Ireland—Commandership of the Army.*

MELBOURNE's position at this time was arduous and anxious.
Responsible as Home Secretary for the peace of the country,
he had to deal continually with incidents and ebullitions of
popular feeling, dangerous to neglect and still more dangerous
to palter with.   Every day agitation out of doors grew more
and more inflamed.   Scotland, usually so quiet, gave forth
wild and unwonted sounds; and Ireland was ablaze with a
fury of its own against Church Establishment.   Bishop
Doyle, who believed the movement for repeal to be delusive,
sought to divert popular attention to the abolition of tithes,
which practically touched the farming classes far more nearly
than any question of representation.   His memorable expression, in a published letter on the subject, became stereotyped
as the motto of every public gathering in the central and
southern portions of the island : " May the hatred of the
people to the exaction of tithes be as lasting as their love of
justice."   Lord Anglesey adopted in principle the views of
Dr. Doyle, and told the Home Secretary that the reduction
of the Anglican establishment in Ireland was the only
antidote to the cry for repeal.   He pointed out that for this
the Presbyterians of the north and the Whig gentry everywhere would coalesce, and that it presented the most feasible

and tangible result which that portion of the empire could gain by Reform. Melbourne, who had voted for concurrent endowment in 1825, as a condition of emancipation, would willingly have promoted a redistribution of Church property, suited to the wants of the three denominations; but his colleagues were engrossed with English and foreign policy: and with Stanley representing the Irish Department, he saw that it was hopeless to raise prematurely the question of the Irish Church Establishment which, sooner or later, he believed must be dealt with. Lord Anglesey's apprehensions and anxieties regarding Repeal he tried to soothe as valetudinarian: for the gallant Marquis was a great sufferer from bodily pain, and was not a little mortified by his unpopularity during his second term of viceregal office. He was more disposed to give heed to the statesmanlike suggestions of Dr. Doyle, whose thoughtful letters were shown him by Sir Henry Parnell. Twice he had succeeded in breaking up the agrarian confederacies that spread terror through his diocese, though he feared their recurrence daily if a change of measures and of men were not speedily adopted.

I have been on the best of terms, wrote the Bishop, with O'Connell since he relinquished the agitation for repeal of the Union, and I would most willingly labour to dissuade him from reopening that question, if the state of Ireland be taken up in a decided way by Government. But, even now, the difficulties created within the last year are great beyond belief, and are every hour increasing. I cannot account on any principle for the errors that have been committed. If anything happens to the Reform Bill, the administration is ruined in both countries; and this, in Ireland, through their own wilful blindness. It is useless to advert to the question of poor laws, or to any other, until the system in this country is changed. All my thoughts are occupied with apprehensions for the future.*

* To Sir H. Parnell, August 8th, 1831.

Lansdowne, Duncannon, and Spring Rice appreciated equally the value of these views, and understood to what they pointed. After many communications with the Chancellor and the Premier, Sir Henry felt himself warranted in telling his correspondent that no insuperable obstacle stood in the way of offering professional rank and office to O'Connell, provided it were ascertained beforehand that he would accept it; and he authorized the Bishop to act upon his own discretion in the matter.* Melbourne had not forgotten the desire of O'Connell in 1827 to have a patent of precedency; and to this distinction he now argued he was more than ever entitled by his transcendent superiority to his rivals at the bar. It was, after all, but the tardy acknowledgment of a debt of justice, which ought to be no longer withheld, and upon the party now in power his recent claims were undeniable for the aid he had rendered in debate on Reform. The sagacious prelate, who was as little of a courtier as a flatterer of the multitude, had urged the expediency of giving some pledge to the popular members in London of substantial changes in Ireland, previous to the close of the session, if the country was not to be thrown into a state of anarchy during the recess.† He thought Government were right in endeavouring to induce O'Connell to take responsible office; and believing him to set some value on his opinion, he promised he would urge it with all his might. In case of disappointment there would be time for further deliberation; but he would risk everything rather than submit to continued abuse of power against right and justice.‡

In reply to another letter from the Secretary at War, after the second Reform Bill had been rejected by the Lords, he said :—

I shall, as you desire, write this evening to Mr. O'Connell. He will be in the hands of the agitators even before my

* September 27th, 1831.
† Bishop Doyle to Sir H. Parnell, October 1st, 1831.
‡ Idem, October 10th, 1831.

letter arrives; but the moment is not one that he should select for agitation, and he may pause. My (first) application to him was more successful than I anticipated; but finding how isolated was the proposal of office made to him, I fully agreed with him that it should be rejected. Does the Government, or any member of it, suppose that, seeing their acts for the last year, we can expect a change if they hesitate to state, however confidentially, that there will be a change, and to what extent? or do they imagine we are such simpletons as to commit ourselves with a bad system, cast from us the means of improvement which we possess, and render ourselves, for base lucre, the byword of the age? I leave home for two or three weeks, and will remain in the neighbourhood of Dublin. I intend to pass a few days with Blake, who is a depositary of all knowledge. I shall not, however, inform him on the subject of O'Connell. I still hope, though but faintly, that your efforts may be successful. I will see O'Connell on going to town.*

At the opening of term the great tribune appeared in court and presented his patent of precedency, which, it is needless to say, could not have been issued without the direct sanction of the Home Secretary and the Chancellor of Ireland, both of whom would doubtless have agreed to follow up this beginning of administrative concession by his appointment as first law officer of the Crown. A brief note from O'Connell to a trusted friend declared that "within an hour he could be Attorney-General." No assurance, however, of even a modified policy, such as Parnell led him to hope for, would be given; and O'Connell, thinking he had been trifled with, renewed his attacks on the Government, and publicly admonished Bishop Doyle against being deluded by viceregal blandishments. The sarcasm was undeserved; but though it wounded the susceptibility of the prelate, it did not warp him from his

* To Sir H. Parnell, October 17th, 1831.

disinterested course. He still confidentially reiterated his advice to those in power that they should "come to some understanding with O'Connell;"* while Stanley held 'office this was impossible, for he regarded such an alliance as derogatory to the position of the Government.

A minority in the Cabinet, consisting of Grey, Lansdowne, Richmond, Palmerston, and Melbourne, would have made concessions of importance to secure a measure of moderate reform. They feared the recurrence of outbreaks like those at Nottingham and Bristol, and, still more, ways of organised agitation becoming habitual in England, which in Ireland had proved so formidable. Grey and Palmerston had several communications in November with Harrowby and Wharncliffe, who were recognised as the spokesmen of a party of compromise supposed to be influential. As long as *pourparler* was devoted to the interchange of regrets at national division, and fears of the subversive tendency of demagogueism, all went well. But, from the first, Melbourne's common sense discerned that they would never be able to agree about details; or, if they did, that one or other of the great parties, now thoroughly roused by conflict, would fly off in a rage from the terms of compromise when clearly placed before them. Matters had not gone very far when the truth of these prognostics appeared. Earl Grey would have risked a good deal to save "his order," which he began to think in jeopardy; but he did not want to throw away his popularity for nothing. Peel had never committed himself broadly or embarrassingly against enfranchisement or disfranchisement, and even the Duke had become a convert to the policy of some change. But neither would endure that the conduct of an affair so all-important should be quietly taken out of their hands by men like the self-appointed mediators; and both refused, consequently, to have anything to do with the negotiation. Disapproval of it spread rapidly on whisper's wing, and when the Premier asked for a list of the peers prepared to take up a neutral position, when the bill

* Letter to Sir H. Parnell, December 23rd, 1831.

a second time should be before the Lords, Wharncliffe was compelled to own that their followers were few.

On the 12th of December Lord J. Russell laid on the table the third edition of the Reform Bill, which left to the freemen their old franchise, adopted the £50 occupation suffrage in counties, and based the disfranchising schedules on a compound ratio of property and population. Some of the more reflecting Conservatives were disposed to acknowledge the conciliatory spirit of these modifications, and would gladly have gone into committee without a division. Sir Robert Peel decided otherwise, knowing that his party in the Upper House remained inexorable, with exception of the fraction who were endeavouring to assume the function and dignity of umpires, and whose secession he felt to be injurious to his authority and influence as leader. He significantly announced that whatever others might do, he would record his opinion on the second reading against the principle of the bill. After two nights' debate, in which Stanley and Macaulay surpassed themselves, 324 voted for the second reading, and but 162 against it.* The preponderance was thus increased by thirty votes above the greatest majority of the previous session.

Melbourne complained that Durham, though adverse to the concessions that had helped to secure this result, would, in his exultation, have used it to crush all further opposition. He had all along been outbidding his colleagues in vehemence of language and advocacy of extreme views. Brougham he hated as a supposed rival in the succession to his father-in-law as head of the Liberal party, whose triumphs were not to end, but only to begin at the passing of the Reform Bill. Every day's delay was mere waste of time. The Premier's reluctance to overbear the Lords filled him alternately with pity and rage, and his taunts and goadings from this time became intolerable. At the Cabinet dinner on the 19th of December, wrote Althorp:—

Durham made the most brutal attack on Lord Grey I ever

* The debate closed on Sunday morning, December 18th, 1831.

heard in my life, and I conclude he will certainly resign. He will put this upon alterations in the bill—most unfairly—because there is no alteration of any consequence in the main principle; and I doubt whether he knows anything about the alterations, as he will not allow anybody to tell him what they are. But if he resigns on this ground it will break up the Government.*

He did not resign, but continued browbeating the Premier; and opposing Palmerston, whom he wanted to supplant in the Foreign Office. Melbourne listened with loathing to his tirades; and on one occasion said, "If I had been Lord Grey I would have knocked him down." After Christmas it became a question whether before the bill was sent to the Upper House power should be demanded to make peers. The veteran chief confessed to his trusted lieutenant with what anxiety he regarded such an alternative, which "he wished to God could be avoided." "Melbourne, Richmond, and Palmerston might in consequence resign; and possibly Lansdowne and Stanley. The Cabinet could not then hold together, and therefore with a view to the eventual success of the measure, it would perhaps be better for them all to make up their minds to resign if again beaten in the Lords."† Brougham was at this time lying ill at his house in Westmoreland; and in opinion he seems to have wavered. To have the power in the last resort was become indispensable, if the ministry were to hold together; and that they should be believed to have it was equally essential to carrying the measure unmutilated through committee in the Commons. When, if ever, it should be exercised, and to what extent, it was premature to determine; but on the 13th of January a minute was agreed to by the Cabinet, reciting their unanimous opinion that it was necessary for them to have the power of making an addition to the peerage for the purpose of carrying the bill; and that the expediency of making such an addition depended on his Majesty being

---

* Althorp to his father, December 20th, 1831.
† Grey to Althorp, January 10th, 1832.

prepared to allow them the discretion of carrying it to the full extent it might be necessary to secure the success of the measure. The Home Secretary and the Lord President shared the first minister's repugnance to the alternative, but it was probably owing in no slight degree to a conviction of their sincerity in this respect, that William IV. was induced to refuse no longer a request so unwelcome. After the rejection of the first bill by the Lords, when the King expressed his desire that ministers should not resign, he stated his belief that no minister could be found to propose a very large creation of peers for the purpose of carrying a new bill, and they certainly had acquiesced in that opinion :—

Things in their progress since had forced upon their consideration what was originally thought impossible ; they had been brought gradually to contemplate what once appeared to be an unqualified evil, as an absolute necessity ; and the King, as these discussions proceeded, was brought at last, though most reluctantly, to confide to them the power which they claimed, to be exercised however only in the last extremity, and on certain conditions.*

Such is the authentic version given at the time by him who was primarily accountable to the sovereign and the nation for counsels which might have been defeated had they been disclosed. Outsiders were divided between misgivings they forebore to express, and impatient unbelief they did not scruple to avow. Even deferential followers who lay nearest the tent of their reticent chief, longed to penetrate the secret of what he would do in extremity, and when he would believe the decisive hour had come. Week after week Althorp and Russell steadily went on working their bill through committee, discussing every insidious amendment with temper and disposing of it handsomely in division. Honest opponents made no more way in public than the Intermediaries in private negotiation. Popular

* Grey to Althorp, March 11th, 1832.

expectancy was calm; but if the peers should misconstrue this for slackening zeal in the cause of Reform, what were ministers prepared to do? Melbourne, when pressed to tell, resorted to his favourite method of defence, and parried Charles Greville's questions by bantering exaggeration and ironical appeals for compassion towards the unfortunate possessors of power—at the risk of being set down for a trifler, or registered in confidential note-book as a recusant at heart ready to go over to the enemy. Hobhouse says Lord Howick urged him to call upon his father and tell him his character would be lost if the bill failed, through his irresolution. In a letter to the *Edinburgh Review,** the present Earl Grey confidently affirms from his own knowledge and recollection that his father "never hesitated in creating peers to whatever extent might be necessary; nor did he ever falter in his determination to fulfil this duty. But he believed it to be of the very highest importance for the future welfare of the nation that the necessity should be averted; and that if it could not in the end be avoided, it ought to be deferred as long as possible." But in February there was a prevalent feeling among the colleagues and friends of the Premier that he was deferring the creation of peers too long. His own explanation of his conduct is to be found in a note on his letter to Sir Herbert Taylor, 10th of February, 1832, in which he told his son that he was quite aware "that the loss of the Reform Bill a second time in the House of Lords would be fatal to his character as a public man, and make his whole long political life a failure; but he must play the game his own way. A premature creation of peers would diminish the chances of success; and he would not suffer himself to be driven into acting until in his own judgment the proper time was come." He thought the motive likely to induce Lords Harrowby and Wharncliffe to vote for the second reading was the desire to prevent what they considered the great evil of creating peers to carry it. But were the step now taken this motive

* May 25th, 1871.

would cease to operate, and they would naturally vote against the bill, and might be followed by no small number of peers.

Meanwhile Harrowby and Wharncliffe, with Charles Greville for their plenipotentiary, clung to the fond illusion that their project of marriage between the party that wanted to go back and the party that wanted to go forward might be realised, and blessed with all the happiness which is proverbially the guerdon of true love. Nobody but the three matchmakers seems to have believed in its feasibility; all the invitations to take part in the eventful ceremonial were refused; and again the critical day was deferred. Nevertheless the busy go-between notes with pensive satisfaction how he and his friends persevered from day to day rebuilding their house of cards and plying Ministers and Opposition chiefs impartially with arguments to prove that theirs was the only plan to save the country. Melbourne's good-nature, and probably too his quiet enjoyment of the ridiculous, encouraged the prince of gossips by throwing him every now and then a sympathetic response, which was duly recounted during the day, and recorded at night as a gratifying proof that in his heart he was with them. One Saturday evening about the middle of February, when we may imagine the Home Secretary trying to get through his letters, the Clerk of the Council dropped in to give him an extra lesson on the sinfulness of making peers to carry the bill, not because the bill was bad, or the country indifferent, but because it might prevent him and other sensible men from coalescing hereafter with those who did not approve of it. He describes the Home Secretary as well inclined to assent to all he said, but being " in one of his listening lazy moods, he was disposed to hear everything and say little *—alternately thinking, no doubt, his visitor a bore, and that it might after all be worth while learning all he had to tell of what was going on among the waverers and waiters upon providence. Next day Palmerston sent to say that he wanted to see him—a proof how much more alert

* Greville's Journal, February 14th, 1832, p. 254.

he was in political exigencies, " and more satisfactory to talk to." So down he trotted to the Foreign Office with a list of trimmers in his pocket who were to turn the balance and save the nation. In strict confidence he showed the names, and then, as a fine stroke of diplomacy, permitted Palmerston to say if he chose on his own authority that he had seen the men in ambush, provided he did not mention any of their names: because, " in fact, not one of them had given any authority to be so counted." * We now understand Melbourne's lazy listening mood when set upon by such a negotiator, who, self-appointed, fancied he could talk reformers and anti-reformers into a new settlement of the representation, for sake of which both should give up a good deal. Palmerston accomplished his purpose in sending for him by telling him certain awful secrets, which he knew he would reveal to his frightened friends, about Lord Grey's waxing wroth and being resolved to make peers. Therewith he presented some rough sketches in *chiaro 'scuro* of the " explosion that must inevitably follow,"† if the bill was thrown out a third time ; a catastrophe they must at any cost prevent. The machinist of impossible compromise undertook to dispute the probability of such an event, and commenced reweaving the Wharncliffe web again. Palmerston having charged him to the muzzle with blank cartridge, took all the rest quietly, and bowed him out with the intimation that he would be delighted to see him again. For another month whispered hints and muttered innuendoes continued without abatement. Sometimes Archbishop Howley's indecision stopped the way ; fragments of letters from Lord Harrowby set people by the ears till the press began to doubt Lord Grey's fidelity to the £10 franchise; and the "Moderate Party," as that nebulous element was called, entertained hopes that even that might be modified. As time wore on other tales got into circulation : one with respect to the right of voting in counties out of freeholds situated in towns was to be given up ; another that Maryle-

---

* Journal, February 14th, 1832, p. 255.   † Idem.

bone only, of the metropolitan cities, was to be enfranchised. The Clerk of the Council seriously believed that Lord Harrowby might have extorted this concession in a conference with Lord Grey, but that he "happened to have a headache." No wonder Brougham and Durham grew uneasy, restless, and tormenting ; and that Melbourne was worried by their forebodings, which his correct appreciation of the character of the Premier and his Home Office introspection of the state of feeling throughout the country made him regard as groundless.

Still anxious doubt overhung the two ensuing months as to what would happen should the possible exigency arise. The bill passed the Commons, without further change of importance, by a majority of 116 ; and, unwilling to risk the consequences of its rejection by the Lords, Althorp supported Brougham and Durham in urging a sufficient creation of peers. Out-voted in the Cabinet, he wrote to the Premier that considering all that had happened he thought they were bound to omit nothing necessary to insure the passing of the measure; and that if by their omission it were lost they would never be forgiven by the nation for the calamities that might ensue. Earl Grey could not venture in reply to say with confidence that the Waverers, as they were called, were strong enough to turn the trembling scale.

The majority against us (in October) was forty-one; the conversions from which we now look forward to a more favourable result on the second reading, would turn against us almost to a man ; many of those on whom we now depend would, I believe, certainly leave us ; and there is no saying how far a defection to which the natural feeling of the House of Lords would tend might be carried. We should be exposed then to a great risk of failure even on the second reading: . . . . and I really believe we should fail. In such a failure you may say our characters would be safe. I doubt it. We should be exposed to attacks of another kind, in which that part of the community which must be regarded as the soundest and the best would probably join.   Even the most violent, who have no affection for us, and whose object it is to vilify all public men, and to wean public opinion from the settled institutions of the Government, would cry out against us, for want of vigour and energy in not having made enough.   What then would be the effect in the country?   Would the indignation directed against the House of Lords be less after the creation of peers, in the event of another failure, than before it; would not all the dangers which we now apprehend be equally in curred? and can you believe that our characters would save us in the general wreck that would ensue?   My belief is the danger of a general combination against the Government would not be less, and that its consequences would be worse.   As at present advised, I do not think anything would induce me to be a consenting party to a large creation of peers.*

A certain deceptive show of success cheered the fainting hopes of compromise when the bill reached the Lords. Bishop Blomfield stood forth like another Aaron with a rod of peace which promised to devour all the rods of war; he was cheered by a few sensible men on both sides, who above all things recoiled from the prospect of recourse to violent measures; and all the extreme politicans on either side of the Woolsack sulked at the conciliatory tone of the Duke and Lord Grey.   Bishop Philpotts scandalised his discreeter brethren in lawn by the vehemence of his antagonism.   He was severely handled by Lord Grey, who towards others was mild and conciliatory, conscious that a harsh or threatening word might turn the balance at the last moment.   Many wavered during that eventful night.   It could hardly be said that Harrowby and Wharncliffe led a compact party of seceders;   for they had no design or capability of

* To Althorp, March 11th, 1832.

welding men together for the purpose of separate action ; and their 'chief function lay in supplying a score or two of Conservative peers with plausible reasons for agreeing to go into committee rather than drive matters to extremity. But it is certain that they were unable to devise, much less to show the way of executing, any definite counter-scheme to be worked out by amendments in detail; and it may with truth be said that the Waverers whose votes were to determine the issue on the second reading had no agree-ment amongst themselves what ought to follow, or how the measure was to be ultimately fashioned. The second read-ing was carried by a majority of nine. Seventeen of their lordships reversed their previous votes, ten abstained from repeating theirs, and twelve whose former absence signified their indifference to Reform mustered in the ranks of Govern-ment to save their order. It was day-dawn on the 14th of April when the memorable result was declared. The san-guine were much elated; but Melbourne said gravely as he quitted the House, "It is not all over yet." *

The Easter holidays were spent in negotiations between Palmerston, Graham, Stanley, and the Duke of Richmond on one side, and Wharncliffe, Haddington, and Lyndhurst on the other, for the Seceders, as they were called, had re-joined the ranks of Opposition, and wished it to be so under-stood. The Premier was ready to make more considerable concessions than previously, and Lyndhurst professed him-self anxious to come to an accommodation. He believed, how-ever, that the principle of some reform having been at length settled by a certain amount of Conservative acqui-escence, ministers could neither carry Schedule A. in the Upper House as then constituted, nor persuade the King to create fifty peers for the purpose; and if not they must either yield in committee or give place to other men. He proposed therefore to begin by turning the bill upside down, and moving that the disfranchising clauses should be post-poned until after the enfranchising clauses had been

* Hobhouse, vol. ii. p. 230.

determined on.   The First Minister declared that to this he
could not agree.   When, therefore, Harrowby and Wharncliffe consented beforehand to vote for it, they knew that
they were insuring a defeat of ministers, who would treat
it as a vote of want of confidence.   No intimation was given
nevertheless by them of the course about to be taken until
the afternoon of the 7th of May, when the peers were about
to go into committee.   This reticence, and the consequent
surprise to which it led, put an end to further parley.
Upon going into committee the Lord Chief Baron proposed
to postpone all the disfranchising clauses with a view of
enforcing amendments of the other portions of the bill, and
virtually hoisting a new standard of Reform inscribed with
the motto, "Creation of new rights without extinction of old
privileges."   Melbourne and Palmerston always said that,
had this been proposed by the Tory Cabinet in 1830, it
would have been carried in both Houses by three to one,
and a decade or two would have elapsed before any serious
attempt was made to extinguish nomination boroughs.
But it was now too late.   Like the rest of his colleagues,
the Home Secretary was now prepared to advise a creation
of peers rather than throw over Schedule A.   Twenty years'
experience of elections had naturally led him to appreciate
highly the convenience of nomination seats ; and he would
sometimes amuse himself and scandalise a Benthamite acquaintance by arguing that if small boroughs were to be
kept they would generally be corrupt ; that it was im-
material to the candidate whether he paid two thousand
pounds to one owner or to two hundred vendors for the
seat; and that public decency was less infringed in the
former case than in the latter.   He loved to play with
the edged tools of argument, when he talked in private and
without reserve.   But to turn gossip of this kind into
grave declarations of opinion, and to found on them re-
flections injurious to common sense and personal honour, is
wholly without justification.   We are asked to believe that
at a ball at the Duchess de Dino's, two nights after he had

helped to carry the second reading of the Reform Bill, Melbourne strove to convince Mr. Greville, then in the confidence of the Opposition, that the Government could not be carried on without the rotten boroughs; and that he did not see why the bill ought not be rejected! What fragments of interrupted talk, or scraps of irony and sarcasm uttered amid the music and bustle of a crowded assembly, may have tickled the ear of the Clerk of the Council, none can tell; but the concatenation of such phrases dropped in such a place, at such a time and by such a man, and the construction put upon them of spontaneous insincerity and wanton treachery to his party, his kindred, and himself, is simply incredible. Lyndhurst's argument for his motion was in effect a declaration against disfranchisement, and in so many words a rejection of the policy three times deliberately adopted within twelve months by the House of Commons. It was carried by a majority of thirty-five, no proxies being available in committee.

In the Chancellor's private room the Premier consulted Holland, Lansdowne, Althorp, and Melbourne; and they were now unanimous that unless peers were created they must resign. The promptitude of acquiescence by the minority who had hitherto deprecated resort to this extreme measure, thus fully indicated their prudence and patriotism. They had persuaded their more eager colleagues to wait until the necessity had been made clear; and thereby exonerated the Cabinet from the responsibility of needlessly wounding the constitution. To have advised the use of the prerogative for the purpose of overbearing the legislative judgment of the peers a day previously, would have exposed them to the imputation of grievous error in calculating the event, which it might always have been said would have gone the other way; or of recklessly humiliating an independent branch of the legislature in their eagerness to secure the success of their bill. No reasonings or protestations could have silenced this reproach. History would have been bound to record how a ministry availed itself of

its popularity out of doors to compel an unwilling monarch
to infringe the constitution when many of the best and wisest
thought there was no actual need of doing so; and the
precedent thus established would ever after have been felt
to overhang freedom of judgment in the Lords. But neither
Melbourne, Lansdowne, or Grey had ever disputed or
doubted that a crisis might come, when to avert revolution
the power of making peers might and ought to be exerted.
The crisis had now arrived; it had been brought about by
their opponents deliberately, and after full warning and discussion; their consciences were therefore free, and without a
dissentient voice they bade their chief upon the morrow tell
the King that unless the unwise majority of peers should
be overborne they could no longer be answerable for the
peace and welfare of the country. A minute of the Cabinet,
drawn by Palmerston with Melbourne's approval, and signed
by all except the Duke of Richmond, recommended an
immediate creation of peers. The Premier and the Chancellor were deputed to lay it before the King, and they
received from his Majesty a peremptory refusal. Ministers
at once resigned. Next day, while hearing a law argument
in court, the Chief Baron received a letter from Sir Herbert
Taylor, requiring his immediate presence in the royal closet.
The incidents that followed are well known: Sir Robert Peel
and the Speaker Manners Sutton, successively declined the
perilous honour of the Premiership; and after the experiment
of a single night's debate, Mr. A. Baring renounced the hopeless attempt of persuading the House of Commons to allow
him to bring in a counter Reform Bill. William IV. was
forced to give way; a sufficient number of the Lords
at his Majesty's private request withdrew from further
opposition; and the bill became law on the 7th of June.

In the struggle which thus ended, the personal popularity
of the sovereign passed away, and thenceforth gave place
to feelings of distrust, rather than dislike, among large
classes of the community. Queen Adelaide was supposed to
have chiefly influenced him in the unfortunate attempt to

displace his ministers, regardless of the decided preference shown them by the House of Commons. Angry invectives and coarse lampoons filled the columns of the journals of widest circulation. The monarch bitterly complained that the authors of these libels were not brought to punishment; and reproached the Home Secretary with not directing the Attorney-General to institute proceedings, as had frequently been done in his brother's reign. Melbourne detested the scurrility of the press, and tried his best to soothe royal susceptibility thus wounded. But he could not, to please the Court, encourage the idea that any good would come of criminal proceedings. He understood too well the futility of such a course, and he was deeply impressed with the conviction that nothing could be more injurious to the interests of monarchy. William IV. listened to his courtly but candid expostulations without being convinced; but he believed in his loyalty and devotion, and continued to repose more confidence in his reliability than in that of any other of his advisers, with the exception of Earl Grey.

Meanwhile, in Ireland, the experiment of government by impartial disregard of all opinions, off-hand snubbings of all suggestions, and the employment of force in repressing all kinds of manifestations, was felt by the Cabinet to be a complete failure. Lord Anglesey pressed for the passing of a Tithe Bill and the redemption of Church lands, the enactment of a poor law and a redistribution of seats in accordance with the altered proportions of population in the three kingdoms since the Union. But Parliament was engrossed with the conflict about the English Reform Bill, and his influence, with his popularity, was gone. Distrust of Stanley characterised his correspondence, which was full of complaints of the ill-usage and ingratitude he had met with from all local factions; and his incessant reiteration of disgust and despair at the position in which he found himself, swayed ministers, no doubt, in neglecting to act upon his recommendations, though it could not justify them in leaving him twelve months longer to be little better than a target whereat conflicting parties fired their insulting pellets, while the country became every day more insubordinate and miserable. No reckless speech in opposition or anonymous invective in the press could depict in darker hues than his own confidential letters the deplorable state of the kingdom of which he was the un-Governor-General. In February he wrote : —

The country is at this moment all but in a state of rebellion. I have shown what additional force will be immediately necessary, which I have rather under than over-rated ; and I conscientiously believe that if our tithe plan were instantly adopted and acted upon, at the same time that a firm determination were shown to enforce the actual laws whilst they last, bad as they are, the country might yet be saved. If we are to act upon a contrary system, I have no hope. Blake goes over immediately. He is perfectly equal to show the practicability of overcoming all the difficulties put forth by Stanley. Indeed, answers to his objections are already sent over to Lord Grey. In the meantime I tremble at every day's post. I cannot cover the whole country, and can only subdue two or three counties at a time, and then fall upon others. But what a miserable state of things! I really doubt if my presence here can be much longer of use. Personally I have nothing to complain of with ministers. All with whom I communicate are apparently full of kindness and confidence. Still there is something, or somebody, too powerful for me to counteract, and therefore I expect mischief. I will not, however, abandon the sinking vessel.*

Elsewhere he describes the relation subsisting between himself and his Chief Secretary, who hardly took the trouble to write to him from London, or to impart his views and projects of legislation. Early in the session he warned Stanley that if the various plans for the improvement of the country were vigorously pushed forward, there would be little

* Private letter to Lord Cloncurry, February 11th, 1832.

need of coercion; but if this were not done (and that promptly), then he had no hesitation in saying that his military means were wholly inadequate; and less than an addition of twenty thousand men could not secure the tranquillity of Ireland.* All this, nevertheless, was not done, nor any material part of it. The Marquis stuck to the ship, which lay helplessly rolling in the trough of the sea of troubles, through many a dark night and dreary day. The Home Secretary continued to write frank and genial letters. Holland's, always witty, were always welcome; Althorp's, considerate and kind. But nothing effectual was done in the way of legislation. A few Whigs were given appointments without distinction or power, and Ponsonby was advanced by his relative, the First Lord of the Treasury, to the exceptionally rich see of Derry. Practically the disregard of the law which proclaimed men of all creeds entitled to trust and employment remained unredressed; and disaffection to misrule grew accordingly.

A bill making the composition for tithes compulsory in Ireland was the only general measure of amelioration for which in 1832 Parliament found time, and, like too many others, it came too late. Animosity to the manner of collection was half forgotten in awakened desire to get rid altogether of a charge upon land which, to the Catholic majority, could never cease to be a badge of conquest. The gentry sympathised with the clergy, who were suddenly reduced to absolute want by the refusal of their dues; and the clergy instinctively looked for sympathy and aid to the few wealthy parishioners of their own communion. Emancipation remained almost a dead letter, its only effect discernible by the peasantry being a rapid multiplication of evictions, stimulated by the abolition of the forty-shilling franchise. And thus the confluent streams of social and sectarian animosity deepened and widened, till order and law seemed everywhere in danger of being swamped in the flood. Melbourne had early foreseen the deplorable consequences of

* Letter to Secretary Stanley, February 6th, 1832.

too long postponing relief from religious disabilities, and the readjustment of the relations between the owners and occupiers of the soil. But while the conflict for Reform lasted no one but Lansdowne, Spring Rice, and Sir H. Parnell had time to give heed to suggestions or effective measures for tranquillising Ireland. The creation of a Board of Works endowed by the Treasury, and the establishment of the system of national education, whose grants in aid of local contribution were furnished from the same imperial source, would in peaceful times have won popular applause, if not gratitude. But in the anarchy of sect and party their effect was inappreciable. The solution of the great disturbing questions was not even attempted. Electoral reform, when England and Scotland had been satisfied, was given to Ireland so grudgingly and with so niggard a hand as to furnish O'Connell with new topics of reproach and upbraiding; and the Tithe Bill of 1832, which if passed three years before might have prevented the guerilla conflicts of Carrickshock and Newtownbarry, was wholly impotent to appease the storm. Lord Anglesey's proposals were in fact overruled at the instance of Stanley, of whom he bitterly complained as thwarting instead of supporting him :—

What a pity (he wrote to Lord Cloncurry) that when there was a scheme worked up by Blake and Griffith, assisted by you, and approved by Lord Plunket and Blackburn, and recommended by me, who was without prejudice and in no respect committed by public declarations or pledges, and had only calmly to listen to the opinions of such able men and then to form my own—what a pity that such a plan should be thrown overboard, and that another of little promise should be substituted.

Melbourne acquiesced doubtingly in a course he felt himself unable to control or guide. Stanley by his courage and eloquence had virtually persuaded Lord Grey to regard

him as Home Secretary for Ireland; and there was quite
enough in the condition of Great Britain to occupy the attention of the Secretary of State. Melbourne himself, it
must be owned, was fascinated by the dauntless energy and
unwavering self-reliance of the Irish Secretary, who began
to be looked upon by many as the coming man of the
party.

Charles Greville notes the substance of his talk with
Melbourne on their way to town from Panshanger, where
they had been staying.* He regretted Lord John's expressions at Torquay about the ballot, which were, he
thought, unwarrantable. Brougham, he said, was "tossed
about in perpetual caprices, fanciful and sensitive, and
actuated by all sorts of littlenesses, even with regard to
people so insignificant that it was difficult to conceive how
he could ever think about them." The Irish question
seemed to him most difficult to settle. Archbishop Howley
was willing to reform the temporalities of the Church, but
not to alienate to other uses any portion of its property.
He evinced no little uneasiness regarding the state of the
country and to this his companion ascribed the desire he
expressed to keep Lord Hill and Lord F. Somerset at the
Horse Guards. But in truth his opinions on this important
subject rested on no transitory apprehension regarding
public tranquillity.

A feeling showed itself early in the new House of
Commons hostile to the influence and independence of the
Horse Guards. Had the Duke of Wellington retained the
command-in-chief, which he took after the death of the
Duke of York with the approval of the whole nation, no idea
of subverting it would have gained ground; but Lord Hill
did not possess equal weight as an administrator; both he and
his Secretary, Lord Fitzroy Somerset, were regarded as party
men, and the insinuation was perpetually reiterated that the
patronage of the army was used for party purposes. Lord
Hill sometimes voted in consonance with his own opinions

* September 28th, 1832.

as a peer; and sometimes stayed away. This did not escape censure in the press and in Parliament; and for not voting for the Reform Bill, Hume and O'Connell had loudly called for his dismissal. It was even mooted in the Cabinet whether he should not be reproved. Melbourne warmly encountered what he deemed an error of executive policy, and his view prevailed. He thought the command of the army ought to be regarded as a neutral trust, to be exercised without regard to the fluctuating politics of the day. He adhered to the policy of Mr. Pitt in this respect, sanctioned by the unqualified approval of Mr. Fox; both of whom in 1788 desired to sever military patronage from that of the administration, in the hope that thereby more thorough confidence should be created in the minds of the officers as to the impartial judgment of their conduct, and their claims to promotion. Government by party he held to be indispensable to the vitality of parliamentary rule, and the dispensation of civil patronage among the adherents of the party in power for the time being, he always vindicated as a necessary concomitant of party government. But he deprecated earnestly the multiplication of prizes to be battled for on the hustings or in the lobby; and having regard to the position of officers, subject as they were to the summary and absolute authority of those above them, and often to their unaccountable and unreasonable caprice, affecting not only their character but their hopes of advancement, he urged strongly the importance of maintaining the theory and the principle that from the sovereign head of the army down through all its grades to the drummer and recruit there ought to be no recognition of political antecedents or party opinions. This was avowedly the sentiment of the Duke of Wellington, and not the sentiment merely, but the administrative rule which he maintained at the Horse Guards. An active and intelligent section of Whigs and Radicals began at this time to advocate the opposite principle, insisting that all control and patronage should be vested in the Secretary for War; who should be held answerable to Parliament for every act of military administration. Sir J. Graham and Mr. Edward Ellice were at all times zealous in their advocacy of this policy, and both pursued its developement as a favourite aim, though neither lived to see its consummation. Grey and Palmerston sided with the Home Secretary; and though they regretted the occasional votes of Lord Hill, they believed him to be an honourable man; and they resisted all attempts to remove him because he did not happen to belong to Brooks's Club. But Greville, in his love of the piquant and epigrammatic, put together frequently odds and ends of opinion dropped in the carelessness of conversation; and then when he came to jot them down, philosophised about them in a fashion not a little calculated to mislead. "It was curious," he wrote of Melbourne, "to see the working and counter-working of his real opinions and principles with his false position, and the mixture of bluntness, facility and shrewdness, discretion, levity, and seriousness, which, colouring his mind and character by turns, made up the strange compound of his thoughts and actions."* How little this kaleidoscopic picture of the man resembled the reality, when, having bid his caricaturist good-morning, he sat down to write confidentially to Bowood, a letter dated the same day enables us correctly to judge :—

Your letter this morning put me in mind of how ill I have fulfilled my promise, of keeping you informed upon the state of Ireland, but I have been in the habit of sending the papers regularly to Grey, and I do not know that you will not give a better judgment if you read the whole of the information together than you would if you had received it in detail. I therefore send you in a box the most material of the letters which have been received. I have perhaps erred rather in this—of sending too many than too few; I add also a copy of a letter from Stanley, which contains his views upon many most important and

* September 28th, 1832.

material points.   The result of the whole appears to me
to be that there is no chance nor thought of any active
and determined resistance to the law in Ireland where it
is adequately enforced, but it is clear that there is a
settled determination not to obey it unless they are compelled to do so.   The tithe is paid wherever a military
force is shown sufficient to compel the payment, but the
barbarous murder at Doneraile and other circumstances
show that the animus is as decided as ever, and will not
scruple any violence or enormity.   The murders, outrages, &c., are dreadful, and will undoubtedly sooner
or later compel the adoption of measures stronger than
the ordinary law.   I have long foreseen this, but such
measures must not be prematurely proposed; you must
carry along with you the public feeling and the general
conviction.   The evil must be so glaring as to be seen
even by the blind, and the necessity so certain as to convince not only the understanding of the prudent, but the
passions of the multitude.   I say nothing of foreign
affairs, you will hear of them from Palmerston.   The
decision of the Conference in which he is now engaged
is of great importance.   From the tone of the Russian
embassy I think they will throw every obstacle in the
way of the adoption of coercive measures.   But our
situation is become embarrassing; and the country is
getting impatient at it.   Grey writes that Althorp and
Brougham are indisposed to any step which may lead to
war; but at the same time alive to the necessity of ful-
filling our engagements.   Grey intended to leave Howick
on the 4th of October, to call at Castle Howard and to
be in town from the 8th to the 10th; but Palmerston
thinks that what he and Graham wrote to him yesterday
will probably induce him to hasten his journey.   In
truth, affairs are rather too important for the absence of
so many ministers at such distances.   Holland is better,
but still very bad, and I should fear his recovery would
be very slow.   She fidgets his life out with anxiety and

solicitude and I am convinced adds a fourth to the time in which he otherwise would get well.*

Melbourne sat to Haydon about this time, who thought him very affable and amiable; he had a fine head, and looked refined and handsome. He asked much about Hazlitt, Leigh Hunt, Keats and Shelley. The artist thought him a delightful, frank, easy, unaffected man of fashion. He says, "I spoke of Lord Durham's return :—Dead silence. I talked of Birmingham. A sort of hint as to Scholefield and Atwood,—a passing opinion, yet confidential." Melbourne said he knew that Lord North often endeavoured to persuade the King not to continue the American War, but that the virulence of the old King's feelings obliged him; and added that the King patronised West against Reynolds because the latter was so intimate with Fox and Burke. With regard to Art, he was afraid history would never have the patronage which portraiture obtained. Haydon said the Government alone could do it. The minister ejaculated, "How?" "First by a committee of the House, then by vote." Melbourne was afraid selections might be invidious. The painter rejoined that the selected would be more likely to be envied than otherwise. He asked, had not sculptors had every opportunity, and had they generally done as well as they ought? Haydon replied " that they had not. But it was no argument, because one class of artists had acted as manufacturers that others must do so too." Melbourne, "then we shall see what a popular Parliament will do. If Hume is not against it your scheme may be feasible." †

* To Lord Lansdowne, September 28th, 1832.
† Haydon's Diary, October to December, 1832.

CHAPTER XX.

EXECUTIVE AND LEGISLATIVE DUTIES.

Coercion Bill—First Factory Act—Mrs. Norton—Home Office patronage—Mr. Disraeli—Viceroyalty of Ireland—Church Temporalities.

STANLEY's brilliant achievements in debate and indefatigable energy in the discharge of the duties of his department won him the reward he coveted—a seat in the Cabinet; and thenceforth the framing of legislative measures and the distribution of Irish patronage were left wholly to him. He had a genuine admiration for Earl Grey, who was older than his father, and to whom from childhood he had been taught to look up. To him he showed a deference and respect which he affected for no other of his colleagues. He had never shown much consideration for the Viceroy's opinions; and not much more for the Chancellor's. The Attorney-General, Blackburn, and the law adviser to the Castle, Mr. (afterwards Baron) Greene, chiefly supplied him with the details of information he wanted, and the forms of legislation he designed. The former was the legitimate successor of Mr. Saurin, with greater versatility and reticence; the latter a timid, hypochondriacal and colourless man, who only required to be wound up once a week to tell punctually on his face at Dublin how the wind blew at Knowsley. Stanley was thenceforth Home Secretary for Ireland, and was the absolute ruler of the country. Unfortunately its condition was one of unparalleled provocation

to high-handed rigour. Agrarian crime desolated whole
counties, and the tithe war raged more fiercely than ever.
O'Connell, incensed at finding himself excluded as completely
as before the passing of the Reform Act, which he had essentially contributed to carry, from all participation or influence
in affairs, gave himself unreservedly to agitation for the Repeal
of the Union. A few Catholic proprietors held aloof, but they
could hardly be said to support the Government; Melbourne,
Althorp, and Grant were for prompt and large measures of
sectarian conciliation; but Stanley declared that "Ireland
must be taught to fear before she could be taught to love;"
and the Premier, and those who sympathised in his personal
resentments and vexations, induced the Cabinet to adopt
the combination of repressive provisions which formed the
first important measure submitted to the new Parliament.
Althorp, overweighted with the business of the Exchequer
and the leadership of the Commons, and who personally
knew nothing of Ireland, stammered through a melancholy
statement of crime and outrage, which he said could only
be quelled by suspending the legal tribunals, by proclaiming
martial law, and at the same time prohibiting by proclamation political meetings. But he failed to persuade
the new House of Commons, for he had failed to be persuaded himself, that these remedies would be effectual. In
common with half the Liberal party, he believed Stanley to
be the truest incarnation of Conservatism in Parliament;
and with his known opinions on the Church question, he
foresaw insuperable difficulty in the way of compensatory
measures of concession, were those of repression once
passed. Unconsciously he betrayed how little his heart was
in the business; and O'Connell's denunciation of the whole
scheme, followed as it was by strong expressions of disapproval from others, rendered it doubtful what the issue
might be. Stanley in half an hour changed the whole
state of affairs. Lord Russell has described it as the most
surprising instance of what intense earnestness, high intellect, reckless courage, and passionate eloquence can

achieve in changing the mood of a popular assembly. Melbourne, who sat under the gallery, said afterwards, " he completely brought back the House to the stern purpose from which it had been wandering, by his incomparable mastery of details. O'Connell felt keenly the odium heaped upon him, during this invective, which held him responsible for all the crime and outrage committed in the land, and the result was practically seen when but a score of English members sided with their Irish colleagues in the division. Lord Grey was delighted with his undaunted lieutenant, and Melbourne began to regard him as next in succession to the headship of the Whig party.

Great as was the effect of Stanley's speech upon the division, Melbourne felt that the minority was well worth considering. It was plain that, out of doors, multitudes thought the bill tyrannical; and he would much rather it had been carried without the triumph of declamation, than, so to speak, by dint of it. Obliged as he was to hear from day to day every popular whisper and murmur through the Dionysian ear of his department, he could not be unconscious that the resistance offered to the measure found prolonged echoes throughout the great cities and towns. O'Connell felt this also, and was not dismayed; he even boasted in his own bantering way at having scared his opponents by his denunciations; every shop window had his likeness by H. B., stretched upon his back as Gulliver, with Anglesey, Stanley, and Althorp eagerly heading the Lilliputians against him. He was supposed to be exclaiming, " I roared so loud, they all ran away, and some of them were hurt by the fall they got jumping off my side, but they soon came back again."

A long arrear of legislative measures of the practical and unpolitical kind had to be worked off; and it remained to be seen how a reconstructed Parliament would deal with them. Revision of the East India Company's Charter, and its renewal on principles of free trade and free colonisation, engrossed the attention of the Board of Control. Abolition

of negro slavery, loudly insisted on by the Liberals when
out of power, could no longer be postponed, and the Colonial
Department was occupied with the details of a legislative
scheme. The Treasury had in hand the important considerations involved in the renewal of the Bank Act; and on
the Home Office devolved the preparation of a Factory Bill
and a new Poor Law. Up to this time the labour of
children was wholly unprotected by any statute law.
Parents and the masters of apprentices might indeed be
called to account for neglect or cruelty by anybody who
witnessed overt acts of ill-usage so heinous as not to admit
of palliation or disproof. But "anybody" practically meant
nobody. Liability to the bondage and brutalisation of premature toil had gradually become the normal condition of
the offspring of the wage classes throughout the manufacturing districts; and in the quickened pace of competition and
stimulated greed of unprecedented gain, the temptations to
use up the otherwise unmarketable capabilities of childhood
had become irresistible. Melbourne called to mind how
Sir Robert Peel, the father of the statesman, had some years
before been the first to denounce publicly the spreading
evil. A select committee had been appointed at his instance
in 1816, which reported important evidence, but made no
definite recommendation; and in 1818 the worthy baronet
brought in a restrictive bill, which had the support of Wilberforce and others who preferred humanity to class interests.
At that time the number of hands engaged in spinning and
weaving cotton was estimated at sixty thousand; Sir Robert
himself stated that he had one thousand apprentices; and that
he knew the necessity of some legal regulation with respect
to that class of persons, which was yearly becoming more
numerous. He therefore called on Parliament to interpose
for the protection of the defenceless ones, whose chances of
health and life were daily sacrificed by employers, making
haste to be rich, at the smallest possible cost in wages. But
the old House of Commons cared for none of these things,
and the Government of which the great manufacturer's

son was a leading member, could not be induced to take up the question. Melbourne had caused inquiries to be made into the actual condition of things in the chief seats of textile industry; and having obtained a body of authentic evidence which placed the magnitude of the abuse beyond all controversy, he had a bill carefully drawn, which with some difficulty he persuaded the Cabinet to sanction, prohibiting the employment for hire of children under nine years of age in any except silk mills, limiting the time for which children under eleven might be employed to nine hours in the day, and forty-eight hours in the week; and providing for attendance at school, with a charge of one penny in the shilling out of the earnings of the child, if the employer required it. Medical aid was established, and inspectors appointed to see that the enactment was obeyed.

Such was the first chapter of what has since been extended into a code of laws for the defence of youth against the cupidity of age; and for the preservation of the moral and material energies of the community from premature exhaustion for the inordinate advantage of a few. The Factory Bill of 1833 encountered sharp opposition in its progress through the legislature. Arguments with which we have since grown familiar, about the right divine of capital to make the most it can of opportunities, and the right divine of parentage to do what it likes with its little ones, were then heard for the first time, from both Radical and Tory benches; and the book of lamentations over trade about to be banished, and foreign rivals about to be enriched in consequence of England's sentimental folly, was then opened, and has not yet been closed. But the Home Secretary was not to be moved by deputations of mill-owners who foretold impending ruin, each to their own particular trade, and all to an unhappy country. He told them that he thought the country was not so unhappy; and (as Macaulay said of the constitution) that it "took a deal of ruining." If the experiment of limiting hours of labour threatened to fail, it could be discontinued; but he was resolved that it should be tried.

One day Mr. Evelyn Denison stopped him at the door of
the Home Office when about to mount his horse, to urge
certain amendments in the education clauses. He bade him
speak to his brother George. "I have been with him,"
said his friend, "for half an hour, but can make no way;"
and on being asked why, he said complainingly, "he damned
me, damned the clauses, and damned the Bill." Melbourne,
by this time in the saddle, replied gravely, "And damn
it, what more could he say?—but I'll see about it."

He had not been long at the Home Office when he received a letter from the grand-daughter of Sheridan, who was
a near relative of Sir James Graham, asking for her husband, Mr Norton, some appointment for which he might be
considered eligible as a member of the bar; and gently pleading, as a claim to consideration, the illustrious memory of
him who had once been the idol of the Whigs, but who had
unrequited passed away while yet they tarried in the wilderness. Recollections of many a brilliant gathering at Melbourne House were awakened by the name

> ———— of that rare gifted man,
> The pride of the senate, the bower, and the hall,
> The orator, dramatist, minstrel who ran
> Through each mode of the lyre and was master of all.

Nor were the more recent memories of the son, still better
known to Melbourne as a contemporary and friend, less calculated to excite his interest. He thought he would answer
the letter in person as he passed by Storey's Gate; and thus
began the intimacy destined to exercise no little influence on
his subsequent life. George Norton, though next in remainder
to his brother Lord Grantley, had but a slender income;
and possessing neither talent or industry to win advancement at the bar, thought he might better his income through
the influence of his wife's family and connections. She was
then but five-and-twenty; possessing hereditary charms of
wit and beauty, and having made good already high pretensions to celebrity in criticism and verse. From the hours
devoted to her children and to her literary pursuits, society

insisted upon stealing not a few, to pay her homage. With her sisters Lady Seymour and Mrs Blackwood she " was everywhere ;" and everywhere men of mark and distinction sought her recognition.   A Secretary of State was now among the number ; and finding in her society attraction and sympathy which he had neither at home nor in the crowd, he was too glad to be received after .a while on the easy footing of an old acquaintance, and soon of a valued friend. A vacancy in the Divisional Magistracy of London enabled him to confer on Mr. Norton the sort of place which he desired.   The work was not laborious, and the salary, though not large,was enough to add materially to the comforts of the unpretentious household.   He professed himself grateful, and did not dis- guise that he was hopeful of greater benefits to come.   He was ever warm in the welcome of his patron, and obsequious in deference to each passing whim.   Only one thing he would not do—attend punctually at his court.   Murmurs on the subject reached Melbourne, and he was vexed. He heard also of disputes between the magistrates, which if made public would be, he thought, unseemly, and tried remonstrance in the way that he supposed least likely to offend.

T. W., as you say, does what he has not the least right to do ; and the worst is, he is not only foolish himself, but is the cause of folly in others.   I had the greatest difficulty in preventing Norton from replying to him in the *Times*.   I was much alarmed at the notion of his doing this, especially as I found him thoroughly impressed with the opinion that he could do it with great cleverness and dexterity. I hate the magistrates writing to the newspapers ; besides people will be sure to say to me,—if the magistrates get squabbling in public, why do you not clear the bench of these fellows altogether ?   They tell me also that Norton does not go to his office early enough.   I should be annoyed at having a complaint made on this subject. Pray dissuade him, gently, from any public exhibitions in the newspapers ; and urge him gently to a little more

activity in the morning. He might surely without difficulty get there by twelve o'clock in the morning. This is
a disagreeable lecturing letter, but still upon matters to
which it is necessary to pay some attention.*

With exceptional colleagues like Mr. Walker, the author
of 'The Original,' and Mr. Hardwicke, both of them men
of attainments and accomplishments, Mr. Norton contrived
to get on better; and when a vacancy subsequently occurred on the Whitechapel bench, "he seemed to think
that he and H. had almost the right to make the appointment, and that everything was to give way to the consideration of giving him a pleasant companion. He said
the bench used, with Walker, to be like a pleasant club,
and that he must have an agreeable fellow to walk to
and fro with."† Melbourne soon discerned, however, how
selfish and unyielding was the temper of the man; and how
unsympathetic was his nature with that of his wife. The
greater portion of their income was the fruit of her literary
toil, and she could not always conceal her disappointment
and chagrin at his insensibility to the continued self-denial
it entailed. She was for some time the editor of a well-known
monthly journal, and afterwards of 'The Keepsake.' And Melbourne, who took daily more interest in her indefatigable
exertions, was ever ready with the suggestion and advice his
fine scholarship and unfailing memory enabled him, without
reference or research, to supply. In weariness of the bickering and spite of party politics, he was glad to spend an hour
without ceremony or notice in society so engaging. He was
for years a frequent visitor at Storey's Gate, and there made
the acquaintance of Mr. R. B. Sheridan and his brothers, of
Albany Fonblanque, who became one of his warmest and
most unwavering adherents; and, as chance would have it, of
a man then but rising into note, who was destined to fill as
high a place in the world's history as himself.

To celebrate her younger brother's birthday, Mrs. Norton

* To the Hon. Mrs. Norton, July 19th, 1831.
† January 27th, 1836.

asked to dinner the other members of her family who were in town, two of her husband's colleagues in the magistracy, Lord Melbourne, and the author of ' Vivian Grey,' in whom she had recently discovered the son of her father's intimate friend.   Young Disraeli was not long returned from his travels in the East, with traits of which he had interested her on the occasion of their first acquaintance.   He had just then been defeated in an attempt to get into Parliament for the borough of Wycombe, where he attributed his failure to want of support by the Whigs.   Mrs. Norton presented him after dinner to the Home Secretary, who had the power, she said, of retrieving the disappointment if he chose; and whose frank and open manner led to a long conversation, in which Mr. Disraeli mentioned the circumstances of his late discomfiture, dwelling on each particular with the emphasis which every young man of ambition since Parliament was invented is sure to lay upon the broken promises and scandalous behaviour of his victorious foes.   The minister was attracted more and more as he listened to the uncommonplace language and spirit of the youthful politician, and thought to himself he would be well worth serving. Abruptly, but with a certain tone of kindness which took away any air of assumption, he said " Well now, tell me,—what do you want to be ?"   The quiet gravity of the reply fairly took him aback—" I want to be Prime Minister."   Melbourne gave a long sigh, and then said very seriously :

No chance of that in our time.   It is all arranged and settled.   Nobody but Lord Grey could perhaps have carried the Reform Bill ; but he is an old man, and when he gives up, he will certainly be succeeded by one who has every requisite for the position, in the prime of life and fame, of old blood, high rank, great fortune, and greater ability.   Once in power, there is nothing to prevent him holding office as long as Sir Robert Walpole. Nobody can compete with Stanley.   I heard him the other night in the Commons, when the party were all divided and breaking away from their ranks, recall them by the mere force of superior will and eloquence : he rose like a young eagle above them all, and kept hovering over their heads till they were reduced to abject submission. There is nothing like him. If you are going into politics and mean to stick to it, I dare say you will do very well, for you have ability and enterprise; and if you are careful how you steer, no doubt you will get into some port at last. But you must put all these foolish notions out of your head; they won't do at all. Stanley will be the next Prime Minister you will see.

How both would have started, had their sybil-like hostess unfolded there and then in prophetic dream the fate in store for each; for the one, that before many months, and for the other after the lapse of five-and-thirty years,—that he should be Prime Minister of England.

His son, though unable to enjoy the sports or share the adventures of youth, was more than ever an object of his solicitude and care. As he grew to man's estate he had improved in person, and in features might be called handsome. He was not without intelligence; amused himself with reading, and occasionally with cards and music. In manner he was affable, and usually gentle in disposition, seldom evincing waywardness or excitability. His father spent some portion of every day with him, and exhausted every artifice of affection to beguile his loneliness and to devise occupations having a tendency to waken him from the apathy of his condition. But the distressing malady to which he was abnormally a victim refused to yield to any kind of treatment, and, though for many years its destructive influence was not generally observable in his bodily frame, it gradually exerted its debilitating sway over the faculties of his mind. The physicians forbade his being left for any time alone, and his father was frequently harassed with apprehension lest he should suffer from the inattention of his attendants. "I have often," said Mrs. Norton, "seen Lord

Melbourne, at his own house, pause in the middle of conversation and remain for some moments listening for some
sound from the adjoining room, where he had left the invalid,
as if he dreaded his being alone." The world knew or recked
not this long protracted trial of his feelings; but that it
weighed upon his spirit and wore the fibre of his mental
elasticity, who can doubt?

On Lord Anglesey's resignation in consequence of ill-
health, the Premier proposed that Melbourne should succeed him in the Viceroyalty of Ireland; and, strange to say,
he did not at first refuse. He was weary of the routine
drudgery of the Home Office, and the irrepressible versatility
and loquacity of the Chancellor left him almost nothing to
do in the House of Lords. The excitement of the Reform
struggle was over; and after three years' Secretaryship of
State he began to feel bored. Ireland was still the difficulty
of the Government, and he fancied that he would find in the
duties of its administration objects of more interest, if not
more usefulness, than those which demanded his attention
at Whitehall. To those who knew his ways and peculia-
rities, and whom observation qualified to judge of the requirements of such a post, it might well seem doubtful
whether he would have suited it, or it would have suited
him. His frankness and love of humour would hardly have
had free play in the mimic pageantry of a court whose
provincialism could not afford to be un-pompous; and he who
had laughed so often at the magnificent airs of his old chief
at the Castle, "the conqueror of Seringapatam," would have
felt himself ineffably ridiculous in the part of mummer
sovereign, with his friend Lady Morgan for Mistress of the
Robes. His sister, Lady Cowper, from whom he had few political thoughts apart, looked incredulous when told that there
was a notion of what she called banishing him to Dublin. He
did not always agree with her in opinion, but he knew her
affection for him, and had the highest estimate of her sagacity
and discernment. He was rather pleased at the offer being
made, but after a day or two he made up his mind that he

would rather not go. It was not easy to find any one fit to
send who would take it ; but upon the whole it was finally
resolved to reappoint Lord Wellesley. Recollections of his
former difficulties, while holding the office in a period of
intense political excitement, were doubtless present to his
mind, and the difference of circumstances was in many
ways disheartening. O'Connell's power and influence were
greatly increased, and the able adviser whom he had then
to lean upon, though still a member of the Government,
could not, as Chancellor, be referred to on all occasions as he
had been when Attorney-General. Lord Wellesley liked to
be considered capable of devising an original policy and
possessing a superior courage requisite for carrying it into
effect ; and it has been conjectured, not unreasonably, that
through Mr. A. B. Blake, O'Connell was again sounded
as to the views he entertained with respect to office. The
great agitator was in the eyes of the noble Marquis simply
an obstacle to be effectually put out of his way if possible.
He looked upon him very much as he had looked upon the
Peishwa as head of the Mahrattas, whom he was quite
willing to take into pay if he desired it, or, if he refused,
to reduce to submission. He was profoundly persuaded
of his own superiority to the rest of mankind, and of the
obligations he owed to fame as a type of transcendent
magnanimity, not to suffer personal prejudice to divert him
from his purpose, or to cherish resentment for abuse and
ridicule as Lord Grey was apt to do. Had he been able to
persuade O'Connell to give up Repeal for the office of chief
adviser of the Crown in Ireland, Lord Wellesley would not
have shrunk from telling the Cabinet that his first act
would be a master-stroke against which he would listen to
no objections ; and if he had not got his way he would not
have hesitated to throw up his office, as more than once in
his lifetime he had done before. It is of course quite possible
that he only thought aloud upon the subject in the presence
of his old confidant, and had not fully made up his mind as
to what he would do ; while an eager and intriguing politican

like Blake, who delighted in mysterious hints and specious
innuendoes, could not refrain from making the most of a
suggestion to O'Connell, and giving him to understand that
all would speedily be settled if he chose.　A sincere Catholic,
and politically a disciple of the school of Burke and Grenville, Blake abhorred the democratic tendencies of agitation, and would readily have made any exertion or sacrifice
to loyalise his fellow-countrymen upon the basis of social
and sectarian equality.　In a word, he was anxious in
1833 for the great experiment in Irish administration
which actually was tried two years later.　But opinion
was not yet ripe; for the present the design fell to the
ground; and except within a very limited circle, nothing
at the time was further known to have been contemplated.
Lady Wellesley was a devout Catholic; and Archbishop
Murray became a more frequent guest at the Phœnix Park,
as did Lord Killeen.　But neither exercised much political
influence over the great body of those who belonged to
their communion.

A remarkable discussion arose in the Lords on the Irish
Church Temporalities Bill, which struck off ten bishoprics
from that establishment, and vested the superfluities of
episcopal and capitular endowments in commissioners for
the bettering of poorer brethren.　The measure was Stanley's
chef d'œuvre in Ireland by alternately humiliating the
rival creeds.　Twenty years before it might have materially
strengthened the Protestant Establishment, and possibly
contributed to prolong its existence.　Even in 1833 the
equity and reasonableness of its provisions reflected a certain degree of credit on its contrivers; but it was treated by
Oxford and Lambeth as the first serious breach in the outworks of national establishment, and while stimulating the
development of the counter-movement afterwards known
as Tractarianism, it evoked thunders of denunciation in the
General Assembly of Scotland and the "no popery" meetings at Exeter Hall.　Haydon, who troubled his head as
little as most men with ecclesiastical apprehensions, went

to hear the debate in the Lords. Nor was his curiosity disappointed :

In the Irish Church debate the Duke spoke well, without hesitation, enforcing what he said with a bend of his head, striking his hand forcibly, and as if convinced, on the papers. He finished, and to my utter astonishment, up starts Melbourne like an artillery rocket. He began in a fury. His language flowed out like fire; he made such palpable hits that he floored the Duke as if he had shot him. But the moment the stimulus was over, his habitual apathy got a head; he stammered, hummed and hawed. It was the most pictorial exhibition of the night. He waved his white hand with the natural grace of Talma, expanded his broad chest, looked right at his adversary like a handsome lion, and grappled him with the grace of Paris.

Resistance throughout the metropolis was organised, during the autumn, to the payment of the window tax. Meetings were held, at some of which Colonel Evans took part, in Westminster; and the collectors hesitated to enforce payment by distress. This was just the sort of case in which the Home Secretary's firmness and decision served to prevent mischievous consequences, which might have readily become wide-spread; but he writes about the matter as quietly as if it were the correction of a clerical error in a turnpike bill:—

I certainly agree with you in all you say, and I hope the matter now stands better than it did. There was some bungling on Thursday in consequence of the Board of Taxes not having had sufficient communication with the sheriffs themselves; but as soon as I heard of it I sent for the latter officers and told them that I looked to them to execute the law, which was accordingly done on Saturday morning, as you will have seen in the newspapers. The effect has been good, and I understand, now, there is a general disposition to pay in the regular course. Meetings,

however, still continue, and Colonel Evans does all he can
to prevent matters from subsiding, but I have every hope
that they will do so in spite of him.   There never was
such a strange fancy as the Chancellor had got into his
head, about proroguing the Parliament before the day to
which it stands prorogued at present.   However, we have
beat him out of it, and everything will go on in the
regular course.*

His manner of dealing with deputations had sometimes
the appearance of levity or whim.   His mood was variable ;
and he indulged now and then in an affectation of ignorance
or indifference shocking to Utilitarians who mistook it for
reality, and grievous to sub-officials who knew it to be but
wayward make-believe.   His pranks at these interviews
were deemed of more consequence than he supposed.   To
seem absorbed in blowing a feather or nursing a sofa-cushion
when giving audience about capital punishment, or receiving
a report on Criminal Law Reform, in preparation for debate,
was, according to Miss Martineau, a " moral offence."   Sydney
Smith, with a juster discrimination, tried to quiz him out of
what he felt to be a fault.

Our Viscount is somewhat of an impostor.   Instead of being
the ignorant man he pretends to be, before he meets the
deputation of tallow chandlers in the morning, he sits
up half the night talking with —— about melting and
skimming, and then, although he has acquired knowledge
enough to work off a whole vat of prime Leicestershire
tallow, he pretends next morning not to know the
difference between a dip and a mould.   I moreover
believe him to be conscientiously alive to the good or evil
that he is doing, but if you had no mind to put or be put
to, the sooner you get out of his way the better.

When the Commissioners of Poor Inquiry in Ireland were
appointed, Archbishop Whately asked for a secretary qualified to aid in organising an efficient staff, and free from the

* To Lord Lansdowne; Home Office, October 29th, 1833.

prejudices likely to embarrass them in the performance of their difficult task. Mr. Senior being consulted, named Mr. Revans, who had distinguished himself in a subordinate capacity under the English Commission, and who had thereby become known to the Home Secretary. As usual, however, in questions of Irish patronage, the claims of others, on the ground of parliamentary influence, were strongly pressed, and the prelate learned with vexation that an individual whom he considered far less fitted for the post, was likely to be appointed. He wrote saying that if they did not nominate Mr. Revans, or some one equally colourless in Irish, and capable in English eyes, he must decline to act. Two days after, the secretary was summoned to the Home Office. " You must be off to Ireland," said Melbourne, as soon as he entered the room. " I have no wish to go," was the rejoinder ; " but if the Government require it, I will only ask that my position may not be worsened by the transfer." " Certainly not," said the minister ; "but talk to Tom Young on the subject, and I will see that the right thing is done. Lose no time about it, as they are waiting for you ; and let me hear how you get on." After some weeks spent in Dublin, Mr. Revans was recalled to London to assist in winding up the affairs of the English Inquiry, and he asked for an interview, to report progress, at Whitehall. On seeing him, Melbourne began with " Well, what sort of team have you got ?" " The wary official," writes Haydon, " hesitated, and said he was not quite sure that he understood the question." " How do the two archbishops pull together ?" " As well as possible," was the reply ; " I only hope we may find no difficulty greater than with them."

" The scene at the Lord Mayor's dinner was exquisite ;
the mischievous air of over-politeness with which Lord
Brougham handed in the Lady Mayoress ; the arch looks
of Lord Melbourne ; the supercilious sneer of Lord Stanley
at a City affair, as he calls it. In the ball-room I said to
Lord Stanley, Lord Melbourne enjoys it. There is nothing

Lord Melbourne does not enjoy, said he. Can there be a finer epitaph on a man? It is true of Lord Melbourne, who is all amiability, good-humour, and simplicity of mind." *

His duties in the House of Lords were manifold and onerous. As having the charge of Government bills originating in that House or sent up from the Commons, he had to master not only the subject of each, but to make himself acquainted with the multifarious details they included, and to give reasons for resisting the changes which an astute and angry Opposition were incessantly attempting to make in them. Grey, Holland, and Plunket dealt ably and eloquently with general principles, on the second reading of the greater measures of the day, and Lansdowne was alike ready to aid in this and in the practical labours of committee. The irrepressible Chancellor took his full share, and something more, of work as well as talk; but to the circumspect and practical Home Secretary his provoking and exaggerative way was sometimes less a help than a hindrance. He had less scruple about compromise than any of his colleagues, when suggested by himself; but he did more than all of them to make compromise difficult by his taunts and jeers at the expense of opponents. Melbourne's uppermost thought, when bringing in or taking up a bill, was so to engineer it as to expose the fewest possible points of attack to his vigilant and out-numbering foes; and for this purpose he often said but little, and refused to be drawn out of his trenches by the most tempting or affronting show of attack. Brougham, on the contrary, was ready to fight any number of duels, rhetorical or conversational, of black-letter law or black-mouthed insinuation, upon any conceivable occasion: and this, in committee, where he could speak any number of times, tried Melbourne's temper sorely. If, he thought, he could only be tethered to the Woolsack for the grand affair of baiting on the second and third reading, and

* 9th Nov. 1833. Haydon's 'Memoirs,' vol. ii. p. 383-4.

let them get through the clauses, deliberatively it would not so much matter: but this was a division of labour to which the noble and learned economist would not by any means agree. At length it came to be tacitly understood that if an amendment was to be peaceably carried it must be arranged with the Home Secretary. Lord Grey's confidence in his judgment and tact left him a wide discretion; and he was able, by his personal influence, to accomplish much that the reporters did not notice at the time, and of which no record is to be found in Hansard. He had, besides, a great variety of business thrown upon him, in preparing the answers to questions to be given by the Premier or by himself, and in dealing with petitions, diversified and often difficult in their character. His laconic method of previous inquiry for these occasions, is indicated in a note to the Secretary of the Treasury.

My DEAR RICE,   Home Office, March 20th, 1834.

When Lord Dundonald received a pardon under the Great Seal, was the fine which had been imposed upon him not repaid to him? I wish to know this because Mr. Butt has given Lord Wynford a petition to the House of Lords in which he alleges this to be the fact, and prays the same from himself.   Yours faithfully.

At the Spring Assizes, 1834, six agricultural labourers were found guilty at Dorchester of belonging to an association bound together by unlawful oaths, and sentenced to transportation for seven years. Surprise and indignation filled the minds of the whole body of trades unionists throughout the kingdom at the severity of the sentence, and with one voice they publicly denounced its execution as unjust. It being resolved that the men should be transported, their immediate removal was thought necessary as the most effectual way to extinguish wild hopes, if not dangerous projects of rescue; they were accordingly sent on board with as little delay as possible and it was announced that the ship had sailed for Sydney. This was regarded as an aggravation of

the injustice; and at public meetings all through the country
Government were denounced as the enemies of the working
classes. This was what came, it was bitterly said, of accepting a measure of reform which enfranchised the whole of
the middle ranks of life, but left without electoral power the
great bulk of those who lived by wage labour. A new movement must be organised to redress the inequality of political
privileges; and, Robert Owen and others added, to secure
an equality of the benefits and blessings of wealth. In the
metropolis the influence of these ideas spread rapidly. Owen
lectured, argued, wrote, and talked himself hoarse in dis-
semination of his fixed idea of mutual support as the one all-
sufficient remedy for the ills of life; and being a thoroughly
earnest and disinterested man, he made such way that even
those who regarded his doctrines as fatuous and dangerous
were compelled to acknowledge his devoted sincerity. To
multitudes out of work, or half starving themselves in the
desperate conflict of strikes, his word seemed a message of
social glad tidings, the like of which had never been heard
before; and when to pecuniary loss and domestic privation
there was added the sting of political wrong, the words of the
theorist were caught up and reiterated with ever-increasing
fervour and force, till they threatened to become like the
breath of the whirlwind. The council of the National Trades
Union, whose affiliated branches were said to contain from
three to four hundred thousand men, published a manifesto
embodying the salient principles of Owenism, and enjoining
practical measures for their realisation. The governing
classes were denounced as idlers, and the trading classes as
profit-mongers who added nothing to the common stock of
the community, but, like their betters, lived upon the fruits
of productive labour.

The best means of enabling the working classes themselves
    to be consumers of the necessaries, commodities, and
    luxuries of life, as well as producers of them, was by
    forming arrangements to prevent the profits of their toil

from going out of the circle of the productive classes into
that of the unproductive. To this end each trade society
must open shops for dealing with each other and profitably
employing their unemployed; no unionist to lay out his
money at any other places than these for all the articles
they could supply. Let the baker's union, in the first
instance, open shops where all unionists could be supplied
with bread or have it baked for them. Butchers' shops,
gardeners, cheesemongers, and other provision dealers,
tailors, shoemakers, and other trades, should do the same.
By these means the producers of real wealth would be
enabled to keep the greater part of the circulating medium
in their own hands, and thereby become what the political
economists have often tauntingly told them to become,
capitalists; and, consequently, they might then give what
directions to industry they should think proper, and no
longer be forced to be slavish suppliants to the upper
classes for leave to toil at what prices they should choose to
offer. Besides, the useful classes would become what they
ought to be, a distinct people from the idle and useless.
Without these arrangements any strike for higher wages
would be fruitless; for if the labourers got higher wages
they would have to pay a higher price for all they consumed, and they might become losers by higher prices, as
the aristocracy would most likely fly to other countries for
a supply of those articles which they now got in England.
The adoption of this plan would force the shop-ocracy into
other and more useful occupations, and to cry for a reduction of taxation.

By way of being practical, the manifesto bade each and every
member of the union refuse to aid in manufacturing any
article of clothing or equipment for the army or police.
In order to make a signal beginning in the complete change
of society on which their organisation was determined, they
summoned all the unions in and around London to meet on
the 21st of April in White Conduit Fields, thence to march

to the Home Office to present, through the Secretary of State, a petition to the King for the immediate recall of the Dorsetshire labourers.

Owen, who heartily abhorred all thoughts of violence and disorder, became uneasy at the feverish symptoms of the excitement he had helped so much to create; and, in his simplicity, wrote to Melbourne, inclosing a copy of the petition, and asking if he would receive deputies from the assembled trades on the appointed day. The minister replied that he would present any memorial reasonably framed, praying for a mitigation of what was felt to be a hardship, if sent to him without menace, ostensible or implied; but that from a multitude threatening to overawe the executive by an array of numbers he would receive nothing. He would be at his office from ten till five o'clock on Monday, and would see them if they came in a peaceful and proper manner. Owen communicated this answer to the council of trades, and prevailed on them to name five of their body whose temper and discretion might be relied on to take charge of the petition; but he strove in vain to dissuade them from accompanying the deputies to Whitehall. Thither the procession must go; its numbers would appal the heart of power; and when it was known they were coming in their might, the officials would not dare to remain at their posts and say them nay. Such being the state of affairs, it became the duty of the Home Secretary to provide for the preservation of public tranquillity. Circulars were addressed to the magistrates desiring them to be on the alert, and directing them to swear in large bodies of special constables in every parish to take charge for the day in their various localities, the police being necessarily concentrated at different points near the projected route. The Guards and other troops received orders to be in readiness whenever called upon, but they were on no account to quit their barracks unless specially required. In the course of Saturday the 19th, notices were issued by the divisional magistrates at the instance of the Home Office to all manufacturers and employers of labour against the dangers of tumult, and recommending them to keep their apprentices at home. All Sunday the town was full of anxiety; Melbourne spent many hours at Whitehall communicating with the various persons in subordinate authority, and endeavouring to impress them all with his own spirit of confidence, that if they only kept their heads cool and refused to be provoked into impatience or ill-humour all would pass off without harm.

From daybreak on the 21st crowds began to assemble at White Conduit House, a tavern which then stood on the rising ground not very far from King's Cross, in the centre of a number of open fields, now no longer recognisable, having been for many years densely covered with buildings. By degrees the unions appeared with their flags and bands, every man in his best attire and wearing the insignia of his trade. When all were assembled, their numbers were estimated from twenty-five to thirty thousand. And as the procession wound its slow length through the streets, the last contingent had not quitted the rendezvous when the head of the column emerged at Charing Cross. The sentries at the Horse Guards and Home Office had been called in for the day, the gates leading into the Park were shut, and not a soldier or constable was to be seen in the neighbourhood of Whitehall. As the cavalcade moved on towards Westminster, Owen and the deputies, accompanied by Dr. Wade, who acted as a sort of chaplain to the association, and appeared in cassock, gown and bands, presented themselves as had been arranged and asked for an interview with the Secretary of State. Melbourne, who had made a point of being seen at one of the front windows, whence he quietly observed the procession, sent the Under-Secretary, Mr. Phillips, to say that he would not receive them, representing as they did a demonstration of physical force meant to overawe the Government; that he had seen a copy of the petition, and did not quarrel with its language; and if that petition were presented on another day and in a becoming manner, he would receive it, and would himself lay it before the King. Melbourne had desired him to add, that he would always be ready to present to His Majesty any petition respectfully worded and delivered to him in a proper manner.

At Kennington they awaited the answer of the deputation charged with the presentation of the petition to the Home Office. The reply was delivered to them by their secretary, Mr. Brown, in these terms :—

Brothers, Lord Melbourne's answer is that he would not receive it in the way it had been presented : but his lordship has condescended to say, that if presented with proper decorum he will himself present it to his Majesty. And now, brothers, it is the order of the Council that you all return promptly and in good order to your several lodges, there to discuss our future proceedings.

Without any expression of feeling, the unions then separated and marched off on their return to their respective districts.* "The conduct of the Government throughout the affair was both courageous and humane, though not without an extra-judicial air." †

The most important measure of 1834 was the New Poor Law, which wrought, as it was designed to do, little less than a revolution in the habits and ideas of the agricultural community; and drew down on those by whom it was carried a weight of obloquy which it is hardly possible for a subsequent generation to estimate or comprehend. Its chief provisions were foreshadowed in the reports of a Commission of Inquiry of the preceding year, in which the most prominent thinkers and writers were Mr. Senior and Mr. Chadwick. The abuses and anomalies which had grown up under the allowance system had long required treatment with a vigorous hand; but the difficulty of the social questions involved, and the unpopularity certain to be provoked by any comprehensive scheme for checking the demoralising practice of undiscriminating relief, had deterred

* *Examiner*, April 27th, 1834.
† 'History of the Half Century,' by W. Wilks, chap. iv. p. 253.

previous administrations from attempting the ungrateful task. Brougham and Althorp it is generally understood were the chief advocates in council for making the attempt. To them must be ascribed the resolve to issue a Commission of Inquiry; and the subsequent persuasion of the Cabinet to embody in legislative form the stringent remedies which the Commission advised. As a Home Office Bill, it would naturally have been introduced by the Minister of the Interior, had he been a member of the House of Commons. But its details had been mainly elaborated under the auspices of the Keeper of the Great Seal and the Chancellor of the Exchequer; and by the latter it was brought in on the 17th of April in a speech of great length and great lucidity. Sir Robert Peel and most of the country gentlemen around him cordially supported its provisions; and with some unessential modifications in committee it passed the Lower House by great majorities. Melbourne willingly complied with the Chancellor's desire to take charge of the measure in the Lords, while the Duke of Wellington gave it a hearty support. In both Houses, nevertheless, humane and thoughtful men pleaded earnestly against some of its more rigorous enactments; and their objections were vehemently enforced by many influential organs of public opinion; above all by the *Times*. The editor, Mr. Barnes, expressed from the outset his aversion from the principles of overruling centralism, refusal of outdoor relief to the able-bodied, and the separation of husband and wife, parent and child, which formed the leading features of the remedial law; and for several years the hardships said to be inseparable from the austere application of these principles formed the theme of the most eloquent contributions to the pages of the great journal. Melbourne had no cordial liking for the bill. Practically he knew little or nothing of the old system of poor relief. His intuitive good sense led him to appreciate the force of the economic objections urged against its continuance; but his lenient and generous nature recoiled from the stern enforcement of novel rules,

for which the habits of the most ignorant and helpless
classes of the community were wholly unprepared. He
acquiesced in the Cabinet because something effectual and
thorough must be done to arrest the downward tendency of
an outworn system; and because he knew not what else
to propose. But he discerned more clearly than others the
consequence to his party of thus making themselves the
legislative protectors of the wealthy and well-to-do, at the
apparent cost of those who live by labour. He shrugged
his shoulders as he perfunctorily said "content," and
muttered to himself something which had very much the
sound of profane swearing.

Upon another question, of engrossing interest, which
was brought to issue in the session of 1834, his views likewise differed materially from those of his leading colleagues.
In their eyes the agitation for the Repeal of the Union was
a mere factious and foolish outcry, incited by one man to
promote his selfish aims, and to gratify his personal spleen.
At any cost he was to be put down. That done, disaffection
to imperial rule and disturbance of social tranquillity would
disappear; and Ireland, with a uniform coinage, mileage,
and postage, would thenceforth become an undistinguishable
part and parcel of an incorporate realm. Melbourne's
sagacity led him to look deeper into things; and while
regarding the proposal to call an independent parliament in
Dublin as delusive, and the threat of separation as chimerical,
he ascribed the demand to general discontent, sectarian
and political, on the part of the Catholic community, for
which there was too much cause. Taken literally, he called
Repeal damned nonsense; but the organised agitation
which used it as a watch-word seemed to him a grave
reproach to Imperial Government at the end of thirty years.
He did not believe that it was the mere reverberation of
one stentorian voice, or that it would cease from troubling
if that voice were mute. O'Connell, on the 23rd of April,
against his own shrewder judgment, consented to bring
forward a motion for a committee to inquire into the means

by which the Union had been carried, and the effects it had produced. After a week's debate, but 37 out of 105 Irish, and but one out of 553 English and Scotch members could be induced to vote for the motion. A joint address to the King pledged both Houses to maintain inviolate the Union as settled in 1800; and a tombstone was thereby supposed to be laid on Irish disaffection. But at Holland House there was no such vain illusion. The warning words of Fox, when his rival was carrying, by equally great majorities, his bill for the union of the three kingdoms, were not forgotten there; and Melbourne's experience of departmental administration served but to confirm his conviction that until equal laws and privileges should be made operative, without regard to creed or race, unity of empire there would never be. He thought if he had power that thus he would shape his policy: but of the possession of such power he did not dream.

END OF VOL. I.